Fathers

For Beth - a very special
sister, I think of you
always!

love
Toni Allison.

Fathers

AN ANTHOLOGY

EDITED AND INTRODUCED BY

LOUISE GUINNESS

CHATTO & WINDUS

LONDON

First published in 1996

1 3 5 7 9 10 8 6 4 2

Selection and Introduction
copyright © Louise Guinness 1996

Louise Guinness has asserted her right under
the Copyright, Designs and Patents Act, 1988
to be identified as the author of this work

First published in Great Britain in 1996 by
Chatto & Windus Limited
Random House, 20 Vauxhall Bridge Road
London SW1V 2SA

Random House Australia (Pty) Limited
20 Alfred Street, Milsons Point, Sydney
New South Wales 2061, Australia

Random House New Zealand Limited
18 Poland Road, Glenfield
Auckland 10, New Zealand

Random House South Africa (Pty) Limited
PO Box 337, Bergvlei, South Africa

Random House UK Limited Reg. No. 954009

Papers used by Random House UK Limited are natural,
recyclable products made from wood grown in
sustainable forests. The manufacturing processes conform
to the environmental regulations of
the country of origin

A CIP catalogue record for this book
is available from the British Library

ISBN: 0 7011 6350 X

Typeset by SX Composing DTP, Rayleigh, Essex

Printed and Bound in Great Britain by
Mackays of Chatham PLC, Chatham, Kent

CONTENTS

To the memory of my father
Patrick Dillon-Malone
1931–72

Good-night; ensured release,
Imperishable peace,
Have these for yours,
While sea abides, and land,
And earth's foundations stand,
An heaven endures.

A.E. Houseman

INTRODUCTION

There are as many different fathers in the world as there are different men, and this book is not an encyclopedia of them. It could not possibly be. This is my own selection of fathers from literature and history – fathers proud and sad and riven by anguish; fathers opinionated, impossible and embarrassing; fathers tender or cold; fathers unreasonable, adoring and adored and those whose brutality and cruelty have indelibly marked their children. The subject is enormous – everybody, after all, has been fathered by somebody – and because of this I had to lay down strict parameters. I decided to choose my fathers from published sources only. There are no anecdotes here. They are taken from poetry and fiction, from biography and autobiography, from diaries, letters and journals and although there is the occasional legend and some extracts from the Bible, I have on the whole concentrated on earthly fathers. God the Father looms on to the pages now and again, but I felt I couldn't go very far down that road, for I would never get back again. The majority are real men either writing about their children or being written about by their children. Fictitious fathers have only been allowed in if, like Shakespeare's Henry IV, the relationship between father and child may be seen to represent a universal tension, or if the novelist succeeds in creating so glorious a character – like Dickens's Wemmick and his Aged Parent – that his presence is enriching and delightful. But one of the most enjoyable discoveries of my research has been the different light thrown on men who are famous for other reasons, when seen in the role of a father. I cannot now think of the theory of evolution without picturing Darwin cooing over his baby and making biographical notes on his infant, his scientific brain just fractionally disabled by helpless tenderness; I cannot hear Winston Churchill quoted without remembering the pathetic letters he wrote to his father from school, hesitatingly asking for an occasional scribble in reply; I think of Boswell in a fuss over his wife's confinement, of Dickens through the eyes of the daughter who doted on him; of Byron, whose little Allegra died, neglected, in a Ravenna convent at the age of five. Nabokov may have written some of the twentieth century's greatest novels, but his name conjures up for me his marvellous agility when pushing a pram, just as I think of Rudyard Kipling's sufferings when his only son was killed in the First World War.

Every discussion and assertion about the bond between a father and child is fettered by the fact that for every new father presented with his infant who is struck, like Laurie Lee, with awe and tenderness, ('she is of course just an ordinary miracle, but is also the particular late wonder of my life'), there will be another who feels nothing at all, another seized by jealousy and another by gnawing doubts. Strindberg's play *The Father* is wholly devoted to an exploration of the madness which takes hold of a man tortured by doubts over his child's paternity. Another might find that, like Levin in *Anna Karenin*, he is overwhelmed by 'such pity for the little creature'. In each individual case, too, the fluid, complicated question of *living* as a father and child means that a single description can do no more than portray the state of the relationship at that moment, true for then but not for always. This is why some fathers, such as Darwin, Thackeray, Oswald Mosley and Evelyn Waugh make more than one appearance here. A single example would be wholly inadequate and misrepresentative. Their children have written about them in so detailed a way, chronicling the relationship in whole volumes devoted to unravelling their complexities. Choosing a sliver from these books would be like holding up a hair from a lion's mane to illustrate the nature of the beast. A true part of the whole picture, but unlikely to enable anyone to grasp the essence of the lion.

Eros is the form of love which has most inspired the poets, yet those fathers who have written about loving their children have produced poetry and prose which is remarkable for its passion and tenderness. The flow of love, which is for so long unrequited by the infant, can be seen as the most pure and generous manifestation of the human spirit. Like all passions this love will bring with it complications. Exasperation is probably the least damaging of the negative emotions. Expectation can turn to disappointment, admiration to disgust and a terrible rage on both sides, if sustained for long enough, can kill all tenderness. Few fathers would go as far as the eighteenth-century eccentric, Captain Thicknesse, who kept up his determined warfare with his sons from beyond the grave. In his will he commanded that his right hand should be cut off after his death and sent to his son in hopes that the sight would remind him of his duty to God and of the father 'who once so affectionately loved him'. And few sons are filled with the loathing that inspired Beverley Nichols to attempt, on three occasions, to murder his father. Nichols describes his father's drunken malice so expertly that the reader cannot help but be on the side of the would-be murderer. 'Our laws are wrong,' he writes. 'Some murders, I can attest, and some attempts at murder, are justified.' When the shell of an unhappy family is cracked open and the rotten kernel exposed the onlookers can be assured of entertainment of a peculiarly compelling kind. 'My father hated me chiefly because I was revolting,' writes Quentin Crisp, 'but also because I was expensive.' George II so hated the Prince of Wales that he was *pleased* when he died. These quarrelsome men – for daughters make few appearances in this section – stomp and flounce and rage and sulk from one end of the section on Feuds and Quarrels to the other. Busily denouncing each other, they fire off letters spluttering with spite and hate: 'You miserable creature' fulminates Lord Queensberry to Alfred Douglas, while Philip Roth's Portnoy describes with glorious relish the almost uncontrollable adolescent detestation which seized him whenever he set eyes on his father's 'ignorant, barbaric carcass'.

The relationship between fathers and sons is altogether more explosive than that between fathers and daughters. I don't think jealousy is the chief cause of this. When jealousy does come into it, the son is more often jealous of the father than the other way round. Nor is it simply the problem caused by the consciousness of mortality when the young buck is seen to challenge the old stag's position at the head of the herd. The reason is that the weight of expectation falls heaviest on the male child, even now. Girls can hate their fathers too but they tend to internalize their bitterness and not to write about it. As Frank Swinnerton writes in his introduction to *A Galaxy Of Fathers*, a biography of five eighteenth-century men of letters, if a man would wish to be immortalized in a biography entirely free from criticism, he should beget a literary daughter. 'She can be relied upon as the acme of loyalty. Even if her father has not been an admirable character she will defend him . . . She will extol his scholarship and his verse, his inventive genius, parental wisdom, social gifts and lovable character, leaving it to men to say he was a criticaster, boaster, sot, bore, liar or gambler. She does this, not from a strained sense of duty, but because she really believes that the man she saw first from her cradle has god-like qualities.' This bluff assertion contains more than a germ of truth, but it is probably becoming less true. The breathless, dewy-eyed tributes paid to their fathers by the likes of Anna Seward (O God bless my aged nursling etc.) and by Thackeray's daughter, the lovely Lady Ritchie, are of their time and are stamped with all the decorum and seemliness of eighteenth- and nineteenth-century ladies. As we move into the twentieth century we find that daughters are beginning to join the backlash against literary hagiography, but even in the cases of Sylvia Plath and Germaine Greer a wistful yearning for love cuts the bitterness. The old tradition is dying hard, I am happy to say. Modern literary daughters can catch at the heart, too, with the sweetness they cast on their father's memories. 'Some daughters may be able to judge their fathers from a distance. I can't,' writes Candida Lycett Green in her preface to the second volume of her father's letters. Both John Betjeman and Cyril Connolly can rejoice from their heavenly perches and congratulate themselves on having begotten literary daughters who so tenderly describe their fathers with pride, humour and love.

The sections on Feuds, Quarrels and Reconciliations and on Bad Fathers feature the dark side of fatherhood, albeit in many instances tilting rather more towards the absurd than the tragic. I have not ignored the darkest side of fatherhood, the crime of sexual abuse; the horror and bitter pain suffered by those who have experienced this ultimate betrayal is not to be denied, but I have kept such extracts down to a minimum because I felt descriptions of these deeds are better placed between the covers of psychological textbooks than in this collection which is, in the end, a celebration of fathers.

The book spans nearly three thousand years, from Homer to Blake Morrison. Human nature has not changed at all – the direct outpourings of love and loss, the bewilderment, frustration and exasperation, all the sorrows and all the joys of parenthood were as familiar to the Ancient People, and before them no doubt to prehistoric man, as they are to us now. What could seem more modern than Homer's portrait of Hector, who removes his plumed helmet to soothe his baby's fears, or Plutarch's description of Cato the Censor who insisted on being present at his son's bathtime, or Theon, writing to his father in the second century, 'If you won't take me with you to Alexandria I won't write to you or speak to you . . .', or Sir William Temple in the seventeenth century complaining to his diary 'holidays too long . . .'? And if only it were true that indifference and cruelty were characteristics of another age. Of course there have been changing fashions in the way we rear and regard our children, as there are in every aspect of life. The philosophy of Thomas Hobbes in the seventeenth century merely compounded Christianity's insistence on the existence of original sin and encapsulated a bleak view of the human spirit – that mankind is essentially vicious and the human child must be trained by nurture to turn from and spurn the base instincts of its nature. A hundred years later Jean-Jacques Rousseau caused a sensation by publishing *Emile*, in which he outlined a revolutionary system for educating children. The child, said Rousseau, must be encouraged to express all the urges of its nature and return to primitive innocence, unfettered by the traditional bonds of formal education. In this way society was to recover a lost purpose and a new virtue. Ironically, Rousseau's Emile was a child of his imagination, invented for the purposes of illustrating the effects of his theory, for although he actually fathered five children he placed each, one after another, in a foundling hospital and knew no more of them than a salmon knows of the results of his spawning on his way upstream. The Victorian father is often regarded as an inhuman automaton, incapable of expressing any exuberant feelings of joy in his offspring or allowing a gesture of affection to break through his stiffness. But this book will do nothing to back up such views. The Victorian fathers featured mostly took a keen and close interest in their children – Darwin, Thackeray and Dickens were all devoted fathers and each of them, too, had to bear the sorrow of one of their children's deaths. Even Prince Albert, so often seen as the personification of rigid Victorian detachment, can be found cavorting with his infants on the carpet at Windsor. Today we pride ourselves on our involvement with our children, for the encouragement given to fathers to enable them to bond with their infants even before birth. Only future generations can judge whether the proliferation of books such as *Partners in Birth*, featuring a caring male, massaging the stomach which contains his embryo, are really any more significant or helpful during childbirth than the brisk, now discredited, attitude of past generations – 'visit your wife from time to time, tell her she is doing splendidly and leave the rest to the doctor'.

Each generation finds fault with the methods their parents used to bring them up, each generation determines not to make the same mistakes and each generation in turn will make a whole set of different mistakes. The cyclical process is destined to repeat itself in a never-ending pattern: young children are welded to their parents by a dependence which develops into a love which idealizes its object and does not judge; with adolescence comes a searing judgment, what Philip Roth calls 'that extended period of rage', a turbulence necessary to effect the painful separation of the child from the parent and the development of the individual. Freud's attempt to explain it all in terms of sexual longings actually brings us no closer to understanding the nature of fatherhood. No one philosopher, however big his brain, no one psychologist, however fat his file of case histories, and no one novelist, poet or dramatist, however great his genius, can ever hope to encompass the myriad facets of the relationship in general, for every abstract analysis becomes meaningless in the face of an individual's particular experience. It is tempting to draw the conclusion that even Shakespeare, about whom Keats once wrote 'He has left nothing to say about nothing or anything', chooses only to present fathers in conflict with their children. All the most significant Shakespearean fathers – Brabantio, Lear, Shylock, Leonato in *Much Ado About Nothing* and Henry IV – would fall effortlessly into the chapter on Feuds, Quarrels and Reconciliations. But there are exceptions: the devoted Egeon and his lost son in *The Comedy of Errors*, Baptista in *The Taming of the Shrew* and the saintly and loving Pericles. Prospero and Miranda hardly represent an ideal father and daughter since his power and her dependence render her too submissive for comfort.

My own particular experience was wholly without conflict, for my father died when I was twelve and so he never suffered from my own extended period of rage. I find it impossible to even imagine any faults in him. He was a gentle, scholarly, humorous man. He had curly black hair which he used to twirl around his fingers when he was lost in thought. He liked to listen to opera and he had a fine singing voice. On long car journeys he sang ballads such as Abdullah Bubbul Ameer – all ninety-four verses – and he tried in vain to teach us to sing in tune. He was very interested in ballet and when he was at Oxford he was the only person who had ever been known to take ballet lessons as well as play rugby for his college. He spoke French like a Frenchman and Greek like an ancient and, unusually for an Irishman, his skin would turn almost black in the sun. He was a religious man, with a strong Catholic faith, but he once told me that he could not believe that God would allow Hell to exist. He was a truly good man, incapable of unkindness in word or deed and I never once heard him raise his voice in anger. He treated us always with such a deep fondness that it is perhaps not surprising that a day does not pass when I do not think of him. I have never stopped missing him or stopped being aware of his absence. He used to read aloud to me from his favourite books, from Lewis Carroll and from Edward Lear, he taught me to love poetry and to believe in angels. He is certainly an angel now and this book is dedicated to his memory.

And Jesus, when he was baptized, went up straightway out of the
water: and, lo, the heavens were opened unto him, and he saw the
Spirit of God descending like a dove, and lighting upon him:
And lo a voice from heaven, saying, This is my beloved Son, in whom
I am well pleased.

Matthew 3: 16–17

ONE

_____

New Fathers

(July 1840): 'He [*i.e.* the baby] is so charming that I cannot pretend to any modesty. I defy anybody to flatter us on our baby, for I defy any one to say anything in its praise of which we are not fully conscious . . . I had not the smallest conception there was so much in a five-month baby. You will perceive by this that I have a fine degree of paternal fervour.'

Charles Darwin (1809–82), letter to W. D. Fox

A GALAXY OF FATHERS

Others grew in the length of their bodies, from whom came the giants, and from them Pantagruel. The first was Chalbroth, who begat Sarabroth, who begat Faribroth, who begat Hurtali – who was a greater consumer of soups and reigned in the time of the Flood – who begat Nimrod, who begat Atlas – who with his shoulders kept the heavens from falling – who begat Goliath, who begat Eryx – who was the inventor of the game of thimble-rigging – who begat Titus, who begat Eryon, who begat Polyphemus, who begat Cacus, who begat Etion – who was the first to get the pox through not having drunk fresh in summer – who begat Enceladus, who begat Ceus, who begat Typhoeus, who begat Aloeus, who begat Otus, who begat Aegeon, who begat Briareus – who had a hundred hands – who begat Porphirio, who begat Adamastor, who begat Antaeus, who begat Agatho, who begat Porus – against whom Alexander the Great fought – who begat Aranthas, who begat Gabbara – who was the first inventor of drinking healths – who begat Goliath of Secundilla, who begat Offot – who had a terribly fine nose through drinking from the cask – who begat Artachaeus, who begat Oromedon, who begat Gemmagog – who was the inventor of pointed shoes – who begat Sisyphus, who begat the Titans, from whom sprang Hercules, who begat Enac – who was very expert in taking little worms out of the hands – who begat Fierabras – who was beaten by Oliver, peer of France and companion of Roland – who begat Morgan – who was the first in this world to play at dice with his spectacles – who begat Fracassus, of whom Merlin Coccai has written, from whom sprang Ferragus, who begat Happemousche – who was the first inventor of smoking ox-tongues over the fire, for until then people salted them as they do hams – who begat Bolivorax, who begat Longys, who begat Gayoffe – whose balls were of poplar and his tool of sorb-apple wood – who begat Maschefain, who begat Bruslefer, who begat Engolevent, who begat Galahad, the inventor of flagons, who begat Mirelangault, who begat Galaffre, who begat Falourdin, who begat Roboastre, who begat Sortibrant Coimbra, who begat Brulant of Mommiré, who begat Bruyer – who was beaten by Ogier the Dane, peer of France – who begat Maubrun who begat Foutasnon, who begat Hacquelebac, who begat Vit-de-grain, who begat Grandgousier, who begat Gargantua, who begat the noble Pantagruel, my master.

Rabelais (c. 1495–c. 1553), *Gargantua and Pantagruel*,
Book 2, Chapter 1, translated by J. M. Cohen

SONG TO BE SUNG

Sung by the Father of Infant Female Children

My heart leaps up when I behold
A rainbow in the sky;
Contrariwise, my blood runs cold
When little boys go by.
For little boys as little boys,
No special hate I carry,
But now and then they grow to men,
And when they do, they marry.
No matter how they tarry,
Eventually they marry.
And, swine among the pearls,
They marry little girls.

Oh, somewhere, somewhere, an infant plays,
With parents who feed and clothe him.
Their lips are sticky with pride and praise,
But I have begun to loathe him.
Yes, I loathe with a loathing shameless
This child who to me is nameless.
This bachelor child in his carriage
Gives never a thought to marriage,
But a person can hardly say knife
Before he will hunt him a wife.

I never see an infant (male),
A-sleeping in the sun,
Without I turn a trifle pale
And think, is *he* the one?

Oh, first he'll want to crop his curls,
And then he'll want a pony,
And then he'll think of pretty girls
And holy matrimony.
He'll put away his pony,
And sigh for matrimony.
A cat without a mouse
Is he without a spouse.

Oh, somewhere he bubbles bubbles of milk,
And quietly sucks his thumbs;
His cheeks are roses painted on silk,
And his teeth are tucked in his gums.
But alas, the teeth will begin to grow,
And the bubbles will cease to bubble;
Given a score of years or so,
The roses will turn to stubble.
He'll send a bond, or he'll write a book,
And his eyes will get that acquisitive look,
And raging and ravenous for the kill,
He'll boldly ask for the hand of Jill.
This infant whose middle
Is diapered still
Will want to marry
My daughter Jill.

Oh sweet be his slumber and moist his middle!
My dreams, I fear, are infanticiddle.
A fig for embryo Lohengrins!
I'll open all of his safety pins,
I'll pepper his powder and salt his bottle,
And give him readings from Aristotle,
Sand for his spinach I'll gladly bring,
And tabasco sauce for his teething ring,
And an elegant, elegant alligator
To play with in his perambulator.
Then perhaps he'll struggle through fire and water
To marry somebody else's daughter!

Ogden Nash (1902–71), *Candy is Dandy*, 1983

QUEEN MARY'S NOSE IS CLUTCHED

We then walked up to the Library, the drawing room, even to our
bedroom, and climbed to the nursery, and the Queen picked up Paul
and played with him. He clutched the royal nose, to her amusement,
and tried to tug at her earrings. She stayed in the nursery for some
time, and seemed delighted with my beloved baby boy, who always
plays up on these occasions. We then took the lift, Her Majesty and I
alone, and shot down, and I showed her into the cloakroom and 'loos'

which we have arranged so gaily. 'Ah', she laughed. 'What a place to keep the family', and she pointed to the Third and Fourth Georges on the walls. I had forgotten them. We then returned to the morning room and although she had sent word not to have tea we had provided lemonade, cakes, etc. . . . At last, at five o-clock the Queen rose and the visit, alas, came to an end. It was a *riotous* success, and one felt it.

The Diary of Chips Channon (1868–1958), 1967

HECTOR AND HIS BABY

Thus having spoke, th'illustrious Chief of *Troy*
Stretch'd his fond Arms to clasp the lovely Boy.
The Babe clung crying to his Nurse's Breast,
Scar'd at the dazling Helm, and nodding Crest.
With secret Pleasure each fond Parent smil'd,
And *Hector* hasted to relieve his Child,
The glitt'ring Terrors from his Brows unbound,
And plac'd the beaming Helmet on the Ground.
Then kist the Child, and lifting high in Air,
Thus to the Gods prefer'd a Father's Pray'r.
  O Thou! whose Glory fills th' Ætherial Throne,
And all ye deathless Pow'rs! protect my Son!
Grant him, like me, to purchase just Renown,
To guard the *Trojans*, to defend the Crown,
Against his Country's Foes the War to wage,
And rise the *Hector* of the future Age!
So when triumphant from successful Toils,
Of Heroes slain he bears the reeking Spoils,
Whole Hosts may hail him with deserv'd Acclaim,
And say, This Chief transcends his Father's Fame:
While pleas'd amidst the gen'ral Shouts of *Troy*,
His Mother's conscious Heart o'erflows with Joy.
  He spoke, and fondly gazing on her Charms
Restor'd the pleasing Burden to her Arms;

Homer (c. 8th century BC), *The Iliad*, translated by Alexander Pope

[8]

She was born in the autumn and was a late fall in my life, and lay purple and dented like a little bruised plum, as though she'd been lightly trodden in the grass and forgotten.

Then the nurse lifted her up and she came suddenly alive, her bent legs kicking crabwise, and her first living gesture was a thin wringing of the hands accompanied by a far-out Hebridean lament.

This moment of meeting seemed to be a birthtime for both of us; her first and my second life. Nothing, I knew, would be the same again, and I think I was reasonably shaken. I peered intently at her, looking for familiar signs, but she was convulsed as an Aztec idol. Was this really my daughter, this purple concentration of anguish, this blind and protesting dwarf?

Then they handed her to me, stiff and howling, and I held her for the first time and kissed her, and she went still and quiet as though by instinctive guile, and I was instantly enslaved by her flattery of my powers.

Only a few brief months have passed since that day, but already I've felt all the obvious astonishments. New-born, of course, she looked already a centenarian, tottering on the brink of an old crone's grave, exhausted, shrunken, bald as Voltaire, mopping, mowing, and twisting wrinkled claws in speechless spasms of querulous doom.

But with each day of survival she has grown younger and fatter, her face filling, drawing on life, every breath of real air healing the birth-death stain she had worn so witheringly at the beginning.

Now this girl, my child, this parcel of will and warmth, fills the cottage with her obsessive purpose. The rhythmic tides of her sleeping and feeding spaciously measure the days and nights. Her frail self-absorption is a commanding presence, her helplessness strong as a rock, so that I find myself listening even to her silences as though some great engine was purring upstairs.

When awake, and not feeding, she snorts and gobbles, dryly, like a ruminative jackdaw, or strains and groans and waves her hands about as though casting invisible nets.

When I watch her at this I see her hauling in life, groping fiercely with every limb and muscle, working blind at a task no one can properly share, in a darkness where she is still alone.

She is of course just an ordinary miracle, but is also the particular late wonder of my life. So each night I take her to bed like a book and lie close and study her. Her dark blue eyes stare straight into mine, but off-centre, not seeing me.

Such moments could be the best we shall ever know – those mid-nights of mutual blindness. Already, I suppose, I should be afraid for her future, but I am more concerned with mine.

I am fearing perhaps her first acute recognition, her first questions, the first man she makes of me. But for the moment I'm safe: she stares idly through me, at the pillow, at the light on the wall, and each is a shadow of purely nominal value and she prefers neither one to the other.

Meanwhile as I study her I find her early strangeness insidiously claiming a family face.

Here she is then, my daughter, here, alive, the one I must possess and guard. A year ago this space was empty, not even a hope of her was in it. Now she's here, brand new, with our name upon her; and no one will call in the night to reclaim her.

Laurie Lee, 'The Firstborn', *I Can't Stay Long*, 1975

ANXIETY SUBDUES A FLUTTER OF JOY

Monday 9th October 1775

My wife having been seized with her pains in the night, I got up about three o'clock, and between four and five Dr Young came. He and I sat upstairs mostly till between three and four, when, after we had dined, her labour became violent. I was full of expectation, and meditated curiously on the thought that it was already certain of what sex the child was, but that I could not have the least guess on which side the probability was. Miss Preston attended my wife close. Lady Preston came several times to inquire, but did not go into the room. I did not feel so much anxiety about my wife now as on former occasions, being better used to an inlying. Yet the danger was as great now as ever. I was easier from the same deception which affects a soldier who has escaped in several battles. She was very ill. Between seven and eight I went into the room. She was just delivered. I heard her say, 'God be thanked for whatever he sends.' I supposed then the child was a daughter. But she herself had not then seen it. Miss Preston said, 'Is it a daughter?' 'No,' said Mrs Forrest, the nurse-keeper, 'it's a son.' When I had seen the little man I said that I should now be so anxious that probably I should never again have an easy hour. I said to Dr Young with great seriousness, 'Doctor, Doctor, let no man set his heart upon anything in this world but land or heritable bonds; for he has no security that anything else will last as long as himself.' My anxiety subdued a flutter of joy which was in my breast.

James Boswell (1740–95), *Boswell's London Journal*

FROST AT MIDNIGHT

The Frost performs its secret ministry,
Unhelped by any wind. The owlet's cry
Came loud – and hark, again! loud as before.
The inmates of my cottage, all at rest,
Have left me to that solitude, which suits
Abstruser musings: save that at my side
My cradled infant slumbers peacefully.
'Tis calm indeed! so calm, that it disturbs
And vexes meditation with its strange
And extreme silentness. Sea, hill, and wood,
This populous village! Sea, and hill, and wood,
With all the numberless goings-on of life,
Inaudible as dreams! the thin blue flame
Lies on my low-burnt fire, and quivers not;
Only that film, which fluttered on the grate,
Still flutters there, the sole unquiet thing.
Methinks, its motion in this hush of nature
Gives it dim sympathies with me who live,
Making it a companionable form,
Whose puny flaps and freaks the idling Spirit
By its own moods interprets, every where
Echo or mirror seeking of itself,
And makes a toy of Thought

But O! how oft,
How oft, at school, with most believing mind,
Presageful, have I gazed upon the bars,
To watch that fluttering *stranger!* and as oft
    With unclosed lids, already had I dreamt
Of my sweet birth-place, and the old church-tower,
Whose bells, the poor man's only music, rang
From morn to evening, all the hot Fair-day,

So sweetly, that they stirred and haunted me
With a wild pleasure, falling on mine ear
Most like articulate sounds of things to come!
So gazed I, till the soothing things, I dreamt,
Lulled me to sleep, and sleep prolonged my dreams!
And so I brooded all the following morn,
Awed by the stern preceptor's face, mine eye
Fixed with mock study on my swimming book:
Save if the door half opened, and I snatched
A hasty glance, and still my heart leaped up,
For still I hoped to see the *stranger's* face,
Townsman, or aunt, or sister more beloved,
My play-mate when we both were clothed alike!

Dear Babe, that sleepest cradled by my side,
Whose gentle breathings, heard in this deep calm,
Fill up the interspersed vacancies
And momentary pauses of the thought!
My babe so beautiful! it thrills my heart
With tender gladness, thus to look at thee,
And think that thou shalt learn far other lore,
And in far other scenes! For I was reared
In the great city, pent 'mid cloisters dim,
And saw nought lovely but the sky and stars.
But *thou*, my babe! shalt wander like a breeze
By lakes and sandy shores, beneath the crags
Of ancient mountain, and beneath the clouds,
Which image in their bulk both lakes and shores
And mountain crags: so shalt thou see and hear
The lovely shapes and sounds intelligible
Of that eternal language, which thy God
Utters, who from eternity doth teach
Himself in all, and all things in himself.
Great universal Teacher! he shall mould
Thy spirit, and by giving make it ask.

Therefore all seasons shall be sweet to thee,
Whether the summer clothe the general earth
With greenness, or the redbreast sit and sing
Betwixt the tufts of snow on the bare branch
Of mossy apple-tree, while the nigh thatch
Smokes in the sun-thaw; whether the eave-drops fall

Heard only in the trances of the blast,
Or if the secret ministry of frost
Shall hang them up in silent icicles,
Quietly shining to the quiet Moon.

Samuel Taylor Coleridge (1772–1849)

A FURIOUS FIT OF PASSION

. . . from six o'clock until ten last night Miss Thackeray roared incessantly in a hearty furious fit of passion wh. wd. have done your heart good to hear. I don't know what it was that appeased her but at the expiration of these four hours the yowling stopped and Miss began to prattle as quietly and gaily as if nothing had happened. What are the mysteries of children? how are they moved I wonder? – I have made Missy lots of pictures, and really am growing quite a domestic character. Kemble's child can sing twelve tunes but is as ugly as sin in revenge. However we must n't brag: for every body who comes into the house remarks Missy's squint that strange to say has grown quite imperceptible to me.

W. M. Thackeray (1811–63), letter to Mrs Carmichael-Smyth, 1839

HER TINY HAND IS CLENCHED

As a father barely out of my teens, I was intoxicated by self-importance. I might not be the star, but I was aware of having a plum part in this traditional drama: prestige without pain. I thought it would be easy for me to turn in a convincing performance without getting too involved. Mine would be a cameo role with a certain amount of glory attached to it by association. I would drink a lot, go unshaved for a day or two, become 'stubbly with goodness'.

For my wife there were no such options available. When a nurse came to shave her there was nothing I could do to save her from defilement. The razor-blade packet had a little blue bird printed on it and we seized on this with relief. Did the NHS have a contract, we asked, with this obscure brand of blunt razor blade? The nurse didn't answer. The blue bird was put away for the scrapbook.

A little while later, when the agony began, Hermine asked me to find one of these inadequate weapons so she could commit suicide. My eyes must have been popping out of my head as I caught my first glimpse of what was really going on here.

'The worst thing was if a nurse came in during a contraction,' she wrote afterwards. 'They didn't seem to understand the mental effort one was making. They would start talking inanely, asking me questions, so that I had to blurt out, "*I am having a contraction!*" I didn't want to alienate them, but if I didn't get them to stop they would go on shouting at me and touching my stomach, which became intolerable.'

She had already had one injection, which was supposed to be enough. The Natural Childbirth was supposed to take care of the rest, but it wasn't working. I should have sat tight, but I was still doing everything I was told by Hermine in those days. I ran all over the hospital, looking for a sister who would sign a chit authorising a nurse to open a cabinet and give my wife another jab.

I think of all those wasted evenings practising natural childbirth, my wife and I breathing heavily in and out while raising our right arm and left leg. The idea was to learn to relax your muscles independently so they didn't get tangled up in the 'natural' birth process. The exercises were so excruciatingly boring we invariably ended up asleep.

'The injection came and I remember no more, till half waking in a new room with a new, lesser pain, I thought vaguely that I was on the lavatory and I began crying because I had given birth unknowingly.'

After all the trouble she'd been to, this is what it came to: I was there and she wasn't; I had seen someone coming out of someone and she hadn't. Whether she blames me for this I don't know. I blame myself.

Our daughter, meanwhile, was fast asleep herself, one little hand showing above the bedclothes. Clenched in it was my heart.

Hugo Williams, *What Shall We Do Now that We Have Done Everything?*, 1993

A BLUSTROUS BIRTH

Pericles.   Now, mild may be thy life!
For a more blusterous birth had never babe;
Quiet and gentle thy conditions! for
Thou art the rudeliest welcome to this world
That e'er was prince's child. Happy what follows!
Thou hast as chiding a nativity
As fire, air, water, earth, and heaven can make,
To herald thee from thy womb. [Poor inch of nature!]
Even at the first thy loss is more than can
Thy portage quit, with all thou canst find here.
Now the good gods throw their best eyes upon't!

William Shakespeare (1564–1616), *Pericles*

A BIOGRAPHICAL SKETCH OF AN INFANT

M. Taine's very interesting account of the mental development of an infant, translated in the last number of MIND (p. 252), has led me to look over a diary which I kept thirty-seven years ago with respect to one of my own infants. I had excellent opportunities for close observation, and wrote down at once whatever was observed. My chief object was expression, and my notes were used in my book on this subject; but as I attended to some other points, my observations may possibly possess some little interest in comparison with those by M. Taine, and with others which hereafter no doubt will be made. I feel sure, from what I have seen with my own infants, that the period of development of the several faculties will be found to differ considerably in different infants.

During the first seven days various reflex actions, namely sneezing, hickuping, yawning, stretching, and of course sucking and screaming, were well performed by my infant. On the seventh day, I touched the naked sole of his foot with a bit of paper, and he jerked it away, curling at the same time his toes, like a much older child when tickled. The perfection of these reflex movements shows that the extreme imperfection of the voluntary ones is not due to the state of the muscles or of the co-ordinating centres, but to that of the seat of the will. At this time, though so early, it seemed clear to me that a warm soft hand applied to his face excited a wish to suck. This must be considered as a reflex or an instinctive action, for it is impossible to believe that experience and association with the touch of his mother's breast could so soon have come into play. During the first fortnight he often started on hearing any sudden sound, and blinked his eyes. The same fact was observed with some of my other infants within the first fortnight. Once, when he was 66 days old, I happened to sneeze, and he started violently, frowned, looked frightened, and cried rather badly: for an hour afterwards he was in a state which would be called nervous in an older person, for every slight noise made him start. A few days before this same date, he first started at an object suddenly seen; but for a long time afterwards sounds made him start and wink his eyes much more frequently than did sight; thus when 114 days old, I shook a paste-board box with comfits in it near his face and he started, whilst the same box when empty or any other object shaken as near or much nearer to his face produced no effect.

Anger. – It was difficult to decide at how early an age anger was felt; on his eighth day he frowned and wrinkled the skin round his eyes before a crying fit, but this may have been due to pain or distress, and not to anger. When about ten weeks old, he was given some rather cold milk and he kept a slight frown on his forehead all the time that he was sucking, so that he looked like a grown-up person made cross from being compelled to do something which he did not like. When nearly four months old, and perhaps much earlier, there could be no doubt, from the manner in which the blood gushed into his whole face and scalp, that he easily got into a violent passion. A small cause sufficed; thus, when a little over seven months old, he screamed with rage because a lemon slipped away and he could not seize it with his hands. When eleven months old, if a wrong plaything was given him, he would push it away and beat it; I presume that the beating was an instinctive sign of anger, like the snapping of the jaws by a young crocodile just out of the egg, and not that he imagined he could hurt the plaything. When two years and three months old, he became a great adept at throwing books or sticks, &c., at anyone who offended him; and so it was with some of my other sons. On the other hand, I could never see a trace of such aptitude in my infant daughters; and this makes me think that a tendency to throw objects is inherited by boys.

Fear. – This feeling probably is one of the earliest which is experienced by infants, as shown by their starting at any sudden sound when only a few weeks old, followed by crying. Before the present one was 4½ months old I had been accustomed to make close to him many strange and loud noises, which were all taken as excellent jokes, but at this period I one day made a loud snoring noise which I had never done before; he instantly looked grave and then burst out crying. Two or three days afterwards, I made through forgetfulness the same noise with the same result. About the same time (*viz.* on the 137th day) I approached with my back towards him and then stood motionless: he looked very grave and much surprised, and would soon have cried, had I not turned round; then his face instantly relaxed into a smile.

Pleasurable Sensations. – It may be presumed that infants feel pleasure whilst sucking, and the expression of their swimming eyes seems to show that this is the case. This infant smiled when 45 days, a second infant when 46 days old; and these were true smiles, indicative of pleasure, for their eyes brightened and eyelids slightly closed. The smiles arose chiefly when looking at their mother, and were therefore probably of mental origin; but this infant often smiled then, and for some time afterwards, from some inward pleasurable feeling, for nothing was happening which could have in any way excited or amused him. When 110 days old he was exceedingly amused by a pinafore being thrown over his face and then suddenly withdrawn; and so he was when I suddenly uncovered my own face and approached his. He then uttered a little noise which was an incipient laugh. Here surprise was the chief cause of the amusement, as is the case to a large extent with the wit of grown-up persons. I believe that for three or four weeks before the time when he was amused by a face being suddenly uncovered, he received a little pinch on his nose and cheeks as a good joke. I was at first surprised at humour being appreciated by an infant only a little above three months old, but we should remember how very early puppies and kittens begin to play. When four months old, he showed in an unmistakable manner that he liked to hear the pianoforte played; so that here apparently was the earliest sign of an aesthetic feeling, unless the attraction of bright colours, which was exhibited much earlier, may be so considered.

Affection. – This probably arose very early in life, if we may judge by his smiling at those who had charge of him when under two months old; though I had no distinct evidence of his distinguishing and recognising anyone, until he was nearly four months old. When nearly five months old, he plainly showed his wish to go to his nurse. But he did not spontaneously exhibit affection by overt acts until a little above a year old, namely, by kissing several times his nurse who had been absent for a short time. With respect to the allied feeling of sympathy, this was clearly shown at 6 months and 11 days by his melancholy face, with the corners of his mouth well depressed, when his nurse pretended to cry. Jealousy was plainly exhibited when I fondled a large doll, and when I weighed his infant sister, he being then 15½ months old. Seeing how strong a feeling jealousy is in dogs, it would probably be exhibited by infants at an earlier age than that just specified, if they were tried in a fitting manner.

. . . I may add that when a few days under nine months old he associated his own name with his image in the looking-glass, and when called by name would turn towards the glass even when at some distance from it. When a few days over nine months, he learnt spontaneously that a hand or other object causing a shadow to fall on the wall in front of him was to be looked for behind. Whilst under a year old, it was sufficient to repeat two or three times at intervals any short sentence to fix firmly in his mind some associated idea. In the infant described by M. Taine the age at which ideas readily became associated seems to have been considerably later, unless indeed the earlier cases were overlooked. The facility with which associated ideas due to instruction and others spontaneously arising were acquired, seemed to me by far the most strongly marked of all the distinctions between the mind of an infant and that of the cleverest full-grown dog that I have ever known. What a contrast does the mind of an infant present to that of the pike, described by Professor Möbius, who during three whole months dashed and stunned himself against a glass partition which separated him from some minnows; and when, after at last learning that he could not attack them with impunity, he was placed in the aquarium with these same minnows, then in a persistent and senseless manner he would not attack them!

Moral Sense. – The first sign of moral sense was noticed at the age of nearly 13 months: I said 'Doddy (his nickname) won't give poor papa a kiss – naughty Doddy'. These words, without doubt, made him feel slightly uncomfortable; and at last when I had returned to my chair, he protruded his lips as a sign that he was ready to kiss me; and he then shook his hand in an angry manner until I came and received his kiss. Nearly the same little scene recurred in a few days, and the reconciliation seemed to give him so much satisfaction, that several times afterwards he pretended to be angry and slapped me, and then insisted on giving me a kiss. So that here we have a touch of the dramatic art, which is so strongly pronounced in most young children. About this time it became easy to work on his feelings and make him do whatever was wanted. When 2 years and 3 months old, he gave his last bit of gingerbread to his little sister, and then cried out with high self-approbation 'Oh kind Doddy, kind Doddy'. Two months later, he became extremely sensitive to ridicule, and was so suspicious that he often thought people who were laughing and talking together were laughing at him. A little later (2 years and 7½ months old) I met him coming out of the dining room with his eyes unnaturally bright, and an odd unnatural or affected manner, so that I went into the room to see who was there, and found that he had been taking pounded sugar, which he had been told not to do. As he had never been in any way punished, his odd manner certainly was not due to fear, and I suppose it was pleasurable excitement struggling with conscience. A fortnight afterwards, I met him coming out of the same room, and he was eyeing his pinafore which he had carefully rolled up; and again his manner was so odd that I determined to see what was within his pinafore, notwithstanding that he said there was nothing and repeatedly commanded me to 'go away,' and I found it stained with pickle-juice; so that here was carefully planned deceit. As this child was educated solely by working on his good feelings, he soon became as truthful, open, and tender, as anyone could desire.

An infant understands to a certain extent, and as I believe at a very early period, the meaning or feelings of those who tend him, by the expression of their features. There can hardly be a doubt about this with respect to smiling; and it seemed to me that the infant whose biography I have here given understood a compassionate expression at a little over five months old. When 6 months and 11 days old he certainly showed sympathy with his nurse on her pretending to cry. When pleased after performing some new accomplishment, being then almost a year old, he evidently studied the expression of those around him. It was probably due to differences of expression and not merely of the form of the features that certain faces clearly pleased him much more than others, even at so early an age as a little over six months. Before he was a year old, he understood intonations and gestures, as well as several words and short sentences. He understood one word, namely, his nurse's name, exactly five months before he invented his first word *mum*; and this is what might have been expected, as we know that the lower animals easily learn to understand spoken words.

Charles Darwin (1809–82), *Mind: a Quarterly Review of Psychology and Philosophy*, vol. 2, July 1877

TO MY SON

Go, and be gay;
You are born into the dazzling light of day.
Go, and be wise;
You are born upon an earth which needs new eyes.
Go, and be strong;
You are born into a world where love rights wrong.
Go, and be brave;
Possess your soul; that you alone can save.

Siegfried Sassoon (1886–1967), *Collected Poems*, 1947

A SAFE DELIVERANCE

1642. My wife now growing bigge & ill, my mother [-in-law] came from Olny to us upon a Tuesday lecture day, April: 12: after sermon, having waited upon God in his house, my wife called her women and God was mercifull to mee in my house, giving her a safe deliverance, & a daughter which on Thursday April: 14 was baptized by the name of Mary, Mr Rich: Harlakenden, Mr John Little, Mrs Mary Mildmay & my wives mother being witnesses. I entertayned my neighbors all about; it cost me 6*l*, & 13*s*. 4*d*. at least: they shewed much love to mee from all parts: God blessed my wife to bee a nurse, and our child thrived, and was even then a pleasant comfort to us: God wash it from its corruption & sanctify it and make it his owne: but it pleased God my wives breasts were sore, wch was a grievance & sad cutt to her, but with use of means in some distance of time they healed up.

The Diary of the Rev. Ralph Josselin 1616–83

NABOKOV THE PRAM-PUSHER

Throughout the years of our boy's infancy, in Hitler's Germany and Maginot's France, we were more or less constantly hard up, but wonderful friends saw to his having the best things available. Although powerless to do much about it, you and I jointly kept a jealous eye on any possible rift between his childhood and our own incunabula in the opulent past, and this is where those friendly faces came in doctoring the rift every time it threatened to open. Then, too, the science of building up babies had made the same kind of phenomenal, streamlined progress that flying or falling had. I, when nine months old, did not get a pound of strained spinach at one feeding or the juice of a dozen oranges per days: and the pediatric hygiene you adopted was incomparably more artistic and scrupulous than anything old nurses could have dreamed up when we were babes.

I think bourgeois fathers – wing-collar workers in pencil-striped pants, dignified, office-tied fathers, so different from young American veterans of today or from a happy, jobless Russian-born expatriate of fifteen years ago – will not understand my attitude toward – our child. Whenever you held him up, replete with his warm formula and grave as an idol, and waited for the postlactic all-clear signal before making a horizontal baby of the vertical one, I used to take part both in your wait and in the tightness of his surfeit, which I exaggerated, therefore rather resenting your cheerful faith in the speedy dissipation of what I felt to be a painful oppression; and when, at last, the blunt little bubble did rise and burst in his solemn mouth, I used to experience a lovely relief while you, with a congratulatory murmur, bent low to deposit him in the white-rimmed twilight of his crib.

You know, I still feel in my wrists certain echoes of the pram-pusher's knack, such as, for example, the glib downward pressure one applied to the handle in order to have the carriage tip up and climb the curb. First came an elaborate mouse-gray vehicle of Belgian make, with fat autoid tires and luxurious springs, so large that it could not enter our puny elevator. It rolled on sidewalks in slow stately mystery, with the trapped baby inside lying supine, well covered with down, silk and fur; only his eyes moved, warily, and sometimes they turned upward with one swift sweep of their showy lashes to follow the receding of branch-pattered blueness that flowed away from the edge of the half-cocked hood of the carriage, and presently he would dart a suspicious glance at my face to see if the teasing trees and sky did not belong, perhaps, to the same order of things as did rattles and parental humor. There followed a lighter carriage, and in this, as he spun along, he would tend to rise, straining at his straps; clutching at the edges; standing there less like the groggy passenger of a pleasure boat than like an entranced scientist in a spaceship; surveying the speckled skeins of a live, warm world; eyeing with philosophic interest the pillow he had managed to throw overboard; falling out himself when a strap burst one day. Still later he rode in one of those small contraptions called strollers; from initial springy and secure heights the child came lower and lower, until, when he was about one and a half, he touched ground in front of the moving stroller by slipping forward out of his seat and beating the sidewalk with his heels in anticipation of being set loose in some public garden. A new wave of evolution started to swell, gradually lifting him again from the ground, when, for his second birthday, he received a four-foot-long, silver-painted Mercedes racing car operated by inside pedals, like an organ, and in this he used to drive with a pumping, clanking noise up and down the sidewalk of the Kurfürstendamm while from open windows came the multiplied roar of a dictator still pounding in his chest in the Neander valley we had left far behind.

Vladimir Nabokov (1899–1977), *Speak, Memory:
An Autobiography Revisited*, 1987

SUCH PITY FOR THE LITTLE CREATURE

Gazing at this pitiful little bit of humanity, Levin searched his soul in vain for some trace of paternal feeling. He could feel nothing but aversion. But when it was undressed and he caught a glimpse of wee, wee little tomato-coloured hands and feet with fingers and toes – the big one distinguishable from the others even – and saw Lizaveta Petrovna bending the sticking-up little arms as if they were soft springs and encasing them in linen garments, such pity for the little creature overwhelmed him, and such fear lest she should hurt it, that he put out a hand to restrain her . . . .

His feelings for this little creature were not at all what he had expected. There was not an atom of pride or joy in them; on the contrary, he was oppressed by a new sense of apprehension – the consciousness of another vulnerable region. And this consciousness was so painful at first, the apprehension lest that helpless being should suffer was so acute, that it drowned the strange thrill of unreasoning joy and even pride which he had felt when the infant sneezed.

Leo Tolstoy (1828–1910), *Anna Karenin*, translated by Rosemary Edmonds

EARLY MORNING FEED

The father darts out on the stairs
To listen to that keening
In the upper room, for a change of note
That signifies distress, to scotch disaster,
The kettle humming in the room behind.

He thinks, on tiptoe, ears a-strain,
The cool dawn rising like the moon:
'Must not appear and pick him up;
He mustn't think he has me springing
To his beck and call,'
The kettle rattling behind the kitchen door.

He has him springing
A-quiver on the landing –
For a distress-note, a change of key,
To gallop up the stairs to him
To take him up, light as a violin,
And stroke his back until he smiles.
He sidles in the kitchen
And pours his tea . . .

And again stands hearkening
For milk cracking the lungs.
There's a little panting,
A cough: the thumb's in: he'll sleep,
The cup of tea cooling on the kitchen table.

Can he go in now to his chair and think
Of the miracle of breath, pick up a book,
Ready at all times to take it at a run
And intervene between him and disaster,
Sipping his cold tea as the sun comes up?

He returns to bed
And feels like something, with the door ajar,
Crouched in the bracken, alert, with big eyes
For the hunter, death, disaster.

Peter Redgrove, *Poems 1954–1987*

NO MAN CAN COPE

My two children were a blessing. They weren't born at home – we had no conveniences. There was no doctor in Big Sur, not even a telephone nearby. From the time they were born, I was a very happy man.

When my children were very small I used to get up at night to feed them. And much more. I changed their diapers too. In those days, I didn't have a car; I would take the dirty diapers in a bag, a big laundry bag, and walk six miles to the hot springs (now taken over by Esalen) and wash them in that hot spring water, then carry them home! Six miles! That's *one* thing I remember about babies. For a time, after my wife left me, I was there with the children alone. That's the hardest thing to ask a man to do – take care of tots from three to five years of age, bouncing with energy, and shut up with them in one room, especially during the rains. In the winter when the rains came we were marooned. I fed them, changed their clothes, washed them, told them stories. I didn't do any writing. I couldn't. By noon every day I was exhausted! I'd say, 'Let's take a nap.' We'd get into bed, the three of us, and then they'd begin scrambling, screaming, fighting with each other. Finally I had to ask my wife to take them. As much as I loved them I couldn't handle the situation. It was something I'll never forget. That experience increased my respect for women, I guess. I realized what a tremendous job women have, married women, cooking meals, doing the laundry, cleaning house, taking care of children, and all that. This is something no man can understand or cope with no matter how hard his work may be.

The kids were fairly close together in age, two and a half years difference. They fought all the time, like sworn enemies. Today, of course they're good friends.

When Val was able to toddle beside me, when she was about three years old, I took her into the forest every day for a long walk beside a narrow stream. I pointed out birds, trees, leaves, rocks, and told her stories. Then I'd pick her up and carry her on my shoulders. I'll never forget the first song I taught her. It was 'Yankee Doodle Dandy.' What joy, walking and whistling with this kid on my back. Anyone who hasn't had children doesn't know what life is. Yes, they were a great blessing.

Henry Miller (1891–1980), *My Life and Times*, 1972

A PRAYER FOR MY DAUGHTER

Once more the storm is howling, and half hid
Under this cradle-hood and coverlid
My child sleeps on. There is no obstacle
But Gregory's wood and one bare hill
Whereby the haystack- and roof-levelling wind,
Bred on the Atlantic, can be stayed;
And for an hour I have walked and prayed
Because of the great gloom that is in my mind.

I have walked and prayed for this young child an hour
And heard the sea-wind scream upon the tower,
And under the arches of the bridge, and scream
In the elms above the flooded stream;
Imagining in excited reverie
That the future years had come,
Dancing to a frenzied drum,
Out of the murderous innocence of the sea.

May she be granted beauty and yet not
Beauty to make a stranger's eye distraught,
Or hers before a looking-glass, for such,
Being made beautiful overmuch,
Consider beauty a sufficient end,
Lose natural kindness and maybe
The heart-revealing intimacy
That chooses right, and never find a friend.

Helen being chosen found life flat and dull
And later had much trouble from a fool,
While that great Queen, that rose out of the spray,
Being fatherless could have her way
Yet chose a bandy-leggèd smith for man.
It's certain that fine women eat
A crazy salad with their meat
Whereby the Horn of Plenty is undone.

In courtesy I'd have her chiefly learned;
Hearts are not had as a gift but hearts are earned
By those that are not entirely beautiful;
Yet many, that have played the fool

For beauty's very self, has charm made wise,
And many a poor man that has roved,
Loved and thought himself beloved,
From a glad kindness cannot take his eyes.

May she become a flourishing hidden tree
That all her thoughts may like the linnet be,
And have no business but dispensing round
Their magnanimities of sound,
Nor but in merriment begin a chase,
Nor but in merriment a quarrel.
O may she live like some green laurel
Rooted in one dear perpetual place.

My mind, because the minds that I have loved,
The sort of beauty that I have approved,
Prosper but little, has dried up of late,
Yet knows that to be choked with hate
May well be of all evil chances chief.
If there's no hatred in a mind
Assault and battery of the wind
Can never tear the linnet from the leaf.

An intellectual hatred is the worst,
So let her think opinions are accursed.
Have I not seen the loveliest woman born
Out of the mouth of Plenty's horn,
Because of her opinionated mind
Barter that horn and every good
By quiet natures understood
For an old bellows full of angry wind?

Considering that, all hatred driven hence,
The soul recovers radical innocence
And learns at last that it is self-delighting,
Self-appeasing, self-affrighting,
And that its own sweet will is Heaven's will;
She can, though every face should scowl
And every windy quarter howl
Or every bellows burst, be happy still.

And may her bridegroom bring her to a house
Where all's accustomed, ceremonious;
For arrogance and hatred are the wares

Peddled in the thoroughfares.
How but in custom and in ceremony
Are innocence and beauty born?
Ceremony's name for the rich horn,
And custom for the spreading laurel tree.

W. B. Yeats (1865–1939), *Collected Poems*, 1933

I MUST LOVE SOMETHING

In November [1816] Shelley wrote to Byron: 'Poor Claire's time approaches, and though she continues as well as women in that situation usually are, I think her spirits begin to fail.' Four months later, in Bath, the child was born. 'I have good news to tell you. Claire is safely delivered of a most beautiful girl. Both the mother and child are well, and Mary describes the latter to be a creature of most exquisite symmetry, and as betraying, even at its birth, a vigour and a sensibility very unusual.' But it was not until four months later that Byron himself first referred to the event, in a letter addressed to Augusta.

'I shall be glad to hear from or of you, and of your children and mine. By the way, it seems that I have got another, a *daughter* by that same lady, whom you will recognize by what I said of her in former letters – I mean *her* who returned to England to become a Mamma incog., and whom I pray the gods to keep there. I am a little puzzled how to dispose of this new production', he added, 'but shall probably send for and place it in a Venetian convent to become a good Catholic, and (it may be) a *Nun*, being a character somewhat wanted in our family.' Nevertheless it is clear that Shelley's description of the baby's beauty touched Byron, even if only in his self-love. 'They tell me it is very pretty, with blue eyes and *dark* hair; and although I never was attached nor pretended attachment to the mother, still in case of the eternal worry and alienation which I foresee about my legitimate daughter, Ada, it may be as well to have something to repose a hope upon. I must love something in my old age, and probably circumstances will render this poor little creature a great and, perhaps, my only comfort . . .'

To be 'a comfort' to Lord Byron – such, then, was to be Allegra's destiny – and this, curiously enough, also was the fate that her mother wished for her. Shelley, from the first, appears to have warned Claire

[27]

that, in giving the child up to Byron, she would have to relinquish her own claims to it, but she was obstinately determined that her baby should have an education 'becoming the child of an English noble-man'. During the first months, however, it was brought up with Shelley's and Mary's own children in their house at Marlow. Shelley loved babies, whether his own or other people's, and justified this love in his own eyes – like his other affections – by a philosophic theory. 'Will your baby tell us anything about pre-existence, Madam?' he asked a complete stranger on Magdalen Bridge, who held in her arms a child a few weeks old – and, at her natural surprise: 'How provok-ingly close are these new-born babes!' he sighed. 'He may fancy per-haps that he cannot [speak] but it is only a silly whim . . . It is not the less certain that all knowledge is reminiscence.'

Iris Origo, *A Measure of Love*, 1957

THE ALMOND TREE

At seven-thirty
the visitors' bell
scissored the calm
of the corridors.
The doctor walked with me
to the slicing doors.

His hand upon my arm,
his voice – I have to tell
you – set another bell
beating in my head:
your son is a mongol
the doctor said.

You turn to the window for the first time
I am called to the cot
to see your focus shift,
take tendril-hold on a shaft
of sun, explore its dusty surface, climb
to an eye you cannot

meet. You have a sickness they cannot heal,
the doctors say: locked in

[28]

your body you will remain.
Well, I have been locked in mine.
We will tunnel each other out. You seal
the covenant with a grin.

In the days we have known one another,
my little mongol love,
I have learnt more from your lips
than you will from mine perhaps:
I have learnt that to live is to suffer,
to suffer is to live.

Jon Stallworthy, *A Familiar Tree*, 1969

A CHANGE OF PLAN

When I was almost forty
I had a daughter whose name was Golden Bells.
Now it is just a year since she was born;
She is learning to sit and cannot yet talk.
Ashamed, – to find that I have not a sage's heart:
I cannot resist vulgar thoughts and feelings.
Henceforward I am tied to things outside myself:
My only reward, – the pleasure I am getting now.
If I am spared the grief of her dying young,
Then I shall have the trouble of getting her married.
My plan for retiring and going back to the hills
Must now be postponed for fifteen years!

Po Chü-i (772–846), 'Golden Bells', translated by Arthur Waley

A DEVIL OF A SPIRIT

'My bastard', wrote Papa, 'came a month ago – a very fine child,
much admired in the gardens and on the Piazza, and greatly caressed
by the Venetians, from the Governatrice downwards.' 'She is very
pretty,' he told Augusta, 'remarkably intelligent, and a great favourite
with everybody; but what is remarkable, she is more like Lady Byron

than her mother – so much so as to stupefy the learned Fletcher [Byron's valet] and astonish me. Is it not odd? I suppose she must also resemble her sister, Ada. She has very blue eyes, and that singular forehead, fair curly hair, and a devil of a Spirit – but that is Papa's!'

Iris Origo, *A Measure of Love*, 1957

BYE BABY BUNTING

Bye, baby bunting,
Daddy's gone a-hunting,
Gone to get a rabbit skin
To wrap the baby bunting in.

SON

While I stood by the bloody bed,
She cried out lonely as a wolf.
I put my hand behind her head.
She was lonely and herself.
A midwife with a witchlike face
Hissed in her ear, 'Push, ducky, push,'
Till from his warm and wanted place
My son came through the burning bush.

Sticky with blood and yellow slime,
He was held up, his back was slapped
Like a drunk's at closing time.
When insecurely he had slipped,
Trailed by a steamy sponge of filth
Into the floodlit theatre, I
Took him inside my arms and felt
How soon our children make us die.

He yelped for air. I took her hand,
But her face was smiled away.
A pride I couldn't understand
Swelled her breasts out like milk. The grey-

[30]

faced witchlike woman in her white
Was smiling also, so I knew
This was an old rite I was at
And was unnecessary to.

I had stood by the bloody bed.
She had cried lonely as a wolf.
I had put my hand behind her head.
She had been lonely and herself.
Now I was lonely and myself,
And standing by the newmade bed,
When he cried lonely as a wolf,
I put my hand behind his head.

Dom Moraes, Collected Poems, 1957

I CROSS THE ROOM TO KISS MY SON

I look down at the heap of manuscript on my desk with a sense of finality. There are nearly thirty years folded away into this small stack of paper. If my son reads it, when he is older, I hope he will understand the person I was, and accept the person I am. I do not hope anything for him, except that he should stay alive and himself.

I have managed that, sometimes with difficulty: what I hoped for as a child has come true, and the vocation I have always held to stays with me. There are new poems somewhere in the rubble of my desk, and there will be others. If I have not written as earthquakingly as I hoped when I was a boy, I have written as well as I could. And the brilliant bit of luck, for which all poets pray, and which they all chase through a lifetime, may yet descend, so that I write one great poem.

They have come downstairs. I cross the room to kiss my son, whose skin has an odour of baby soap and milk. He has English apples for cheeks, but somewhere behind them is a tinge of gold and olive, the colour of the country from which I came.

Dom Moraes, My Son's Father, 1968

TWO

Bad Fathers

I ask questions of the past but I don't expect answers. Though I shared a house and a crime with my father, I scarcely knew the man. Mine is not a story of the boot, but of the imprint of that boot on flesh: imprinting.

This I do know: my father was not a monster. His life was a bud that never opened, blighted by the first frost. His crime became his prison, his guilt his bars. He served his sentence as I have served mine, but his was for life, whereas I got off after forty-seven years for reasonably good behavior.

Sylvia Fraser, *My Father's House*, 1987

BANANAS

On one occasion, just after the war, the first consignment of bananas reached Britain. Neither I, my sister Teresa nor my sister Margaret had ever eaten a banana throughout the war, when they were unprocurable, but we had heard all about them as the most delicious taste in the world. When this first consignment arrived, the socialist government decided that every child in the country should be allowed one banana. An army of civil servants issued a library of special banana coupons, and the great day arrived when my mother came home with three bananas. All three were put on my father's plate, and before the anguished eyes of his children, he poured on cream, which was almost unprocurable, and sugar, which was heavily rationed, and ate all three. A child's sense of justice may be defective in many respects, and egocentric at the best of times, but it is no less intense for either. By any standards, he had done wrong. It would be absurd to say that I never forgave him, but he was permanently marked down in my estimation from that moment, in ways which no amount of sexual transgression would have achieved. It had, perhaps, the effect on my estimation of him that the Lavery and Great Débâcles combined had on his of me. From that moment, I never treated anything he had to say on faith or morals very seriously.

Auberon Waugh, *Will This Do?*, 1991

VILE BODIES

Monday 23 December 1946

The presence of my children affects me with deep weariness and depression. I do not see them until luncheon, as I have my breakfast alone in the library, and they are in fact well trained to avoid my part of the house; but I am aware of them from the moment I wake. Luncheon is very painful. Teresa has a mincing habit of speech and a pert, humourless style of wit; Bron is clumsy and dishevelled, sly, without intellectual, aesthetic or spiritual interest; Margaret is pretty and below the age of reason. In the nursery whooping cough rages I believe. At tea I meet the three elder children again and they usurp the drawing-room until it is time to dress for dinner. I used to take some pleasure in inventing legends for them about Basil Bennett, Dr Bedlam and the Sebag

Montefiores. But now they think it ingenious to squeal: 'It isn't true.' I taught them the game of draughts for which they show no aptitude.

The frost has broken and everything is now dripping and slushy and gusty. The prospect of Christmas appalls me and I look forward to the operating theatre as a happy release.

Evelyn Waugh, Diaries, edited by Mark Amory, 1976

AN UNSUITABLE COMPANION

To Laura Waugh   AUGUST 1945

White's
25 August 1945

Darling Laura

I have regretfully come to the conclusion that the boy Auberon is not yet a suitable companion for me.

Yesterday was a day of supreme self-sacrifice. I fetched him from Highgate, took him up the dome of St Pauls, gave him a packet of triangular stamps, took him to luncheon at the Hyde Park Hotel, took him on the roof of the hotel, took him to Harrods & let him buy vast quantities of toys (down to your account), took him to tea with Maimie who gave him a pound and a box of matches, took him back to Highgate, in a state (myself not the boy) of extreme exhaustion. My mother said 'Have you had a lovely day?' He replied 'A bit dull'. So that is the last time for some years I inconvenience myself for my children. You might rub that in to him.

I had a very enjoyable evening getting drunk at the House of Commons with Hollis & Fraser and the widow Hartington (who is in love with me I think) & Driberg & Nigel Birch & Lord Morris and Anthony Head & my communist cousin Claud Cockburn.

Last night I dined with Maimie. Vsevolode kept going to bed and coming down again.

London is fuller & noisier than ever.

All my love
Evelyn

Evelyn Waugh, Letters, edited by Mark Amory, 1980

ABRAHAM AND ISAAC

And Abraham called the name of his son that was born unto him, whom Sarah bare to him, Isaac.

And Abraham circumcised his son Isaac being eight days old, as God had commanded him.

And Abraham was an hundred years old, when his son Isaac was born unto him.

Genesis 21: 3–5

And it came to pass after these things, that God did tempt Abraham, and said unto him, Abraham: and he said, Behold, *here* I *am.*

And he said, Take now thy son, thine only *son* Isaac, whom thou lovest, and get thee into the land of Moriah; and offer him there for a burnt offering upon one of the mountains which I will tell thee of.

And Abraham rose up early in the morning, and saddled his ass, and took two of his young men with him, and Isaac his son, and clave the wood for the burnt offering, and rose up, and went unto the place of which God had told him.

Then on the third day Abraham lifted up his eyes, and saw the place afar off.

And Abraham said unto his young men, Abide ye here with the ass; and I and the lad will go yonder and worship, and come again to you.

And Abraham took the wood of the burnt offering, and laid *it* upon Isaac his son; and he took the fire in his hand, and a knife; and they went both of them together.

And Isaac spake unto Abraham his father, and said, My father: and he said, Here *am* I, my son. And he said, Behold the fire and the wood: but where *is* the lamb for a burnt offering?

And Abraham said, My son, God will provide himself a lamb for a burnt offering: so they went both of them together.

And they came to the place which God had told him of; and Abraham built an altar there, and laid the wood in order, and bound Isaac his son, and laid him on the altar upon the wood.

And Abraham stretched forth his hand, and took the knife to slay his son.

And the angel of the LORD called unto him out of heaven, and said, Abraham, Abraham: and he said, Here *am* I.

And he said, Lay not thine hand upon the lad, neither do thou any thing unto him: for now I know that thou fearest God, seeing thou hast not withheld thy son, thine only *son* from me.

And Abraham lifted up his eyes and looked, and behold behind *him* a ram caught in a thicket by his horns: and Abraham went and took the ram, and offered him up for a burnt offering in the stead of his son.

Genesis 22: 1–13

STUDY OF A FIGURE IN A LANDSCAPE, 1952

after Francis Bacon

> – Did your bowels move today?
> – Yes, Daddy.
> – At what time did your bowels move today?
> – At eight o'clock, Daddy.
> – Are you sure?
> – Yes, Daddy.
> – Are you sure that your bowels moved today?
> – I am, Daddy.
> – Were you sitting down in the long grass?
> – I was, Daddy.
> – Are you telling me the truth?
> – I am, Daddy.
> – Are you sure you are not telling me a lie?
> – I am, Daddy.
> – You are sure that your bowels moved today?
> – I am, Daddy, but please don't beat me, Daddy.
> Don't be vexed with me, Daddy.
> I am not absolutely sure, Daddy.
> – Why are you not absolutely sure?
> – I don't know, Daddy.
> – What do you mean you don't know?
> – I don't know what bowels are, Daddy.
> – What do you think bowels are?
> – I think bowels are wheels, Daddy.
> Black wheels under my tummy, Daddy,
> – Did your black wheels move today?
> – They did, Daddy.
> – Then your bowels definitely did move today.
> – Yes, Daddy.

– You should be proud of yourself.
– Yes, Daddy.
– Are you proud of yourself?
– Yes, Daddy.
– Constipation is the curse of Cain.
– Yes, Daddy.
– You will cut and reap the corn today.
– Yes, Daddy.
– Every day be sure that your bowels move.
– Yes, Daddy.
– If your bowels do not move, you are doomed.
– Yes, Daddy.
– Are you all right?
– No, Daddy.
– What in the name of the Mother of God
And the dead generations is the matter with you?
– I want to go to the toilet, Daddy.
– Don't just stand there, run for it.
– Yes, Daddy.
– Are you in your starting blocks?
– Yes, Daddy.
– When I count to three, leap from your starting blocks.
– I can't, Daddy.
– Can't can't.
– Don't, Daddy, don't, Daddy, don't, Daddy, don't.

Paul Durcan, *A Snail in My Prime*, 1993

A DEFICIENCY OF TENDERNESS

In his views of life he partook of the character of the Stoic, the Epicurean, and the Cynic, not in the modern but the ancient sense of the word. In his personal qualities the Stoic predominated. His standard of morals was Epicurean, inasmuch as it was utilitarian, taking as the exclusive test of right and wrong, the tendency of actions to produce pleasure or pain. But he had (and this was the Cynic element) scarcely any belief in pleasure; at least in his later years, of which alone, on this point, I can speak confidently. He was not insensible to pleasures; but he deemed very few of them worth the price which, at least in the present state of society, must be paid for them. The greater number of miscarriages in life, he considered to be attributable to the over-valuing of pleasures. Accordingly, temperance, in the large sense intended by the Greek philosophers – stopping short at the point of moderation in all indulgences – was with him, as with them, almost the central point of educational precept. His inculcations of this virtue fill a large place in my childish remembrances. He thought human life a poor thing at best, after the freshness of youth and of unsatisfied curiosity had gone by. This was a topic on which he did not often speak, especially, it may be supposed, in the presence of young persons: but when he did, it was with an air of settled and profound conviction. He would sometimes say, that if life were made what it might be, by good government and good education, it would be worth having: but he never spoke with anything like enthusiasm even of that possibility. He never varied in rating intellectual enjoyments above all others, even in value as pleasures, independently of their ulterior benefits. The pleasures of the benevolent affections he placed high in the scale; and used to say, that he had never known a happy old man, except those who were able to live over again in the pleasures of the young. For passionate emotions of all sorts, and for everything which has been said or written in exaltation of them, he professed the greatest contempt. He regarded them as a form of madness. 'The intense' was with him a bye-word of scornful disapprobation. He regarded as an aberration of the moral standard of modern times, compared with that of the ancients, the great stress laid upon feeling. Feelings, as such, he considered to be no proper subjects of praise or blame. Right and wrong, good and bad, he regarded as qualities solely of conduct – of acts and omissions; there being no feeling which may not lead, and does not frequently lead, either to good or to bad actions: conscience itself, the very desire to act right, often leading people to act wrong. Consistently carrying out the doctrine, that the object of praise and blame should be the discouragement of wrong conduct and the encouragement of right, he refused to let his praise or blame be influenced by the motive of the agent. He blamed as severely what he thought a bad action, when the motive was a feeling of duty, as if the agents had been consciously evil doers. He would not have accepted as a plea in mitigation for inquisitors, that they sincerely believed burning heretics to be an obligation of conscience. But though he did not allow honesty of purpose to soften his disapprobation of actions, it had its full effect on his estimation of characters. No one prized conscientiousness and rectitude of intention more highly, or was more incapable of valuing any person in whom he did not feel assurance of it. But he disliked people quite as much for any other deficiency, provided he thought it equally likely to make them act ill. He disliked, for instance, a fanatic in any bad cause, as much or more than one who adopted the same cause from self-interest, because he thought him even more likely to be practically mischievous. And thus, his aversion to many intellectual errors, or what he regarded as such, partook, in a certain sense, of the character of a moral feeling. All this is merely saying that he, in a degree once common, but now very unusual, threw his feelings into his opinions; which truly it is difficult to understand how any one who possesses much of both, can fail to do. None but those who do not care about opinions, will confound this with intolerance. Those, who having opinions which they hold to be immensely important, and their contraries to be prodigiously hurtful, have any deep regard for the general good, will necessarily dislike, as a class and in the abstract, those who think wrong what they think right, and right what they think wrong: though they need not therefore be, nor was my father, insensible to good qualities in an opponent, nor governed in their estimation of individuals by one general presumption, instead of by the whole of their character. I grant that an earnest person, being no more infallible than other men, is liable to dislike people on account of opinions which do not merit dislike; but if he neither himself does them any ill office, nor connives at its being done by others, he is not intolerant: and the forbearance which flows from a conscientious sense of the importance to mankind of the equal freedom of all opinions, is the only tolerance which is commendable, or, to the highest moral order of minds, possible.

It will be admitted, that a man of the opinions, and the character, above described, was likely to leave a strong moral impression on any mind principally formed by him, and that his moral teaching was not likely to err on the side of laxity or indulgence. The element which was chiefly deficient in his moral relation to his children was that of tenderness. I do not believe that this deficiency lay in his own nature. I believe him to have had much more feeling than he habitually showed, and much greater capacities of feeling than were ever developed. He resembled most Englishmen in being ashamed of the signs of feeling, and by the absence of demonstration, starving the feelings themselves. If we consider further that he was in the trying position of sole teacher, and add to this that his temper was constitutionally irritable, it is impossible not to feel true pity for a father who did, and strove to do, so much for his children, who would have so valued their affection, yet who must have been constantly feeling that fear of him was drying it up at its source.

J. S. Mill (1806–73), Autobiography, 1873

THE FOND FATHER

Of Baby I was very fond,
She'd won her father's heart;
So, when she fell into the pond,
It gave me quite a start.

Harry Graham (1874–1936), Ruthless Rhymes, 1900

A TRUE PORTRAIT OF MY PROGENITOR

I attribute the following to Pappie: (1) the undermining of his children's health, and their rotting teeth, to absolutely irregular feeding and living, cheap adulterated food, and general unsanitary conditions of life; (2) the handicap of his children's chances in life (whereby

Poppie's chance, for example, is quite ruined); (3) Mother's unhealth; unhappiness, weakening mind, and death, to his moral brutality and the Juggernaut he made life with him, and to his execrable treatment of her even up to her last day; and (4), indirectly, Georgie's death, for if Georgie had been properly doctored or in a hospital, he would have lived. Besides these, he is pulling down his children's characters with him as he sinks lower. It's a pretty list on paper yet somewhat understated. 'Moral brutality' does not convey to the stranger mind the eternity of abuse that in memory impinges monotonously on my accustomed ear at will. It was a constant threat of his to Mother, 'I'll break your heart! I'll break your bloody heart!' It must be admitted that this was exactly what he did, but not of set purpose. He saw that his callous habit of commonplace gluttony, as graceless and dull a routine as the rest of his life, would have this effect, and it eased his ill nature to think so. He uses the threat to us, now, but adds, 'I'll break your stomach first though, ye buggers. You'll get the effects of it later on. Wait till you're thirty and you'll see where you'll be.' He has made the house what it has always been by his unlovely nature and his excellent appetite for whiskey and water, and that he has any pension left to live upon is due to the influence of friends and consideration for the family dependent on him. He was near being left without. Here is one of my Book of Days. On Thursday the 27th April [1905] I was up fairly early – 8 perhaps – and the day went according to my plan till a certain hour. Pappie was defendant in an appeal case and expected the case to be called. He was going to defend the action himself. I went down to see. I did not see, for it was not called, and I came home at six. Pappie was not in, there was no light, and no meal. I had wasted my day waiting for him in the Four Courts – a snobbish, utterly stupid, noisy hole – while he was getting drunk in some bar parlour or snug. I was irritated, for I knew he had money. I sat down heavily on the table and cursed his name vehemently. Poppie, who had been moping over the fire in the dark with the children, began to ease her own irritation and her tongue on me. I cursed at her like Pappie's son and went out. I was happy out – but what to do in such a house? Answer advertisements? Is anything more futile and disheartening? And what to do out? Aunt Josephine was laid up, so they would not be out, and my customary relief was blocked. I walked out to Dollymount by myself, then I came home, after nine. Pappie was not in yet. I had been speculating by outward signs about it while I knocked and had given myself hope. I cursed again violently for perhaps a minute, and was silent. Afterwards I went up to bed. It was partly stomach anger, it was partly a fanning of resentment into violent hatred, but it was deep irritation at myself far more than these. For some idea of amiability I had lived with him for some days and had consented not [to] go with those my thoughts should have chosen. Lâche! I had acted the part of companion to him – 'acted' is the word, for I knew that my slight, perceptible dislike for him was as constant and unchanging as my slight, perceptible pity for Mother. I felt my pride outwitted and humiliated. After ten Pappie came in with few pence left. We – and the children – had fasted 14 hours. I heard his drunken intonations in the dark downstairs, and then the saddening flow. This is a true portrait of my progenitor: the leading one a dance and then the disappointing, baffling, baulking and turning up drunk – the business of breaking hearts.

Stanislaus Joyce (1884–1955), *The Dublin Diary of Stanislaus Joyce*, 1962

BY THE EXETER RIVER

'What is it you're mumbling, old Father, my Dad?
Come drink up your soup and I'll put you to bed.'

'By the Exeter River, by the river, I said.'

'Stop dreaming of rivers, old Father, my Dad,
Or save all your dreaming till you're tucked in bed.'

'It was cold by the river. We came in a sled.'

'It's colder to think of, old Father, my Dad,
Than blankets and bolsters and pillows of bed.'

'We took off his dress and the cap from his head.'

'Outside? In the winter? Old Father, my Dad,
What can you be thinking? Let's get off to bed.'

'And Sally, poor Sally I reckon is dead.'

'Was she your old sweetheart, old Father, my Dad?
Now lean on my shoulder and come up to bed.'

'We drowned the baby. I remember we did.'

Donald Hall, *The One Day, Poems, 1947–1990*, 1991

MALICIOUS FREDERICK WILLIAM

To those who look upon royal life as invariably a scene of unmixed indulgence, the following description of the family circle of the King of Prussia, father to the great Frederick, may convey some instruction. It has been gathered from the accounts left us by his own daughter, the Princess Royal, afterwards Margravine of Bareith. 'His children,' she tells us, 'were all obliged to be in his apartment by nine o'clock every morning, and durst not leave his presence till night, upon any account. He was too restless to lie in bed, and being troubled with the gout, sat up in a large arm-chair, which was provided with castors, that he might be rolled about all over the palace, and be able to pursue any of the family who might chance to require a drubbing. His regular employment, during the whole day, was to abuse and torment young Frederick and the princess; the former getting no other name than *le coquin de Fritz*, and the latter, *la canaille Anglaise* (from the project to unite her to our Prince of Wales). This was not, however, the worst of it. His majesty, as well from a motive of economy, as from a spirit of maliciousness, pretended to be a disciple of the good old system of starving; ordered soup for his children, made of salt and water; and as he always himself performed the office of carver, made a point of helping every other person at table, except them. At times, however, he would pretend to give them a festival; and then would force them to eat and drink such disgusting and unwholesome things: *Ce qui nous obligoit quelquefois de rendre en sa présence tout ce que nous avions dans le corps.* Once his daughter Frederica ventured to murmur a little at this way of living; which put his majesty into so furious a rage, that he threw the plates at their heads, and fell a brandishing his crutches about him in the most death-like style; and when the affrighted flock took to their heels, pursued them in his rolling car as long as one of them was to be seen.'

Percy Anecdotes, 1823

Frederick William was deeply disappointed by his son, the future Frederick the Great, who in his youth seemed more interested in French culture, music, and literature than in the military virtues. The father's disaffection turned to actual hatred, and his treatment became so harsh that the young prince decided to run away, with the aid of two accomplices, Lieutenants Katte and Keith. Their plan was discovered; Keith escaped, but the prince and Katte were captured and court-martialed. Katte was sentenced to life imprisonment, Frederick to solitary confinement. Frederick William, deciding that Katte's sentence was too lenient, had him beheaded in the presence of Prince Frederick.

This drastic measure had the desired effect; Frederick asked the king's pardon and began to apply himself to acquiring the Prussian military philosophy.

The Faber Book of Anecdotes

THE SADDEST STORY EVER TOLD

In the course of the evening they came into the drawing-room and as an especial treat were to sing some of their hymns to me instead of saying them, so that I might hear how nicely they sang. Ernest was to choose the first hymn and he chose one about some people who were to come to the sunset tree. I am no botanist, and do not know what kind of a tree a sunset tree is, but the words began, 'Come, come, come; come to the sunset tree for the day is past and gone.' The tune was rather pretty and had taken Ernest's fancy, for he was unusually fond of music and had a sweet little child's voice which he liked using.

He was, however, very late in being able to sound a hard C or K, and instead of saying 'Come,' he said 'tum, tum, tum.'

'Ernest,' said Theobald from the armchair in front of the fire where he was sitting with his hands folded before him, 'don't you think it would be very nice if you were to say "come" like other people, instead of "tum"?'

'I do say tum,' replied Ernest, meaning that he had said 'come'.

Theobald was always in a bad temper on Sunday evening. Whether it is that they are as much bored with their day as their neighbours, or whether they are tired, or whatever the cause may be, clergymen are seldom at their best on Sunday evening; I had already seen signs that evening that my host was cross, and was a little nervous at hearing Ernest say so promptly, 'I do say tum,' when his papa had said he did ⸺ should.

⸺ oticed the fact that he was being contradicted in a ⸺ ad been sitting in an armchair in front of the fire with

[46]

his hands folded, doing nothing, but he got up at once and went to the piano.

'No Ernest, you don't,' he said; 'you say nothing of the kind, you say "tum" not "come". Now say "come" after me, as I do.'

'Tum,' said Ernest at once, 'is that better?' I have no doubt he thought it was, but it was not.

'Now Ernest, you are not taking pains: you are not trying as you ought to do. It is high time you learned to say "come"; why Joey can say "come", can't you, Joey?'

'Yeth I can,' replied Joey promptly, and he said something which was not far off 'come'.

'There, Ernest, do you hear that? There's no difficulty about it nor shadow of difficulty. Now take your own time; think about it and say "come" after me.'

The boy remained silent for a few seconds and then said 'tum' again.

I laughed, but Theobald turned to me impatiently and said, 'Please do not laugh Overton, it will make the boy think it does not matter, and it matters a great deal'; then turning to Ernest he said, 'Now Ernest, I will give you one more chance, and if you don't say "come" I shall know that you are self-willed and naughty.'

He looked very angry and a shade came over Ernest's face, like that which comes upon the face of a puppy when it is being scolded without understanding why. The child saw well what was coming now, was frightened, and of course said 'tum' once more.

'Very well Ernest,' said his father catching him angrily by the shoulder. 'I have done my best to save you but if you will have it so you will,' and he lugged the little wretch out of the room crying by anticipation. A few minutes more and we could hear screams coming from the dining-room across the hall which separated the drawing-room from the dining-room, and knew that poor Ernest was being beaten.

'I have sent him to bed,' said Theobald, as he returned to the drawing-room, 'and now, Christina, I think we will have the servants in to prayers,' and he rang the bell for them, red-handed as he was.

Samuel Butler (1835–1902), *The Way of All Flesh*, 1903

HE LEFT ME ALL HIS RICHES

My father died a month ago
And left me all his riches;
A feather bed, and a wooden leg,
And a pair of leather breeches.

He left me a teapot without a spout,
A cup without a handle,
A tobacco pipe without a lid,
And half a farthing candle.

Nursery rhyme

NEVER MIND DADDY

'It just happened,' he said hoarsely. 'I don't know – I don't know.

'After her mother died when she was little she used to come into my bed every morning, sometimes she'd sleep in my bed. I was sorry for the little thing. Oh, after that, whenever we went places in an automobile or a train we used to hold hands. She used to sing to me. We used to say, "Now let's not pay any attention to anybody else this afternoon – let's just have each other – for this morning you're mine."' A broken sarcasm came into his voice. 'People used to say what a wonderful father and daughter we were – they used to wipe their eyes. We were just like lovers – and then all at once we were lovers – and ten minutes after it happened I could have shot myself – except I guess I'm such a God-damned degenerate I didn't have the nerve to do it.'

'Then what?' said Doctor Dohmler, thinking again of Chicago and of a mild pale gentleman with a pince-nez who had looked him over in Zurich thirty years before. 'Did this thing go on?'

'Oh, no! She almost – she seemed to freeze up right away. She'd just say, "Never mind, never mind, Daddy. It doesn't matter. Never mind.'

'There were no consequences?'

'No.' He gave one short convulsive sob and blew his nose several ... ow there're plenty of consequences.'

F. Scott Fitzgerald (1896–1940), *Tender Is the Night*, 1934

A LUDICROUS DISPROPORTION

He was far too manly and generous to strike a child for the gratification of his anger; and he was too impulsive ever to punish a child in cold blood and on principle. He therefore relied wholly on his tongue as the instrument of domestic discipline. And here that fatal bent towards dramatisation and rhetoric (I speak of it the more freely since I inherit it) produced a pathetic yet comic result. When he opened his mouth to reprove us he no doubt intended a short well-chosen appeal to our common sense and conscience. But alas, he had been a public speaker long before he became a father. He had for many years been a public prosecutor. Words came to him and intoxicated him as they came. What actually happened was that a small boy who had walked on damp grass in his slippers or left a bathroom in a pickle found himself attacked with something like Cicero on Catiline, or Burke on Warren Hastings; simile piled on simile, rhetorical question on rhetorical question, the flash of an orator's eye and the thundercloud of an orator's brow, the gestures, the cadences and the pauses. The pauses might be the chief danger. One was so long that my brother, quite innocently supposing the denunciation to have ended, humbly took up his book and resumed his reading; a gesture which my father (who had after all only made a rhetorical miscalculation of about a second and a half) not unnaturally took for 'cool, premeditated insolence'. The ludicrous disproportion between such harangues and their occasions puts me in mind of the advocate in Martial who thunders about all the villains of Roman history while meantime *lis est de tribus capellis –*

> *This case, I beg the court to note,*
> *Concerns a trespass by a goat.*

My poor father, while he spoke, forgot not only the offence, but the capacities, of his audience. All the resources of his immense vocabulary were poured forth. I can still remember such words as 'abominable', 'sophisticated' and 'surreptitious'. You will not get the full flavour unless you know an angry Irishman's energy in explosive consonants and the rich growl of his R's. A worse treatment could hardly have been applied. Up to a certain age these invectives filled me with boundless terror and dismay. From the wilderness of the adjectives and the welter of the unintelligible, emerged ideas which I thought I understood only too well, as I heard with implicit and literal belief that our Father's ruin was approaching, that we should all soon beg our bread in the streets, that he would shut up the house and keep us at school all the year round, that we should be sent to the colonies and there end in misery the career of crime on which we had, it seemed, already embarked. All security seemed to be taken from me; there was no solid ground beneath my feet. It is significant that at this time if I woke in the night and did not immediately hear my brother's breathing from the neighbouring bed, I often suspected that my father and he had secretly risen while I slept and gone off to America – that I was finally abandoned. Such was the effect of my father's rhetoric up to a certain age; then, quite suddenly, it became ridiculous. I can even remember the moment of the change, and the story well illustrates both the justice of my father's anger and the unhappy way in which he expressed it.

C. S. Lewis (1898–1963), *Surprised by Joy*, 1955

A LITTLE WHELP IS WHIPPED

A very sullen-faced man stood at the corner of O'Connell Bridge waiting for the little Sandymount tram to take him home. He was full of smouldering anger and revengefulness. He felt humiliated and discontented; he did not even feel drunk; and he had only twopence in his pocket. He cursed everything. He had done for himself in the office, pawned his watch, spent all his money; and he had not even got drunk. He began to feel thirsty again and he longed to be back again in the hot, reeking public-house. He had lost his reputation as a strong man, having been defeated twice by a mere boy. His heart swelled with fury and, when he thought of the woman in the big hat who had brushed against him and said *Pardon!* his fury nearly choked him.

His tram let him down at Shelbourne Road and he steered his great body along in the shadow of the wall of the barracks. He loathed returning to his home. When he went in by the side-door he found the kitchen empty and the kitchen fire nearly out. He bawled upstairs:

'Ada! Ada!'

His wife was a little sharp-faced woman who bullied her husband when he was sober and was bullied by him when he was drunk. They had five children. A little boy came running down the stairs.

'Who is that?' said the man, peering through the darkness.

'Me, pa.'

'Who are you? Charlie?'

'No, pa. Tom.'

'Where's your mother?'

'She's out at the chapel.'

'That's right . . . Did she think of leaving any dinner for me?'

'Yes, pa. I –'

'Light the lamp. What do you mean by having the place in darkness? Are the other children in bed?'

The man sat down heavily on one of the chairs while the little boy lit the lamp. He began to mimic his son's flat accent, saying half to himself: '*At the chapel. At the chapel, if you please!*' When the lamp was lit he banged his fist on the table and shouted:

'What's for my dinner?'

'I'm going . . . to cook it, pa,' said the little boy.

The man jumped up furiously and pointed to the fire.

'On that fire! You let the fire out! By God, I'll teach you to do that again!'

He took a step to the door and seized the walking-stick which was standing behind it.

'I'll teach you to let the fire out!' he said, rolling up his sleeve in order to give his arm free play.

The little boy cried 'O, *pa!*' and ran whimpering round the table, but the man followed him and caught him by the coat. The little boy looked about him wildly but, seeing no way of escape, fell upon his knees.

'Now, you'll let the fire out the next time!' said the man, striking at him vigorously with the stick. 'Take that, you little whelp!'

The boy uttered a squeal of pain as the stick cut his thigh. He clasped his hands together in the air and his voice shook with fright.

'O, pa!' he cried. 'Don't beat me, pa! And I'll . . . I'll say a *Hail Mary* for you . . . I'll say a *Hail Mary* for you, pa, if you don't beat me . . . I'll say a *Hail Mary* . . .'

James Joyce (1882–1941), 'Counterparts', *Dubliners*, 1914

DO NOT TOUCH THIS ONE

Though I would later see indelible signs of my father's violence, I never experienced it in the unrestricted way that my brothers did. In fact, I remember being hit by my father on only one occasion. The cause of the spanking is vague – which only goes to support Frank's belief that all you truly carry away from such an incident is the bitterness of the punishment. I think I probably did something like drawing on a wall with a crayon or sassing my mother, and my father deemed that the act called for a whipping. I remember that he undressed me and stood me in front of him as he unbuckled his belt – a wide, black leather belt with a gleaming silver buckle – and pulled it from around his waist. This whole time he was telling me what my whipping was going to be like, how badly it was going to hurt. I remember I felt absolute terror in those moments – nobody had ever hit me before for any reason, and the dread of what was about to happen felt as fearful as the idea of death itself. My father was going to *hit* me, and it was going to hurt. It seemed horribly threatening – like the sort of thing I might not live through – and it also seemed horribly unjust.

My father doubled his belt over and held it in his hand. Then he sat down on his chair, reached out and took me by the arm and laid me across his lap. The next part is the only part I don't recall. I know I got whipped and that I cried out, but I can't remember a thing about the blows or the pain, or whether it was even truly bad. All I remember is that a few moments later I was standing in front of him again, this time held in my mother's embrace. 'That's enough, Frank,' she said. 'You've gone too far. You're not going to do to *this* one what you did to the others.' I stood there, looking at my father, rubbing my naked, sore butt, crying. I remember that what had really hurt me was that I felt I had lost my father's love, that the man I trusted most had hurt me in a way I had never expected. My father was smiling back at me – a smile that was meant to let me know that he was proud with what he had just done, that he enjoyed the power and the virtue of this moment. I looked back at him and I said: 'I hate you.'

I know it is the only time I ever said that to him in my life, and I cannot forget what those words did to his face. His smile fell – indeed, his whole face seemed to fall into a painful fear or sense of loss. He laid his belt on his desk and sat studying the floor, with a weary look of sadness.

Mikal Gilmore, *Shot in the Heart*, 1994

RIGHT AGAIN

An aerosol can of bug-spray swept by us one day. Father did not question where it came from – he was too busy railing about it. And plastic jugs on the current. He railed more. He railed against fat people and politicians and banks and breakfast cereal and scavengers – there were turkey buzzards and muddy vultures right overhead. He bawled them out, he cursed machines.

'I look forward to the day when I can cut this outboard loose – turn it into the meatgrinder it really is.' All machines were gravediggers, he said. Leave them alone for a minute and they bury themselves. That's all they were good for – holes.

'I had a Hole once.'

He smacked his lips, congratulating himself.

'I made ice out of fire!'

He named our floating hut the *Francis Lungley*, then changed it to the *President Fox*, and finally scratched *Victory* on its side with a nail. He said it was the world. It was twenty-seven feet long and six feet wide. He and Mother had the 'Master Cabin' (the cookstove, the chair, the pelican-feather bed). With the excess weight of timbers thrown overboard or cut for fuel, our craft moved more easily in the water, with the hefty grace of a canal boat, or a motorized barge in the Connecticut Valley. As soon as we were past the cut-off, where branches banged our roof, we plugged along the creek, staying midstream. Anywhere, Father said, as long as it was against the current.

We entered the Patuca that first day. We were surprised that the great river had been flowing all this time beyond the swamp to the east of our little Laguna Miskita – four hours' chug. But the river was hidden. We did not see it until we were almost on top of it. Father said he was not surprised at all – right again! The rain had swelled it over its red banks and into the trees and made it silent and so wide that in some reaches it hardly seemed to flow at all.

Father worked the boat along the edge of the submerged banks, where the current was easy. We made slow progress, but as Father said, 'Where's the fire? What's the rush? This isn't a vacation – this is life.'

At night we tied up to a tree and ate and slept with our smudge-pots going, to drive off the mosquitos. When a cloud of mosquitos approached, its millions drooped over us like a terrible net and made a loud high-pitched hum, the sound a radio makes between stations.

With the river murmuring past us, slurping at our logs, Father said that in all the world we were the last ones left. If we yelled for help, no one would come. Oh, we might meet stragglers, we might bump into savages, or even see whole villages on high ground that had been spared. But we were the only ones who knew that a catastrophe had taken place – the fire that had been followed by the thunder of war and the flood had been general throughout the earth. How could anyone here in Mosquitia know that America had been wiped out? It was man's narrow conceit that rain fell on him alone. But Father knew it was global. At each stage, he said, he had predicted what was to come. Even Americans themselves had seen the handwriting on the wall – they had talked about nothing else! But while they had sat and complained and twiddled their thumbs, Father had taken countermeasures to prevent our destruction.

'I may have exaggerated at times,' he said. 'But that was only to convince you of its seriousness, and get you moving. You're hard people to organize. Half the time you don't even believe me!'

What did it matter, he said, if he had been wrong about picky little things? He had been vindicated by great events. And what we had seen over the past year was the highest form of creation. He had outwitted the spectre which haunted the world, by removing us from a fragile and temporary civilization. All worlds ended, but Americans had been sure that, in spite of the obvious flaws, theirs would last. Not possible! But Father would carry us safely upriver.

'Farter,' Jerry said. 'Farter, farter, farter.'

Father did not hear him. He was shouting, 'How can I be wrong if I'm going against the current?'

The coast was death. The current tended that way. So it stood to reason that it flowed from life – mountains and springs. There among the volcanos of Olancho, we would make our home.

This was what he told us at night, in the cabin, when we were tied to a tree and the frogs croaked and drawled outside. During the day he still talked, but with the outboard going we hardly heard a word he said.

The river seemed to swell out of the ground. It flooded the jungle. This was a wilderness of water. Tree stumps with crooked uprising roots tumbled past us. It rained less often – a sprinkle in the morning, a downpour in the afternoon. But, as Father said, we were waterproof. And we saved the rainwater to drink. The sun on the river turned the muddy current to brass. It gave the jungle a nice bright smack. Shining through the morning mist it thickened the air with gold-spangled smoke that danced between the boughs. In places, there were clouds of white butterflies – regattas of them tacking just above the water. Or blue ones, as big as sparrows working their tottery wings so shyly they moved like beautiful scraps of silk flung out of the trees.

Two or three times a day we saw Zambus or Miskitos in cayukas slipping quickly downstream. Often, they waved to us, but the current took them so fast that no sooner had we spotted them than they were below us and around the bend.

'He's a goner,' Father usually said, as one went past. 'He's a dead man. A zombie, not a Zambu. Going down to die.'

They were wet, but they looked perfectly normal, paddling in their grubby underwear, riding across the fumbles of the current.

Jerry said that one of these days he was going to hop into our dugout and let the current take him to the coast. Father got wind of this, maybe from one of the twins, and ordered him into the dugout.

'In you go!'

Then Father cast it off and let it zoom downriver. Jerry was too terrified to paddle. He hung on to the seat and crouched with his head down and howled. When Jerry had almost travelled out of sight, Mother said, 'Allie, do something!' and Father snatched up a line. It was attached to the dugout. He jerked it, toppling Jerry on to his face. Jerry was shaking as Father towed him and the dugout back.

'That was insane!' Mother said.

'I proved my point. I got my wish.'

'What if the rope had snapped?'

'Then Jerry would have got *his* wish,' Father said. 'Anyone want to try it? I might just decide to let you go next time. Down the drain. Anyone interested?'

Another day, he caught me snoozing over the sounding chain. He punished me by putting me into the dugout and towing me behind the boat ('I sure hope that line doesn't snap! Better sit still!'), while my little canoe rocked and slewed in its wake.

We passed flooded villages. They were deserted – the wooden bones of huts standing in water, huts tipped over, others with fractured roofs, no more. These dead empty huts proved Father right. He said the people had been swept away – those were the folks in the long-johns we saw paddling down the drain to be swallowed by the sea.

'They won't need these,' he said, as he picked alligator pears, and limes and papayas and plantains off their trees. We found bags of rice and beans in some of these empty villages.

Father said, 'This isn't a raid. It's not theft. And it's certainly not scavenging. They don't need this where they are.'

But sometimes the birds beat us to it.

'Scavengers!'

One day we thought we saw an airplane, but our outboard was so loud we could not hear the plane's engines. Father said it was a turkey buzzard. What human had the sense to come here? This was the emptiest part of the map. In the whole world, this part of Honduras was the safest and least known – the last wilderness.

Paul Theroux, The Mosquito Coast, 1981

HOW NOT TO BEHAVE

When little Margaret grows up do *not* behave like John Barrymore did with his daughter Diana. John Barrymore who was sitting with Errol Flynn said as Diana passed by 'Ever f–d her?' Errol Flynn had, but as the girl was sixteen, he thought it wise to show surprise and denial – 'Don't miss it,' said Barrymore, 'she's terrific.'

Ann Fleming (1913–81), P. S. in a letter to Evelyn Waugh, 1958

HE WAS ALWAYS SHOWING OFF

A boy wants something very special from his father. You are always hearing it said that fathers want their sons to be what they feel they cannot themselves be but I tell you it also works the other way. I know that, as a small boy, I wanted my father to be a certain thing he was not, could not be. I wanted him to be a proud silent dignified one. When I was with other small boys and he passed along the street, I wanted to feel in my breast the glow of pride.

'There he is. That is my father.'

But he wasn't such a one. He couldn't be. It seemed to me then that he was always showing off. Let's say someone in our town had got up a show. They were always doing it. At that time it would have been the G.A.R., the Grand Army of the Republic. They did it to raise some money to help pay the rent of their hall.

So they had a show, the druggist in it, the fellow who clerked in the shoe store. A certain horse doctor was always in such shows in our town and, to be sure, a lot of women and girls. They got as many in it as they could so that all of the relatives of the actors would come. It was to be, of course, a comedy.

And there was my father. He had managed to get the chief comedy part. It was, let's say, a Civil War play and he was a comic Irish soldier. He had to do the most absurd things. They thought he was funny, but I didn't think so.

I thought he was terrible. I didn't see how Mother could stand it. She even laughed with the others. It may be that I also would have laughed if it hadn't been my father.

Or there was a parade, say on the Fourth of July or on Decoration Day. He'd be in that too. He'd be right at the front of it. He had got himself appointed Grand Marshall or some such office, had got, to ride in the parade, a white horse hired from a livery stable.

He couldn't ride for shucks. He fell off the horse and everyone hooted with laughter but he did not care. He even seemed to like it. I remember one such occasion when he had done something ridiculous, and right out on the main street too, when I couldn't stand it. I was with some other boys and they were laughing and shouting at him and he was shouting back at them and having as good a time as they were. I ran away. There was an alleyway back of the stores on Main Street and I ran down that. There were some sheds, back of the Presbyterian church, where country people stabled horses during church on Sundays and I went in there. I had a good long cry.

Sherwood Anderson (1876–1941), *Memoirs: A Critical Edition*, 1942

ROUSSEAU'S FOUNDLINGS

He who contributed most to the population of the Foundling Hospital was always most applauded. I caught the infection; I formed my manner of thinking upon that which I saw prevalent amongst very amiable and, in the main, very honourable people. I said to myself, 'Since it is the custom of the country, one who lives here may follow it.' Here was the expedient for which I was looking. I cheerfully resolved to adopt it, without the least scruples on my own part; I only had to overcome those of Thérèse, with whom I had the greatest trouble in the world to persuade her to adopt the only means of saving her honour. Her mother, who, in addition, was afraid of this new embarrassment in the shape of a number of brats, supported me, and Thérèse at last yielded. We chose a discreet and safe midwife, one Mademoiselle Gouin, who lived at the Pointe Saint-Eustache, to take care of this precious charge; and when the time came, Thérèse was taken to her house by her mother for her accouchement. I went to see her several times, and took her a monogram, which I had written on two cards, one of which was placed in the child's swaddling clothes, after which it was deposited by the midwife in the office of the hospital in the usual manner. The following year the same inconvenience was remedied by the same expedient, with the exception of the monogram, which was forgotten. On my side there was no more reflection, no greater approval on the mother's; she obeyed with a sigh . . . at last Madame la Maréchale pushed her kindness so far as to express a wish to remove and adopt one of my children. She knew that I had put a monogram upon the eldest one's linen; she asked me for the duplicate of it, and I gave it to her. In the search she employed La Roche, her *valet de chambre* and confidential servant, whose inquiries proved useless; he found out nothing, although only twelve or fourteen years had elapsed; if the registers of the Foundling Hospital had been regularly kept, or if the inquiry had been properly conducted, the mark ought not to have been so difficult to discover. However that may be, I was less annoyed at his failure than I should have been, if I had followed the child's career from its birth. If, with the assistance of the information afforded, any child had been presented to me as mine, the doubt, whether it really was so, or whether another had been substituted for it, would have tormented my heart with uncertainty, and I should not have enjoyed in all its charm the true feeling of nature, which, in order to be kept alive, must be kept up by constant familiarity, at least during infancy. The continued absence of a child whom one does not yet know, weakens and at last utterly destroys the feelings of a parent; it is impossible to love a child which has been put out to nurse as much as one which is brought up at home. This reflection may extenuate the effects of my faults, but only aggravates their origin.

Never, for a single moment in his life, could Jean Jacques have been a man without feeling, without compassion, or an unnatural father. I may have been mistaken, never hardened. If I were to state my reasons, I should say too much. Since they were strong enough to mislead me, they might mislead many others, and I do not desire to expose young people, who may read my works, to the danger of allowing themselves to be misled by the same error. I will content myself with observing, that my error was such that, in handing over my children to the State to educate, for want of means to bring them up myself, in deciding to fit them for becoming workmen and peasants rather than adventurers and fortune-hunters, I thought that I was behaving like a citizen and a father, and considered myself a member of Plato's Republic. More than once since then, the regrets of my heart have told me that I was wrong; but, far from my reason having given me the same information, I have often blessed Heaven for having preserved them from their father's lot, and from the lot which threatened them as soon as I should have been obliged to abandon them. If I had left them with Madame d'Epinay or Madame de Luxembourg, who, from friendship, generosity, or some other motive, expressed themselves willing to take charge of them, would they have been happier, would they have been brought up at least as honest men? I do not know; but I do know that they would have been brought up to hate, perhaps to betray, their parents; it is a hundred times better that they have never known them.

My third child was accordingly taken to the Foundling Hospital, like the other two. The two next were disposed of in the same manner, for I had five altogether. This arrangement appeared to me so admirable, so rational, and so legitimate, that, if I did not openly boast of it, this was solely out of regard for the mother; but I told all who were acquainted with our relations. I told Grimm and Diderot. I afterwards informed Madame d'Epinay, and, later, Madame de Luxembourg, freely and voluntarily, without being in any way obliged to do so, and when I might easily have kept it a secret from everybody; for Gouin was an honourable woman, very discreet, and a person upon whom I could implicitly rely. The only one of my friends to whom I had any interest in unbosoming myself was M. Thierry, the physician who attended my poor 'aunt' in a dangerous confinement. In a word, I made no mystery of what I did, not only because I have never known how to keep a secret from my friends, but because I really saw no harm in it. All things considered, I chose for my children what was best, or, at least, what I believed to be best for them. I could have wished, and still wish, that I had been reared and brought up as they have been.

J. J. Rousseau (1712–78), *The Confessions*, privately printed 1904

DADDY UP WORRIED

Without a word of warning he bolted every door and window in the house and waited up.

When he heard the latch of the back door being raised, he was dozing in darkness. Then he heard various windows being tried. Softly he went to the back door and drew the bolt and as soon as he heard returning footsteps he opened the door.

'This is a nice hour,' he said.

'I was in town. I couldn't get a lift back. I had to walk.'

'What were you doing in town?'

'There was a dance.'

'Did you ask to go to the dance?'

'No.'

'No *what*? No, pig!'

'No, Daddy.'

Moran beckoned him to come in and as he was passing him in the narrow hallway he seized him and struck him violently about the head. 'I'll teach you to come in at this hour! I'll teach you to go places without asking! There must have been drink at this hooley as well!'

Sheltered by his sisters, Michael was unused to any blows and angrily cried out as soon as he was struck. There would have been a violent struggle but for Rose's appearance.

'What an hour to come in at, Michael! You have Daddy up worried about you the whole night.'

'I couldn't get a lift. He hit me,' the boy cried.

'You haven't seen the end of this by half. I'll teach you one good lesson. Nobody's coming into this house at any old hour of the night they like while I'm in charge here.'

'Everyone's tired now. We'll get to bed. Anything that has to be gone into can be gone into in the morning,' Rose said.

Moran glared at her. He seemed about to brush her out of the way to seize the boy but drew back. 'You can thank your lucky stars the woman's here.'

'He hit me,' the boy sobbed.

'And I'll damn well show you what it is to be hit the next time you come into the house at this hour. You're not going to do anything you like while I'm here.'

'I'll go away,' the boy shouted self-pityingly.

'Everybody's tired. Look at the time it is. You can't be coming in at this time. You had poor Daddy and everybody else worried to death about you,' Rose scolded and managed to shepherd both men to their rooms without further trouble.

'I'll see that gentleman in the morning,' Moran warned. 'He need-n't think he's getting away with anything in this house.'

John McGahern, *Amongst Women*, 1990

JEALOUS GEORGE IV

Her life in London was arranged for her by the Regent almost down to the shape of a sandwich she might offer to a guest. Charlotte and her watchful guardians were to go occasionally to the play or opera, also sometimes to a dinner or party at Carlton House. As companion she was to have the Duchess of Leeds' daughter, Catherine Osborne, 'an elegant little girl of fifteen, who danced well, could play a little on the pianoforte, and speak a little French.' She sounds a youthful but complete bore, and this seems to have been Charlotte's opinion, for though she was extremely kind to her, as she always was to everyone she had to do with, this 'elegant' child never appears to have become part of her life, but remained merely a figure that moved about and mimed its small part. All the entertaining Charlotte was to do at Warwick House was to give 'parties of young ladies not presented – that is to say, children's balls.' In everything the Regent was determined to keep her back and treat her as if she had not come out, even to the point of the Duchess of Leeds opening all her letters. For each year as Charlotte grew from child to woman the Regent's jealousy increased; he was, says Henry Brougham, jealous of her 'to a degree of insanity.' Caroline had already come between him and his popularity with the nation, and now in the people's growing feeling for Charlotte the Regent saw that affection which he considered ought to belong to him being given to his child. Naturally the fact of Charlotte being Caroline's daughter did not endear her to him, and her taking her mother's side embittered him still more. And, apart from these considerations, Charlotte as a human being made no appeal to him whatever. In a life that he had found full of frets and difficulties he asked that women should act as consolatory balm, and in this eager, stammering schoolgirl, her mind filled with ideas that ran counter to his, and stamping her foot as she talked, there was no balm to be found. No; as far as he was concerned, Charlotte was nothing but a perpetual annoyance, a perpetual reminder of things he would sooner forget.

D. Creston, *The Regent and His Daughter*, 1932

I CANNOT MAKE HIM A HERO

In my notebook I wrote: 'No matter how I try, no matter how loyal I feel, I cannot make this man a hero. He was the one who lost his head when all around were keeping theirs. He tried to chicken out; he exaggerated his symptoms to the investigating officers and they believed him. He tried to impose on them; they believed him and treated him courteously, but he failed, because conditions were too grim for his malaise to be significant. Other people were working on, trying to conceal the fact that their chests were filling up with muck, and here is No. 254380 trying to get invalided out with a chest that despite his heavy smoking rings clear as a bell. They ask for sputum to examine and he can produce none. Perhaps I am having to face the fact that Daddy was a bounder. I think of Mr Adman's satiric smile and my heart fails. I remember the fear and shame in Daddy's eyes. I wonder if he could not love me any more because he had let me down.'

Germaine Greer, *Daddy We Hardly Knew You*, 1989

FREELY MOVED TO TEARS

By comparison with his sister, the Prince was timid and passive and easily cowed by the forceful personality of his father. When Prince Philip upbraided his son for a deficiency in behaviour or attitude, he easily drew tears to the child's eyes. According to a close friend, 'Philip was trying to bring up a son who would be able to take over as King in a tough world. Certainly Charles wasn't a cry-baby, but he was terribly sensitive. Prince Philip didn't quite realise how sensitive he was. Another child might not have noticed but Charles used to curl up . . . He just shrank.' Determined to prepare his son for the rigours that lay ahead, the Duke of Edinburgh was to put the relationship between father and son severely to the test. Even at this stage, though the bonds of love were by all accounts strong, they were already strained by impatience on the one side and trepidation on the other . . .

Despite the intense pleasure that the entire family derived from the sporting life at Sandringham and Balmoral, the Prince was frequently subdued and withdrawn, serious to the point of solemnity. To friends and relatives it was also clear that the Duke of Edinburgh found this demeanour irksome, a reaction which seemed only to exacerbate his son's tendency to retreat from the family fray. Princess Anne, who was now the dominant sibling, seemed very obviously her father's favourite. Openly indulging her often brash and obstreperous behaviour, he was quick to rebuke his son, in public no less than in private, for inconsequential errors. Indeed, he often seemed intent not merely on correcting the Prince but even mocking him as well, so that he seemed to be foolish and tongue-tied in front of friends as well as family. To their distress and embarrassment, the small boy was frequently brought to tears by the banter to which he was subjected and to which he could find no retort. On occasion, even his closest friends found the Duke's behaviour inexplicably harsh. One remembers that after a paternal reprimand at lunch, 'the tears welled into his eyes with a whole table full of people staying there . . . And I thought how could you do that?' Another, who both liked and admired the Duke 'enormously', observed the 'belittling' of the Prince and drew the conclusion that the father thought the son was 'a bit of a wimp . . . and Charles realised what his father thought, and it hurt him deeply'. A close relation, who is today on intimate terms with both men, would recall 'the rough way' the father addressed the son: 'very bullying . . . which had the effect of driving Charles more and more back into his shell'. According to one otherwise devoted retainer, 'Prince Philip did rather jump down his throat. Charles was frightened of him.' As an adult, the Prince was to remember these moments but would balance them against other aspects of his father's character: the patience with which he taught his son to make models, the readings from Longfellow's *Hiawatha*, and the visits to meet 'characters' like the actor James Robertson Justice and the dinghy sailor Uffa Fox, all of which were to leave the abiding impression that even if his childhood had difficulties, his father was at least trying to do his best and that even if there were moments of misery at home, there was also much happiness.

Observing friends were also frustrated by the failure of the child's mother to intervene by protective word or gesture. She was not indifferent so much as detached, deciding that in domestic matters she would submit entirely to the father's will. It was the more perplexing because they otherwise had every reason to believe that both parents had a deep if inarticulate love for their son, and that this love was reciprocated. They had seen them all together shooting or fishing or out on horseback; they had watched the games they played, and they knew that both parents could be found in the nursery seeing their children to bed and reading them to sleep. So witnessing this behaviour, loyal friends drew the conclusion that Prince Philip hectored his son because it was the only means he knew to achieve his supreme objective – to mould a prince for kingship.

Jonathan Dimbleby, *The Prince of Wales*, 1994

NASTY AND BRUTISH

Dad was brutal too. He drowned our dog's puppies. He put them all in a sack and shut me in my room, because I had asked for one to be saved and wouldn't stop whining about it. He just walked down to the river and dumped them in, keeping them under until they were dead. Once I brought a fieldmouse home. I held it out in my cupped hands, very pleased to have such a warm, living thing to play with. But Dad took it away from me. He threw it on the floor and crushed it under his foot. It squeaked.

Christine Keeler, *Scandal*, 1989

THE FIRST SIGHT OF A MONSTER

The first time I remember my father he was lying dead drunk on the dining-room floor.

He had clutched the table-cloth as he fell, and the carpet was littered with silver, broken glass, fruit and spilled wine. A decanter of port which he had been holding had broken in his hand; there was blood flowing from his wrist, and it mingled with the wine which had drenched his shirt. My eldest brother, Paul, was trying to bind his wrist with a napkin. Paul was then twelve years old. My other brother, Alan, who had come running to fetch me out of bed, was nine.

I was six.

Lying there on the floor, with groans coming from his open lips, with his moustache dyed dark from the wine into which he had plunged his face, with his glazed eyes rolling to and fro, my father looked like a great animal that had been wounded in the chase. A dangerous animal too, who might get up, who might stagger about again, and bite and claw and kill.

As he lifted his head his eyes ceased to roll, and focused themselves slowly, relentlessly, on me. I wanted to run away, but my legs did not seem to belong to me. I could feel them shaking in my pyjama trousers. Still he stared, and suddenly he spat out a couple of words, in a strangled voice. I did not understand the words; at the age of six I was not so versed in obscene language as I was to become, under my father's tuition, at the age of nine. But I knew that the words boded no good. They were a threat from which I must escape. So I threw myself from my brother's arm and ran from the room, screaming in an agonized treble . . . 'Daddy's drunk, daddy's drunk.'

II

In this book I must try not to let the vision be blurred by the miasma of hatred which, even to this day, seems to rise through the soil of his grave. For that grave is also my mother's resting-place, and it is her picture that I wish to paint. If only his image did not rise before me so constantly, getting in the way, like a slime over the canvas! That is an ugly phrase, reeking of hatred. Can they be reconciled – the truth and the hatred? Are they one and the same?

Yes, they are, and both are stranger than fiction. I would not dare to write a novel in which a small boy behaved as I did then. The reader would condemn him as an intolerable little prig.

This is what happened.

I ran straight from the dining-room, through the hall, and down the long corridor past the billiards-room. I pushed open the swing door that led to the servants' hall. And I threw myself into the kitchen, where the cook was sitting over the fire, reading aloud to another maid.

'Daddy's drunk,' I kept crying. 'Daddy's drunk.'

The tears streamed down my face and my body would not stop trembling. I think that Alan had followed me and was trying to tell me not to say such things before cook. I cannot be quite sure, but I think so. The next moments are very clear indeed.

I fell on my knees by a kitchen chair, and prayed aloud. 'Oh, God . . . daddy's drunk . . . please make him well.' The kindly, troubled face of the cook loomed over me, but I thrust her aside. 'Please, God, do not let him hurt my mother. Please make him well. Oh, God . . . daddy's drunk . . . drunk.'

The face of the cook, and behind it, the face of the big kitchen clock. The hard feel of the chair on my elbows. The rungs of the chair through which I was staring, as though they were bars through which I might see some glimpse of God. And the constant shrill cry of that word 'drunk' which I did not understand, but which I knew, with the intuition of childhood, was associated with madness, and disaster and death.

Beverley Nichols (1901–83), *Father Figure*, 1972

THREE

Petitions, Admonitions, Advice and

Exasperation

God good in preserving An in a milke bowle, and Jane from swoun-ing who let her fall in, and, John in falling from ye top of ye schoole staires; God give his angels charge over us.

1 Sept 1653, *The Diary of the Rev. Ralph Josselin, 1616–83*

SOME USELESS ADVICE FROM SCOTT FITZGERALD

August 8, 1933
La Paix, Rodgers' Ford,
Towson, Maryland.

Dear Pie:

I feel very strongly about you doing duty. Would you give me a little more documentation about your reading in French? I am glad you are happy – but I never believe much in happiness. I never believe in misery either. Those are things that you see on the stage or the screen or the printed page, they never really happen to you in life.

All I believe in in life is the rewards for virtue (according to your talents) and the *punishments* for not fulfilling your duties, which are doubly costly. If there is such a volume in the camp library, will you ask Mrs Tyson to let you look up a sonnet of Shakespeare's in which the line occurs *Lilies that fester smell far worse than weeds.*

Have had no thoughts today, life seems composed of getting up a *Saturday Evening Post* story. I think of you, and always pleasantly; but if you call me 'Pappy' again I am going to take the white cat out and beat his bottom *hard, six times for every time you are impertinent.* Do you react to that?

I will arrange the camp bill.

Half-wit, I will conclude. Things to worry about:

Worry about courage
Worry about cleanliness
Worry about efficiency
Worry about horsemanship . . .

Things not to worry about:

Don't worry about popular opinion
Don't worry about dolls
Don't worry about the past
Don't worry about the future
Don't worry about growing up
Don't worry about anybody getting ahead of you
Don't worry about triumph
Don't worry about failure unless it comes through your own fault
Don't worry about mosquitos
Don't worry about flies
Don't worry about insects in general

Don't worry about parents
Don't worry about boys
Don't worry about disappointments
Don't worry about pleasures
Don't worry about satisfactions
Things to think about:
What am I really aiming at?
How good am I really in comparison to my contemporaries in regard to:
(a) Scholarship
(b) Do I really understand about people and am I able to get along with them?
(c) Am I trying to make my body a useful instrument or am I neglecting it?
With dearest love,
Daddy

F. Scott Fitzgerald (1896–1940) *Letters*, 1964

A PEDOBAPTIST EXPOSED

I slept in a little bed in a corner of the room, and my Father in the ancestral four-poster nearer to the door. Very early one bright September morning at the close of my eleventh year, my Father called me over to him. I climbed up, and was snugly wrapped in the coverlid; and then we held a momentous conversation. It began abruptly by his asking me whether I should like to have a new mamma. I was never a sentimentalist, and I therefore answered, cannily, that that would depend on who she was. He parried this, and announced that, any way, a new mamma was coming; I was sure to like her. Still in a non-committal mood, I asked: 'Will she go with me to the back of the lime-kiln?' This question caused my Father a great bewilderment. I had to explain that the ambition of my life was to go up behind the lime-kiln on the top of the hill that hung over Barton, a spot which was forbidden ground, being locally held one of extreme danger. 'Oh! I daresay she will,' my Father then said, 'but you must guess who she is.' I guessed one or two of the less comely of the female 'saints,' and, this embarrassing my Father – since the second I mentioned was a married woman who kept a sweet-shop in the village – he cut my inquiries short by saying, 'It is Miss Brightwen.'

So far so good, and I was well pleased. But unfortunately I remembered that it was my duty to testify 'in season and out of season.' I therefore asked, with much earnestness, 'But, Papa, is she one of the Lord's children?' He replied, with gravity, that she was. 'Has she taken up her cross in baptism?' I went on, for this was my own strong point as a believer. My Father looked a little shame-faced, and replied: 'Well, she has not as yet seen the necessity of that, but we must pray that the Lord may make her way clear before her. You see, she has been brought up, hitherto, in the so-called Church of England.'

Our positions were now curiously changed. It seemed as if it were I who was the jealous monitor, and my Father the deprecating penitent. I sat up in the coverlid, and I shook a finger at him. 'Papa,' I said, 'don't tell me that she's a pedobaptist?' I had lately acquired that valuable word, and I seized this remarkable opportunity of using it. It affected my Father painfully, but he repeated his assurance that if we united our prayers, and set the Scripture plan plainly before Miss Brightwen, there could be no doubt that she would see her way to accepting the doctrine of adult baptism. And he said we must judge not, lest we ourselves be judged. I had just enough tact to let that pass, but I was quite aware that our whole system was one of judging, and that we had no intention whatever of being judged ourselves. Yet even at the age of eleven one sees that on certain occasions to press home the truth is not convenient.

Edmund Gosse (1849–1928), *Father and Son*, 1907

THE MARXIAN WAY

Summer, 1940

Dear Arthur:

Glad to hear from you and to know that you are recovering. I am also pleased to learn that you have a rich dame who wants to put you up while you are recuperating. How does she have her money? Is it in jewels or securities, or just plain gold? Some night, when you are grappling with her in the moonlight, you might find out. Do it discreetly, for God's sake. Don't come out bluntly and say, 'How much dough have you got?' That wouldn't be the Marxian way. Use finesse.

Well, I will leave the whole thing to you.
    Love,
    Padre

Groucho Marx (1895–1977), *The Groucho Letters*, 1967

SOME STRANGE CAUTIONS

It was during the visit to my father at Monte Carlo that he issued the wildest and most terrifying of all his warnings to me. Readers of those books of mine in which my father occurs may remember that he was wont to give strange cautions to those round him. As he grew older these seemed to become more unexpected and frequent. We had been talking the previous evening of my projected first visit to the United States early in the New Year. In the morning he sent for me to his room. As I entered, he said: 'Good morning, Osbert, come in and shut the door . . . There are two things of which I should warn you before you start for America.'

My heart sank at the familiar opening, usually the preliminary to trouble.

'What are they, Father?'

'Never play with a dead cat, and above all never make friends with a monkey.'

Even I, accustomed though I was to receiving from him cautions at once morbid and startling, was on this occasion somewhat disconcerted, because the warnings thus addressed to me seemed to fit in with no proclivities of my nature of which I was conscious. Good heavens, what could he mean? Indeed, I was so much taken aback that I rather foolishly asked: 'Why?', and received a yet more bewildering Delphic reply delivered in his most withering style:

'Because if you do you'll get diphtheria!'

The explanation proved to be that my father had read in one of the papers of an outbreak in New York of this illness, which a small boy had developed; and the child had been seen playing in Central Park, throwing the body of a dead cat up in the air and catching it over and over again. The second warning derived also from a newspaper, in the columns of which he had read how some children had been observed, pressed against the bars of a cage in the Zoo, talking for a long time to a great ape, and that in view of the fact that the animal had devel-

[72]

oped diphtheria the next day, it was surmised in medical circles that the children, who fell ill a week or two later, had contracted the disease from their anthropoid chum. (My father was fond of animals, and I have often seen him go up to the cage of a monkey, and talk to the sad-eyed but insouciant inmate . . . His special interest in the simian tribes was no doubt a tribute to the part they played in the evolutionary theories of his great hero Charles Darwin.) That, however, which rendered my father's warnings disturbing as well as entertaining was that you could not just dismiss them, because you never knew what might not come next, and because often under their *prima facie* absurdity would lurk, hidden by piles of rubbish though it might be, an unexpected truth. Equally, his mind, with its conflicting streaks of conventional and unconventional, on occasions enabled him to arrive at startling but perhaps correct conclusions – as, for example, when we entered into argument about a contemporary trial for murder; in the course of our dispute I opined that the man found guilty was plainly a lunatic and should, therefore, not be executed: my father agreed, rather surprisingly, that the man was mad, but added: 'and one of his delusions may be that he can always commit a murder with absolute impunity'.

My father had a great belief in 'Looking Ahead', which had become with him a special process and one which was concerned with material affairs and not, as might have been presumed from its name, with some spiritual state in the future. No, 'Looking Ahead' was included in good management and was avoided whenever possible by my mother. The concentration necessary to its formulation sometimes gave 'Looking Ahead' an impression of insensibility which was not altogether deserved. It had to be impersonal as a proposition in geometry, and who has ever complained that Euclid was heartless? . . . My mother related to me one of the most singular instances of it. The scene had taken place in March 1916, while I was in the trenches. My father had one morning rushed like a whirlwind into the room, and said at great speed: 'I have just been looking ahead. We may hear at any moment that Osbert's been killed, and the other dear boy will probably go too; in which case you will certainly pass away, and what I want to know is, would the money in your settlement be available for the sons of my second marriage?'

Osbert Sitwell (1892–1969), *Tales My Father Taught Me*, 1962

ONE PENIS IS ENOUGH

Dear Son

I am sorry to heare Mr Bishop is so much his owne foe. Surely his brayne is not right. Probably you may heare agayne of him before hee returnes into his country. Hee seemed to bee fayre conditiond when hee was in these parts, though very hypochondriacall sometimes. Mr Hombarston whenever his brayne is distemper'd, resolves upon a journey to London, & there showes himself, acts his part & returnes home better composed, as hee did the last time. Hee would not bee persuaded to bleed agayne before hee went. If the dolphin were to bee showed for money in Norwich, little would bee gott. If they showed it in London, they are like to take out the viscera & salt the fish & then the dissection will bee inconsiderable. You may remember the dolphin opened when the King was heere & Dr Clark was at my howse, when you tooke a draught of severall parts very well, which Dr Clark had sent unto him. Bartholinus hath the Anatome of one in his centuries. You may observe therein the odde muscle whereby it spouts out water, the odde Larynx like a goose head, the flattish heart, the Lungs, the *Renes racemosi*, the penis, the multiple stomack &c. When wee wasshed that fish a kind of cuticule came of in severall places on the sides & back. Your mother hath an art to dresse & cooke the flesh so as to make an excellent savory dish of it, & the King being at Newmarket I sent collars thereof to his table, which were well liked of.

Though you must take the paynes to compose a new sett of Lectures, yet I do not see why you should not retaine the greatest and necessarie part for information of the Auditors, although you may alter or adde some things as observation or reading shall informe you, or as you find they are not cleare enough or fully enough expressed, & some remarkable observations may bee retained, as that of the *papillae pyramidalis* in the elephants skinne, with some hint that the appositenesse & aptnesse therein would not bee omitted, though showne & produced to serve for illustration before, for there will bee many present next time which were not nowe, & some absent which were now present.

De pulmone.

The Lungs taking up a considerable part of the chest, it may seeme something strange that the chest may bee runne through, or traversely pierced through both sides, & yet the Lungs escape & have no hurt, butt this notwithstanding may happen, if the thrust bee made at the expiration and when the Lungs subside.

De pene.

Some have queried why since nature hath been so sollicitous about the provisions for generation, this penis is only single and not double in masles, which Sinibaldus thincks sufficiently answered when hee sayth. *Absit certe, nimius est unus.* O no. God forbid, one is to much. However, the question is not altogether groundlesse, for in some animals this part is double, as in the viper, Sinibaldus, lib. 3. tractat 1. cap 8. Which you need not quote as to the place.

de cuticula aut cute

Many, especially yong persons, are sayd to bee goose skinned, wherein the parts are a little elevated, whereof I have heard an odde observation, which I cannot as yet confirme, that those who have such skinns have not had the *lues venerea.*

You have also divers parts to handle which were not treated in your last, as the *Mesenterium*, Thymus, Larynx & its cartilages, wherein you may help yourself in Casserius also *de dentibus*, for the barber chirurgeons sake that they may have a Theoricall knowledge of those parts wherin they are often practicall.

I shall returne the lect. upon the first good opportunity that you may have them by you to make use of & send hints as they occurre.

Your loving father

T.B.

June 14.

[1676]

Sir Thomas Browne (1605–82), Letter to his son Edmund, 1676

A PIECE OF WORLDLY ADVICE

When we reached the booking-office at Victoria, where my father was getting a return ticket and a half to Tunbridge Wells, I saw what I thought was a bright new farthing on the ground in front of me.

'Pappa,' I called, 'there's a golden farthing on the ground.'

My father looked round.

'Put your foot on it, you little duffer,' he said sharply.

This I did, and when he had got the tickets my father bent down and picked up half a sovereign.

'Don't shout out like that when you find a piece of gold. Anybody hearing you might have claimed that he had just dropped it.'

This within my recollection is the first piece of purely worldly advice I ever received.

Compton Mackenzie (1883–1972), My Life and Times, Octave I, 1963

AN AIR OF DOUCEUR

CCXIV

BATH, *October* 19, 1753.

MY DEAR FRIEND,

Of all the various ingredients that compose the useful and necessary art of pleasing, no one is so effectual and engaging as that gentleness, that *douceur* of countenance and manners, to which you are no stranger, though (God knows why) a sworn enemy. Other people take great pains to conceal or disguise their natural imperfections; some by the make of their clothes, and other arts, endeavour to conceal the defects of their shape; women who unfortunately have natural bad complexions lay on good ones; and both men and women, upon whom unkind nature has inflicted a surliness and ferocity of countenance, do at least all they can, though often without success, to soften and mitigate it; they affect *douceur*, and aim at smiles, though often in the attempt, like the Devil in Milton, they *grin horrible a ghastly smile*.* But you are the only person I ever knew, in the whole course of my life, who not only disdain, but absolutely reject and disguise a great advantage that nature has kindly granted. You easily guess I mean *countenance*; for she has given you a very pleasing one; but you beg to be excused, you will not accept it; on the contrary, take singular pains to put on the most *funeste*, forbidding, and unpleasing one, that can possibly be imagined. This one would think impossible; but you know it to be true. If you imagine that it gives you a manly, thoughtful, and decisive air, as some, though very few of your countrymen do, you are most exceedingly mistaken; for it is at best the air of a German corporal, part of whose exercise is to look fierce, and to *blasemeer-op*.

You will say, perhaps, What, am I always to be studying my countenance, in order to wear this *douceur*? I answer, No, do it but for a fortnight, and you will never have occasion to think of it more. Take

[76]

but half the pains to recover the countenance that nature gave you, that you must have taken to disguise and deform it as you have, and the business will be done. Accustom your eyes to a certain softness, of which they are very capable, and your face to smiles, which become it more than most faces I know. Give all your motions, too, an air of *douceur*, which is directly the reverse of their present celerity and rapidity. I wish you would adopt a little of *l'air du couvent* (you very well know what I mean) to a certain degree; it has something extremely engaging; there is a mixture of benevolence, affection, and unction in it; it is frequently really sincere, but is almost always thought so, and consequently pleasing. Will you call this trouble? It will not be half an hour's trouble to you in a week's time. But suppose it be, pray tell me, why did you give yourself the trouble of learning to dance so well as you do? It is neither a religious, moral, or civil duty. You must own, that you did it then singly to please, and you were in the right on't. Why do you wear your fine clothes, and curl your hair? Both are troublesome; lank locks, and plain flimsy rags, are much easier. This, then, you also do in order to please, and you do very right. But then, for God's sake, reason and act consequentially; and endeavour to please in other things too, still more essential, and without which the trouble you have taken in those is wholly thrown away.

You show your dancing, perhaps, six times a year, at most; but you show your countenance, and your common motions every day, and all day. Which, then, I appeal to yourself, ought you to think of the most, and care to render easy, graceful, and engaging? *Douceur* of countenance and gesture can alone make them so. You are by no means ill-natured; and would you then most unjustly be reckoned so? Yet your common countenance intimates, and would make anybody, who did not know you, believe it. *A propos* of this, I must tell you what was said the other day to a fine lady whom you know, who is very good-natured, in truth, but whose common countenance implies ill-nature, even to brutality. It was Miss Hamilton, Lady Murray's niece, whom you have seen, both at Blackheath and at Lady Hervey's. Lady Murray was saying to me, that you had a very engaging countenance, when you had a mind to it, but that you had not always that mind; upon which Miss Hamilton said, that she liked your countenance best, when it was as glum as her own. Why then, replied Lady Murray, you two should marry; for, while you both wear your worst countenances, nobody else will venture upon either of you; and they call her now Mrs. Stanhope! . . .

I do not yet hear one jot the better for all my bathings and pumpings, though I have been here already full half my time. I consequently go very little into company, being very little fit for any. I hope you keep company enough for us both; you will get more by that than I shall by all my reading. I read singly to amuse myself, and fill up my time, of which I have too much; but you have two much better reasons for going into company, Pleasure and Profit. May you find a great deal of both, in a great deal of company! Adieu.

* *Paradise Lost*, ii, 846.

Lord Chesterfield (1694–1773)

A PRIVATE FAREWELL

Prince Andrei had been summoned to his father's study, where the old prince wished to bid him a private farewell. All were waiting for them to come out.

When Prince Andrei went into the study the old man, the spectacles of old age on his nose and wearing a white dressing-gown in which he never received anyone except his son, was sitting at the table writing. He glanced round.

'Are you off?' And he went on writing.

'I have come to say good-bye.'

'Kiss me here,' and he indicated his cheek. 'Thank you, thank you!'

'Why do you thank me?'

'Because you don't dilly-dally, because you aren't tied to your wife's apron-strings. The service before everything. Thank you, thank you!' And he went on writing so vigorously that his quill spluttered and squeaked. 'If you have anything to say, say it. I can attend to these two things at once,' he added.

'About my wife . . . I am so sorry to leave her on your hands . . .'

'Why talk nonsense? Say what it is you want.'

'When the time comes, send to Moscow for an *accoucheur* . . . Get him here.'

The old prince stopped writing and pretending not to understand fixed his son with stern eyes.

'I know that if nature does not do her work no one can help,' said Prince Andrei, obviously embarrassed. 'I know that not more than one in a million cases goes amiss, but this is her whim and mine. People have been telling her things, she has had a dream, and she's frightened.'

[78]

'H'm . . . H'm . . .' growled the old man, taking up his pen again. 'I'll see to it.'

He signed his name with a flourish, and suddenly turned to his son with a laugh.

'It's a bad business, eh?'

'What is, father?'

'Your wife!' said the old prince with blunt significance.

'I don't understand,' said Prince Andrei.

'Yes, there's nothing to be done about it, my young friend,' said the prince. 'They're all alike; and there's no getting unmarried again. Never fear, I won't tell anyone; but you know yourself it's the truth.'

He grasped his son's hand with his small bony fingers, shook it, looked him straight in the face with keen eyes which seemed to see through a person, and again laughed his chilly laugh.

The son sighed, thereby admitting that his father had read him correctly. The old man continued to fold and seal his letters, snatching up and throwing down wax, seal and paper with his habitual rapidity.

'What can you do? She's a beauty. I'll see to everything. Make your mind easy,' said he abruptly, as he sealed the last letter.

Andrei was silent. It was both pleasant and painful that his father understood him. The old man got up and handed the letter to his son.

'Come,' said he, 'don't worry about your wife. Whatever can be done shall be done. Now listen. Give this letter to Mihail Ilarionovich.' (This was Kutuzov.) 'I have asked him to make use of you in proper places, and not keep you too long as an adjutant: it's a nasty job! Tell him that I remember him with affection. Write and let me know how he receives you. If he gives you a proper welcome, stay with him. The son of Nikolai Andreich Bolkonsky need serve no one on sufferance. Now come here.'

He spoke so rapidly that half his words were left unfinished, but his son was used to understanding him. He led him to a desk, threw back the lid, pulled open a drawer and drew out a manuscript-book filled with his own bold, angular, close handwriting.

'I am sure to die before you. So remember, these are my memoirs to be given to the Emperor after my death. Now here is a bank-note and a letter: it is a prize for anyone who writes a history of Suvorov's campaigns. Send it to the Academy. Here are some jottings for you to read after I am gone. You will find them worth your while.'

Andrei did not tell his father that he would no doubt live a long time yet. He felt it better not to say that.

'I shall carry out your wishes, father,' he said.

'Well, now, good-bye.' He gave his hand to be kissed, and embraced his son. 'Remember one thing, Prince Andrei: if you get killed, it will be a grief to me in my old age . . .' He paused abruptly and then in a scolding voice suddenly cried: 'But if I were to hear that you had not behaved like the son of Nikolai Bolkonsky, I should be – ashamed!'

'You need not have said that to me, father,' replied the son with a smile.

The old man did not speak.

'There's another thing I wanted to ask you,' continued Prince Andrei. 'If I am killed and if I have a son, keep him here with you, as I was saying yesterday. Let him grow up under your roof . . . Please.'

'Not let your wife have him?' said the old man, and he laughed.

They stood in silence, facing one another. The old man's keen eyes gazed straight into his son's. There was a tremor in the lower part of the old prince's face.

'We have said good-bye . . . now go!' said he suddenly. 'Go!' he shouted in a loud, angry voice, opening the study door.

'What is it? What has happened?' asked Prince Andrei's wife and sister as Prince Andrei came out and they caught a momentary glimpse of the old man in his white dressing-gown, without his wig and wearing his spectacles, as he appeared at the door shouting irately.

Prince Andrei sighed and made no reply.

'Well!' said he, turning to his wife. And this 'Well!' sounded like a cold sneer, as though he were saying: 'Now go through your little per-formance.'

'André, already?' said the little princess, turning pale and fixing terror-stricken eyes on her husband.

He embraced her. She shrieked and fell swooning on his shoulder.

He warily released the shoulder she leant on, glanced into her face and carefully laid her in an armchair.

'Adieu, Marie,' said he gently to his sister, taking her by the hand and kissing her, and hastened out of the room.

The little princess lay in the armchair, Mademoiselle Bourienne chafing her temples. Princess Maria, supporting her sister-in-law, con-tinued to look with her beautiful eyes dim with tears at the door through which Prince Andrei had disappeared, and she made the sign of the cross after him. From the study came the sounds of the old man blowing his nose with sharp angry reports like pistol shots. Hardly had Prince Andrei left the room before the study door was flung open and the stern figure of the old man in his white dressing-gown looked out.

'Gone, has he? Well, and a good thing too!' said he, and looking furiously at the fainting little princess he shook his head reprovingly and slammed the door.

Leo Tolstoy (1828–1910), *War and Peace*, translated by Rosemary Edmonds

THE PONY

Magnificent Father, Lucrezia and I are trying who can write best. She writes to grandmother Lucrezia, I, my father, to you. The one who obtains what he asks for will win. Till now Lucrezia has had all she wished for. I, who have always written in Latin in order to give a more literary tone to my letters, have not yet had that pony you promised me so that I am laughed at by all. See to it therefore, Your Magnificence that she should not always be the winner.

26th May, 1479

Magnificent Father mine, – That pony does not come, and I am afraid that it will remain so long with you that Andrea will cause it to change from a beast to a man, instead of curing its hoof. – We are all well and studying. Giovanni is beginning to spell. By this letter you can judge where I am in writing; as for Greek I keep myself rather in exercise by the help of Martino than make any progress. Giuliano laughs and thinks of nothing else; Lucrezia sews, sings, and reads; Maddalena knocks her head against the wall, but without doing herself any harm, Luisa begins to say a few little words; Contessina fills the house with her noise . . . Nothing is wanting to us save your presence.

Magnificent Father mine, – I fear that some misfortune has happened to that pony, for had it been well I know you would have sent it to me as you promised. I beg of you therefore as a grace that you will take this fear from me; for I think of it night and day, and until the pony comes I shall have no peace. In case that one cannot come be pleased to send me another. For, as I have already written to you, I am here on foot, and sometimes it is necessary for me to go in the company of my friends. See to this therefore, Your Magnificence.

Magnifico Patri meo, – I cannot tell you, Magnificent Father, how glad I am to have the pony, and how his arrival incites me to work. If

[81]

I desire to praise him, *Ante diem clauset componet vesper Olympo.* He is so handsome and so perfect that the trumpet of Maronius would hardly suffice to sing his praises. You may think how I love him; particularly when his joyous neighs resound and rejoice all the neighbourhood. I owe you and I send you many thanks for such a fine gift and I shall try and repay you by becoming what you wish. I promise you that I shall try with all my heart.

Piero de' Medici (1471–1503), from letters to his father Lorenzo the Magnificent

AN UNHAPPY ALTERNATIVE

Mrs. Bennet rang the bell, and Miss Elizabeth was summoned to the library.

'Come here, child,' cried her father as she appeared. 'I have sent for you on an affair of importance. I understand that Mr. Collins has made you an offer of marriage. Is it true?' Elizabeth replied that it was. 'Very well – and this offer of marriage you have refused?'

'I have, Sir.'

'Very well. We now come to the point. Your mother insists upon your accepting it. Is not it so, Mrs. Bennet?'

'Yes, or I will never see her again.'

'An unhappy alternative is before you, Elizabeth. From this day you must be a stranger to one of your parents. – Your mother will never see you again if you do *not* marry Mr. Collins, and I will never see you again if you *do*.'

Jane Austen (1775–1817), *Pride and Prejudice*

THE LADY'S NEW-YEAR'S GIFT: OR, ADVICE TO A DAUGHTER

I find, that even our most pleasing thoughts wil bee unquiet; they wil bee in motion; and the mind can have no rest whilst it is possessed by a darling passion. You are at present the chief object of my care, as wel as of my kindness, which sometimes throweth mee into visions of your being happy in the World, that are better suited to my partial wishes, than to my reasonable hopes for you. At other times, when my fears prevaile, I shrink as if I was struck, at the prospect of danger, to which a young woman must bee exposed. By how much the more lively, so much the more lyable you are to bee hurt; as the finest plants are the soonest nipped by the Frost. Whilst you are playing full of innocence, the spitefull World wil bite, except you are guarded by your caution. Want of care therefore, my Dear child, is never to bee excused; since, as to this World, it hath the same effect as want of virtue. Such an early sprouting Witt requireth soe much the more to bee sheltered by some Rules, like something strewed upon tender flowers to preserve them from being blasted. You must take it wel to bee pruned by soe kind a hand as that of a Father. There may be some bitterness in meer obedience: The natural love of liberty may help to make the commands of a Parent harder to goe down: some inward resistance there wil be, where power and not choice maketh us move. But when a Father layeth aside his authority, and persuadeth onely by his kindnesse, you will never answer it to good nature, if it hath not weight with you . . .

But I must restrain my thoughts, which are full of my dear Child, and would overflow into a Volume, which would not be fit for a New-year's guift. I wil conclude with my warmest wishes for all that is good to you. That you may live soe as to be an Ornament to your Family, and a Pattern to your Sex; That you may be blessed with a Husband that may value, and with Children that may inherit, your vertue; that you may shine in the world by a true light, and silence Envy by deserving to be esteemed; that wit and vertue may both con-spire to make you a great figure. When they are seperated, the first is so empty, and the other so faint, that they scarce have right to be com-mended. May they therefore meet and never part; Let them be your guardian Angels, and be sure never to stray out of the distance of their joynt protection. May you so raise your Character, that you may help to make the next Age a better thing, and leave Posterity in your debt for the advantage it shal receive by your Example.

Let me conjure you, *My Dearest*, to comply with this kind ambition of a father, whose thoughts are soe engaged in your Behalfe, that he reckoneth your happiness to be the greatest part of his own.

1st Marquess of Halifax (1633–95)

ADVICE TO A SON

Never trust a white man,
Never kill a Jew,
Never sign a contract,
Never rent a pew.
Don't enlist in armies;
Nor marry many wives;
Never write for magazines;
Never scratch your hives.
Always put paper on the seat,
Don't believe in wars,
Keep yourself both clean and neat,
Never marry whores.
Never pay a blackmailer,
Never go to law,
Never trust a publisher,
Or you'll sleep on straw.
All your friends will leave you
All your friends will die
So lead a clean and wholesome life
And join them in the sky.

Berlin, 1931

Ernest Hemingway (1899–1961), *Omnibus: Almanach auf das Jahr 1932*

I WILL MAKE YOU AMENDS ONE DAY

Paris
April 18??

... The 200 francs which you kindly sent me at the beginning of the
month won't last beyond the 3rd or 4th of May, as I was obliged to
give 50 fr. which were overdue for manuscript paper and copying that
I had to pay for. Then I bought a hat which cost me 20 fr. I had my
boots repaired for 14 fr. And I had two pairs of shoes made, 14 fr. I
am also going to make a request, my dear Papa, which may strike you
as tactless. I have an intense desire to acquire the complete works of
Volney, made up, as you know, of the *Ruins, Travels in Syria,* the

Description of the United States, the *Letters on Greece*, and the *Researches into Ancient History*. This superb edition, the only one that exists, is on the point of going out of print, the Government has forbidden a reprinting, and the price is rising all the time. Three months ago it was selling for 40 fr., at the moment it can't be had for less than 64, and in spite of this there are only twenty copies left.

Farewell, dear Papa, please believe that I am not so far from being what you wish me to be, and that one day I will make you amends for the pain I have caused you.

Your respectful and loving son,

H. Berlioz

Hector Berlioz (1803–69), letter to his father

SEND ME A FINE HATT

And therfore, I besech you to send a servant of yours to my lady and me, and shew now by your fatherly kyndnesse that I am your child; for I have sent you dyverse messuages and wryttings, and I had never answere againe. Wherfore, yt is thought in this parties, by those persones that list better to say ill than good, that ye have litle favor unto me; the which error ye may now quench, yf yt will like you to be so good and Kynd father unto me. Also I beseech you to send me a fine hatt and some good cloth to make me some kevercheffes.

Dorothy Plumpton, (c. 1490–c. 1540) letter to Sir Robert Plumpton, c. 1500

LITTLE TEMPLES

1796

22nd March   Children do not think at all, or think only of themselves: giddy, selfish, capricious.

23rd June   Octavius's propensity to perverseness must be checked. Children when young are always bickering. To be a parent without an assistant is a hard task. Always doing something to discompose and interrupt tranquillity.

27th June   Much discomposed to-day with the children: difficult to please or keep them in humour with one another, envious and jealous. 13th July   Am discomposed with Octavius, who grows very rude and troublesome. Holidays too long. What uneasiness do children give one from the very first.

William Johnson Temple (1628–99), *Diaries*

MR BRONTË IS SURPRISED

Now, however, when the demand for the work had assured success to *Jane Eyre*, her sisters urged Charlotte to tell their father of its publication. She accordingly went into his study one afternoon after his early dinner, carrying with her a copy of the book, and two or three reviews, taking care to include a notice adverse to it.

She informed me that something like the following conversation took place between her and him. (I wrote down her words the day after I heard them; and I am pretty sure they are quite accurate.)

'Papa, I've been writing a book.'

'Have you, my dear?'

'Yes; and I want you to read it.'

'I am afraid it will try my eyes too much.'

'But it is not in manuscript; it is printed.'

'My dear! you've never thought of the expense it will be! It will be almost sure to be a loss, for how can you get a book sold? No one knows you or your name.'

'But, papa, I don't think it will be a loss; no more will you, if you will just let me read you a review or two, and tell you more about it.'

So she sat down and read some of the reviews to her father; and then, giving him the copy of *Jane Eyre* that she intended for him, she left him to read it. When he came in to tea he said, 'Girls, do you know Charlotte has been writing a book, and it is much better than likely?'

Elizabeth Gaskell (1810–65), *The Life of Charlotte Brontë*, 1857

THACKERAY BANISHES BONNETS

A momentous event for the children was when their father took them abroad for six weeks in the summer of 1851. Anny was fourteen, Minny eleven. They went without a maid and it was all adventure and thrill.

'I suppose the outer circuit of my own very limited wanderings must have been reached at the age of thirteen or thereabouts, when my father took me and my little sister for the grand tour of Europe. We had, of course, lived in Paris and spent our summers in quiet country places abroad with our grandparents, but this was to be something different from anything we had ever known before at St. Germains or Montmorenci among the donkeys; Switzerland, and Venice, and Vienna, Germany and the Rhine! Our young souls thrilled with expectation. And yet those early feasts of life are not unlike the miracle of the loaves and the fishes; the twelve basketfuls that remain in after years are certainly even more precious than the feast itself.

'We started one sleety summer morning. My father was pleased to be off, and we were enchanted. He had brought a gray wide-awake hat for the journey, and he had a new sketch book in his pocket, besides two smaller ones for us, which he produced as the steamer was starting. We sailed from London Bridge, and the decks were all wet and slippery as we came on board. We were scatter-brained little girls, although we looked demure enough in our mushroom hats and waterproofs. We also had prepared a travelling trousseau . . . which consisted I remember of a draught board, a large wooden work-box, a good many books, paint boxes, and other odds and ends; but I felt that whatever else might be deficient our *new bonnets* would bring us triumphantly out of every crisis. They were alike, but with a difference of blue and pink wreaths of acacia, and brilliant in ribbons to match, at a time when people affected less dazzling colours than they do now. Alas! for human expectations! When the happy moment came at last, and we had reached foreign parts and issued out of the hotel dressed and wreathed and triumphantly splendid, my father said "My dear children go back and put those bonnets away in your box, and don't ever wear them any more!" How the sun shone as he spoke; how my heart sank under the acacia trees. My sister was eleven years old, and didn't care a bit; but at thirteen and fourteen one's clothes begin to strike root. I felt disgraced, beheaded of my lovely bonnet, utterly crushed, and I turned away to hide my tears.'

Anne Thackeray Ritchie (1837–1919), *Recollections*

'I think it fit and agreeable to the affection I bear thee, to help thee with such rules and advertisements for the squaring of thy life, as are rather gained by experience, than much reading; to the end that entering into this exorbitant age, thou mayest be the better prepared to shun those scandalous courses whereunto the world and the lack of experience may easily draw thee.'

1 When it shall please God to bring thee to man's estate, use great providence and circumspection in choosing thy wife; for from thence will spring all thy future good or evil; . . .let her not be poor, how generous soever; for a man can buy nothing in the market with gentility; nor choose a base and uncomely creature altogether for wealth; for it will cause contempt in others and loathing in thee; neither make choice of a dwarf, or a fool; for by the one you shall beget a race of pigmies, the other will be thy continual disgrace, and it will irke thee to hear her talk; for thou shalt find it, to thy great grief, that there is nothing more fulsome than a she-fool . . .

Bring thy children up in learning and obedience, yet without outward austerity. Praise them openly, reprehend them secretly. Give them good countenance and convenient maintenance according to thy ability; otherwise thy life will seem their bondage and what portion thou shalt leave them at thy death, they will thank death for it, and not thee. And I am persuaded that the foolish cockering of some parents, and the over-stern carriage of others, causeth more men and women to take ill courses, than their own vicious inclinations. Marry thy daughters in time, lest they marry themselves. And suffer not the sons to pass the Alps, for they shall learn nothing there but pride, blasphemy, and atheism. And if by travel they get a few broken languages, that shall profit them nothing more than to have one meat served in divers dishes. Neither, by my consent, shalt thou train them up in wars; for he that sets up his rest to live by that profession, can hardly be an honest man or a good Christian . . . Besides it is a science no longer in request than use; for soldiers in peace, are like chimneys in summer.

Live not in the country without corn and cattle about thee; for he that putteth his hand to the purse for every expense of household, is like him that putteth water in a sieve . . . Be not served with kinsmen, or friends, or men intreated to stay; for they expect much and do little.

Undertake no suit against a poor man without receiving much

wrong; for besides that thou makest him thy compeer, it is a base conquest to triumph where there is so small resistance . . .

Be sure to keep some great man thy friend, but trouble him not with trifles; compliment him often with many, yet small gifts, and of little charge; and if thou hast cause to bestow any great gratuity, let it be something which may be daily in sight; otherwise in this ambitious age, thou shalt remain like a hop without a pole, live in obscurity, and be made a football for every insulting companion to spurn at.

Towards thy superiors be humble, yet generous, with thine equals familiar, yet respective; towards thine inferiors show much humanity, and some familiarity; as to bow the body, stretch forth the hand, and to uncover the head, with such like popular compliments. The first prepares thy way to advancement, the second makes thee known for a man well bred; the third gains a good report, which once got is easily kept; for high humilities take such deep root in the minds of the multitude, as they are easilier gained by unprofitable courtesies, than by churlish benefits; yet I advise thee not to affect or neglect popularity too much. Seek not to be Essex; shun to be Raleigh.

Be not scurrilous in conversation nor satirical in thy jests; the one will make thee unwelcome to all company, the other pull on quarrels, and get thee hatred of thy best friends. Jests, when any of them savour of truth, leave a bitterness in the minds of those which are touched; and, albeit I have already pointed at this inclusively; yet I think it necessary to leave it to thee as a special caution, because I have seen many so prone to quip and gird, as they would rather lose their friend than their jest; and if, perchance, their boiling brain yield a quaint scoff, they will travail to be delivered of it as a woman with child. These nimble fancies are but the froth of wit.

William Cecil, Lord Burghley (1520–98), advice to his son Robert,
1st Earl of Salisbury

BE MERRY, BUT NOT INSOLENT

My Son,

That I see you not before my parting, impute to this great occasion, wherein time is so precious; but that shall, by God's grace, be recompensed by your coming to me shortly, and continual residence with me ever after. Let not this news make you proud or insolent, for a king's son ye were, and no more are ye now; the augmentation that is hereby like to fall to ye, is but in cares and heavy burden. Be merry, but not insolent; keep a greatness, but *sine fastu*; be resolute, but not wilful; be kind, but in honourable sort. Choose none to be your playfellows but of honourable birth; and, above all things, never give countenance to any, but as ye are informed they are in estimation with me.

Look upon all Englishmen that shall come to visit you as your loving subjects, not with ceremoniousness as towards strangers, but with that heartiness which at this time they deserve. This gentleman whom the bearer accompanies, is worthy, and of good rank, and now my family servitor; use him, therefore, in a more homely, loving sort than others.

I send ye herewith my book lately printed. Study and profit in it, as ye would deserve my blessing; and as there can nothing happen unto you whereof ye will not find the general ground therein, if not the particular point touched, so must ye level every man's opinions or advices with the rules there set down, allowing and following their advices that agree with the same, mistrusting and frowning upon them that advise ye to the *contraire*. Be diligent and earnest in your studies, that at your meeting with me I may praise ye for your progress in learning. Be obedient to your master for your own weal, and to procure my thanks; for in reverencing him, ye obey me and honour yourself. Farewell.

Your loving father,
James R.

James I (1566–1625) letter to Prince Henry

MY TWO BOY ADVENTURERS

My sweet boys,

I write this now, my seventh letter, unto you upon the 17th of March, sent in my ship called the *Adventurer*, to my two boy-adventurers, whom God ever bless. . . . I send you your robes of the order, which ye must not forget to wear on St. George's Day, and dine together in them – if they can come in time – which I pray God they may, for it will be a goodly sight for the Spaniards to see my boys dine in them.

I send you also the jewels as I promised, some of mine and such of yours – I mean both of you – as are worthy the sending, ay, or my Baby's presenting his mistress. I send him an old double cross of Lorrain, not so rich as ancient, and yet not contemptible for the value; a good looking-glass with my picture in it, to be hung at her girdle, which ye must tell her ye have caused it so to be enchanted by art-magic, that whensoever she shall be pleased to look in it, she shall see the fairest lady that either her brother or your father's dominions can afford.

Ye shall present her with two fair long diamonds, set like an anchor, and a fair pendent diamond hanging in them. Ye shall give her a goodly rope of pearls, ye shall give a carquanet or collar, thirteen great ballas rubbies, and thirteen knots or conques of pearls; and ye shall give her a head-dressing of two and twenty great pear pearls. . .

And for my Baby's own wearing, ye shall have two good jewels of your own, your round broach of diamonds, and your triangle diamond with the great round pearl. . . . Ye have also good diamond buttons of your own, to be set to a doublet or jerkin. as for your first, it may serve for a present to a Don.

As for thee, my sweet gossip, I send thee a fair table diamond – which I would once have given thee before, if thou would have taken it – for wearing in thy hat, or where thou pleases; and if my Baby will spare thee the two long diamonds in form of an anchor, with the pendent diamond, it were fit for an admiral to wear, and he hath enough better jewels for his mistress. Though he is of thine own, [I send] thy good old jewel, thy three pindars diamonds, the picture case I gave Kate, and the great diamond chain I gave her (who would have sent thee the least pin she had, if I had not stayed her).

If my Baby will not spare the anchor from his mistress, he may well lend thee his round broach to wear, and yet he shall have jewels to wear in his hat for three great days.

And now for the form of my Baby's presenting of his jewels to his mistress: I leave that to himself, with Steenie's advice, and my Lord of Bristol's. Only I would not have them presented all at once, but at the more sundry times the better, and I would have the rarest and richest kept hindmost. I have also sent four other crosses, of meaner value, with a great pointed diamond in a ring, which will save charges in presents to Dons, according to their quality. But I will send with the fleet divers other jewels for presents, for saving charges (whereof we have too much need); for till my Baby's coming away, there will be no need of giving presents to any but her.

Thus you see how, as long as I want the sweet company of my boys' conversation, I am forced, yea, and delight to converse with them by long letters. God bless you both, my sweet boys, and send you, after a successful journey, a joyful happy return in the arms of your dear dad.

James R.

From Newmarket on St. Patrick's Day, who, of old, was too well patronized in the country you are in.

James I (1566-1625), letter to Henry and Charles, 1623

AN HONOUR OR A DISGRACE

'You are now launching into a scene of Life, where You may either prove an Honour or a Disgrace to Your Family. It would be very unbecoming of the love I have for my Children if I did not at this serious moment give You Advice how to conduct yourself. Had I taken the common method of doing it in Conversation, it would soon have been forgot: therefore I prefer this mode, as I trust you will frequently peruse this, as it is dictated from no other motive than the anxious feelings of a Parent, that his child may be happy, and deserve the approbation of Men of Worth and Integrity.

'You should never lose sight', urged the King, 'of the certainty that every thought as well as action, is known to the All wise Disposer of the Universe and that no solid comfort ever in this World can exist, without a firm reliance on His Protection . . . these reflections are still more necessary to be foremost in the minds of those at Sea . . . therefore, I strongly recommend the habitual reading of the Holy Scriptures and Your more and more placing that reliance on the Divine Creator, which is the only real means of obtaining that peace of mind, that alone can fit a Man for arduous undertaking.

'Remember You are now quitting home, where it has been the object of those who were placed about You to correct Your faults, yet keep them out of sight of the World. Now You are entering into a Society of about seven hundred persons, who will watch every step You take, will freely make their remarks, and communicate them to the whole Fleet; thus what would I hope have been cured must now be instantly avoided, or will be forever remembered to Your disadvantage.

[92]

'Though when at home a Prince, on board the *Prince George* You are only a Boy learning the Naval Profession; but the Prince so far accompanies You that what other Boys might do, You must not. It must never be out of Your thoughts that more Obedience is necessary from You to Your Superiors in the Navy, more Politeness to Your Equals and more good nature to Your Inferiors, than from those who have not been told that these are essential to a Gentleman.'

George III (1738–1820), to his son Prince William, 13 June, 1779

TO HIS LITTLE SON BENEDICT FROM THE TOWER OF LONDON

Sweet Benedict, whilst thou art young,
And know'st not yet the use of tongue,
Keep it in thrall whilst thou art free:
Imprison it or it will thee.

John Hoskyns (1566–1638), *Oxford Book of Children's Verse*

FOUR

Doting and Indulgent Fathers

Miss Thackeray on seeing her new sister wanted to poke one of her
eyes out and said teedle deedle, wh. is considered very clever.

W.M. Thackeray (1811–63), letter to George Wright, 1838

THE INDULGENCE OF HENRY FOX

With his children Holland was always a welcome comrade. No
amount of personal care or sorrow could lessen his sympathy with
their smallest interests; no amount of money seemed too great for the
indulgent father to bestow upon their follies; and yet few children
have ever been more expensive luxuries than Stephen and Charles
James Fox. Both of them were inveterate and most unlucky gamblers,
and it was not a rare occurrence for one or the other of them to lose
ten thousand pounds in a single night's play. Yet seldom, as far as we
know, did Holland show the least displeasure at such antics. His fortune was theirs – to save or to squander.

T.W. Riker, *Henry Fox, the Politician and the Man*, 1911

Better testimony to his marvellous, but not ungraceful, precocity than the
admiration of an indulgent father is given by Charles Fox himself, who
remembered being present in the room when his mother made a
desponding remark about his passionate temper. 'Never mind,' said
Henry Fox, always for leaving both well and ill alone. 'He is a very sensible little fellow, and will learn to cure himself.' 'I will not deny,' said
Charles, when he told the story, 'that I was a very sensible little boy; a
very clever little boy. What I heard made an impression on me, and was
of use to me afterwards.' If he mended his faults so readily, it certainly is
a pity that he did not overhear more of the parental criticisms; for of correction and reprimand he received little or none. 'Let nothing be done to
break his spirit,' Lord Holland used to say. 'The world will do that business fast enough.' The impression left by the father's subservience to all
the child's whims and fancies is preserved in many well-known anecdotes
which for the most part are probably mythical. The shortest, and best, of
these stories is to the effect that Charles declared his intention to destroy
a watch. 'Well!' said Lord Holland; 'if you must, I suppose you must.'

George Trevelyan, *The Early History of Charles James Fox*, 1881

A CREAM BATH

Once a grand dinner was held at Holland House for some visiting
foreign dignitaries. The Fox children were brought in for dessert.
Charles, still a toddler in petticoats, said he wanted to bathe in a huge

bowl of cream that stood on the table. Despite Caroline's remonstrances, Fox ordered the dish to be put down on the floor and there, in full view of some of Europe's most powerful politicians, the little boy slopped and slid to his heart's content in the cool, thick liquid. Another time Fox lifted Charles up on the table and put him on top of a prize joint of roast beef so that the child could sit astride the symbol of England itself, a living image of Fox's hopes for his sons.

Stella Tillyard, *Aristocrats*, 1994

FOND FATHERS

The warlike Agesilaus was, within the walls of his own house, one of the most tender and playful of men. He used to join with his children in all their innocent gambols, and was once discovered by a friend, showing them how to ride upon a hobby-horse. When his friend expressed some surprise at beholding the great Agesilaus so employed, 'Wait,' said the hero, 'till you are yourself a father, and if you then blame me, I give you liberty to proclaim this act of mine to all the world.'

The grave Socrates was once surprised in nearly a similar situation by Alcibiades, and made nearly the same answer to the scoffs of that gay patrician. 'You have not,' said he, 'such reason as you imagine to laugh so, at a father playing with his child. You know nothing of that affection which parents have to their children; restrain your mirth till you have children of your own, when you will, perhaps, be found as ridiculous as I now seem to you to be.'

The elder Cato, in the busiest periods of his life, always found time to be present at the bathing and dressing of his son; and when he grew up, would not suffer him to have any other master than himself. Being once advised to resign the boy to the care of some learned servant, he replied, that 'He could not bear that any servant should pull his son by the ears, or that his son should be indebted for his learning and education to any other than himself.'

Charles the Great was so fond a father, that he never dined nor supped without his children at table; he went no where, but he took them along with him; and when he was asked why he did not marry his daughters, and send his sons abroad to see the world, his reply was, 'That he was sure he could not be able to bear their absence.'

Percy Anecdotes, 1823

MISSING MY DAUGHTER

This wall-paper has lines that rise
Upright like bars, and overhead,
The ceiling's patterned with red roses.
On the wall opposite the bed
The staring looking-glass encloses
Six roses in its white of eyes.

Here at my desk, with note-book open
Missing my daughter, makes those bars
Draw their lines upward through my mind.
This blank page stares at me like glass
Where stared-at roses wish to pass
Through petalling of my pen.

An hour ago, there came an image
Of a beast that pressed its muzzle
Between bars. Next, through tick and tock
Of the reiterating clock
A second glared with the wide dazzle
Of deserts. The door, in a green mirage,

Opened. In my daughter came.
Her eyes were wide as those she has,
The round gaze of her childhood was
White as the distance in the glass
Or on a white page, a white poem.
The roses raced around her name.

Stephen Spender (1909–95), *Collected Poems*, 1985

A LITTLE WENCH IS FOUND

At last – oh, sight of joy! – this lane, the longest in the world, was coming to an end, was opening on a broad high-road, where there was actually a coach passing! And there was a finger-post at the corner: she had surely seen that finger-post before – 'To St. Oggs, 2 miles.' The gypsy really meant to take her home, then: he was probably a good man, after all, and might have been rather hurt at the thought that she didn't like coming with him alone. This idea became stronger as she felt more and more certain that she knew the road quite well, and she was considering how she might open a conversation with the injured gypsy, and not only gratify his feelings but efface the impression of her cowardice, when, as they reached a cross-road, Maggie caught sight of some one coming on a white-faced horse.

'Oh, stop, stop!' she cried out. 'There's my father! Oh, father, father!'

The sudden joy was almost painful, and before her father reached her, she was sobbing. Great was Mr. Tulliver's wonder, for he had made a round from Basset, and had not yet been home.

'Why, what's the meaning o' this?' he said, checking his horse, while Maggie slipped from the donkey and ran to her father's stirrup.

'The little miss lost herself, I reckon,' said the gypsy. 'She'd come to our tent at the far end o' Dunlow Lane, and I was bringing her where she said her home was. It's a good way to come arter being on the tramp all day.'

'Oh, yes, father, he's been very good to bring me home,' said Maggie. 'A very kind, good man!'

'Here, then, my man,' said Mr. Tulliver, taking out five shillings. 'It's the best day's work *you* ever did. I couldn't afford to lose the little wench; here, lift her up before me.'

'Why, Maggie, how's this?' he said, as they rode along, while she laid her head against her father, and sobbed. 'How came you to be rambling about and lose yourself?'

'Oh, father,' sobbed Maggie, 'I ran away because I was so unhappy – Tom was so angry with me. I couldn't bear it.'

'Pooh, pooh,' said Mr. Tulliver, soothingly, 'you mustn't think o' running away from father. What 'ud father do without his little wench?'

'Oh, no, I never will again, father – never.'

George Eliot (1819–80), *The Mill on the Floss*

HARTLEY COLERIDGE IN RAPTURES

Hartley returns his love to you; he talks often about you. I hear his voice at this moment distinctly; he is below in the garden, shouting to some foxgloves and fern, which he has transplanted, and telling them what he will do for them if they grow like good boys! This afternoon I sent him naked into a shallow of the river Greta; he trembled with the novelty, yet you cannot conceive his raptures.

God bless you!
I remain, with affectionate esteem,
Yours sincerely,
S. T. Coleridge.

Letter to James West Tobin, 25 July 1800

NOTHING BUT IN CARE OF THEE

Miranda. Had I been any god of power, I would
Have sunk the sea within the earth, or ere
It should the good ship so have swallow'd, and
The fraughting souls within her.
Prospero. Be collected:
No more amazement: tell your piteous heart
There's no harm done.
Miranda. O, woe the day!
Prospero. No harm.
I have done nothing but in care of thee,
Of thee, my dear one, thee, my daughter, who
Art ignorant of what thou art; nought knowing
Of whence I am, nor that I am more better
Than Prospero, master of a full poor cell,
And thy no greater father.
Miranda. More to know
Did never meddle with my thoughts.

William Shakespeare (1564–1616), *The Tempest*

PROUD STEELE

The Children do come on so well that it would make ev'n me
Covetous to put them in a condition equal to the good Genius, I blesse
God, they seem to be off. Moll is the noisiest little Creature in the
World, and as active as a Boy. Madam Betty is the Gravest of
Matrons in her Airs and Civilities. Eugene a most Beautifull and Lusty
Child.

Sir Richard Steele (1672–1729), letter to Lady Steele, 25 February 1716–17

Your Son at the present writing is mighty well employed in Tumbling on the Floor of the room and Sweeping the sand with a Feather. He grows a most delightfull Child, and very full of Play and Spiritt. He is also a very great Scholar. He can read His Primer, and I have brought down my Virgil. He makes most shrewd remarks upon the Pictures. We are very intimate Freinds and Play fellows. He begins to be very ragged and I hope I shall be pardoned if I equip Him with new Cloaths and Frocks or what Mrs. Evans and I shall think for His Service.

Sir Richard Steele (1672–1729), letter to Lady Steele, 16 March 1716–17

WITCHES IN DISGUISE

To *Candida Betjeman*   The Athenaeum
18 October 1949   Pall Mall SW1

Dear Candida,
I am very pleased to have your nice letter and I am sorry I have not a nice postcard to send to you like Mummy did. Here are some fairies

but I think they are witches pretending to be fairies. I liked the drawing you did of trees and flowers and yourself.

Here I am sitting in this
club.

Love from Daddy

John Betjeman (1906–84), letter to Candida Betjeman

MY LITTLE BEAUTIFUL CHILD

Saighton,
Nov. 6, 1895

MY DEAR CHARLES, –

What can you think of my silence? I postponed my reply until my return here from visiting; but – you will sorrow with us to hear – no sooner was I back than my little Percy was severely injured by a fall from his pony. His thigh is broken and alas! very near the socket. Dear Charles, I cannot tell you what the last 48 hours have been; but now there is a lull in the fearful pain. I was more than an hour with him on the ground, alone, before help came. I can't think of it without strangling. Then I got him on to a plank and into a cart. His courage and beauty made it harder not to break down. As I carried the plank into the house, after all that pain and cold and fear of the unknown, he hailed Cuckoo with a cheery voice as he passed her.

I cut him out of his little clothes and boots, for he would allow no one else to touch him. When the Doctor said it was his thigh I broke down, but I pulled myself together for I was the one person he trusted, and stood by him while he took the ether, and pulled his poor beautiful little leg while they set it; and yesterday I held him fast with two hands for 14 hours while he rode out the storm of pain. His Mother, thank God! was away until late last night, when the very worst was over.

Yesterday was more terrible than any horror I had ever imagined; but, it brought us together in such a fire of agony, that I believe to-day, as I have never yet been able to believe, that neither death nor any eternity after death can ever part me from my little beautiful child. He believed that my hands helped him, and fixed his fever-bright eyes on mine with love and trust even as the paroxysms came on, calling out 'hold me tighter, Papa, hold me tighter, here it comes.' Well, to-day he is not in such pain, and I have never felt such gratitude to God! Dear Charles! forgive all this . . .

Yours ever,
GEORGE WYNDHAM

George Wyndham (1863–1913), letter to Charles T. Gatty,

TO HIS SWEETEST CHILDREN

I hope that a letter to all of you may find my four children in good
health and that your father's good wishes may keep you so. In the
meantime, while I make a long journey, drenched by a soaking rain,
and while my mount, too frequently, is bogged down in the mud, I
compose these verses for you in the hope that, although unpolished,
they may give you pleasure. From them you may gather an indication
of your father's feelings for you – how much more than his own eyes
he loves you; for the mud, miserably stormy weather, and necessity
for driving a diminutive horse through deep waters have not been able
to distract his thoughts from you or to prevent his proving that, wherever he is, he thinks of you. For instance, when and it is often – his
horse stumbles and threatens to fall, your father is not interrupted in
the composition of his verses. Poetry often springs from a heart which
has no feeling; these verses a father's love provides – along with a
father's natural anxiety. It is not so strange that I love you with my
whole heart, for being a father is not a tie which can be ignored.
Nature in her wisdom has attached the parent to the child and bound
them spiritually together with a Herculean knot. This tie is the source
of my consideration for your immature minds, a consideration which
causes me to take you often into my arms. This tie is the reason why
I regularly fed you cake and gave you ripe apples and pears. This tie
is the reason why I used to dress you in silken garments and why I
never could endure to hear you cry. You know, for example, how
often I kissed you, how seldom I whipped you. My whip was invariably a peacock's tail. Even this I wielded hesitantly and gently so that
sorry welts might not disfigure your tender seats. Brutal and unworthy to be called father is he who does not weep himself at the tears of
his child. How other fathers act I do not know, but you know well
how gentle and devoted is my manner towards you, for I have always
profoundly loved my own children and I have always been an indulgent parent – as every father ought to be. But at this moment my love
has increased so much that it seems to me I used not to love you at all.
This feeling of mine is produced by your adult manners, adult despite
your tender years; by your instincts, trained in noble principles which
must be learned; by your pleasant way of speaking, fashioned for clar-
ity; and by your very careful weighing of every word. These characteristics of yours so strangely tug at my heart, so closely bind me to
you, my children, that my being your father (the only reason for many

a father's love) is hardly a reason at all for my love of you. Therefore, most dearly beloved children all, continue to endear yourselves to your father and, by those same accomplishments which make me think that I had not loved you before, make me think hereafter (for you can do it) that I do not love you now.

Sir Thomas More (1478–1535)

DON'T LET YOUR DAUGHTERS MARRY

'It's easy to see that you love your father and mother!' said the old man, clutching Eugène's hand with both his feeble, trembling hands. 'Do you understand that I am going to die without seeing them, without seeing my girls? I have been thirsty for ten years, and *they* have never quenched my thirst. My sons-in-law killed my daughters. Yes, I was bereaved of daughters when they got married. Fathers, tell the Chambers they must pass a law against marriages! Don't let your daughters marry, if you love them. A son-in-law is a scoundrel who spoils everything in a girl's heart, he corrupts her whole nature. Let there be no more marriages! They carry off our daughters, and rob us of them, and we are left alone when we come to die. Pass a law for dying fathers. It is shocking! It cries for vengeance! They would come if my sons-in-law did not prevent them. Kill them! Strike down Restaud, kill the Alsatian, they are my murderers! Death or my daughters! Ah! this is the end, I am dying and they are not with me! Dying without them! Nasie, Delphine, why do you not come? Your father is going –'

'Dear Father Goriot, keep calm, there, there, stay quiet; set your heart at rest; don't think.'

'Not to see them – there is death's sting!'

Honoré de Balzac (1799–1850), *Old Goriot*, translated by
Marion Ayton Crawford

A CURE FOR THE SUFFERINGS OF MISUNDERSTOOD YOUTH

D'Israeli's cure for the sufferings of misunderstood youth was a toy, a guinea, or – when his runaway son had been found sleeping on a tomb in Hackney churchyard – a pony. At last the discovery that the boy was scribbling verses roused him. Isaac was packed off, 'like a bale of goods,' to a tutor in Amsterdam. Thence he returned, at the age of eighteen, long-haired, a reader of Voltaire, and a disciple of Rousseau. To the request that he would proceed to Bordeaux and take up a post that had been procured for him in a sound commercial house, he replied by proffering 'a poem of considerable length, which he wished to publish, against commerce, which was the corruption of man.' There was nothing for it but to hide him again on the Continent.

D.L. Murray, *The Life of Disraeli*, 1908

ALICE IN THE WHITE HOUSE

Alice's antics scandalized the staid society of Washington during her father's tenure at the White House. When a visitor objected to the girl's wandering in and out of the president's office while he was discussing important business with her father, Roosevelt said, 'I can be president of the United States or I can control Alice. I cannot possibly do both.'

Marcus Connelly, *Voices Offstage: A Book of Memoirs*, 1968

FATHER'LL TAKE YOUR PART

Mrs. Tulliver's scream made all eyes turn towards the same point as her own, and Maggie's cheeks and ears began to burn, while uncle Glegg, a kind-looking, white-haired old gentleman, said –

'Heydey! what little gell's this – why, I don't know her. Is it some little gell you've picked up in the road, Kezia?'

'Why, she's gone and cut her hair herself,' said Mr. Tulliver in an under-tone to Mr. Deane, laughing with much enjoyment. 'Did you ever know such a little hussy as it is?'

'Why, little Miss, you've made yourself look very funny,' said uncle Pullet, and perhaps he never in his life made an observation which was felt to be so lacerating.

'Fie, for shame!' said aunt Glegg, in her loudest, severest tone of reproof. 'Little gells as cut their own hair should be whipped and fed on bread and water – not come and sit down with their aunts and uncles.'

'Ay, ay,' said uncle Glegg, meaning to give a playful turn to this denunciation, 'she must be sent to jail, I think, and they'll cut the rest of her hair off there, and make it all even.'

'She's more like a gypsy nor ever,' said aunt Pullet in a pitying tone, 'it's very bad luck, sister, as the gell should be so brown – the boy's fair enough. I doubt it'll stand in her way i' life to be so brown.'

'She's a naughty child, as'll break her mother's heart,' said Mrs. Tulliver, with the tears in her eyes.

Maggie seemed to be listening to a chorus of reproach and derision. Her first flush came from anger, which gave her a transient power of defiance, and Tom thought she was braving it out, supported by the recent appearance of the pudding and custard. Under this impression, he whispered, 'Oh, my! Maggie, I told you you'd catch it.' He meant to be friendly, but Maggie felt convinced that Tom was rejoicing in her ignominy. Her feeble power of defiance left her in an instant, her heart swelled, and, getting up from her chair, she ran to her father, hid her face on his shoulder, and burst out into loud sobbing.

'Come, come, my wench,' said her father, soothingly, putting his arm round her, 'never mind; you was i' the right to cut it off if it plagued you, give over crying: father'll take your part.'

Delicious words of tenderness! Maggie never forgot any of these moments when her father 'took her part;' she kept them in her heart, and thought of them long years after, when every one else said that her father had done very ill by his children.

George Eliot (1819–80), *The Mill on the Floss*

A GRAND POWER OF IMAGINATION

The little child is perpetually prattling about you all: and walks in the Shondileasy, with Ganny and Aunty and Polie just as if she were in France instead of here. There is a grand power of imagination about these little creatures, and a creative fancy and belief that is very curious to watch: it fades away in the light of common day.

W.M. Thackeray (1811–63), letter to Mrs Carmichael-Smyth, 1839

MON PETIT FILS

Mon petit fils qui n'as encore rien vu
A ce matin, ton père te salue . . .

Jan, petit Jan, viens voir ce tant beau monde,
Ce ciel d'azur, ces estoiles luisantes,
Ce soleil d'or, cette grant terre ronde.
Cette ample mer, ces rivières bruyantes,
Ces beaux oyseaux qui chantent à paissantes;
Viens voir le tout à souhait et désir.

Petit enfant! peux-tu le bienvenu
Etre sur terre, où tu n'apportes rien,
Mais où tu viens comme un petit ver nu?
Tu n'as de drap, ni linge que soit tien,
Or ny argent, n'aucun bien terrein.
A père et mère apportes seulement
Peyne et soucy et voilà tout ton bien.
Pauvre enfant, tu viens bien povrement.

De ton honneur ne veuil plus être chiche,
Petit enfant de grand bien puissant,
Tu viens au monde aussi grand, aussi riche
Que le roy, et aussi florissant.
Ton héritage est le ciel splendissant;
Tes serviteurs sont les anges sans vice;
Ton trésorier, c'est le Dieu Tout-puissant:
Grâce divine est ta mère nourrice.

Anon, in *The Vagabond Path: An Anthology*, compiled by Iris Origo, 1972

A DEVOTED FATALIST

H.N. TO B.N. & N.N.

12th December, 1942
Sissinghurst

I am not really worried about you two. I do not suppose that many
fathers are as devoted to their sons as I am, but I am a fatalist about
such things. I worry much less than I used to when Ben was scrubbing
floors at Chatham and I would think about how miserable he must be.
It would be no relief to me to feel that you were safe again in Scotland,
and I have a vicarious excitement in imagining the adventures which
you must be experiencing. That is what one is always told about old
men – how they sit sipping sherry in their Pall Mall clubs and relishing the ardours of the younger generation. But it is not that. I know
you will pass through many hours of agony and fear. But I also know
that it has been a dead weight on my life never to have known the dan-
gers of the last war and never to have discovered whether I am a hero
or a coward.

BEN HURT

A young man called Captain Haycock, who was in photographic
interpretation with Ben, says that he has heard that Ben was knocked
down by a lorry on 15th December and injured his head. He is in hospital and they think he will be there for four weeks.
Diary, 21 December 1944

The thought of Ben in pain and suffering all alone in Italy is something that brings a stab to my heart like an exposed nerve.
Diary, 22 December 1944

MY EYES ARE BLINDED WITH TEARS

DIARY

25th October, 1942

Ben and I walk round to the Temple Underground, carrying his big
fibre suit-case and his funny little handbag. We have to wait some
time for the train, but eventually it lumbers through the tunnel. We sit

beside each other for the short journey between the Temple and Charing Cross. I cannot speak. When the train stops, I get up and go. 'Goodbye, Benzie.' 'Goodbye, Daddy.' I close the carriage doors behind me. I stand there waiting for the train to go out. It jerks away, taking Ben to Paddington and then to Bristol and then to Avonmouth and then to Lagos and then to Cairo. My eyes are blinded with tears.

Sir Harold Nicolson (1886–1968), *Letters and Diaries*, 1968

AN ABUNDANCE OF BLUD

1588. Jan. 1st, abowt nine of the clok afternone, Michel, going chilyshly with a sharp stik of eight ynches long and a little wax candell light on the top of it, did fall uppon the playn bords in Marie's chamber, and the sharp point of the stik entred throwgh the lid of his left ey toward the corner next the nose, and so persed throwgh, insomuch that great abundance of blud cam out under the lid, in the very corner of the sayd eye; the hole on the owtside is not bygger then a pyn's hed; it was anoynted with St. John's oyle. The boy slept well. God spede the rest of the cure! The next day after it apperid that the first towch of the stikes point was at the very myddle of the apple of the ey, and so (by God's mercy and favor) glanced to the place where it entred; with the strength of his hed and the fire of his fulness, I may make some shew of it to the prayse of God for his mercies and protection.

John Dee (1527–1608), *The Diary of Dr Dee*

WANTON THROWING

1591. June 27th, Arthur wownded on his hed by his own wanton throwing of a brik-bat upright, and not well avoyding the fall of it agayn, at Mr. Harberts abowt sonn-setting. The half-brik weighed 2½lb.

John Dee (1527–1608), *The Diary of Dr Dee*

'You're not going to find it easy to break it to them. They are always discussing what we are going to do in two weeks' time.'

'No, it won't be easy. The Devil got into me today to annoy Father: he ordered one of his peasants to be flogged the other day – and quite right too; yes, yes, and you needn't look at me with such horror – he did quite right, because the fellow's a thief and a frightful drunkard. But Father hadn't expected me "to have received information on this head" as they say. He was quite overcome, and now I shall have to disappoint him into the bargain. Never mind! He'll get over it.'

Bazarov had said 'never mind!' but the whole day passed before he plucked up courage to tell Vasily Ivanovich of his intention. In the end it was not until he was actually bidding him good night in the study that he said with a strained yawn:

'Ah yes, I almost forgot to ask you. Would you give orders for Fyedot to be ready with a change of horses for us tomorrow?'

Vasily Ivanovich was dumbfounded.

'Surely Mr Kirsanov isn't leaving us?'

'Yes, he is, and I'm going with him.'

Vasily Ivanovich spun round where he stood.

'You're leaving?'

'Yes, I must. You will make arrangements about the horses, won't you?'

'Very well,' stammered the old man, 'a change of horses – very well – only – only . . . How is this?'

'I shall have to stay with him for a little while. Then I'll return here.'

'Yes! for a little while . . . Very well.' Vasily Ivanovich drew out his handkerchief and almost bent double over the business of blowing his nose. 'Ah well! Everything will come all right. I thought that you would be with us a bit longer. Three days . . . That's, that's rather short after three years; rather short, Yevgeny!'

'But I'm telling you I shall be back soon. I'm obliged to go.'

'Obliged – oh well! Duty must always be our first consideration. Send about the horses, then? Very well. Of course Arina and I were not expecting this. She's begged some flowers from the woman down the way, wanted to put them in your room.' (Vasily Ivanovich did not mention how every morning at crack of dawn, standing bare-legged in his slippers, he would confer with Timofeyich and, producing one bank-note after another with shaking fingers, would send him off to make various purchases, setting particular store by eatables and red wine, which, in so far as he had been able to tell, the young people had particularly enjoyed.) 'The main thing is freedom; that is my maxim – no use interfering – no . . .'

He suddenly broke off and made for the door.

'We'll see each other again soon, Father, honestly.'

But Vasily Ivanovich just made a gesture with his hand without turning round and went out. Back in his bedroom he found his wife in bed and began to say his prayers in a whisper so as not to waken her. However, she did wake up.

'Is that you, Vasily Ivanovich?' she asked.

'Yes, Mother.'

'Have you just come from Yevgeny? You know, I'm worried; do you think he sleeps well on the sofa? I told Anfisushka to give him your camp mattress and the new pillows; I would have given him our feather mattress only I seem to remember that he doesn't like a soft bed.'

'Never mind, Mother, don't worry. He's all right. God, have mercy upon us sinners,' he went on with his prayers under his breath. Vasily Ivanovich wished to spare his old lady; he could not bring himself to tell her what sorrow awaited her before she slept.

Bazarov and Arkady left the following day. From early morning all was dejection in the house; Anfisushka kept on dropping things; even Fed'ka couldn't make out what was going on and ended by taking off his boots. Vasily Ivanovich bustled around more than ever before. He was evidently determined to put a good face on things, spoke loudly and stamped his feet, but his face was drawn and he avoided looking directly at his son. Arina Vlas'evna was quietly weeping; she would have succumbed completely and lost all self-control had not her husband devoted two whole hours to talking her round earlier that morning. When Bazarov, after repeated promises to return in not more than a month's time, had finally torn himself from their reluctant arms and had taken his place in the tarantass; when the horses started off and the bells on their harness began to tinkle and the wheels were set in motion; when there was already nothing left to look after and the dust was laid and Timofeyich, all bent and tottering on his feet, had wandered aimlessly back into his little room; when the two old people found themselves alone in the house, which also seemed to have suddenly shrunk and grown decrepit: Vasily Ivanovich, who but a few moments earlier had still been waving his handkerchief bravely from the porch, sank on to a chair and dropped his head on his breast. 'He's deserted us, left us,' he muttered, 'gone; he feels bored with us now. I'm alone now, all alone!' he repeated several times and each time stretched his hand in front of him, the index finger sticking out pathetically as though to illustrate his own isolation.

Ivan Turgenev (1818–83), *Fathers and Children*, translated by Avril Pyman

A COAT OF MANY COLOURS

These are the generations of Jacob. Joseph, being seventeen years old, was feeding the flock with his brethren; and the lad *was* with the sons of Bilhah, and with the sons of Zilpah, his father's wives: and Joseph brought unto his father their evil report.

Now Israel loved Joseph more than all his children, because he was the son of his old age: and he made him a coat of *many* colours.

And when his brethren saw that their father loved him more than all his brethren, they hated him, and could not speak peaceably unto him.

Genesis 37: 2–4

HIS FATHER GOT HIM WITH A GREATER GUST

for several Mothers bore
To Godlike *David*, several Sons before.
But since like slaves his bed they did ascend,
No True Succession could their seed attend.
Of all this Numerous Progeny was none
So Beautifull, so brave as *Absolon*:
Whether, inspir'd by some diviner Lust,
His Father got him with a greater Gust;
Or that his Conscious destiny made way,
By manly beauty to Imperiall sway.
Early in Foreign fields he won Renown,
With Kings and States ally'd to *Israel*'s Crown:
In Peace the thoughts of War he coud remove,
And seem'd as he were only born for love.
What e'r he did was done with so much ease,

In him alone, 'twas Natural to please.
His motions all accompanied with grace;
And *Paradise* was open'd in his face.
With secret Joy, indulgent *David* view'd
His Youthfull Image in his Son renew'd:
To all his wishes Nothing he deny'd,
And made the Charming *Annabel* his Bride.
What faults he had (for who from faults is free?)
His Father coud not, or he woud not see.
Some warm excesses, which the Law forbore,
Were constru'd Youth that purg'd by boyling o'r:
And *Amnon*'s Murther, by a specious Name,
Was call'd a Just Revenge for injur'd Fame.
Thus Prais'd, and Lov'd, the Noble Youth remain'd,
While *David*, undisturb'd, in *Sion* raign'd.

John Dryden (1631–1700), *Absalom and Achitophel*, 13–42

CIGARS, WHISKY AND AFTERSHAVE

My father came back from the war. He was resplendent in a correspondent's uniform: he brought with him a Gurkha kukri to hang like
a moon on his study wall, a dented American Army helmet, and hundreds of presents. He had flown the Hump, and walked with Stilwell
on the long retreat from Burma. He was unscratched, intact: my
mother became hysterically gay, and for days the flat was a roar of
parties. During these parties my father would enter my bedroom every
fifteen or twenty minutes, and, since the noise always kept me awake,
would talk to me, stroke my hair, or read me a story. In this way he
spent as much time with me as he did at the party. When he left me
he would hold me hard against his shark-skin dinner jacket for a
moment. My elbows bumped against the buttons, but I inhaled the
delicious smell of cigars, whisky, aftershave with deep pleasure. Once
I demanded, 'Why do you come in so often, Daddy? Mummy only
comes in at bedtime.' He said humbly, 'I haven't seen you for a long
while, son, and I just want to make sure you're all right.' In a curious,
patronising way, I felt touched.

Dom Moraes, *My Son's Father*, 1968

HE WOULD TOLERATE ALMOST ANYTHING

Except when we failed in respect for people and things, he would tolerate almost anything my brothers and I did, whether it was getting poor marks in the classroom, playing truant from school, making a noise while he was working, dirtying the floors, overturning a full dish, singing improper songs or tearing our clothes. I know now that he begged my mother to shut her eyes to certain pranks, such as when I made Gabrielle believe that goat-droppings were olives. Just as she started to put some in her mouth, my mother, who was easily disgusted, cried out, and so saved Bee-bon from an unpleasant experience. Then from her pocket she took a little knife, which she always carried, and began cutting a switch off a bush. My father had all he could do to persuade her not to use it on me. On the other hand, he scolded me one day when I helped myself to some Brie cheese by cutting off the soft point at the end of the piece, thereby depriving the rest of the family of the centre, which is the most delicate part because farthest from the rind. He called me a cad, which, coming from him, was as derogatory as possible. In the Renoir household caddishness ranked even below bad manners. Not being frank, beating around the bush, or being affected or ill-mannered, irritated my father. He thought being over-polite was impolite, and it made him want to be rude. To him it was only a caricature of the courtesy of former days, a sign of the conceit of the middle classes, who imagine that they can raise themselves to the level of aristocrats by discarding simplicity.

Jean Renoir (1894–1979), *Renoir, My Father*, 1962

TELEMACHUS

This is my son, mine own Telemachus,
To whom I leave the sceptre and the isle –
Well-loved of me, discerning to fulfil
This labour, by slow prudence to make mild
A rugged people, and thro' soft degrees
Subdue them to the useful and the good.
Most blameless is he, centred in the sphere
Of common duties, decent not to fail

In offices of tenderness, and pay
Meet adoration to my household gods,
When I am gone.

Alfred Tennyson (1809–92), 'Ulysses'

A FREE AND UNCONVENTIONAL UPBRINGING

By the standards of any period, the upbringing was free and unconventional. The children were not required to be tidy or punctual or
even very clean, and my grandfather benevolently allowed them to
take every kind of risk with horses and firearms. 'Nigs has been very
hard put to it to find something to do,' he writes of his fourth son when
still a schoolboy, 'having tried all the weapons in the gun-cupboard in
succession – some in the riding school and some, he tells me, in his own
room – and having failed to blow his fingers off, he has been driven to
reading Sydney Smith's essays and studying Hogarth's pictures.'

Nor were his children made to be silent or acquiescent in the presence of their elders. Middle-aged visitors were disconcerted to find
their views disputed politely – my grandfather's belief in liberty did not
include the liberty to be rude – but firmly by a boy or girl of twelve. As
a matter of fact, the children were more polite to visitors than to their
father; a foreign girl staying at Hatfield thought that 'goose' must be a
word of endearment, since she had heard it so often used by the Cecil
children when addressing their father. He does not seem to have
addressed them as geese – on the contrary, 'My father talks to me as if
I was an ambassador,' said one of his sons, 'and I must say I do like it.'
This did not imply, however, that his father deferred to his opinions.
He was not in the habit of deferring to any ambassador's opinions.
Treating his son on equal terms meant that he made no concession to
youthful ignorance or stupidity. 'Would you mind defining?' he would
ask courteously and formidably; or, in answer to some excited state-
ment, 'do let us look at the question chemically', by which he meant
with scientific detachment. Humorously and relentlessly, he kept his
children's minds at work, questioning vague statements and deflating
cloudy sentimentalities, especially if they involved praise for some
quixotic but foolish action. 'A display of moral vanity masquerading
as virtue': so he would describe it.

He also refused to make up his children's minds for them. If one of them asked him for his advice on a course of action, he would give what he considered to be the facts necessary to know in order to form a decision; and then, 'Now it is for you to decide,' he would remark, and decline to say any more. This method presented a teen-aged boy or girl with an ordeal. The children were inexperienced; they admired their father and wanted very much to do what he thought right. Often, in frustration, one of them would ask another to try diplomatically to find out their father's true opinion. Once his children had grown up, my grandfather was even more determined to let them judge for themselves. He thought it morally wrong to exert pressure to influence a grown son or daughter's choice in the matter of marriage or profession. He remembered how he had suffered from his own father's interference, and he resolved to be as different from him as possible.

David Cecil (1902–85), *The Cecils of Hatfield House*, 1973

LORD HIPPO

Despairing, maddened and distraught
He utterly collapsed and sought
His sire,

the Earl of Potamus,
And brokenly addressed him thus:
'Dread Sire – to-day – at Ascot – I . . .'

His genial parent made reply:
'Come! Come! Come! Come! Don't look so glum!
Trust your Papa and name the sum . . .
WHAT?

. . . Fifteen hundred thousand? . . . Hum!
However . . . stiffen up, you wreck;
Boys will be boys – so here's the cheque!'
Lord Hippo, feeling deeply – well,
More grateful than he cared to tell –
Punted the lot on Little Nell: –
And got a telegram at dinner
To say

that he had backed the Winner!

Hilaire Belloc (1870–1953), *Cautionary Tales for Children*, 1908

DEAR MAN, DON'T

'Think what your mother's been to you, Jon! She has nothing but you;
I shan't last much longer.'

'Why not? It isn't fair to – Why not?'

'Well,' said Jolyon, rather coldly, 'because the doctors tell me I
shan't; that's all.'

'Oh! Dad!' cried Jon, and burst into tears.

This downbreak of his son, whom he had not seen cry since he was
ten, moved Jolyon terribly. He recognized to the full how fearfully
soft the boy's heart was, how much he would suffer in this business,
and in life generally. And he reached out his hand helplessly – not
wishing, indeed not daring to get up.

'Dear man,' he said, 'don't – or you'll make me!'

John Galsworthy (1867–1933), 'The Forsyte Saga', III, *To Let*, 1921

BABY LOVE

He [Cato] was also a good father, a considerate husband, and a
household manager of no mean talent, nor did he give only a fitful
attention to this, as a matter of little or no importance. Therefore I
think I ought to give suitable instances of his conduct in these relations. He married a wife who was of gentler birth than she was rich,
thinking that, although the rich and the high-born may be alike given
to pride, still, women of high birth have such a horror of what is dis-
graceful that they are more obedient to their husbands in all that is
honourable. He used to say that the man who struck his wife or child,
laid violent hands on the holiest of holy things. Also that he thought
it more praiseworthy to be a good husband than a great senator, nay,
there was nothing else to admire in Socrates of old except that he was
always kind and gentle in his intercourse with a shrewish wife and
stupid sons. After the birth of his son, no business could be so urgent,
unless it had a public character, as to prevent him from being present
when his wife bathed and swaddled the babe. For the mother nursed
it herself, and often gave suck also to the infants of her slaves, that so
they might come to cherish a brotherly affection for her son. As soon
as the boy showed signs of understanding, his father took him under

his own charge and taught him to read, although he had an accomplished slave, Chilo by name, who was a school-teacher, and taught many boys. Still, Cato thought it not right, as he tells us himself, that his son should be scolded by a slave, or have his ears tweaked when he was slow to learn, still less that he should be indebted to his slave for such a priceless thing as education. He was therefore himself not only the boy's reading-teacher, but his tutor in law, and his athletic trainer, and he taught his son not merely to hurl the javelin and fight in armour and ride the horse, but also to box, to endure heat and cold, and to swim lustily through the eddies and billows of the Tiber. His History of Rome, as he tells us himself, he wrote out with his own hand and in large characters, that his son might have in his own home an aid to acquaintance with his country's ancient traditions. He declares that his son's presence put him on his guard against indecencies of speech as much as that of the so-called Vestal Virgins, and that he never bathed with him.

Plutarch (c. AD 46–120), *Parallel Lives*, translated by Bernadette Perrin

THE CHILD AT THE WINDOW

Remember this, when childhood's far away;
The sunlight of a showery first spring day;
You from your house-top window laughing down,
And I, returned with whip-cracks from a ride,
On the great lawn below you, playing the clown.
Time blots our gladness out. Let this with love abide . . .

The brave March day; and you, not four years old,
Up in your nursery world – all heaven for me.
Remember this – the happiness I hold –
In far off springs I shall not live to see;
The world one map of wastening war unrolled,
And you, unconscious of it, setting my spirit free.

For you must learn, beyond bewildering years,
How little things beloved and held are best.
The windows of the world are blurred with tears,
And troubles come like cloud-banks from the west.
Remember this, some afternoon in spring,

When your own child looks down and makes your sad heart sing.

Siegfried Sassoon (1886–1967), Collected Poems, 1947

A SWEET LETTER

. . . my father was giving me an allowance of £350 a year, a substantial sum in those days; he never interfered with me in any way and seldom asked questions. His feeling for me may be seen in a short letter he wrote me during my last term at Cambridge:

> 'My dear lad,
> I asked Nancy [my sister] last night whether you were really hard up and I gathered that you were. Now I want you to drop me a line and let me know if you ever find funds running low, as all I have is at your disposal as you ought to know and there need never be reservations between us. My faith in you is as my affection for you and knows no bounds.
> Your old Dad.'

No son could ever have received from his father a sweeter letter than that; how saddening it is to read it now. The very boundlessness of his faith in me contributed, as time went on, to my anxiety. For I could not write, and if he did ask questions on his return from his office in the evenings: 'Well, old boy, what have you been doing today?' I felt ashamed and evasive, for I had done nothing.

J.R. Ackerley (1896–1967), My Father and Myself, 1968

AN UNUSUAL GLIMPSE OF PRINCE ALBERT

Although it does not accord with the popular conception of the Prince Consort, he was most at his ease and most relaxed in the company of his children. We see him in the closing months of his life playing with the infant Princess Beatrice; he would envelop her in one of those vast, well laundered, Victorian dinner-napkins, lift her up as if she were in a hammock and swing her through his legs; the child would shout with glee, while the Duchess of Kent stood by chuckling in her rich guttural German laughter. Always on New Year's Eve there was a children's dance at Windsor and the Prince joined in with the activity of a boy. Although in the words of the Queen 'he danced lightly and beautifully', she goes on to say that 'he disliked it in general' but on these occasions he capered and pirouetted with a zest which inspired them all. At the country dance, which was the prelude to the playing in of the New Year, he would skip down the middle and then with twinkling feet dance Poussette. He would then run back to help the children and his amused laughter at their awkward fixes could be heard above the music.

. . . On the last Christmas of the Prince's life people were amused to notice Prince Arthur, who had been given a splendid pop-gun, taking a quick pot-shot at his father and then by way of amends ceremoniously presenting arms. The Queen's sister, recalling the delightful terms which bound the children to their father, observed that in their company 'he was so like a child'.

On the elder children his influence was abiding and their affection for him was unbounded – perhaps in excess of what they felt for the Queen. They seem to have been able to pierce through the shyness which veiled his intensely affectionate nature and to appreciate not only the loving-kindness of his heart but the quality of his character. When the Princess Royal married she confided to the Queen, 'I think it will kill me to take leave of dear Papa'. On the day after they parted, when they had driven together through heavy snow and cheering crowds to the terminus of the North Kent Railway, he wrote:

'I am not of a demonstrative nature and therefore you can hardly know how dear you have always been to me, and what a void you have left behind in my heart: yet not in my heart for there assuredly you will abide henceforth, as till now you have done, but in my daily life, which is evermore reminding my heart of your absence.'

Roger Fulford, *The Prince Consort*, 1949

A FATHER FIRST AND FOREMOST

'That monster will capitulate when I say to him, "You must do a deal with me! If you want your son give my daughter back her property, and leave her free to do as she pleases."'

'Oh, Father!'

'Yes, your father, Nasie, a father first and foremost! That rascal of a great lord had better not ill-treat my daughters. Thunder and lightning! I don't know what fiery blood runs in my veins: I have tiger's blood in me, I could crunch the bones of those two men. Oh, children, is that what your life is? The thought of it is death to me. And what will become of you when I am gone? Fathers ought to live as long as their children. God, how badly Your world is arranged! And yet You have a Son, if what they tell us is true. You should save us from suffering through our children. My darlings, my darlings, to think that it should be sorrow that brings you to me. Your tears are all you let me know of you. Ah! well, yes, yes, you love me, I see that. Come and shed your tears here. My heart is big enough to hold all your troubles. Yes, even if my heart is broken each piece will make a father's heart again. If only I could take all your troubles on me and suffer for you! Ah! when you were little things, how happy you were! –'

> Honoré de Balzac (1799–1850), *Old Goriot*, translated by Marion
> Ayton Crawford

GOD BLESS YOU

. . . my father had such an intense dislike for leave-taking that he always, when it was possible, shirked a farewell, and we children, knowing this dislike, used only to wave our hands or give him a silent kiss when parting. But on this Monday morning, the seventh, just as we were about to start for London, my sister suddenly said: 'I *must* say good-bye to papa,' and hurried over to the châlet where he was busily writing. As a rule when he was so occupied, my father would hold up his cheek to be kissed, but this day he took my sister in his arms saying: 'God bless you, Katie,' and there, 'among the branches of the trees, among the birds and butterflies and the scent of flowers,' she left him, never to look into his eyes again.

> Mamie Dickens (1838–96), *My Father as I Recall Him*

FIVE

Absent Fathers

TO APOLLO FROM HIS SON

... dearest father, and I pray to God that you are prosperous and successful and that we may receive you home in good health. I have indeed told you before of my grief at your absence from among us, my fear being that something dreadful might happen to you and that we may not find your body. Indeed I have often wished to tell you that in view of the unsettled state of things I wanted to stamp a mark on you ...

Third or fourth century AD

FOR A FATHERLESS SON

You will be aware of an absence, presently,
Growing beside you, like a tree,
A death tree, color gone, an Australian gum tree –
Balding, gelded by lightning – an illusion,
And a sky like a pig's backside, an utter lack of attention.

But right now you are dumb.
And I love your stupidity,
The blind mirror of it. I look in
And find no face but my own, and you think that's funny.
It is good for me

To have you grab my nose, a ladder rung.
One day you may touch what's wrong
The small skulls, the smashed blue hills, the godawful hush.
Till then your smiles are found money.
26 September 1962

Sylvia Plath (1932–63), *Collected Poems*, 1981

LET THE INDIANS HAVE AMERICA

To the Reverend William Hazlitt
Address: The Rev. Mr. Hazlitt/London/To the care of Mr. David
Lewis

12 of Novr[1786]

My Dear papa
   I shall never forget that we came to america. If we had not came to
america we should not have been away from one and another, though
now it can not be helped, I think for my part that it would have been
a great deal better if the white people had not found it out. Let the
[Indians have] it to themselves for it was made for them, I have got a
little of my grammar sometimes I get three pages and sometimes but

one I do not sifer any at all. mamma peggy and Jacky are very well
and I am to

  I still remain your most
  affectionate son
  William, Hazlitt

William Hazlitt (1778–1830), letter to his father

I WILL COME BACK TO THEE SOON

[c. 30 or 31 May 1822]

My dear little baby,
  The only comfort or tie poor Father has left! I send thee a pound to
spend. Be happy as thou canst, my love, and I will come back to thee
soon, that is, before the holidays, and we will go to Winterslow Hut
together, and seek for peace. I have got a hundred pound since I came,
and hope before that is spent, to recover spirits to work and support
thy little life. Call on Mr. Patmore, my dear, and tell him to write
what he knows to poor Father and to intreat Mr. Colburn without
loss of time to send the new volume of Table Talk to Mr. Jeffrey, if he
has not sent it to me already, or we shall miss another Review. I got
the 100£ from Mr. Jeffrey, and it has perhaps saved us both from
ruin. I was so ill in the Steam-Boat, but am a little better. I will write
to you again soon to tell you when I shall be up. Farewel, my blessed
child. Thy mother is to take the oath next Tuesday, the only thing that
can save me from madness. Once more, farewel. I have got a present
of a knife for thee. Every one pities poor father, but the monster who
has destroyed him. Your ever
  affectionate parent,
  W. H.

William Hazlitt (1778–1830), letter to Willie Hazlitt Junior

A SCATOLOGICAL IMPROPRIETY

Red in the face, he tried to disengage himself from her embrace.
Desperately she clung. 'But I'm Linda, I'm Linda.' The laughter
drowned her voice. 'You made me have a baby,' she screamed above

the uproar. There was a sudden and appalling hush; eyes floated uncomfortably not knowing where to look. The Director went suddenly pale, stopped struggling and stood, his hands on her wrists, staring down at her, horrified. 'Yes, a baby – and I was its mother.' She flung the obscenity like a challenge into the outraged silence; then, suddenly breaking away from him, ashamed, ashamed, covered her face with her hands, sobbing. 'It wasn't my fault, Tomakin. Because I always did my drill, didn't I? Didn't I? Always . . . I don't know how . . . If you knew how awful, Tomakin . . . But he was a comfort to me, all the same.' Turning towards the door, 'John!' she called. 'John!'

He came in at once, paused for a moment just inside the door, looked round, then soft on his moccasined feet strode quickly across the room, fell on his knees in front of the Director, and said in a clear voice: 'My father!'

The word (for 'father' was not so much obscene as – with its connotation of something at one remove from the loathsomeness and moral obliquity of child-bearing – merely gross, a scatological rather than a pornographic impropriety), the comically smutty word relieved what had become a quite intolerable tension. Laughter broke out, enormous, almost hysterical, peal after peal, as though it would never stop. My father – and it was the Director! My *father*! Oh Ford, oh Ford! That was really too good. The whooping and the roaring renewed themselves, faces seemed on the point of disintegration, tears were streaming. Six more test-tubes of spermatozoa were upset. My *father*!

Pale, wild-eyed, the Director glared about him in an agony of bewildered humiliation.

My *father*! The laughter, which had shown signs of dying away, broke out again more loudly than ever. He put his hands over his ears and rushed out of the room.

Aldous Huxley (1894–1963), Brave New World, 1932

THE TRUISMS

His father gave him a box of truisms
Shaped like a coffin, then his father died;
The truisms remained on the mantelpiece
As wooden as the playbox they had been packed in
Or that other his father skulked inside.

Then he left home, left the truisms behind him
Still on the mantelpiece, met love, met war,
Sordor, disappointment, defeat, betrayal,
Till through disbeliefs he arrived at a house
He could not remember seeing before,

And he walked straight in; it was where he had come from
And something told him the way to behave.
He raised his hand and blessed his home;
The truisms flew and perched on his shoulders
And a tall tree sprouted from his father's grave.

Louis MacNeice (1907–63), *Collected Poems*, 1966

SOLITARY TREES GROW STRONG

On November 24 [1895] Winston went to Dr Roose's and was shown a telegram just received from Madras that stated that Lord Randolph's condition had become very much worse and that it had been decided to cut short the tour and to return to England immediately. Lord and Lady Randolph reached London on December 24. Despite a few misleading symptoms of recovery there was now no hope that he could live and the family awaited his death with miserable resignation. 'For a month,' Winston wrote in the Life of his father, 'at his mother's house, he lingered pitifully, until very early in the morning of 24 January 1895 the numbing fingers of paralysis laid that weary brain to rest.' Seventy years to the day Winston himself was to die. On January 28 Lord Randolph was buried in Bladon churchyard, and a memorial service was held for him in Westminster Abbey.

Winston was just twenty at the time of his father's death and must henceforward be regarded as a man and no longer a boy. Despite his lack of means he plainly felt himself responsible for the small family – there was only his mother and Jack. Both his grandfathers, the Duke and Leonard Jerome, had been dead for some time. His grandmother Jerome was to die within a few months; so too was Everest. The old Duchess died four years later. These three Churchills were to be alone in the world. Lady Randolph still had her private income which she quickly dissipated or mortgaged; and their fortunes were to be increasingly dependent on the impecunious gentleman cadet who was shortly to receive the Queen's Commission in the 4th Hussars with pay of £120 per annum. Within the confinements of his slender means and the limitations of the career to which he was committed – the only one for which he had any training – he was his own master. He had a stout heart, an audacious spirit, colossal ambition, a late-maturing but massive brain from which elements of genius cannot be excluded, a sharp sword; and he was soon to fashion himself a valuable and rewarding pen, which was in the next few years, combined with his thirst for adventure, to liberate him from the thraldom of penury and open all doors during the seventy years that lay ahead.

'It is said', Winston was to write nearly forty years later in his Life of Marlborough, 'that famous men are usually the product of an unhappy childhood. The stern compression of circumstances, the twinges of adversity, the spur of slights and taunts in early years, are needed to evoke that ruthless fixity of purpose and tenacious mother-wit without which great actions are seldom accomplished.' And in 1898 he wrote of the Mahdi: 'Solitary trees, if they grow at all, grow strong; and a boy deprived of a father's care often develops, if he escapes the perils of youth, an independence and vigour of thought which may restore in after life the heavy loss of early days.'

There was now no one to help him – or stand in his way; for if Lord Randolph had lived, even in better health, he would have been an obstacle to Winston's career and prospects which were soon to burgeon. He was free to leave the nest and soar through many hazards to the empyrean.

Randolph S. Churchill (1911–68), *The Biography of Winston Churchill*, 1966

NELSON'S DAUGHTER

Victory, October 19th 1805

My dearest Angel, – I was made happy by the pleasure of receiving your letter of September 19th, and I rejoice to hear that you are so very good a girl, and love my dear Lady Hamilton, who most dearly loves you. Give her a kiss for me. The Combined Fleets of the Enemy are now reported to be coming out of Cadiz; and therefore I answer your letter, my dearest Horatia, to mark to you that you are ever uppermost in my thoughts. I shall be sure of your prayers for my safety, conquest, and speedy return to dear Merton, and our dearest

good Lady Hamilton. Be a good girl, mind what Miss Connor says to you. Receive, my dearest Horatia, the affectionate Parental Blessing of your Father,
NELSON & BRONTE.

Horatio Nelson (1758–1805), letter to Horatia Nelson Thompson

AN ELUSIVE MAN

We boys never knew any male authority. My father left us when I was three, and apart from some rare and fugitive visits he did not live with us again. He was a knowing, brisk, elusive man, the son and the grandson of sailors, but having himself no stomach for the sea he had determined to make good on land. In his miniature way he succeeded in this. He became, while still in his middle teens, a grocer's assistant, a local church organist, an expert photographer, and a dandy. Certain portraits he took of himself at that time show a handsome though threadbare lad, tall and slender, and much addicted to gloves, high'collars, and courtly poses. He was clearly a cut above the average, in charms as well as ambition. By the age of twenty he had married the beautiful daughter of a local merchant, and she bore him eight children – of whom five survived – before dying herself still young. Then he married his housekeeper, who bore him four more, three surviving, of which I was one. At the time of this second marriage he was still a grocer's assistant, and earning nineteen shillings a week. But his dearest wish was to become a Civil Servant, and he studied each night to this end. The First World War gave him the chance he wanted, and though properly distrustful of arms and battle he instantly sacrificed both himself and his family, applied for a post in the Army Pay Corps, went off to Greenwich in a bullet-proof vest, and never permanently lived with us again.

He was a natural fixer, my father was, and things worked out pretty smoothly. He survived his clerk-stool war with a War Office pension (for nervous rash, I believe), then entered the Civil Service, as he had planned to do, and settled in London for good. Thus enabling my Mother to raise both his families, which she did out of love and pity, out of unreasoning loyalty and a fixed belief that he would one day return to her . . .

Laurie Lee, *Cider with Rosie*, 1959

FATHER IN A PIE

'Now, my dears,' said old Mrs. Rabbit one morning, 'you may go into the fields or down the lane, but don't go into Mr. McGregor's garden: your Father had an accident there; he was put in a pie by Mrs. McGregor.'

Beatrix Potter (1866–1943), *The Tale of Peter Rabbit*, 1902

FROM THE TEMPLE OF LONGING

The moment the children climb
into my ex-wife's car they buckle
themselves into a faraway look.
The little one
never cries, the eldest
counts white hairs that sneak
like the future up the side of his arm.
Camel, tent, oasis, storm – their ancestors
longed to pause and longed even more
to press on. But on a cobalt dark
night like this, following
an invisible need at the other
end of a leash, I want to hear
from my wild nomads dreaming
on the other side of the state. I want
to hear them say papa, it's alright,
don't cry – always thirsty at three a.m.
for something more than water. Maybe
you think this is all about a dime-
a-dozen emotional flotsam who left a furious
marriage only to miss his children from one
school holiday to the next, who exaggerates
the tangled heartworms that pressed
his ribcage when his
parents divorced. Maybe you just
want to tell me that children

are not that fragile. But I wonder
what I would hear, a dozen
years from now, waiting for the last
solar eclipse of the century, my arms relaxed
around my teenage boys, hovering
over a jerryrigged
cardboard theater, watching
the little moon erase the little sun -
I wonder what they would say
in that strange light, if I asked them
to remember.

Roger Weingarten, *New American Poets of the 90s*, 1991

HARE NOT APPARENT

My father never once noticed my existence during his long stay at the
Rectory. On the last day before he left, my mother said laughingly,
'Really, Francis, I don't think you have ever found out that such a
little being as Augustus is in existence here.' He was amused, and said,
'Oh no, really!' and he called me to him and patted my head, saying,
'Good little Wolf: good little Wolf!' It was the only notice he ever
took of me.

Augustus Hare (1834–1903), *The Story of My Life*

I HAD NO SOUL

A father would have weighted me with a certain stable obstinacy.
Making his moods my principles, his ignorance my knowledge, his
disappointments my pride, his quirks my law, he would have inhab-
ited me. That respectable tenant would have given me self-respect,
and on that respect I would have based my right to live. My begetter
would have determined my future. As a born graduate of the Ecole
Polytechnique, I would have felt reassured forever. But if Jean-
Baptiste Sartre had ever known my destination, he had taken the

secret with him. My mother remembered only his saying, 'My son won't go into the Navy.' For want of more precise information, nobody, beginning with me, knew why the hell I had been born. Had he left me property, my childhood would have been changed. I would not be writing, since I would be someone else. House and field reflect back to the young heir a stable image of himself. He touches himself on *his* gravel, on the diamond-shaped panes of *his* veranda, and makes of their inertia the deathless substance of his soul. A few days ago, in a restaurant, the owner's son, a little seven-year-old, cried out to the cashier, 'When my father's not here, *I'm* the boss!' There's a man for you! At his age, I was nobody's master and nothing belonged to me. In my rare moments of lavishness, my mother would whisper to me, 'Be careful! We're not in our own home!' We were never in our own home, neither on the Rue le Goff nor later, when my mother remarried. This caused me no suffering since everything was loaned to me, but I remained abstract. Worldly possessions reflect to their owner what he is: they taught me what I was not. *I was not* substantial or permanent, *I was not* the future continuer of my father's work, *I was not* necessary to the production of steel. In short, I had no soul.

Jean-Paul Sartre (1905–80), *Words*, 1964

TWO JAILBIRDS MEET

We approached timidly and slowly towards one another, filled with fear and welcome. I noticed that he was trembling, his lips were shaking and lightning shot from his eyes. I spoke to him quietly in English.

– Phwat is yer nam?

He spoke voice-brokenly and aimlessly.

– Jams O'Donnell!' said he.

Wonder and joy swept over me as flashes of lightning out of the celestial sky. I lost my voice and I nearly lost my senses again.

My father! my own father!! my own little father!!! my kinsman, my progenitor, my friend!!!! We devoured one another with our eyes eagerly and I offered him my hand.

– The name and surname that's on me, said I, is also Jams O'Donnell. You're my father and it's clear that you've come out of the jug.

– My son! said he. My little son!! my little sonny!!!

He took hold of my hand and ate and swallowed me with his eyes. Whatever flood-tide of joy had come over him at that time, I noticed that the ugly fellow had little health; certainly, he had not benefited from the bout of joy which he derived from me at that hour in the station; he had become as white as snow and saliva dripped from the edges of his lips.

– I'm told, said I, that I've earned twenty-nine years in the same jug.

I wished that we had had conversation and that the eerie staring, which was confusing us both, should cease. I saw a softness creep into his eyes and quiet settle over his limbs. He beckoned with his finger.

– Twenty-nine years I've done in the jug, said he, and it's surely an unlovely place.

– Tell my mother, said I, that I'll be back . . .

A strong hand suddenly grasped the back of my rags, rudely sweeping me away. A peeler was assaulting me. I was sent into a running bound by a destructive shove in the small of the back.

– *Kum along blashketman!* said the peeler

I was cast into a coach and we set out on our journey without delay. Corkadoragha was behind me – perhaps for ever – and I was on my way to the faraway jail. I fell on the floor and wept a headful of tears.

Yes! that was the first time that I laid eyes on my father and that he laid eyes on me; one wee moment at the station and then – separation for ever. Certainly, I suffered Gaelic hardship throughout my life – distress, need, ill-treatment, adversity, calamity, foul play, misery, famine and ill-luck.

I do not think that my like will ever be there again!

Flann O'Brien (1911–66), *The Poor Mouth*, 1941

A MEAN TRICK

Sperm Doctor Guilty of Tricking Women

An infertility doctor was convicted here [Alexandria, Virginia] of defrauding patients by artificially inseminating them with his own sperm while claiming to use other donors.

Cecil Jacobson, aged 55, was also found guilty of fraud for tricking women into believing that they were pregnant. He was convicted on 52 counts of fraud and perjury. He appeared to show no emotion when the jury foreman, Daniel Richard, announced the verdict.

Jacobson faces a jail term of up to 280 years and $500,000 (£290,000) in fines at his sentencing scheduled for May 8.

Jacobson is credited with introducing amniocentesis, which detects foetal abnormalities, in America. Randy Bellows, the prosecutor, had described Jacobson as 'a man who routinely lies to his patients'. James Tait, the defence counsel, called him a medical pioneer who acted 'out of love, out of a desire to help people'.

Jacobson admitted he had occasionally used his own sperm for artificial insemination when other donors were not available. He said he did not know how many children he had fathered. His lawyer said his action was not illegal, in any case. 11 people testified that Jacobson had promised to match the physical characteristics and religion of patients' husbands.

The prosecution said genetic tests showed that Jacobson was 99.9% likely to be the father of 15 children by unsuspecting patients. Over all, by the prosecution's account, he may have fathered up to 75 children. One woman testified that she noticed her daughter's resemblance to Jacobson in a photograph taken when the infant was 3 days old.

The Times, 5 March 1992

FATHERS

My father may be often in my dreams
Yet (since he died when I was young) play parts –
Or be himself – and stay unrecognized.

In any case dreaming often modifies
The features of the characters we know,
Though usually telling us who's really meant.

Like useful footnotes to an allegory.
This morning speckled foam fell in the basin:
Watching my father shave came flooding back

From over fifty years. His cut-throat razor,
Black beard, seemed things of fascinated love –
And now replace the visage and his speech.

Did he imagine (as I sometimes do)
His son would one day reach the age of sixty,
Himself being almost *ipso facto* dead?

Worse, in his final illness did he think
How he would leave a foolish child of eight,
Himself being hardly out of folly's years?

Roy Fuller (1912–91), *Collected Poems*, 1962

WHAT WAS IT . . .?

What was it that my father said
To my cocooned and dreaming head?
He sat there, dazed, and I was not
Surprised to see he was not dead.
I talked on like an idiot:

The multitudinous happenings
Since he had left us, publishings,
Memorials, his personal things,
How I'd looked after their removal,
Hoping I met with his approval.

And yet all this was to protect
Him from the certain ill-effect
Of his decline, the little chance
Of permanent deliverance.
His face took on a radiance.

With all my silly chatter done,
I put my arms about him, knew
His real dying had begun
And knew this miracle was true,
Occasion for a last adieu.

John Fuller, from 'Star-gazing', *Stones and Fires*, 1996

WAS I IN YOUR WALLET?

We used to have a picture of me in my buttoned-up coat with a velvet
collar, the kind we called a Prince Edward coat, standing on the hard

sand at Elwood Beach, smiling up at someone much taller than me with my eyes all crinkled up. Mother laughed when she mentioned it, because Daddy had buttoned the coat up wrong, which I never noticed when the snapshot was still to be seen. Mother had jettisoned it now of course along with almost all my books, all the china and furniture we grew up with and all the letters Daddy ever wrote her. All I saw when I looked at that picture was the sharp delight on my baby face and the eyes shut against the glare of the sky. The person I was smiling up at, whose shadow falls across the sand wrinkles at the edge of Port Philip Bay almost to the round toes of my patent leather shoes, was Daddy. Daddy must have taken me for a walk by ourselves with the camera loaded and ready. Daddy knew he was going away, perhaps forever, but I did not.

No wonder I hate being photographed. Being photographed is the prelude to being deserted. You look up and beam all your love and trust into the shiny eye at the end of the pleated bellows, because Daddy tells you to. Watch the birdie. Say cheese. And I said cheese so hard up into the light that my eyes filled with tears. And then he was gone.

Was I in your wallet at least, Papa? Perhaps I did ride with you in your wallet. Next to pictures of mother with her hennaed pompadour, in clinging crêpe and crisp sharkskin, or hanging on your arm in Collins Street with the tiny felt hat tipped over her eye. Perhaps you did show me when the other men showed their children, but then I forget. In your job there was no fraternising.

Germaine Greer, *Daddy We Hardly Knew You*, 1989

I WISH YOU WOULD COME

Winston to Lord Randolph

8 October 1887   Brighton

Dearest Father,

I am very glad to hear that I am going to Harrow & not to Winchester. I think I shall pass the Entrance Examination, which is not so hard as Winchester. I shall know by the time I go there the 1st 2nd and part of the 3rd books of Euclid. In arithmetic we are doing 'Square Root' and have quite mastered Decimal fractions & Rule of three. Greek, however is my weakest subject as I have yet to learn the

Verbs in μ which are very hard. Will you send me some of your autographs. We are, at the end of the term going to act Molière's '*Médecin Malgré lui*'. I take the part of 'Martine'.

We are getting up a Greek play too, in which, there are only 2 characters one of whom is myself. The Play is called 'The Knights' by 'Aristophanes'. Of course we are only doing one extract but I think it will prove very amusing to all. I wish you would come to the distribution of prizes at the end of this term, but I suppose it is impossible. The weather, today is moderately fine, but we have had some severe storms. I went to see Grandmamma a fortnight ago, & she read me your speech on the Distribution of Prizes for the school of Art, it was just the sort of speech for school boys. You had great luck in Salmon fishing, I wish I had been with you I should have liked to have seen you catch them. Did you go to Harrow or Eton? I should like to know.

Please do not forget the autographs.

With Love & Kisses I remain, Your loving son
WINSTON S. CHURCHILL

It seems strange that a boy of nearly thirteen who was about to go to Harrow should not have known that his father had been to Eton. The implication is a remoteness between father and son and an excessive parental disposition to decide things above a child's head without any reference to the child. An agreeable contrast is afforded by Winston's treatment of his own son more than thirty years later; when he gave his son the choice of Eton or Harrow, the latter inspected both institutions, and opted for Eton.

Randolph S. Churchill (1911–68), Winston Churchill, 1966

I KNOW THAT YOU ARE BUSY

9 December 1883   Ascot

My dear Papa

I hope you are quite well. We had gymnastic trials yesterday. I got 39 marks out of 90. I beat some of the boys in two classes above me. The play room is getting ready for concert we are learning to sing for it. It is about 75 feet long & 20 broad and lighted by 920 cp [candlepower] lamps it will show a very bright light wont it.

With love and kisses I remain yours affet
WINSTON

X one big kiss and a lot of little ones.

[3 December 1882]   Ascot
My dear Papa,
   I am very happy at chool. You will be very plesed to hear I spent a
very happy birthday. Mrs Kynersley gave me a little bracket. I am
going to send a Gazette wich I wish you to read.
                           With love and kisses, I remain your loving son
                                                                    WINSTON

5 April 1885   Brighton
My darling Papa,
   I hope you are quite well. The weather continues very fine though
there has been a little rain lately. I have been our riding with a gentleman who thinks that Gladstone is a brute and thinks that 'the one
with the curly moustache ought to be Premier.' The driver of the
Electric Railway said 'that Lord R. Churchill would be Prime
Minister.' Cricket has become the foremost thought now. Every body
wants your Autograph but I can only say I will try, and I should like
you to sign your name in full at the end of your letter. I only want a
scribble as I know that you are very busy indeed. With love and kisses.
                                               I remain your loving son
                                                                    WINSTON

     Winston Churchill (1874–1965), letters to Lord Randolph Churchill

                        PLUS ÇA CHANGE . . .

Theon to his father Theon, greeting. It was a fine thing not to take me
with you to town! If you won't take me with you to Alexandria, I
won't write to you or speak to you or say good-bye to you. If you go
to Alexandria, I won't ever take your hand nor greet you again. That
is what will happen if you won't take me. Mother said to Archelaus
'It quite upsets him to be left behind.' It was good of you to send me
a present the day you sailed. Send me a lyre, now, I beg you. If you
don't, I won't eat, I won't drink. That's that.

   Oxyrhyncus Papyri, CXIX, 2nd or 3rd century AD, translated by F. A. Wright

NO WANT OF AFFECTION

The following little note was written by the King to Elizabeth while he was in detention on the Isle of Wight.

                                        Newport, 14th October
Dear daughter,

It is not want of affection that makes me write so seldom to you but want of matter such as I could wish; and indeed I am loth to write to those I love when I am out of humour (as I have been these days by-past), lest my letters should trouble those I desire to please.

But having this opportunity, I would not lose it; though at the time I have nothing to say, but God bless you! So I rest
Your loving father,
Charles R.

Charles I (1600–49), to his daughter, Princess Elizabeth, 1648

TO MY DAUGHTER BETTY

In wiser days, my darling rosebud, blown
To beauty proud as was your Mother's prime.
In that desired, delayed, incredible time,
You'll ask why I abandoned you, my own,
And the dear heart that was your baby throne,
To dice with death. And oh! they'll give you rhyme
And reason: some will call the thing sublime,
And some decry it in a knowing tone.
So here, while the mad guns curse overhead,
And tired men sigh with mud for couch and floor,
Know that we fools, now with the foolish dead,
Died not for flag, nor King, nor Emperor,
But for a dream, born in a herdsman's shed,
And for the secret Scripture of the poor.

T. M. Kettle, written four days before his death in action, 1916, *Up The Line to Death*, 1964

POOR JACK

The child of a drunken sailor asked him for bread. Irritated by his request, the dissolute father spurned him from him with his foot, and the child fell in the sea, from the beach. Nothing could be done from the shore, and the child soon disappeared; but the arm of Providence was extended over him, and by clinging to an oar, or raft, that he came near, he floated, till picked up by a vessel then under weigh. The child could only tell them his name was Jack, but the humanity of the crew led them to take care of him. Poor Jack, as he grew up, was promoted to wait on the officers, received instruction easily, was quick and steady, and served in some actions. In the last, he had obtained so much promotion, that he was appointed to the care of the wounded seamen. He observed one with a Bible under his head, and showed him so much attention, that the man, when he was near dying, requested Jack to accept this Bible, which had been the means of reclaiming him from the ways of sin. By some circumstances, Poor Jack recognized, in the penitent sailor, his once cruel father.

Such was the affecting story, as related at a meeting of the Brighton Bible Society, by a stranger, who requested permission to address the company. It made a powerful impression on all present; which was not lessened, when the speaker added, with a modest bow, 'And, ladies and gentlemen, I am poor Jack.'

Percy Anecdotes, 1823

OH! MY DADDY!

Bobby was left standing alone, the Station Cat watching her from under the bench with friendly golden eyes.

Of course you know already exactly what was going to happen. Bobbie was not so clever. She had the vague, confused, expectant feeling that comes to one's heart in dreams. What her heart expected I can't tell – perhaps the very thing that you and I know was going to happen – but her mind expected nothing; it was almost blank, and felt nothing but tiredness and stupidness and an empty feeling like your body has when you have been on a long walk and it is very far indeed past your proper dinner time.

Only three people got out of the 11.54. The first was a country-woman with two baskety boxes full of live chickens who stuck their russet heads out anxiously through the wicker bars; the second was Miss Peckitt, the grocer's wife's cousin, with a tin box and three brown-paper parcels; and the third –

'Oh! my Daddy, my Daddy!' That scream went like a knife into the heart of everyone in the train, and people put their heads out of the windows to see a tall pale man with lips set in a thin close line, and a little girl clinging to him with arms and legs, while his arms went tightly round her.

E. Nesbit (1858–1924), *The Railway Children*, 1906

SIX

Revered Fathers

My love for my father has never been touched or approached by any other love. I hold him in my heart of hearts as a man apart from all other men, as one apart from all other beings.

Mamie Dickens (1838–96), *My Father as I Recall Him*

A FATHER AND A FLEDGLING OWL

The time was late May, 1914.

The place, Ennistymon House, County Clare.

In this memory I am three years old and standing at the top of the stairs in a white winceyette nightgown. The stairs lead down to the hall in a wide curve of shallow steps. From below, a shadowy journey away it seemed to me, my father is shouting for me to come down. He is long-legged, giant-sized and his voice reverberates against the pan-elling. The prospect appals me, I ought to be in bed, and I peep through the banisters. The next moment I am snatched up into my father's arms, kidnapped, nursery rules broken, and as we leap down the stairs I feel the draught in my hair from the open front door. We jump the stone steps in front of the house, rush across the lawn, and I am dropped with my bare feet on the damp grass. The lawn, with a copper beech at the edge standing like a sentinel, is a platform high above the river. My father flings himself down on his hands and knees in front of a clump of pampas grass and half disappears inside it. The cold sound of the waterfall drifts up through the mist in the valley. It is dusk, the rooks in the rookery are silent, the hooded crows are already roosting in the copper beech above my head. My father backs out of the pampas grass with a short-eared owl in his arms. The owl's astonished speckled head swivels around and I see its yellow eyes. In my arms it is quiet and feathery and I cannot find a piece of solid to hold and hug it tight. My father dives into the pampas grass again and brings out a fledgeling owl, immense staring eyes in a ball of fluff.

I seem to remember a fuss. If I don't, I remember another fuss of the same kind. For the pattern of this owl episode was to be repeated many times. My mother or Sophy the nurse protesting because the rules had been broken. 'The child over excited . . . a cold . . . bare feet on the wet grass . . .' My father roared, his arms flaying the air, 'What was a cold or a restless night?' An owl to hug was more important, a miracle I would remember for the rest of my life. My father was always to set the world topsy-turvy for a touch of magic, for a grand gesture.

Nicolette Devas, Two Flamboyant Fathers, 1966

We his children all took especial pleasure in the games he played at with us, but I do not think he romped much with us; I suppose his health prevented any rough play. He used sometimes to tell us stories, which were considered specially delightful, partly on account of their rarity.

The way he brought us up is shown by a little story about my brother Leonard, which my father was fond of telling. He came into the drawing-room and found Leonard dancing about on the sofa, which was forbidden, for the sake of the springs, and said, 'Oh, Lenny, Lenny, that's against all rules,' and received for answer, 'Then I think you'd better go out of the room.' I do not believe he ever spoke an angry word to any of his children in his life; but I am certain that it never entered our heads to disobey him. I well remember one occasion when my father reproved me for a piece of carelessness; and I can still recall the feeling of depression which came over me, and the care which he took to disperse it by speaking to me soon afterwards with especial kindness. He kept up his delightful, affectionate manner towards us all his life. I sometimes wonder that he could do so, with such an undemonstrative race as we are; but I hope he knew how much we delighted in his loving words and manner. How often, when a man, I have wished when my father was behind my chair, that he would pass his hand over my hair, as he used to do when I was a boy. He allowed his grown-up children to laugh with and at him, and was generally speaking on terms of perfect equality with us.

He was always full of interest about each one's plans or successes. We used to laugh at him, and say he would not believe in his sons, because, for instance, he would be a little doubtful about their taking some bit of work for which he did not feel sure that they had knowledge enough. On the other hand, he was only too much inclined to take a favourable view of our work. When I thought he had set too high a value on anything that I had done, he used to be indignant and inclined to explode in mock anger. His doubts were part of his humility concerning what was in any way connected with himself; his too favourable view of our work was due to his sympathetic nature, which made him lenient to every one.

He kept up towards his children his delightful manner of expressing his thanks; and I never wrote a letter, or read a page aloud to him, without receiving a few kind words of recognition. His love and goodness towards his little grandson Bernard were great; and he often spoke of the pleasure it was to him to see 'his little face opposite to him' at luncheon. He and Bernard used to compare their tastes; *e.g.*, in liking brown sugar better than white, &c.; the result being, 'We always agree, don't we?'

Francis Darwin (ed.) (1848–1925), *Life and Letters of Charles Darwin*, 1887

TO THE REVEREND SHADE OF HIS RELIGIOUS FATHER

That for seven *lusters* I did never come
To do the rites to thy religious tomb;
That neither hair was cut, or true tears shed
By me, o'er thee (*as justments to the dead*),
Forgive, forgive me; since I did not know
Whether thy bones had here their rest or no.
But now 'tis known, behold! behold, I bring
Unto thy ghost th'effused offering:
And look, what smallage, night-shade, cypress, yew,
Unto the shades have been, or now are due,
Here I devote; and something more than so;
I come to pay a debt of birth I owe.
Thou gav'st me life (but mortal); for that one
Favour I'll make full satisfaction;
For my life mortal, rise from out thy hearse,
And take a life immortal from my verse.

Robert Herrick (1591–1674)

HIS SHLONG WAS LIKE A FIRE HOSE

I stand at attention between his legs as he coats me from head to toe with a thick lather of soap – and eye with admiration the baggy substantiality of what overhangs the marble bench upon which he is seated. His scrotum is like the long wrinkled face of some old man with an egg tucked into each of his sagging jowls – while mine might hang from the wrist of some little girl's dolly like a teeny pink purse. And as for his *shlong*, to me, with that fingertip of a prick that my mother likes to refer to in public (once, okay, but that once will last a lifetime) as my 'little thing,' his *shlong* brings to mind the fire hoses coiled along the corridors at school. *Shlong*: the word somehow catches exactly the brutishness, the *meatishness*, that I admire so, the sheer mindless, weighty, and unselfconscious dangle of that living piece of hose through which he passes streams of water as thick and strong as rope.

Philip Roth, *Portnoy's Complaint*, 1969

THE AGED PARENT

'You wouldn't mind being at once introduced to the Aged, would you? It wouldn't put you out?'

I expressed the readiness I felt, and we went into the castle. There, we found sitting by a fire, a very old man in a flannel coat – clean, cheerful, comfortable, and well cared for, but intensely deaf.

'Well, aged parent,' said Wemmick, shaking hands with him in a cordial and jocose way, 'how am you?'

'All right, John; all right!' replied the old man.

'Here's Mr. Pip, aged parent,' said Wemmick, 'and I wish you could hear his name. Nod away at him, Mr. Pip; that's what he likes. Nod away at him, if you please, like winking!'

'This is a fine place of my son's, sir,' cried the old man, while I nodded as hard as I possibly could. 'This is a pretty pleasure-ground, sir. This spot and these beautiful works upon it ought to be kept together by the nation, after my son's time, for the people's enjoyment.'

'You're as proud of it as Punch, ain't you, Aged?' said Wemmick, contemplating the old man, with his hard face really softened. '*There's* a nod for you' – giving him a tremendous one. '*There's* another for you' – giving him a still more tremendous one. 'You like that, don't you? If you're not tired, Mr. Pip – though I know it's tiring to strangers – would you tip him one more? You can't think how it pleases him.'

I tipped him several more, and he was in great spirits. We left him bestirring himself to feed the fowls, and we sat down to our punch in the arbour, where Wemmick told me as he smoked a pipe that it had taken him a good many years to bring the property up to its present pitch of perfection.

'Is it your own, Mr. Wemmick?'

'Oh, yes,' said Wemmick. 'I have got hold of it a bit at a time. It's a freehold, by George!'

'Is it, indeed? I hope Mr. Jaggers admires it?'

'Never seen it,' said Wemmick. 'Never heard of it. Never seen the Aged. Never heard of him. No; the office is one thing, and private life is another. When I go into the office, I leave the castle behind me, and when I come into the castle, I leave the office behind me. If it's not in any way disagreeable to you, you'll oblige me by doing the same. I don't wish it professionally spoken about.'

Of course I felt my good faith involved in the observance of his request. The punch being very nice, we sat there drinking it and talking, until it was almost nine o'clock. 'Getting near gun-fire,' said Wemmick then, as he laid down his pipe; 'it's the Aged's treat.'

Proceeding into the castle again, we found the Aged heating the poker, with expectant eyes, as a preliminary to the performance of his great nightly ceremony. Wemmick stood with his watch in his hand until the moment was come for him to take the red-hot poker from the Aged, and repair to the battery. He took it, and went out, and presently the stinger went off with a bang that shook the crazy little box of a cottage as if it must fall to pieces, and made every glass and tea-cup in it ring. Upon this the Aged – who I believe would have been blown out of his arm-chair but for holding on by the elbows – cried out exultingly, 'He's fired! I heerd him!' and I nodded at the old gentleman until it is no figure of speech to declare that I absolutely could not see him.

Charles Dickens (1812–70), *Great Expectations*

DOSTOEVSKY THE FATHER

. . . now and then, when Mlle Dostoevsky forgets the political rancours of the moment and the complex effect of the Norman strain upon the Lithuanian temperament, she opens the study door and lets us see her father as she saw him. He could not write if he had a spot of candle-grease on his coat. He liked dried figs and kept a box of them in a cupboard from which he helped his children. He liked eaude-Cologne to wash with. He liked little girls to wear pale green. He would dance with them and read aloud Dickens and Scott. But he never spoke to them about his own childhood. She thinks that he dreaded discovering signs of his father's vices in himself; and she believes that he 'wished intensely to be like others.' At any rate, it was the greatest pleasure of her day to be allowed to breakfast with him and to talk to him about books. And then it is all over. There is her father laid out in his evening dress in his coffin; a painter is sketching him; grand dukes and peasants crowd the staircase; while she and her brother distribute flowers to unknown people and enjoy very much the drive to the cemetery.

Virginia Woolf (1882–1941), review of *Fyodor Dostoevsky* by Aimée Dostoevsky, in *The Times Literary Supplement*, 1922

A SINGULAR VOLATILITY

On his moral character I shall scarcely presume to dwell. The philosophic sweetness of his disposition, the serenity of his lot, and the elevating nature of his pursuits, combined to enable him to pass through life without an evil act, almost without an evil thought. As the world has always been fond of personal details respecting men who have been celebrated, I will mention that he was fair, with a Bourbon nose, and brown eyes of extraordinary beauty and lustre. He wore a small black velvet cap, but his white hair latterly touched his shoulders in curls almost as flowing as in his boyhood. His extremities were delicate and well-formed, and his leg, at his last hour, as shapely as in his youth, which showed the vigour of his frame. Latterly he had become corpulent. He did not excel in conversation, though in his family circle he was garrulous. Everything interested him, and blind and eighty-two he was still as susceptible as a child. One of his last acts was to compose some verses of gay gratitude to his daughter-in-law, who was his London correspondent, and to whose lively pen he was indebted for constant amusement. He had by nature a singular volatility which never deserted him. His feelings, though always amiable, were not painfully deep, and amid joy or sorrow the philosophic vein was ever evident. He more resembled Goldsmith than any man that I can compare him to; in his conversation, his apparent confusion of ideas ending with some felicitous phrase of genius, his naïveté, his simplicity not untouched with a dash of sarcasm affecting innocence – one was often reminded of the gifted friend of Burke and Johnson. There was however one trait in which my father did not resemble Goldsmith; he had no vanity. Indeed, one of his few infirmities was rather a deficiency of self-esteem.

Memoir of Isaac Disraeli by his son Benjamin, in *The Life of Benjamin Disraeli*, by William Flavelle Moneypenny, 1910

KIND CYRIL CONNOLLY

As a child I believed that it was his tremendous age which made him so knowledgeable. Now I know it was nothing to do with his years; that he was just indefatigably curious and clever.

He could imitate the mating call of a hippopotamus, describe the history and tenets of Buddhism (explaining the differences between the three principal schools thereof) and recite yards of poetry by heart. He knew Latin, Greek, French, geography, history and literature.

He was also very funny. He invented humorous songs and ditties, and made up stories about landmarks which we passed on car journeys. An ordinary house became the lair where a giant kept his toothbrush; another was compulsorily purchased – in his imagination only – as a store for his books. He was also a brilliant mimic.

He could be kind. When, at 11, I knitted a hat for him – it looked like an aborted tea cosy – he wore it up to London on the train.

My father had learned to drive before the days of compulsory tests, and he sometimes spluttered along in second gear for what felt like miles. I dreaded my schoolfriends seeing our car straining and lurching and often told him to hurry up, which made him drive, smirking mischievously, all the slower.

Cressida Connolly, *Daily Mail*, 25 March 1995

THE SACRED GHOST OF ANCHISES

But old Anchises, in a flow'ry vale,
Review'd his muster'd race, and took the tale:
Those happy spirits, which, ordain'd by fate,
For future beings and new bodies wait –
With studious thought observ'd th' illustrious throng,
In nature's order as they pass'd along:
Their names, their fates, their conduct, and their care,
In peaceful senates and successful war.
He, when Aeneas on the plain appears,
Meets him with open arms, and falling tears.
'Welcome,' he said, 'the gods' undoubted race!
O long expected to my dear embrace!
Once more 't is giv'n me to behold your face!
The love and pious duty which you pay
Have pass'd the perils of so hard a way.
'T is true, computing times, I now believ'd
The happy day approach'd; nor are my hopes deceiv'd.
What length of lands, what oceans have you pass'd;
What storms sustain'd, and on what shores been cast?
How have I fear'd your fate! but fear'd it most,
When love assail'd you, on the Libyan coast.'
To this, the filial duty thus replies:
'Your sacred ghost before my sleeping eyes
Appear'd, and often urg'd this painful enterprise.
After long tossing on the Tyrrhene sea,
My navy rides at anchor in the bay.
But reach your hand, O parent shade, nor shun
The dear embraces of your longing son!'
He said; and falling tears his face bedew:
Then thrice around his neck his arms he threw;
And thrice the flitting shadow slipp'd away,
Like winds, or empty dreams that fly the day.

Virgil (70–19BC), *The Aeneid*, translated by John Dryden

WHAT GENTLE SYMPATHY

Always visibly happy in the happiness of others, especially of children, our father entered into all our pleasures, and soothed and cheered us in all our little griefs with such overflowing tenderness, that it was no wonder we almost worshipped him. My first recollection of him is of his carrying me up to his private room to prayers, in the summer evenings, about sunset, and rewarding my silence and attention afterwards with a view of the flower-garden through his prism. Then I recall the delight it was to me to be permitted to sleep with him during a confinement of my mother's – how I longed for the morning, because then he would be sure to tell me some fairy tale, of his own invention, all sparkling with gold and diamonds, magic fountains and enchanted princesses. In the eye of memory I can still see him as he was at that period of his life, – his fatherly countenance, unmixed with any of the less loveable expressions that, in too many faces, obscure that character – but pre-eminently *fatherly*; conveying the ideas of kindness, intellect, and purity; his manner grave, manly, and cheerful, in unison with his high and open forehead: his very attitudes, whether as he sat absorbed in the arrangement of his minerals, shells, and insects – or as he laboured in his garden until his naturally pale complexion acquired a tinge of fresh healthy red; or as, coming lightly towards us with some unexpected present, his smile of indescribable benevolence spoke exultation in the foretaste of our raptures.

Never can I forget my first excursion into Suffolk, in company with my parents. It was in the month of September, 1791 – (shortly after my mother had recovered from her confinement with her fourth son, *Edmund Burke* Crabbe, who died in infancy,) – that, dressed in my first suit of boy's clothes, (and that scarlet), in the height of a delicious season, I was mounted beside them in their huge old gig, and visited the scenes and the persons familiar to me, from my earliest nursery days, in their conversation and anecdotes. Sometimes, as we proceeded, my father read aloud; sometimes he left us for a while to botanise among the hedgerows, and returned with some unsightly weed or bunch of moss, to him precious. Then, in the evening, when we had reached our inn, the happy child, instead of being sent early as usual to bed, was permitted to stretch himself on the carpet, while the reading was resumed, blending with sounds which, from novelty, appeared delightful, – the buzzing of the bar, the rattling of wheels, the horn of the mail-coach, the gay clamour of the streets – every thing to excite and astonish, in the midst of safety and repose. My father's countenance at such moments is still before me; – with what gentle sympathy did he seem to enjoy the happiness of childhood!

The Life of George Crabbe (1754–1832), by his son, George Crabbe

THEY CAME TO SHOOT MY FATHER

I obeyed my father as much as most boys do; but there was one curious thing over which he seemed to exert all his personal force, all that was left to him as he grew old, and even more, as though he called up hidden reserves of power; and that was that one day in that room he might say to me 'Look at the picture,' and if ever he did I was to go immediately to a little Dutch picture at the end of the room and watch it; I forget for how long, but I was to watch it minutely. And, if ever he said those words, I was never to think that he did not mean them, or that it was a joke, or that there was time to spare. He told me this often. Why? He never told me why.

Well, there we were sitting, and the house was all shut up; my father always went round every shutter himself to see they were properly fastened, and I used to think it rather unnecessary, for we knew everybody all round us; but once when I said something of this to my father he had replied: 'You never know who might come over the bog.' And certainly on the other side of the bog there were hills of which we knew nothing. Yet the idea that, even over there, could be anyone with enmity for my father, seemed, I remember, absurd to me: for one thing he did not seem active enough to have his share of such enmities; but that was a boy's idea, forgetting he had been younger.

We were talking when at all about Lisronagh, for I wanted quietly to find out what day I might go; when the housemaid brought in the milk, a tumbler of plain milk which he used to mix with the whiskey himself, after tasting the milk to see that it was not sour. The housemaid left the room, and he put his hand to the tumbler that stood on a table beside him. I can see him now more clearly than I can picture faces seen yesterday; tall and thin, with fine profile, with the firelight in his greying beard. And I was talking of Lisronagh. I thought he would have let me go next day, till he said definitely: 'Not this week.' I remember the words because they fell on my ears with such a sense of disaster, yearning as I was to get to Lisronagh before the geese had gone, and because they were the last words but four that I ever heard him say. He lifted the glass of milk to his lips and then put it down again, and turned to me and said: 'Look at the picture.' And he said it with none of the authority I had expected, if ever I really expected he would say those words at all, with less authority by far than that with which he forbade me to go to Lisronagh; but as though he were very tired.

I did as I had been taught. I went without thinking he did not mean it, or that there was time to spare: I went to the little Dutch picture and gazed at the tiny figures, skating past churches and windmills over grey ice. The picture was near the door, the only door in the room, which was shut, until it was opened from outside, and four tall men came in. Then I looked round, and my father was gone.

I saw at once that the men were from the other side of the bog; they were dark and strange and like none of our men. They peered round the room, then one of them looked at me fixedly and said: 'There is no one we have a greater respect for than your father, but it is a pity he mixed himself up with politics the way he did; and it's the way it is we want to speak to him, and no one could be sorrier than myself that I have to say it.'

Then I knew they had come to shoot my father.

So I said: 'He is up in his room, but I'll go and fetch him.'

'You will not, sir,' said the same man. 'But we will come with you.'

So they looked amongst all the curtains in the library, and behind a sofa that there was, and found nothing, and then I walked slowly up the stairs, and they came with me. So slowly I went that one of them shouted: 'Come *on*, now.' And at that I started forward and ran up a few steps, and fell at the top of a flight. I got up slowly, and then limped a little. All this gained time.

When we came to the door of my father's room I knocked, but they shoved in past me. The room was in darkness and I got a match for them and lit a candle: they looked round the room carefully, and we gained time there.

I said: 'He must be in his study.' And then I added: 'Perhaps he is in another bedroom. Shall we go there first?'

But the man who had spoken before said: 'You will go to the study.' So I did as he told me and we all went downstairs. All the time I was calculating how far my father could have got. How he had got out of the library I had no idea; there was only one door and all the shutters were shut; but gone he had. And even if he went by some narrow passage, and difficult steps in the dark, I calculated that with our various trifling delays, that all add up, he had gone by now as far as we had, and that that should have just taken him clear of the house. He would make of course for the stables: that was a hundred yards. And then he would have to get in, and saddle his horse and get out again, and past the gate by the house, before one could think him safe.

When we entered the study I think they saw at a glance that my father was not there, and never had been. It was not only that the fire was unlighted, but the look and feel of the room told you at once that it never was used by anyone. And indeed, except for meals, we never used any room at all but the library. And they all looked at me in a rather nasty way.

'If you don't show us where he is, we'll burn the house,' said one of them that had not spoken before.

'You will not,' I said, looking straight at him.

And his face fell at that, and I saw the eyes of all of them turn downwards. For they knew, whoever they were or wherever they came from, that we kept a piece of the true Cross at High Gaut, and had done for ages, ever since it had been granted to us for the help my family gave in a war of one of the popes. I saw they were thinking of it, and did not have to remind them that if a man burned that, the flames might not be so easily quenched. They would flicker about his soul all through eternity.

But you do not always know, when you invoke powers like that, whom in the end they will benefit. The leader turned to me and told me to get the cross. It was a crystal cross and part of the crystal was hollow, and in the hollow the piece of the true Cross was. I knew what they wanted it for: they were going to swear me on it. And I grew suddenly afraid of the cross, and afraid of the men.

I had to get it: it was in that very room; in a little golden box on a marble table. It was never locked up; there was no need for that. I went across the room to get it, and they all drew their pistols as I went. They took them out of their pockets, in which I knew they had them, but they had not shown them before. Now they were getting annoyed because they had not found my father, and I saw that they were not going to let me escape from swearing to them on the Cross. They were long, single-barrelled pistols, old even then; nothing like the automatics they use nowadays.

When I came back with the relic I saw that they had me covered. I came up to them and lifted it in my hand, and they all dropped on their knees. 'Do you swear,' said the leader, kneeling before me, but still covering me with the long black pistol, 'to the best of your knowledge and your belief that you father is still in this house?'

And while he spoke I heard the clip clop, clip clop, of my father's horse coming out of the stables. But it was only coming at a walk. That was of course so as to make less noise, and then there was a gate that he would have to open, but somehow I had thought he would gallop. Almost at once he got on to the grass, and they had not heard him, but he had to come right past the house. I could still hear every step of the horse, but I suppose it is easier to hear what you are listening for, if you are listening as I was; while they were all watching me and the cross that I held and waiting for me to speak, and they never heard the horse coming by on the grass. But they would have if I hadn't spoken just when I did. He wasn't safe till he'd opened the gate another fifty yards on. 'I swear,' I said, 'to the best of my knowledge and my belief,' speaking slowly, spinning it out as long as I could, to drown the noise of the hooves, 'that my father is in this house.'

I suppose one puts one's soul in danger oftener than one thinks, and in less good causes. The risk frightened me when I took it. If it wasn't the true Cross, and (God help me) I've sometimes doubted it, then no harm was done. If it was, could it be on the side of these four men and against my father? But I was not easy about what I'd done, for a single moment, till I went to Father McGillicud and told him all. 'And would you murder your father,' he said, 'and with the true Cross in your hand?' Then I knew that I'd done right.

Lord Dunsaney (1878–1957), *The Curse of the Wise Woman*, 1933

ADORED OSCAR WILDE

It was only during these early years that I knew my father; after 1895 I never saw him again. Most small boys adore their fathers, and we adored ours; and as all good fathers are, he was a hero to us both. He was so tall and distinguished and, to our uncritical eyes, so handsome. There was nothing about him of the monster that some people who never knew him and never even saw him have tried to make him out to be. He was a real companion to us, and we always looked forward eagerly to his frequent visits to our nursery. Most parents in those days were far too solemn and pompous with their children, insisting on a vast amount of usually undeserved respect. My own father was quite different; he had so much of the child in his own nature that he delighted in playing our games. He would go down on all fours on the nursery floor, being in turn a lion, a wolf, a horse, caring nothing for his usually immaculate appearance. And there was nothing half-hearted in his methods of play. One day he arrived with a toy milk-cart drawn by a horse with real hair on it. All the harness undid and took off, and the churns with which the cart was filled could be removed and opened. When my father discovered this he immediately went downstairs and came back with a jug of milk with which he pro-ceeded to fill the churns. We then all tore round the nursery table, slopping milk all over the place, until the arrival of our nurse put an end to that game.

Like other fathers, he mended our toys; he spent most of one after-noon repairing a wooden fort that had come to pieces in the course of various wars, and when he had finished he insisted upon everyone in the house coming to see how well he had done it and to give him a little praise. He also played with us a great deal in the dining-room, which was in some ways more suited to romping than the nursery, as there were more chairs and tables and sideboards to dodge through, and more room to clamber over Papa as well.

When he grew tired of playing he would keep us quiet by telling us fairy stories, or tales of adventure, of which he had a never-ending supply. He was a great admirer of Jules Verne and Stevenson, and of Kipling in his more imaginative vein. The last present he gave me was *The Jungle Book*; he had already given me *Treasure Island* and Jules Verne's *Five Weeks in a Balloon*, which were the first books I read through entirely by myself. He told us all his own written fairy stories suitably adapted for our young minds, and a great many others as well. There was one about the fairies who lived in the great bottles of coloured water that chemists used to put in their windows, with lights behind them that made them take on all kinds of different shapes. The fairies came down from their bottles at night and played and danced and made pills in the empty shop. Cyril once asked him why he had tears in his eyes when he told us the story of *The Selfish Giant*, and he replied that really beautiful things always made him cry.

Vyvyan Holland (1886–1967), *Son of Oscar Wilde*, 1954

Memorandum that in his Utopia his lawe is that the young people are to see each other stark-naked before marriage. Sir [William] Roper, of Eltham in Kent, came one morning, pretty early, to my lord, with a proposall to marry one of his daughters. My lord's daughters were then both together a bed in a truckle-bed in their father's chamber asleep. He carries Sir [William] into the chamber and takes the sheet by the corner and suddenly whippes it off. 'They lay on their Backs, and their smocks up as high as their armpitts. This awakened them, and immediately they turned on their Bellies. Quoth Roper, I have seen both sides, and so gave a patt on her Buttock he made choice of, sayeing, Thou art mine.' Here was all the trouble of the wooeing. This account I had from my honoured friend old Mris. Tyndale, whose grandfather Sir William Stafford was an intimate acquaintance of this Sir W. Roper, who told him the story.

. . . AND INVENTS A PRODIGIOUS DRAGON

His discourse was extraordinary facetious. Riding one night, upon the suddaine, he crossed himself *majori cruce*, crying out 'Jesu Maria! doe not you see that prodigious dragon in the sky?' They all lookt-up, and one did not see it, nor the tother did not see it. At length one had spyed it, and at last all had spied. Wheras there was no such phantôme; only he imposed on their phantasies.

. . . A FATHER'S HEAD PRESERVED

His head was upon London bridge: there goes this story in the family, *viz.* that one day as one of his daughters was passing under the bridge, looking on her father's head, sayd she, 'That head haz layn many a time in my lapp, would to God it would fall into my lap as I passe under.' She had her wish, and it did fall into her lappe, and is now preserved in a vault in the cathedrall church at Canterbury.

John Aubrey (1626–97), Brief Lives

SIR THOMAS MORE IN THE TOWER

When Sir Thomas More came from Westminster to the Tower-ward again, his daughter, my wife, desirous to see her father, whom she thought she should never see in this world after, and also to have his final blessing, gave attendance about the Tower Wharf, where she knew he should pass by, before he could enter into the Tower. There tarrying for his coming, as soon as she saw him, after his blessing upon her knees reverently received, she hasting towards him, and without consideration or care of herself, pressing in among the midst of the throng and company of the guard, that with halberds and bills went round about him, hastily ran to him, and there openly in the sight of them all, embraced him, took him about the neck and kissed him. Who well liking her most natural and dear daughterly affection towards him, gave her his fatherly blessing, and many godly words of comfort besides. From whom after she was departed, she not satisfied with her former sight of him, and like one that had forgotten herself, being all ravished with the entire love of her dear father, having respect neither to herself, nor to the press of the people and the multitude that were about him, suddenly turned back again, ran to him as before, took him about the neck, and divers times together most lovingly kissed him; and at last, with a full heavy heart, was fain to depart from him: the beholding whereof was to many of them that were present thereat so lamentable, that it made them for very sorrow thereof to mourn and weep.

More wrote his last letter to his daughter in the Tower, with a piece of coal, on 5 July 1535:

I cumber you, good Margaret, much; but I would be sorry if it should be any longer than tomorrow. For tomorrow is Saint Thomas's Even and the Utas of Saint Peter; and therefore tomorrow long I to go to God. It were a day very and convenient for me, etc, I never liked your manner toward me better than when you kissed me last; for I love when daughterly love and dear charity hath no leisure to look for worldly courtesy. Farewell, my dear child, and pray for me, and I shall for you and all your friends, that we may merrily meet in heaven . . .

William Roper (1498–1578), The Life of Sir Thomas More

FOLLOWER

My father worked with a horse-plough,
His shoulders globed like a full sail strung
Between the shafts and the furrow.
The horses strained at his clicking tongue.

An expert. He would set the wing
And fit the bright steel-pointed sock.
The sod rolled over without breaking.
At the headrig, with a single pluck

Of reins, the sweating team turned round
And back into the land. His eye
Narrowed and angled at the ground,
Mapping the furrow exactly.

I stumbled in his hob-nailed wake,
Fell sometimes on the polished sod;
Sometimes he rode me on his back
Dipping and rising to his plod.

I wanted to grow up and plough,
To close one eye, stiffen my arm.
All I ever did was follow
In his broad shadow round the farm.

I was a nuisance, tripping, falling,
Yapping always. But today
It is my father who keeps stumbling
Behind me, and will not go away.

Seamus Heaney, *Selected Poems*, 1980

HE REMINDS ME WHAT IS GOOD

23RD SEPTEMBER, 1882, 10 PM
Have just come back from a shooting expedition on horseback. Papa,
Lev and me, with the hounds, a long way, beyond Yassenki, and we
got three hares. One Papa spotted and we all three rode up and saw it
lying there. It was terribly jolly. I did not get one. Two more were put

up. I was so beside myself with delight at their taking me that I couldn't keep my mouth in place; it stretched to my ears. We started out at mid-day and got back at eight; I don't feel in the least exhausted. On Monday Papa came back with Lev . . . He decided to take him away from school and have him taught at home. Mamma was very annoyed at first, but now seems to have made her peace about it. I was very glad to see Papa, and he was so sweet and touching, buying chairs and carriages for us in Moscow. I was also glad because he always reminds me what is good and what is bad. I mean, not the fact that he speaks to me of it, but that when he is near I can sense clearly what is worth thinking about and worrying over, and what is not; what is important in life and what are trifles. I do not remember what we were talking of, only it was something about death, and Papa said that the world is like a river: men are born and produce still more people, and die and that is like the flow of a river, and the current carries with it models of fine or worthless people, good and bad and all sorts – well, it's also our duty to leave the pattern we want on that river.

From *The Tolstoy Home: Diaries of Tatiana Tolstoy*, (1864-1950)

YOUR FATHER'S EYES ARE BLUE AGAIN

My mother has come back from her cataract operation. For years she has felt hemmed in by the murk. The colours amaze her.

'Your father's eyes are blue again.'

My father has the most beautiful blue eyes I have ever seen in a man. I do not say this because he is my father. They are mariner's eyes, level and steady. On the Malta convoys they scanned the surface of the sea for mines, or the horizon for an enemy warship. They are the eyes of a man who has never known the meaning of dishonesty. They have never tempted him to anything mean or shoddy.

My mother's eyes are brown and lively, with suggestions of Southern ancestry.

When my mother, Margharita, was in hospital he found a photograph I had feared was lost. He had it taken at Hove in 1940 before going to sea. The photo shows the clear blue eyes, that can only be blue, gazing squarely at the camera from under the patent leather peak of his naval officer's cap. My mother kept it by her bedside. I would kiss it before going to bed. My first memory of him is on my third birthday, the 13th of May 1943. He took us bicycling near Flamborough Head, the grey Yorkshire headland that Rimbaud may have seen from a brig and put into his prose-poem *Promontoire*.

He rigged up an improvised saddle for me on his crossbar, with stirrups of purple electric wire. I pointed to a squashed brown thing on the road.

'What's that, daddy?'

'I don't know.'

He did not want me to see something dead.

'Well, it looks to me like a piece of hedgehog.'

My father was not looking in the box of old photos for the one of himself, but for one of his father's yacht, the *Aireymouse*. In the Twenties and Thirties my grandfather, a Birmingham lawyer, owned a vessel of legendary beauty. She was a teak, clipper-bowed ketch built at Fowey in Cornwall in 1898; she had once been rigged as a cutter. An aireymouse is a bat and, under her bowsprit, there was the figurehead of a bat with outstretched wings. The bat had disappeared by my father's day. *Aireymouse* had brown sails dyed with cutch-bark, a brass ship's bell, and a gold line from stem to stern.

My grandfather died in 1933, and *Aireymouse* had to be sold. She needed expensive repairs to her stanchions. Neither my father nor his brothers and sister could afford them. They sold her for £200. For my father alone it was the loss of a lover.

He had other boats – the *Nocteluca*, the *Dozmaree*, the *Nereid*, the *Sunquest* – but he shared them with others, and none matched the boat of his dreams.

I do not think he could bring himself to find out what had happened to *Aireymouse*. He heard rumours. In Guernsey a car had driven over the pier and landed on her deck – without doing too much damage. Or she was a rotting house-boat in the mud of a West Country creek. Or an incendiary bomb had hit her in the War. He came to accept that she was gone, but never quite believed it. On our sailing holidays we all believed that one golden evening, off Ushant or in the Race of Alderney, two sails would appear on the horizon and the ethereal craft would heave into view. My father would raise his binoculars and say the words he yearned to say: 'It's *Aireymouse*.'

He became resigned. My parents no longer went to sea. They bought a camping van and travelled all over Europe. My father kept a sailor's log-book of their journeys, and read road-maps as if they were charts.

He had also dreamed of making one trade-wind passage to the

West Indies. He never found the time to get away. Too many people depended on his legal advice. He would come home exhausted in the evenings after grappling with the problems of National Health Service hospitals. After his retirement, he had an arthritic hip and I feared he would go into decline. Once the operation had been performed, he was young again.

Four years ago my brother took him on the trade-wind passage. The boat was a modern yacht to be delivered to Antigua. But the owners had made her top-heavy with expensive junk. In a following sea, she did a fifty-degree roll and they had to turn back to the Cape Verde Islands. My father looked younger than ever after his adventure, but it was a disappointment.

Three days before Margharita went to hospital, he found himself talking on the phone to a man who said: 'I've been looking for you for a long time.' Was Charles Chatwin related to the pre-war owners of *Aireymouse*?

'I am,' said my father. 'She was our boat.'

'I've bought her,' the man said.

The man had found her up the River Dart. He fell in love with her and bought her. He took her to a yard in Totnes. The deck was gone. Many of the oak timbers were gone. But the teak hull was in perfect condition.

'I'm going to reconstruct her,' the man said. Could he count on Charles's help?

Charles will be eighty this year.

Let us pray he will sail on *Aireymouse*.

Bruce Chatwin (1940–89), *What Am I Doing Here?*, 1989

AN EXPLOSIVE GOD

My father was no ordinary cosy daddy figure. I did not run to him crying with a bruised knee; we never kissed or cuddled. My father was an explosive god. To call such a man 'Daddy' would have reduced him to domestic size. Domesticated gods are no longer worthy of the name. I called my father by his first name, Francis. I think of him as Francis, and henceforth I shall write of him as Francis.

Francis lived on theories. With his grand scale personality he imposed them on his family; some were fun, some were awful. I was an early victim.

I was a pale, frail looking child. 'A diet of larks' tongues' my mother complained, when I would not eat. The Macnamara reputation for toughness, courage and wild deeds, appeared to be threatened by the unpromising material that I seemed to be. 'County Clare, the land of the Macnamaras famous for their courage' the father of Oscar Wilde, Sir William Wilde, wrote in a book on the history and archaeology of the West of Ireland. However, confronted by a daughter that looked a born coward, Francis was not going to take any chances. He had a remedy, a theory. He never had any doubts about his theories, even when they went wrong.

My next memory illustrates his theory about my courage or lack of it, though it must have taken place a year or so later. Francis walked me down to the sea at Lahinch by the meandering path along the river. Lahinch Bay concealed a drowned village, and he pointed to the sea where waves broke in swirling foam over the steeple of the village church. 'In rough weather the bell can be heard . . .'

On the way home we took a short cut across the boggy fields. These were intersected by streams and drainage dykes. With a run and his long legs Francis could leap over them. I couldn't. So he threw me over. I remember being picked up, swung in his arms as he took aim and I gathered momentum; one, two, three, and the rush of air as my skirt went over my head; then the thud of landing on the sludgy bank. It was a jolly experience, and Francis was excited too, a young father of twenty-nine who enjoyed the exercise and at the same time improved his daughter's moral fibre. For he was careful to explain that this experience would toughen me and make me a brave woman. There seemed to be a lot of dykes between us and home. A dyke wider than the others stopped us, and for some time we looked without success for a narrow place to cross. Francis measured the distance with his eye, picked me up, swung, and away I flew and landed short. The cold water was a shock. I paddled like a dog for the bank, and crawled out with the grit of mud on my arms and legs. Francis landed beside me. He must have had qualms about our reception from Sophy for he carried me on his shoulders the rest of the way, and to avoid more dykes, followed the river path. By then it was getting dark and the mist was rising over the water. High on Francis's shoulders I rode above the mist; out of reach of the bogies lurking among the ferns. Though cold and muddy, I felt like a princess.

Nicolette Devas, *Two Flamboyant Fathers*, 1966

RUDOLF HESS

When my father flew to Scotland on 10 May 1941 I was three-and-a-half years old. I can still see his worried face as he pulled me out of the garden pond, and I can still hear his comforting voice as he disentangled me, screaming in panic, from a bat that had caught itself in my hair and carried it to the window, releasing it into the night. These are my only personal memories of my father from that time. I remember nothing at all of my godfather, Adolf Hitler.

Wolf Rudiger Hess, *My Father Rudolf Hess*, 1986

THE MOST ADORING FATHER

Ever since she could remember he had been everything in life to her. She had had no thought since she grew up for anybody but her father. There was no room for any other thought, so completely did he fill her heart. They had done everything together, shared everything together, dodged the winters together, settled in charming places, seen the same beautiful things, read the same books, talked, laughed, had friends, – heaps of friends; wherever they were her father seemed at once to have friends, adding them to the mass he had already. She had not been away from him a day for years; she had had no wish to go away. Where and with whom could she be so happy as with him? All the years were years of sunshine. There had been no winters; nothing but summer, summer, and sweet scents and soft skies, and patient understanding with her slowness – for he had the nimblest mind – and love. He was the most amusing companion to her, the most generous friend, the most illuminating guide, the most adoring father; and now he was dead, and she felt nothing.

Elisabeth Von Arnim (1866–1941), *Vera*, 1921

She had moved from the wall of the garret, very near to the bench on which he sat. There was something awful in his unconsciousness of the figure that could have put out its hand and touched him as he stooped over his labour.

Not a word was spoken, not a sound was made. She stood, like a spirit, beside him, and he bent over his work.

It happened, at length, that he had occasion to change the instrument in his hand, for his shoemaker's knife. It lay on that side of him which was not the side on which she stood. He had taken it up, and was stooping to work again, when his eyes caught the skirt of her dress. He raised them, and saw her face. The two spectators started forward, but she stayed them with a motion of her hand. She had no fear of his striking at her with the knife, though they had.

He stared at her with a fearful look, and after a while his lips began to form some words, though no sound proceeded from them. By degrees, in the pauses of his quick and laboured breathing, he was heard to say:

'What is this?'

With the tears streaming down her face, she put her two hands to her lips, and kissed them to him; then clasped them on her breast, as if she laid his ruined head there.

'You are not the gaoler's daughter?'

She sighed 'No.'

'Who are you?'

Not yet trusting the tones of her voice, she sat down on the bench beside him. He recoiled, but she laid her hand upon his arm. A strange thrill struck him when she did so, and visibly passed over his frame; he laid the knife down softly, as he sat staring at her.

Her golden hair, which she wore in long curls, had been hurriedly pushed aside, and fell down over her neck. Advancing his hand by little and little, he took it up and looked at it. In the midst of the action he went astray, and, with another deep sigh, fell to work at his shoe-making.

But not for long. Releasing his arm, she laid her hand upon his shoulder. After looking doubtfully at it, two or three times, as if to be sure that it was really there, he laid down his work, put his hand to his neck, and took off a blackened string with a scarp of folded rag attached to it. He opened this, carefully, on his knee, and it contained a very little quantity of hair: not more than one or two long golden hairs, which he had, in some old day, wound off upon his finger.

He took her hair into his hand again, and looked closely at it. 'It is the same. How can it be! When was it! How was it!'

As the concentrating expression returned to his forehead, he seemed to become conscious that it was in hers too. He turned her full to the light, and looked at her.

'She had laid her head upon my shoulder, that night when I was summoned out – she had a fear of my going, though I had none – and when I was brought to the North Tower they found these upon my sleeve.' "You will leave me them? They can never help me to escape in the body, though they may in the spirit." Those were the words I said. I remember them very well.'

He formed this speech with his lips many times before he could utter it. But when he did find spoken words for it, they came to him coherently, though slowly.

'How was this? – *Was it you?*'

Once more, the two spectators started, as he turned upon her with a frightful suddenness. But she sat perfectly still in his grasp, and only said, in a low voice, 'I entreat you, good gentlemen, do not come near us, do not speak, do not move!'

'Hark!' he exclaimed. 'Whose voice was that?'

His hands released her as he uttered this cry, and went up to his white hair, which they tore in a frenzy. It died out, as everything but his shoemaking did die out of him, and he refolded his little packet and tried to secure it in his breast; but he still looked at her, and gloomily shook his head.

'No, no, no; you are too young, too blooming. It can't be. See what the prisoner is. These are not the hands she knew, this is not the face she knew, this is not a voice she ever heard. No, no. She was – and He was – before the slow years of the North Tower – ages ago. What is your name, my gentle angel?'

Hailing his softened tone and manner, his daughter fell upon her knees before him, with her appealing hands upon his breast.

'O, sir, at another time you shall know my name, and who my mother was, and who my father, and how I never knew their hard, hard history. But I cannot tell you at this time, and I cannot tell you here. All that I may tell you, here and now, is, that I pray to you to touch me and to bless me. Kiss me, kiss me! O my dear, my dear!'

His cold white head mingled with her radiant hair, which warmed and lighted it as though it were the light of Freedom shining on him.

'If you hear in my voice – I don't know that it is so, but I hope it is – if you hear in my voice any resemblance to a voice that once was sweet music in your ears, weep for it, weep for it! If you touch, in touching my hair, anything that recalls a beloved head that lay in your breast when you were young and free, weep for it, weep for it! If, when I hint to you of a Home there is before us, where I will be true to you with all my duty and with all my faithful service, I bring back the remembrance of a Home long desolate, while your poor heart pined away, weep for it, weep for it!'

She held him closer round the neck, and rocked him on her breast like a child.

'If, when I tell you, dearest dear, that your agony is over, and that I have come here to take you from it, and that we go to England to be at peace and at rest, I cause you to think of your useful life laid waste, and of our native France so wicked to you, weep for it, weep for it! And if, when I shall tell you of my name, and of my father who is living, and of my mother who is dead, you learn that I have to kneel to my honoured father, and implore his pardon for having never for his sake striven all day and lain awake and wept all night, because the love of my poor mother hid his torture from me, weep for it, weep for it! Weep for her, then, and for me! Good gentlemen, thank God! I feel his sacred tears upon my face, and his sobs strike against my heart. O, see! Thank God for us, thank God!'

He had sunk in her arms, and his face dropped on her breast: a sight so touching, yet so terrible in the tremendous wrong and suffering which had gone before it, that the two beholders covered their faces.

When the quiet of the garret had been long undisturbed, and his heaving breast and shaken form had long yielded to the calm that must follow all storms – emblem to humanity, of the rest and silence into which the storm called Life must hush at last – they came forward to raise the father and daughter from the ground. He had gradually dropped to the floor, and lay there in a lethargy, worn out. She had nestled down with him, that his head might lie upon her arm; and her hair drooping over him curtained him from the light.

Charles Dickens (1812–70), A Tale of Two Cities

A SERENE CORPSE

Green Park Bgs Tuesday Eveng, Janry 22d.

My dearest Frank

I wrote to you yesterday; but your letter to Cassandra this morning, by which we learn the probability of your being by this time at Portsmouth, obliges me to write to you again, having unfortunately a communication as necessary as painful to make to you. – Your affectionate heart will be greatly wounded, & I wish the shock could have been lessen'd by a better preparation; – but the Event has been sudden, & so must be the information of it. We have lost an Excellent Father. – An Illness of only eight & forty hours carried him off yesterday morning between ten & eleven. He was seized on saturday with a return of the feverish complaint, which he had been subject to for the three last years, evidently a more violent attack from the first, as the applications which had before produced almost immediate relief, seemed for some time to afford him scarcely any. – On Sunday however he was much better, so much so as to make Bowen quite easy, & give us every hope of his being well again in a few days. – But these hopes gradually gave way as the day advanced, & when Bowen saw him at ten that night he was greatly alarmed. – A Physician was called in yesterday morning, but he was at that time past all possibility of cure – & Dr Gibbs & Mr Bowen had scarcely left his room before he sunk into a Sleep from which he never woke. – Everything I trust & beleive was done for him that was possible! – It has been very sudden! – within twenty four hours of his death he was walking with only the help of a stick, was even reading! – We had however some hours of preparation, & when we understood his recovery to be hopeless, most fervently did we pray for the speedy release which ensued. To have seen him languishing long, struggling for Hours, would have been dreadful! – & thank God! we were all spared from it. Except the restlessness & confusion of high Fever, he did not suffer – & he was mercifully spared from knowing that he was about to quit the Objects so beloved, so fondly cherished as his wife & Children ever were. – His tenderness as a Father, who can do justice to? – My Mother is tolerably well; she bears up with great fortitude, but I fear her health must suffer under such a shock. – An express was sent for James, & he arrived here this morning before eight o'clock. – The Funeral is to be on Saturday, at Walcot Church. – The Serenity of the Corpse is most delightful! – It preserves the sweet, benevolent smile which always distinguished him. – They kindly press my Mother to remove to Steventon as soon as it is all over, but I do not beleive she will leave Bath at present. We must have this house for three months longer, & here we shall probably stay till the end of that time. –

We all unite in Love, & I am affec:ly Yours

JA.

Capt. Austen
HMS *Leopard*
Portsmouth

Jane Austen (1775–1817), letter to Francis Austen

THE KINDEST AND GENTLEST OF MEN

My father was only forty-six when he died, an age at which most authors and artists enter upon the period of their greatest achievements. But apart from the letter to Lord Alfred Douglas known as *De Profundis*, and *The Ballad of Reading Gaol*, he wrote nothing after 1895. The spark of genius in him was extinguished by prison life, and it could never be rekindled. He constantly spoke of work which he had in mind, but when it came to actual writing he began to be assailed by doubts and problems; doubts as to how any work of his would be received, and problems as to whether it was humanly possible for him to reconstruct his literary life.

More books have been written, in more languages, about Oscar Wilde than about any literary figure who has lived during the past hundred years. But as people recede further and further into the past, they are apt to assume the aspect of effigies from which all humanity has departed; and when other people write about them they hack them about to make them fit into a pattern of their own making until no flesh and blood remains. This is especially true of Oscar Wilde. Most of the people who have written about him have treated him like a beetle under a microscope, to be examined and dissected and analysed as psychological problem – not as a human being at all. If they have mentioned any human qualities it has always been in parentheses, as it were, and almost on a note of surprise and deprecation. And yet the most outstanding aspect of my father's character was his great humanity, his love of life and of his fellow-men and his sympathy with suffering. He was the kindest and gentlest of men, and he hated to see anyone suffer. None of his biographers, not even Frank Harris, has suggested that he ever did a mean or an unkind act. Many stories are told of how he helped people in distress, even when he was himself in want.

Once in Reading Gaol he discovered that three small children were in the same place for the heinous crime of poaching rabbits; a fine which neither they nor their parents were able to pay had been inflicted upon them and they were sent to prison in default. This may seem incredible to us now, but not much more than a hundred years earlier they would probably have been publicly hanged. My father was deeply distressed that children who might be the same age as his own could be so barbarously treated by a self-righteous community, and he managed to get a note through to one of the warders with whom he was on good terms, asking what he could do to help and offering to pay the fine. 'Please do this for me,' the note went on to say; 'I must get them out. Think what a thing it would be for me to be able to help three little children. If I can do this by paying the fine, tell the children that they are to be released tomorrow by a friend, and ask them to be happy and not to tell anyone.' And the children were freed.

Vyvyan Holland (1886–1967), *Son of Oscar Wilde*, 1954

THE EMBODIMENT OF ROMANCE

I think it was at Sutton Hoo also, or it may have been at Leiston, that I remember my father riding by early one sunny morning on his chestnut mare called Butterfly. The sun was shining and there was a jingling from silver chains in his bridle. His sword was by his side in a brown leather sheath. He seemed to embody all I had heard of romance and chivalry as he smiled down at me and rode on his way to go on parade with his regiment.

At this time also I remember watching my father shave. He used a cut-throat razor which he wiped clean of white lavender-scented shaving soap made grey by the stubbles he had cut. He used to make faces so as to stretch the skin of his chin to be smooth for the edge of the razor. He knew that I thought this funny and made special faces when I came to watch. I use a safety razor myself and I used at one time, some thirty years later I suppose, to get my children to read me passages for their education while I shaved. My wife would first teach each one to read, and then they would come on to me and read aloud. But my enjoyment of my father's shaving had nothing didactic about it.

Bryan Guinness (1909–92), Dairy Not Kept, 1975

ODYSSEUS AND LAERTES

So he found his father alone in the vineyard digging about one of the plants. He had on him a dirty old shirt full of patches, with patched leather gaiters to save his shins from scratches, and leather gauntlets against the brambles. On his head he wore a goatskin hat, in the care-lessness of his sorrow.

When Odysseus saw him at last, worn with age and full of sorrow, he stood still under a spreading pear-tree and the tears came into his eyes. What should he do? . . .

Laertes answered: 'If you are really Odysseus my son come home again, give me a clear sign to prove that you speak the truth.'

Odysseus said: 'That wound first of all – look, here it is for you to see! You remember how the boar gashed me with his tusk as I ran on him? . . . Yes and let me tell you the trees you gave me in this jolly orchard, when I was a little boy and went round the garden with you and begged for each! We walked among these very trees, you told me their names every one! Thirteen pear trees you gave me and ten apples, forty figs; rows of vines you promised, fifty of them bearing at different times through the vintage, with grapes of all sorts, whenever Zeus made them heavy in the season of the year!'

The old man's knees crickled under him, and his heart melted, as he heard the signs recounted which he knew so well; he laid his arms about his son's neck, and Odysseus held him fainting.

Homer (8th century BC), The Odyssey, Books XIX and XXIV,
translated by W. H. D. Rouse

NOBODY EVER THOUGHT OF SUCH DROLL
THINGS

'After my father's return from America he took an apartment in Paris for the autumn months, and it was then that he told us he had made a plan for wintering in Rome. It almost seems to me now that all the rest of my life dates in some measure from those old Roman days, which were all the more vivid because my sister and I were still spectators and not yet actors in the play. I was just sixteen, my sister was thirteen.

'We started early in December 1853, my father, my sister and I. He had his servant with him, for already his health had begun to fail. We reached Marseilles in bitter weather late one night. We laid our travelling plaids upon our beds to keep ourselves warm, but though we shivered, our spirits rose to wildest pitch next morning in the excitement of the golden moment. The wonderful sights in the streets are before me still – the Jews, Turks, dwellers in Mesopotamia, chattering in gorgeous colours and strange languages; the quays, the crowded shipping, the amethyst water. I can still see in a sort of mental picture a barge piled with great golden onions, floating along one of the quays, guided by a lonely woman in blue rags with a coloured kerchief on her head. "There goes the Lady of Shalot," said my father: and when we looked at him rather puzzled, for we knew nothing of onions and very little of Tennyson in those days, he explained that a shalot was a species of onion, and after a moment's reflection we took in his little joke, feeling that nobody ever thought of such droll things as he did. Then we reached our hotel again where there were Turks still drinking coffee under striped awnings, and a black man in a fez, and a lank British diplomat, with a very worn face, who knew my father, arriving from some outlandish place with piles of luggage; and we caught sight of the master of the hotel and his family gathered round a soup tureen in a sort of glass conservatory, and so went upstairs to rest and refresh ourselves before our start that evening. All this splendour and novelty and lux mundi had turned our heads, for we forgot our warm wraps and half our possessions at the hotel, and did not discover, till long after the steamer had started with all of us on board, how many essentials we had left behind.

Anne Thackeray Ritchie (1837–1919), *Recollections*

GOD BLESS YOU, MY BOY

In the year 1869, after I had been at college about a year, I was fortunate enough to gain one of the principal scholarships at Trinity Hall, Cambridge – not a great thing, only £50 a year; but I knew that this success, slight as it was, would give him intense pleasure, so I went to meet him at Higham Station upon his arrival from London to tell him of it. As he got out of the train I told him the news. He said, 'Capital! capital!' – nothing more. Disappointed to find that he received the news apparently so lightly, I took my seat beside him in the pony carriage he was driving. Nothing more happened until we had got half-way to Gad's Hill, when he broke down completely. Turning towards me with tears in his eyes and giving me a warm grip of the hand, he said, 'God bless you, my boy; God bless you!' That pressure of the hand I can feel now as distinctly as I felt it then, and it will remain as strong and real until the day of my death.

Henry Dickens (1849–1933), *Memories of My Father*, 1928

DEMETRIUS

Demetrius, the King of Macedon, was remarkable both for his filial and his parental affection. His father, Antigonus, after giving audience one day to Ptolemy and Lysimachus, the ambassadors of Cassauder, called them back, because his son, Demetrius, coming in warm from hunting, went into his father's apartment, saluted him, and then sat down with his javelin in his hand. When the ambassadors demanded what his pleasure was? he replied, 'Tell your masters upon what terms my son and I live.'

When Demetrius had succeeded to the throne, and was imprisoned by Seleucus, he wrote a letter to his son Antigonus, entrusting to him the management of his affairs in Greece. He exhorted him to govern his subjects justly, to act with moderation, and to look upon his father as dead; and conjuring him never to part with a single city, in order to procure his liberation. Such a letter as this, might, in the cold policy of statesmen, have exculpated Antigonus for making the best terms he could, without any consideration for his father; but his filial affection at once overcame all questions of state policy, and he immediately

[177]

offered to his enemy, Seleucus, not only all the cities and provinces that he held in Greece, but his own person, as a hostage for his father's liberty.

This was refused by Seleucus; but Antigonus still continued to solicit it by the most pressing importunities and offers, as long as his father lived. He even went into deep mourning, during the whole of his father's captivity of three years, and never once during the whole of that time, partook of any feasts or diversions. When Antigonus was informed of the death of his father, and that his ashes were on the way from Syria, he sailed with a noble fleet to the Archipelago to meet them. He deposited the ashes of his father in a golden urn, which, when he entered the harbour of Corinth, he placed in the poop of the royal galley. He placed his own crown upon it, and covered it with a canopy of purple; sitting by it all the time, clothed in deep mourning.

Percy Anecdotes, 1823

HOW GREAT HE WAS

I know I have an onerous task. But I love my father and want to show the world how great he was: how he was, unlike most of us, interested in things other than himself; how he revealed the divine in the ordinary and enriched so many people's lives; how he laughed an inordinate amount and when he put his head back and opened his mouth and shook with laughter you couldn't help laughing too; how he joked about the clergy and obscure denominations (I was not brought up to count my cherry stones, 'big house, little house, pigsty, barn', but, 'church, chapel, agnostic, free thinker'); above all, how strongly he believed. I remember once my brother fell down the ladder from the apple loft at Farnborough and his best friend Terry Carter came into the kitchen and said to my parents, 'Paul's dead.' We all rushed out and found him unconscious, but alive. Later my father walked across to the church and stayed there for over an hour. I asked his secretary Miss Webb what he was doing and she said he was thanking God.

I want to show how my father is not categorizable; how his architectural tastes were catholic and all-embracing, from the stone dwellings on St Kilda to the wild buildings of Gaudi and the brick galleries of Jim Stirling; how he did not necessarily love all things

Victorian, as is popularly supposed, but only a carefully selected proportion; how he never accepted the mediocre and how he was England's grand champion not of conservation, with all the stuffiness and fossilizing academicism that the word now implies, but of safeguarding what he called 'indeterminate beauty' – the last thing on any official list, because of its indefinable quality . . .

His great gift to anyone who came in contact with him was to talk about *them*, to bring *them* from the shadows into the limelight, however briefly, and leave them with a feeling of self-worth. He never saw things in terms of his own achievement and seldom kept his own writings. By the end of his life his library included few of his own books. When he was twenty-nine years old, my father was asked to list his chief interests, dislikes and hopes for an anthology. Characteristically he wrote to the editor, 'This has cost me sweat and blood. I cannot write about myself, just as some people can't sign their names.' Among his chief interests he listed: ecclesiastical architecture of the late eighteenth and early nineteenth centuries; box pews and three-decker pulpits; Irish peers, Irish architecture and pre-Celtic Twilight Irish poetry, written in English; Salkeld's Catalogue; branch railways; suburbs; provincial towns; steam trains. His dislikes included aeroplanes; main roads; insurance companies; 'development'; local councils; and materialism, dialectical or otherwise; and his hopes were for a Triumph of Christianity and a town plan for England. He stuck to his guns.

Candida Lycett-Green, Preface to *The Letters of John Betjeman*, vol. 1, 1994

THE POINT OF BEING ALIVE

Writing about the last ten years of my father's life was a painful experience, as I recorded his friends dying and his own health deteriorating. When I had to face writing the last chapter and selecting the letters for it, I found myself making any excuse not to begin. Of course I was in floods of tears writing the last paragraph. What woman in my shoes wouldn't have been? I had lived so close to my father for the last four years and suddenly I was reliving the experience of his death.

For a time after finishing the book I felt bereft. I needed him to turn to. He understood better than anyone the point of being alive – how terrible it is a lot of the time and how wonderful at others. Now, later, I can go back to his poetry and recall him with an overwhelming vividness. No father could leave a greater gift to a daughter.

Candida Lycett-Green, Preface to *The Letters of John Betjeman*, vol. 2, 1994

SEVEN

Bereaved Fathers

'Heaven will be no heaven to me if Octavius is not there.'
May 1783

George III (1738–1820), on the death of his beloved Octavius, aged four

ON HIS FIRST SONNE

Farewell, thou child of my right hand, and joy;
My sinne was too much hope of thee, lov'd boy,
Seven yeeres thou'wert lent to me, and I thee pay,
Exacted by thy fate, on the just day.
O, could I lose all father, now. For why
Will man lament the state he should envie?
To have so soone scap'd worlds, and fleshes rage,
And, if no other miserie, yet age?
Rest in soft peace, and, ask'd, say here doth lye
BEN. JONSON his best piece of *poetrie*.
For whose sake, hence-forth, all his vowes be such,
As what he loves may never like too much.

Ben Jonson (1572/3–1637), *Epigrammes*, 1616

PRESENCE OF MIND

When, with my little daughter Blanche,
I climbed the Alps, last summer,
I saw a dreadful avalanche
About to overcome her;
And, as it swept her down the slope,
I vaguely wondered whether
I should be wise to cut the rope
That held us twain together.

I must confess I'm glad I did,
But still I miss the child – poor kid!

Harry Graham (1874–1936), *Ruthless Rhymes*, 1900

Off the Erl Hugelyn of Pyze the langour
Ther may no tonge telle for pitee.
But litel out of Pize stant a tour,
In which tour in prisoun put was he,
And with hym been his litel children thre;
The eldest scarsly fyf yeer was of age.
Allas, Fortune! it was greet crueltee
Swiche briddes for to putte in swich a cage!

Dampned was he to dyen in that prisoun.
For Roger, which that bisshop was of Pize,
Hadde on hym maad a fals suggestioun,
Thurgh which the peple gan upon hym rise,
And putten hym to prisoun, in swich wise
As ye han herd, and mete and drynke he hadde
So smal, that wel unnethe it may suffise,
And therwithal it was ful povre and badde.

And on a day bifil that in that hour
Whan that his mete wont was to be broght,
The gayler shette the dores of the tour.
He herde it wel, but he spak right noght,
And in his herte anon ther fil a thoght
That they for hunger wolde doon hym dyen.
'Allas!' quod he, 'allas, that I was wroght!'
Therwtih the teeris fillen from his yen.

His yonge sone, that thre yeer was of age,
Unto hym seyde, 'Fader, why do ye wepe?
Whanne wol the gayler bryngen oure potage?
Is ther no morsel breed that ye do kepe?
I am so hungry that I may nat slepe.
Now wolde God that I myghte slepen evere!
Thanne sholde nat hunger in my wombe crepe;
Ther is no thyng, save breed, that me were levere.'

Thus day by day this child bigan to crye,
Til in his fadres barm adoun it lay,
And seyde, 'Farewel, fader, I moot dye!'
And kiste his fader, and dyde the same day.

And whan the woful fader deed it say,
For wo his armes two he gan to byte,
And seyde, 'Allas, Fortune, and weylaway!
Thy false wheel my wo al may I wyte.'

His children wende that it for hunger was
That he his armes gnow, and nat for wo,
And seyde, 'Fader, do nat so, allas!
But rather ete the flessh upon us two.
Oure flessh thou yaf us, take oure flessh us fro,
And ete ynogh,' – right thus they to hym seyde.
And after that, withinne a day or two,
They leyde hem in his lappe adoun and deyde.

Hymself, despeired, eek for hunger starf;
Thus ended is this myghty Erl of Pize.
From heigh estaat Fortune awey hym carf.
Of this tragedie it oghte ynough suffise;
Whoso wol here it in a lenger wise,
Redeth the grete poete of Ytaille
That highte Dant, for he kan al devyse
Fro point to point, nat o word wol he faille.

Geoffrey Chaucer (c.1343–1400), 'The Monk's Tale', *The Canterbury Tales*

IN MEMORIAM

Private D. Sutherland killed in action in the German trench, May
16th, 1916, and the others who died.

So you were David's father,
And he was your only son,
And the new-cut peats are rotting
And the work is left undone,
Because of an old man weeping,
Just an old man in pain,
For David, his son David,
That will not come again.

Oh, the letters he wrote you,
And I can see them still,

Not a word of the fighting
But just the sheep on the hill
And how you should get the crops in
Ere the year get stormier,
And the Bosches have got his body,
And I was his officer.

You were only David's father,
But I had fifty sons
When we went up in the evening
Under the arch of the guns,
And we came back at twilight –
O God! I heard them call
To me for help and pity
That could not help at all.

Oh, never will I forget you,
My men that trusted me,
More my sons than your fathers',
For they could only see
The little helpless babies
And the young men in their pride.
They could not see you dying,
And hold you while you died.

Happy and young and gallant,
They saw their first-born go,
But not the strong limbs broken
And the beautiful men brought low,
The piteous writhing bodies,
They screamed 'Don't leave me, sir,'
For they were only your fathers
But I was your officer.

E. A. Mackintosh (1893–1916), *Up The Line to Death*, 1964

A SOLEMN STILLNESS REIGNED

The joy which Peter the Great felt at the birth of his first son, by the
Empress Catharine, was only equalled by his affliction on the death of
the child, at the age of two years. On the birth of the infant, whom

Peter, in a letter to Field Marshal Scheremeteff, called a recruit sent from God, he ordered the whole army to rejoice. When the child died, the czar burst into tears, and abandoned himself to a despair from which the most fearful consequences were apprehended, until they were averted by the care and unremitted attentions of Catharine, and the ingenuity and firmness of the patriotic senator Dolgerucki.

The czar had shut himself up for three days and three nights in his closet, without seeing any person, not even his beloved Catharine. He lay on his camp bed, took neither victuals nor drink, nor could he be diverted from his grief, to attend to the most important affairs. The course of justice was suspended, the dispatches of ambassadors and generals were unanswered, and the most important operations of war were at a stand; the functions of the senate, the admiralty, and the college of war, were all suspended; and a solemn stillness, accompanied with terror and suspense, reigned at court.

Percy Anecdotes, 1823

A LITTLE ANGEL SENT TO HEAVEN

What shall I say to you about our little darling who is gone? – I don't feel sorrow for her, and think of her only as something charming that for a season we were allowed to enjoy: when Anny was very ill dying as I almost thought, it seemed to me wrong to pray for her life, for specific requests to God are impertinencies I think, and all we should ask from him is to learn how to acquiesce and now I would be almost sorry – no that is not true – but I would not ask to have the dear little Jane back again and subject her to the degradation of life and pain. O God watch over us too, and as we may think that Your Great heart yearns towards the innocent charms of these little infants, let us try and think that it will have tenderness for us likewise who have been innocent once, and have, in the midst of corruption, some remembrances of good still. Sometimes I fancy that at the judgement time the little one would come out and put away the sword of the angry angel I think her love for us and her beautiful purity would melt the Devil himself – Nonsense, you know what I mean. We have sent to Heaven a little angel who came from us & loved us and God will understand her language & visit us mildly – Why write you this mad stuff dearest Mother? – God bless you and all besides I shall write G.M: and thank

her for her money & use it too –
  Your affte W M T

W.M. Thackeray (1811–63), letter to Mrs Carmichael Smyth, March 1839

THE NETTLES

This, then, is the grave of my son,
Whose heart she won! And nettles grow
Upon his mound; and she lives just below.

How he upbraided me, and left,
And our lives were cleft, because I said
She was hard, unfeeling, caring but to wed.

Well, to see this sight I have fared these miles,
And her firelight smiles from her window there,
Whom he left his mother to cherish with tender care!

It is enough. I'll turn and go;
Yes, nettles grow where lone lies he,
Who spurned me for seeing what he could not see.

Thomas Hardy (1840–1928), *Moments of Vision*, 1925

A GIRL OF THREE

Ruined and ill, – a man of two score;
Pretty and guileless, – a girl of three.
Not a boy, – but still better than nothing:
To soothe one's feeling, – from time to time a kiss!
There came a day, – they suddenly took her from me;
Her soul's shadow wandered I know not where.
And when I remember how just at the time she died
She lisped strange sounds, beginning to learn to talk,
Then I know that the ties of flesh and blood
Only bind us to a load of grief and sorrow.
At last, by thinking of the time before she was born,
By thought and reason I drove the pain away.

Since my heart forgot her, many days have passed
And three times winter has changed to spring.
This morning, for a little, the old grief came back,
Because, in the road, I met her foster-nurse.

Po Chü-i (772–846), 'Remembering Golden Bells', translated by Arthur Waley

THE JOY OF THE HOUSEHOLD

'Our poor child, Annie, was born in Gower Street, on March 2, 1841, and expired at Malvern at mid-day on the 3rd of April, 1851.

'I write these few pages, as I think in after years, if we live, the impressions now put down will recall more vividly her chief characteristics. From whatever point I look back at her, the main feature in her disposition which at once rises before me, is her buoyant joyousness, tempered by two other characteristics, namely, her sensitiveness, which might easily have been overlooked by a stranger, and her strong affection. Her joyousness and animal spirits radiated from her whole countenance, and rendered every movement elastic and full of life and vigour. It was delightful and cheerful to behold her. Her dear face now rises before me, as she used sometimes to come running downstairs with a stolen pinch of snuff for me her whole form radiant with the pleasure of giving pleasure. Even when playing with her cousins, when her joyousness almost passed into boisterousness, a single glance of my eye, not of displeasure (for I thank God I hardly ever cast one on her), but of want of sympathy, would for some minutes alter her whole countenance.

'The other point in her character, which made her joyousness and spirits so delightful, was her strong affection, which was of a most clinging, fondling nature. When quite a baby, this showed itself in never being easy without touching her mother, when in bed with her; and quite lately she would, when poorly, fondle for any length of time one of her mother's arms. When very unwell, her mother lying down beside her, seemed to soothe her in a manner quite different from what it would have done to any of our other children. So, again, she would at almost any time spend half an hour in arranging my hair, 'making it,' as she called it, 'beautiful,' or in smoothing, the poor dear darling, my collar or cuffs – in short, in fondling me.

'Besides her joyousness thus tempered, she was in her manners remarkably cordial, frank, open, straightforward, natural, and without

[189]

any shade of reserve. Her whole mind was pure and transparent. One felt one knew her thoroughly and could trust her. I always thought, that come what might, we should have had in our old age, at least one loving soul, which nothing could have changed. All her movements were vigorous, active, and usually graceful. When going round the Sand-walk with me, although I walked fast, yet she often used to go before, pirouetting in the most elegant way, her dear face bright all the time with the sweetest smiles. Occasionally she had a pretty coquettish manner towards me, the memory of which is charming. She often used exaggerated language, and when I quizzed her by exaggerating what she had said, how clearly can I now see the little toss of the head, and exclamation of, "Oh, papa, what a shame of you!" In the last short illness, her conduct in simple truth was angelic. She never once complained; never became fretful; was ever considerate of others, and was thankful in the most gentle, pathetic manner for everything done for her. When so exhausted that she could hardly speak, she praised everything that was given her, and said some tea "was beautifully good." When I gave her some water, she said, "I quite thank you;" and these, I believe, were the last precious words ever addressed by her dear lips to me.

'We have lost the joy of the household, and the solace of our old age. She must have known how we loved her. Oh, that she could now know how deeply, how tenderly, we do still and shall ever love her dear joyous face! Blessings on her!

'April 30, 1851.'

Charles Darwin (1809–82), Memoirs

DEATH OF A SON

(who died in a mental hospital aged one)

Something has ceased to come along with me.
Something like a person: something very like one.
    And there was no nobility in it
      Or anything like that.

    Something was there like a one year
Old house, dumb as stone. While the near buildings
    Sang like birds and laughed
      Understanding the pact

They were to have with silence. But he
Neither sang nor laughed. He did not bless silence
　　Like bread, with words.
　　　　He did not forsake silence.

　But rather, like a house in mourning
Kept the eye turned in to watch the silence while
　　The other houses like birds
　　Sang around him.

And the breathing silence neither
Moved nor was still.

　I have seen stones: I have seen brick
But this house was made up of neither bricks nor stone
　　But a house of flesh and blood
　　　　With flesh of stone

　And bricks for blood. A house
Of stones and blood in breathing silence with the other
　　Birds singing crazy on its chimneys.
　　　　But this was silence,

　This was something else, this was
Hearing and speaking though he was a house drawn
　　Into silence, this was
　　　　Something religious in his silence,

　Something shining in his quiet,
This was different this was altogether something else:
　　Though he never spoke, this
　　　　Was something to do with death.

　And then slowly the eye stopped looking
Inward. The silence rose and became still.
The look turned to the outer place and stopped,
　　　With the birds still shrilling around him.
　　　　And as if he could speak

He turned over on his side with his one year
Red as a wound
He turned over as if he could be sorry for this
And out of his eyes two great tears rolled, like stones,
　　and he died.
                                   Jon Silkin, *The New Poetry*, 1962

MY POOR LITTLE BOY

My dear Robert

I am quite sure you will feel with me. My poor little boy got strangled in being born. I would not send the notice of my misfortune to
the Times and I have had to write some 60 letters. If you desire to
know about it ask Edmund Lushington to show you that letter which
I wrote to him. My wife has been going on very well since; but last
night she lost her voice and I thought I should lose *her*: she is however
free from all danger this morning according to my medical man. I
have suffered more than ever I thought I could have done for a child
still born: I fancy I should not have cared so much if he had been a
seven months spindling, but he was the grandest-looking child I had
ever seen. Pardon my saying this. I do not speak only as a father but
as an Artist – if you do not despise the word from German associa-
tions. I mean as a man who has eyes and can judge from seeing.

I refused to see the little body at first, fearing to find some pallid
abortion which would have haunted me all my life – but he looked (if
it be not absurd to call a newborn babe so) even majestic in his
mysterious silence after all the turmoil of the night before.

He was – not born, I cannot call it born for he never breathed – but
he was released from the prison where he moved for nine months – on
Easter Sunday. Awful day! We live close upon an English-church
chapel. The organ rolled – the psalm sounded – and the wail of a
woman in her travail – of a true and tender nature suffering, as it
seemed intolerable wrong, rose ever and anon.

But ask Edmund for the account and God bless you and your wife,
dear Robert

For ever and ever

A. Tennyson

Alfred Tennyson (1809–92), letter to Robert Monteith, April 1851

A PRODIGY FOR WITT AND UNDERSTANDING

1658. 27 Jan. After six fits of a quartan ague with which it pleased
God to visit him, died my deare son Richard, to our inexpressible
griefe and affliction, 5 yeares and 3 days old onely, but at that tender

age a prodigy for witt and understanding; for beauty of body a very angel; for endowment of mind of incredible and rare hopes. To give onely a little taste of some of them, and thereby glory to God, who out of the mouths of babes and infants does sometimes perfect his praises: at 2 yeares and halfe old he could perfectly reade any of the English, Latine, French, or Gottic letters, pronouncing the three first languages exactly. He had before the 5th yeare, or in that yeare, not onely skill to reade most written hands, but to decline all the nouns, conjugate the verbs regular, and most of the irregular; learn'd out Puerilis, got by heart almost the entire vocabularie of Latine and French primitives and words, could make congruous syntax, turne English into Latine, and *vice versa*, construe and prove what he read, and did the government and use of relatives, verbs, substantives, elipses, and many figures and tropes, and made a considerable progress in Comenius's Janua; began himselfe to write legibly, and had a stronge passion for Greeke. The number of verses he could recite was prodigious, and what he remember'd of the parts of playes; which he would also act; and when seeing a Plautus in one's hand, he ask'd what booke it was, and being told it was comedy, and too difficult for him, he wept for sorrow. Strange was his apt and ingenious application of fables and morals, for he had read Aesop; he had a wonderful disposition to mathematics, having by heart divers propositions of Euclid that were read to him in play, and he would make lines and demonstrate them. As to his piety, astonishing were his applications of Scripture upon occasion, and his sense of God; he had learn'd all his Catechisme early, and understood the historical part of the Bible and New Testament to a wonder, how Christ came to redeeme mankind, and how, comprehending these necessarys himselfe, his godfathers were discharg'd of their promise. These and the like illuminations far exceeded his age and experience, considering the prettinesse of his addresse and behaviour, cannot but leave impressions in me at the memory of him. When one told him how many dayes a Quaker had fasted, he replied that was no wonder, for Christ had said man should not live by bread alone, but by the Word of God. He would of himselfe select the most pathetic psalms, and chapters out of Job, to reade to his mayde during his sicknesse, telling her when she pitied him that all God's children must suffer affliction. He declaim'd against the vanities of the world before he had seene any. Often he would desire those who came to see him to pray by him, and a yeare before he fell sick, to kneel and pray with him alone in some corner. How thankfully would he receive admonition, how soon be reconciled! how indifferent, yet continualy chereful! He would give grave advice to his brother John, beare with his impertinencies, and say he was but a child. If he had heard of or saw any new thing, he was unquiet till he was told how it was made; he brought to us all such difficulties as he found in books, to be expounded. He had learn'd by heart divers sentences in Latin and Greeke, which on occasion he would produce even to wonder. He was all life, all prettinesse, far from morose, sullen, or childish in any thing he said or did. The last time he had ben at church (which was at Greenwich), I ask'd him, according to costome, what he remembered of the sermon; two good things, father, said he, *bonum gratiae* and *bonum gloriae*, with a just account of what the preacher said. The day before he died he cal'd to me, and in a more serious manner than usual told me that for all I loved him so dearly I should give my house, land, and all my fine things, to his brother Jack, he should have none of them; the next morning, when he found himself ill, and that I persuaded him to keepe his hands in bed, he demanded whether he might pray to God with his hands unjoyn'd; and a little after, whilst in greate agonie, whether he should not offend God by using his holy name so often calling for ease. What shall I say of his frequent pathetical ejaculations utter'd of himselfe; Sweete Jesus save me, deliver me, pardon my sinns, let thine angels receive me! So early knowledge, so much piety and perfection! But thus God having dress'd up a Saint fit for himselfe, would not longer permit him with us, unworthy of the future fruites of this incomparable hopefull blossome. Such a child I never saw: for such a child I blesse God in whose bosome he is! May I and mine become as this little child, who now follows the child Jesus that Lamb of God in a white robe whithersoever he goes; Even so, Lord Jesus, *fiat voluntas tua!* Thou gavest him to us, Thou hast taken him from us, blessed be the name of the Lord! That I had any thing acceptable to Thee was from thy grace alone, since from me he had nothing but sin, but that Thou hast pardon'd! blessed be my God for ever, amen!

John Evelyn (1620–1706), *Diary*

JEREMY TAYLOR SUFFERS

Deare Sir, I am in some little disorder by reason of the death of a little child of mine, a boy that lately made us very glad: but now he rejoyces in his little orbe, while we thinke, and sigh, and long to be safe as he is.

Jeremy Taylor (1613–67), letter to John Evelyn

O ABSALOM, MY SON

And the king said unto Cushi, *Is* the young man Absalom safe? And Cushi answered, The enemies of my lord the king, and all that rise against thee to do thee hurt, be as that young man is.
And the king was much moved, and went up to the chamber over the gate and wept: and as he went, thus he said, O my son Absalom, my son, my son Absalom! would God I had died for thee, O Absalom, my son, my son!

II Samuel 18: 32–3

LAMENTS

Just as an olive seedling, when it tries
To grow up like the big trees towards the skies
And sprouts out of the ground, a single stalk,
A slender, leafless, twigless, living stick;
And which, if lopped by the swift sickle's blade
Weeding out thorns and nettles, starts to fade
And, sapped of natural strength, cut off, forlorn,
Drops by the tree from whose seed it was born –
Growing before her parents' caring eyes,
She'd barely risen above ground when Death
Felled the dear child with his infectious breath
At our very feet. Hard-eyed Persephone,
Were all those tears of no avail to me?

Sweet girl, I wish that you had either never
Been born or never died! For you to sever
All your attachments, take such early leave –
What else, what else can I do now but grieve?
You were like one of those recurrent dreams
About a crock of gold, fool's gold that gleams
And tempts our greed but, when we wake at dawn,
Our hands are empty and the gleam is gone.
Dear daughter, this you did in your own way:
Your light appeared to me but would not stay.
It was as if you wanted to destroy
My very soul by robbing all its joy.
The shock of sudden death tore it in two:
One half stayed grieving, one half fled with you.
Here is your epitaph. Stonecutters, hone
The chisels sharp and cut the words in stone:
'Ursula Kochanowski lies beneath,
Her father's joy that slipped his loving hands.
Learn from this grave the ways of careless Death:
The green shoot is mown down – the ripe crop stands.'

Jan Kochanowski (1530–84), translated by Stanislaw Baranczak and
Seamus Heaney, *Times Literary Supplement*, October 1995

A BOXE OF SWEET OINTMENT

[1650] May. 26. This morning all our hopes of Maries life was gone,
to the Lord I have resigned her and with him I leave her, to receive her
into his everlasting armes, when he seeth best, shee rests free from
much paine wee hope in regard shee maketh no dolour the lord makes
us willing shee should bee out of her paine, and why are wee at any
times unwilling, when god is about such a worke, that he should take
them up into his glory, this day the word was made merveylous comfortable to mee, my heart could not but mourne over and for my babe,
but I left it with the lord, and was quiett in my spirit, in gods taking
it, to whom, I did freely resigne it, my litle sonne in all peoples eyes is
a dying child, lord they will bee done, thou art better to mee then
sonnes and daughters, though I value them above gold and jewells,
my navel continued well this weeke for which I blesse god, my bile

grew sorer, and my carnels in my flanke, which god I trust will ordaine for an aboundance of good unto mee,

MAY 27. This day a quarter past two in the afternoone my Mary fell asleepe in the Lord, her soule past into that rest where the body of Jesus, and the soules of the saints are, shee was: 8 yeares and 45 dayes old when shee dyed, my soule had aboundant cause to blesse god for her, who was our first fruites, and those god would have offered to him, and this I freely resigned up to him(,) it was a pretious child, a bundle of myrrhe, a bundle of sweetnes, shee was a child of ten thousand, full of wisedome, woman-like gravity, knowledge, sweet expre[*ssions of god, apt in her learning,*] tender hearted and loving, an [*obed*]ient child [*to us.*] it was free from [*the rudenesse of*] litle children, it was to us as a boxe of sweet ointment, which now its broken smells more deliciously then it did before, Lord I rejoyce I had such a present for thee, it was patient in the sicknesse, thankefull to admiracion; it lived desired and dyed lamented, thy memory is and will bee sweete unto mee,

The Diary of Ralph Josselin 1616–83

MY MOST DEARE CHILD ASCENDED

[1673] June 15. about one a clocke in the morning my eldest sonne Thomas and my most deare child ascended early hence to keepe his everlasting Sabbath with his heavenly father, and Saviour with the church above(,) his end was comfortable, and his death calme, not much of pain til the Satturday afore. in my course this morning I read Josh; I: which had words of comfort, god making his word my counsellor and comfort(.) He was my hope. but some yeares I have feared his life, god hath taken all my first brood but Jane. lett all live in thy sight sanctified(.) a wett morning, the heavens for some time have mourned over us.

The Diary of Ralph Josselin 1616–83

My son! and what's a son? A thing begot
Within a pair of minutes – thereabout;
A lump bred up in darkness, and doth serve
To ballast these light creatures we call women;
And, at nine months' end, creeps forth to light.
What is there yet in a son,
To make a father dote, rave, or run mad?
Being born, it pouts, cries, and breeds teeth.
What is there yet in a son? He must be fed,
Be taught to go, and speak. Ay, or yet
Why might not a man love a calf as well?
Or melt in passion o'er a frisking kid,
As for a son? Methinks, a young bacon,
Or a fine little smooth horse colt,
Should move a man as much as doth a son;
For one of these, in very little time,
Will grow to some good use; whereas a son,
The more he grows in stature, and in years,
The more unsquar'd, unbevell'd, he appears,
Reckons his parents among the rank of fools,
Strikes care upon their heads with his mad riots;
Makes them look old, before they meet with age.
This is a son! – And what a loss were this,
Consider'd truly? – O, but my Horatio
Grew out of reach of these insatiate humours:
He lov'd his loving parents;
He was my comfort, and his mother's joy,
The very arm that did hold up our house;
Our hopes were storëd up in him,
None but a damnëd murderer could hate him . . .
Well, heaven is heaven still!
And there is Nemesis, and Furies,
And things call'd whips,
And they sometimes do meet with murderers:
They do not always 'scape, that is some comfort.
Ay, ay, ay; and then time steals on,
And steals, and steals, till violence leaps forth
Like thunder wrappëd in a ball of fire,

And so doth bring confusion to them all.

Thomas Kyd (c.1557–c.1595), *The Spanish Tragedy*, 1594

I LOVED THE BOY

2 December 1812
Wednesday Evening
My dear Friend,
   Symptoms of the measles appeared upon my Son Thomas last
Thursday; he was most favorable held till tuesday, between ten and
eleven at that hour was particularly lightsome and comfortable; without any assignable cause a sudden change took place, an inflamma-
tion had commenced on the lungs which it was impossible to check
and the sweet Innocent yielded up his soul to God before six in the
evening. He did not appear to suffer much in body, but I fear something in mind as he was of an age to have thought much upon death
a subject to which his mind was daily led by the grave of his Sister.
My Wife bears the loss of her Child with striking fortitude. My Sister
was not at home but is returned to day, I met her at Threlkeld. Miss
Hutchinson also supports her sorrow as ought to be done. For myself
dear Southey I dare not say in what state of mind I am; I loved the Boy
with the utmost love of which my soul is capable, and he is taken from
me – yet in the agony of my spirit in surrendering such a treasure I feel
a thousand times richer than if I had never possessed it. God comfort
and save you and all our friends and us all from a repetition of such
trials – O Southey feel for me! If you are not afraid of the complaint,
I ought to have said if you have had it come over to us! Best love from
everybody – you will impart this sad news to your Wife and Mrs
Coleridge and Mrs Lovel and to Miss Barker and Mrs Wilson. Poor
woman! she was most good to him – Heaven reward her.
   Heaven bless you
   Your sincere Friend
W. Wordsworth

Will Mrs Coleridge please to walk up to the Calverts and mention
these afflictive news with the particulars. I should have written but my
sorrow over-powers me.

William Wordsworth (1770–1850), letter to Robert Southey

Byron's love for Allegra had only existed in so far as he identified her with himself, and in this attitude he persisted. 'It is my present intention', he wrote to John Murray, 'to send her remains to England for sepulture in Harrow Church . . . in what ship I know not' – but Teresa was seeing to the details. A few weeks later he added: 'There is a spot in the churchyard, near the footpath, on the brow of the hill looking towards Windsor; and a tomb under a large tree (bearing the name of Peachie, or Peachey), where I used to sit for hours and hours when a boy; this was my favourite spot; but, as I wish to erect a tablet to her memory, the body had better be deposited in the Church, near the door. On the left hand as you enter, there is a monument with a tablet containing these words:

"When Sorrow weeps o'er Virtue's sacred dust,
Our tears become us, and our Grief is just;
Such were the tears she shed, who grateful pays
This last sad tribute of her love and praise."

I recollect them (after seventeen years) not from anything remarkable in them, but because from my seat in the Gallery I had generally my eyes turned towards that monument; as near it as convenient I would wish Allegra to be buried, and on the wall a marble tablet placed, with these words:

In memory of
Allegra
daughter of G.G. Lord Byron,
who died at Bagnacavallo,
in Italy, April 20th, 1822,
aged five years and three months
"I shall go to her, but she shall not return to me."
2nd Samuel, XII, 23.'

Byron's wishes encountered many obstacles. When the news of the child's death reached Pisa, Lega Zambelli had at once replied to Ghigi that 'Mylord, inconsolable, approves all that has been done and authorizes you to pay the Professors and everyone else.' And in a later letter he had told him that, since 'Protestants are not allowed holy ground in Catholic countries', Byron desired to send the child's body back to his own land, on a ship from Livorno. Whereupon Ghigi – so flustered and distressed that he 'wished he had never met the noble

Lord' – gave orders for the little body to be embalmed, ordered a double coffin of lead and oak, a box for the child's heart and another for its entrails. He observed, however, that the apothecary 'will expect to be well paid for the embalming, as is usual for such unusual operations, which are generally performed only on the great'. The whole convent, he added, had been much upset, 'the nuns greatly disturbed and Suor Marianna so distressed that she has taken to her bed'. As for himself, 'I cannot describe the obstacles, the trouble and the unforeseen expense'. At last he sent off the little coffin and the two boxes to Livorno, accompanied (since he felt that a priest should be present) by his own brother-in-law, Don Gaetano Fabiani, and another man. But when the sad little cortège arrived in Pisa, Byron refused even to see them. 'They have come back' [to Ravenna], wrote Ghigi, 'much mortified that Mylord would not receive them, and I too blush that it should one day be known (for now we strive to conceal it) that this was so. I too believe that Mylord is very sensitive and much grieved, but I am also aware that every man has his pride – and one must not, on account of one's own grief, forget what is due to others.' But Lega's answer only contained a lame apology, and a request that Ghigi should procure some Romagnole truffles for Mylord!

Even then, the correspondence was not yet over. For many months Lega continued to haggle over the bills for the coffin, the undertaker and the embalmment (on the ground that 'the amount of spices consumed would suffice for a grown-up person'), until at last in disgust Ghigi wrote: 'If he will not pay the 300 *scudi* which are due, let him pay whatever sum he pleases. I must not and cannot believe in such baseness in the noble lord. I am not an Englishman, but in my sentiments I am as noble as any of them.' He was, however, never paid in full, as is shown by a detailed account which he sent in, after Byron's death, to his executors.

Thus the strife to which poor little Allegra had given rise by the mere fact of her existence continued even after her death.

Iris Origo, (1902–88) A Measure of Love, 1957

MY LOST WILLIAM

Where art thou, my gentle child?
Let me think thy spirit feeds,

With its life intense and mild,
The love of living leaves and weeds,
Among these tombs and ruins wild; –
Let me think that, through low seeds
Of sweet flowers and sunny grass,
Into their hues and scents may pass
A portion . . .

P.B. Shelley (1792–1822), quoted in Neville Rogers, 'Shelley and the West Wind',
London Magazine, June 1956

SUCH POTENT GRIEF

Florence, 22 May 1563

Messer Benedetto, whom I greatly esteem, you must know that I have
lost my only son, when he was almost reared, and meseems that in all
my life I have had nothing in the world that gave me so much pleasure,
as he. Now death has robbed me of him within four days; and my grief
was so potent that I verily believed I should depart with him, since for
evident reasons I may not hope ever again to possess such a treasure.

And since it gave me pleasure to make him some small renown, the
Brothers of the Annunciation have graciously permitted me to make
a monument for him, until such time as it may please God that I go to
sleep by his side in whatsoever humble tomb my poverty may allow
me to prepare. Meanwhile I purpose to design this monument with
two Cherubs, their faces in their hands, and betwixt them an epitaph
the which I now submit to you in my own rough words, for I know
that you, with your admirable skill, will express the matter far better
than I could do; and I commit me to your infallible judgment, whether
it please you to compose it in Latin or in Tuscan. And if I weary you
with this, forgive me, and command me, for I am ever at your service
in like manner.

My notion, which I would desire you to express, is thus:
    Giovan Cellini, Benvenuto's only son,
    Lies here, remov'd by death in tender years.
    Ne'er have the Furies with their murderous shears
    From Pole to Pole more hopes destroyed in one.

Benvenuto Cellini (1500–71), letter to Benedetto Varchi

A STUPENDOUS SHOCK

Since Charlotte had been taken ill on Monday evening messengers had been sent at intervals to the Regent, who was in Suffolk shooting at Lord Hertford's. When, however, on Wednesday he received a letter from one of the doctors saying that Charlotte's recovery would be slow, he suddenly took fright, and refusing even to wait for fresh horses to be put in the post-chaise that had brought the message, scrambled inside, and set off precipitately for Carlton House . . .

Two hours after Charlotte's death, that is to say at four o'clock on Thursday morning, the Regent's post-chaise reeled into the courtyard of Carlton House. The Regent went indoors, and up to his bed. Three hours passed, and then, a little before seven, the Duke of York arrived with Lord Bathurst. They asked that the Regent should be wakened and told they were there. This was done, and they both went to his room. Lord Bathurst, without any preamble, told him what had happened.

Little affection though the Regent had for Charlotte, the shock was stupendous. Striking his forehead with his hands, he bowed downwards without a word.

D. Creston, *The Regent and His Daughter*, 1932

IT'S SOMETHING TO HAVE BRED A MAN

12 November, 1915

Our boy was reported 'wounded & missing' since Sep. 27 – the Battle of Loos and we've heard nothing official since that date. But all we can pick up from the men points to the fact that he is dead and probably wiped out by shell fire. However, he had his heart's desire and he didn't have a long time in trenches. The Guards advanced on a front of two platoons for each battalion. He led the right platoon over a mile of open ground in face of shell and machine-gun fire and was dropped at the further limit of the advance, after having emptied his pistol into a house full of German m.g's. His C.O. and his Company Commander told me how he led 'em and the wounded have confirmed it. He was senior ensign tho' only 18 yrs and 6 weeks, and worked like the devil for a year at Warley and knew his Irish to the ground. He was reported on as one of the best of the subalterns and was gym instructor and signaller. It was a short life. I'm sorry that all the years' work ended in that one afternoon but – lots of people are in our position – and it's something to have bred a man. The wife is standing it wonderfully tho' she, of course, clings to the bare hope of his being a prisoner. I've seen what shells can do, and I don't.

Rudyard Kipling (1865–1936), letter to Brigadier L. C. Dunsterville

JACOB CANNOT BE COMFORTED

And they took Joseph's coat, and killed a kid of the goats, and dipped the coat in the blood;

And they sent the coat of *many* colours, and they brought *it* to their father; and said, This have we found: know now whether it *be* thy son's coat or no.

And he knew it, and said, *It is* my son's coat; an evil beast hath devoured him; Joseph is without doubt rent in pieces.

And Jacob rent his clothes, and put sackcloth upon his loins, and mourned for his son many days.

And all his sons and all his daughters rose up to comfort him; but he refused to be comforted; and he said, For I will go down into the grave unto my son mourning. Thus his father wept for him.

Genesis 37: 31–5

POOR MR CRAWLEY

He was recalling all the facts of his life, his education, which had been costly, and, as regarded knowledge, successful; his vocation to the church, when in his youth he had determined to devote himself to the service of his Saviour, disregarding promotion or the favour of men; the short, sweet days of his early love, in which he had devoted himself again, – thinking nothing of self, but everything of her; his diligent working, in which he had ever done his very utmost for the parish in which he was placed, and always his best for the poorest; the success of other men who had been his compeers, and, as he too often told himself, intellectually his inferiors; then of his children, who had been carried off from his love to the churchyard, – over whose graves he himself had stood, reading out the pathetic words of the funeral service with unswerving voice and a bleeding heart; and then of his children still living, who loved their mother so much better than they loved him.

Anthony Trollope (1815–82), *The Last Chronicle of Barset*

OF MY DEARE SONNE, GERUASE BEAUMONT

Can I, who have for others oft compil'd
The Songs of Death, forget my sweetest child,
Which like a flow'r crusht, with a blast is dead,
And ere full time hangs downe his smiling head,
Expecting with cleare hope to live anew,
Among the Angels fed with heav'nly dew?
We haue this signe of Ioy, that many dayes,
While on the earth his struggling spirit stayes,
The name of *Iesus* in his mouth containes,
His onely food, his sleepe, his ease from paines.
O may that sound be rooted in my mind,
Of which in him such strong effect I find.
Deare Lord, receive my Sonne, whose winning love
To me was like a friendship, farre above
The course of nature, or his tender age,
Whose lookes could all my bitter griefes asswage;
Let his pure soule ordain'd sev'n yeeres to be
In that fraile body, which was part of me,
Remaine my pledge in heav'n, as sent to shew,
How to this Port at ev'ry step I goe.

John Beaumont (1582–1627), *New Oxford Book of English Verse, 1250–1950*,
ed. Helen Gardner, 1981

LORD ULLIN'S DAUGHTER

A chieftain to the Highlands bound
  Cries 'Boatman, do not tarry!
And I'll give thee a silver pound
  To row us o'er the ferry.'

'Now who be ye would cross Lochgyle,
  This dark and stormy water?'
'O, I'm the chief of Ulva's isle,
  And this Lord Ullin's daughter.

'And fast before her father's men
  Three days we've fled together,
For, should he find us in the glen,
  My blood would stain the heather.

'His horsemen hard behind us ride;
  Should they our steps discover,
Then who will cheer my bonny bride
  When they have slain her lover?'

Outspoke the hardy Highland wight
  'I'll go, my chief! I'm ready;
It is not for your silver bright,
  But for your winsome lady.

'And, by my word! the bonny bird
  In danger shall not tarry;
So, though the waves are raging white
  I'll row you o'er the ferry.'

By this the storm grew loud apace,
  The water-wraith was shrieking;
And in the scowl of heaven each face
  Grew dark as they were speaking.

But still, as wilder blew the wind,
  And as the night grew drearer,
Adown the glen rode armèd men –
  Their trampling sounded nearer.

'O haste thee, haste!' the lady cries,
  'Though tempests round us gather;

I'll meet the raging of the skies,
    But not an angry father.'

The boat has left a stormy land,
    A stormy sea before her, –
When, oh! too strong for human hand,
    The tempest gathered o'er her.

And still they rowed amidst the roar
    Of waters fast prevailing:
Lord Ullin reached that fatal shore, –
    His wrath was changed to wailing.

For sore dismayed, through storm and shade,
    His child he did discover:
One lovely hand she stretched for aid,
    And one was round her lover.

'Come back! come back!' he cried in grief
    Across the stormy water:
'And I'll forgive your Highland chief,
    My daughter! oh my daughter!'

'Twas vain: the loud waves lashed the shore,
    Return or aid preventing;
The waters wild went o'er his child,
    And he was left lamenting.

Thomas Campbell (1777–1844), *Palgrave's Golden Treasury*, 1929

PRIAM, ACHILLES AND HECTOR'S BODY

. . . he high Olympus reacht. The king then left his coach
To grave Idaeus, and went on, made his resolv'd approach
And enterd in a goodly roome, where with his Princes sate
Jove-lov'd Achilles at their feast; two onely kept the state
Of his attendance, Alcimus and Lord Automedon.
At Priam's entrie a great time Achilles gaz'd upon
His wonderd-at approch, nor eate: the rest did nothing see
While close he came up, with his hands fast holding the bent knee
Of Hector's conqueror, and kist that large man-slaughtring hand
That much blood from his sonnes had drawne. And as in some

[207]

strange land

And great man's house, a man is driven (with that abhorr'd dismay
That followes wilfull bloodshed still, his fortune being to slay
One whose blood cries alowde for his) to pleade protection
In such a miserable plight as frights the lookers on:
In such a stupefied estate Achilles sate to see,
So unexpected, so in night, and so incrediblie,
Old Priam's entrie. All his friends one on another star'd
To see his strange lookes, seeing no cause. Thus Priam then prepar'd
His sonne's redemption: 'See in me, O godlike Thetis' sonne,
Thy aged father, and perhaps even now being outrunne
With some of my woes, neighbour foes (thou absent) taking time
To do him mischiefe, no meane left to terrifie the crime
Of his oppression; yet he heares thy graces still survive
And joyes to heare it, hoping still to see thee safe arrive
From ruin'd Troy. But I (curst man) of all my race shall live
To see none living. Fiftie sonnes the Deities did give
My hopes to live in – all alive when neare our trembling shore
The Greeke ships harbor'd – and one wombe nineteene of those sons
    bore.
Now Mars a number of their knees hath strengthlesse left, and he
That was (of all) my onely joy and Troy's sole guard, by thee
(Late fighting for his countrey) slaine, whose tenderd person now
I come to ransome. Infinite is that I offer you,
My selfe conferring it, exposde alone to all your oddes,
Onely imploring right of armes. Achilles, feare the gods,
Pitie an old man like thy sire – different in onely this,
That I am wretcheder, and beare that weight of miseries
That never man did, my curst lips enforc't to kisse that hand
That slue my children.' This mov'd teares; his father's name did stand
(Mention'd by Priam) in much helpe to his compassion,
And mov'd Æacides so much he could not looke upon
The weeping father. With his hand, he gently put away
His grave face; calme remission now did mutually display
Her powre in either's heavinesse. Old Priam, to record
His sonne's death and his deathsman see, his teares and bosome
    pour'd
Before Achilles. At his feete he laid his reverend head.
Achilles' thoughts now with his sire, now with his friend, were fed.
Betwixt both Sorrow fild the tent. But now Æacides
(Satiate at all parts with the ruth of their calamities)

Start up, and up he raisd the king. His milke-white head and beard
With pittie he beheld, and said: 'Poore man, thy mind is scar'd
With much affliction. How durst thy person thus alone
Venture on his sight that hath slaine so many a worthy sonne,
And so deare to thee? Thy old heart is made of iron. Sit
And settle we our woes, though huge, for nothing profits it.
Cold mourning wastes but our lives' heates. The gods have destinate
That wretched mortals must live sad. Tis the immortall state
Of Deitie that lives secure. Two Tunnes of gifts there lie
In Jove's gate, one of good, one ill, that our mortalitie
Maintaine, spoile, order; which when Jove doth mixe to any man,
One while he frolicks, one while mourns. If of his mournfull Kan
A man drinks onely, onely wrongs he doth expose him to.
Sad hunger in th' abundant earth doth tosse him to and froe,
Respected nor of gods nor men. The mixt cup Peleus dranke;
Even from his birth heaven blest his life; he liv'd not that could thanke
The gods for such rare benefits as set foorth his estate.
He reign'd among his Myrmidons most rich, most fortunate,
And (though a mortall) had his bed deckt with a deathlesse Dame.
And yet withall this good, one ill god mixt, that takes all name
From all that goodnesse – his Name now (whose preservation here
Men count the crowne of their most good) not blest with powre to
    beare
One blossome but my selfe, and I shaken as soone as blowne.
Nor shall I live to cheare his age and give nutrition
To him that nourisht me. Farre off my rest is set in Troy,
To leave thee restlesse and thy seed. Thy selfe, that did enjoy
(As we have heard) a happie life – what Lesbos doth containe
(In times past being a blest man's seate), what the unmeasur'd maine
Of Hellespontus, Phrygia, holds, are all said to adorne
Thy Empire, wealth and sonnes enow – but, when the gods did turne
Thy blest state to partake with bane, warre and the bloods of men
Circl'd thy citie, never cleare. Sit downe and suffer then.
Mourne not inevitable things; thy teares can spring no deeds
To helpe thee, nor recall thy sonne: impacience ever breeds
Ill upon ill, makes worst things worse. And therefore sit.' He said:
'Give me no seate, great seed of Jove, when yet unransomed
Hector lies ritelesse in thy tents: but daigne with utmost speed
His resignation, that these eyes may see his person freed,
And thy grace satisfied with gifts. Accept what I have brought,
And turne to Phthia; tis enough thy conquering hand hath fought

Till Hector faltred under it, and Hector's father stood
With free humanitie safe.' He frown'd, and said: 'Give not my blood
Fresh cause of furie. I know well I must resigne thy sonne –
Jove by my mother utterd it; and what besides is done,
I know as amply, and thy selfe, old Priam, I know too.
Some god hath brought thee, for no man durst use a thought to go
On such a service; I have guards, and I have gates to stay
Easie accesses. Do not then presume thy will can sway
Like Jove's will, and incense againe my quencht blood, lest nor thou
Nor Jove gets the command of me.' This made the old king bow,
And downe he sate in feare; the Prince leapt like a Lion forth,
Automedon and Alcimus attending; all the worth
Brought for the body they tooke downe and brought in, and with it
Idaeus, herald to the king; a cote embroderd yet,
And two rich cloakes, they left to hide the person. Thetis' sonne
Cald out his women to annoint and quickly overrunne
The Corse with water, lifting it in private to the coach
Lest Priam saw and his cold blood embrac't a fierie touch
Of anger at the turpitude prophaning it and blew
Againe his wrath's fire to his death. This done, his women threw
The cote and cloake on; but the Corse Achilles' owne hand laide
Upon a bed, and, with his friends, to chariot it convaide.

Homer (c.8th C. BC), *The Iliad*, translated by George Chapman (1559–1634),

EIGHT

Fathers and Their Flights of Fancy

AUGUST 16. Lupin positively refused to walk down the Parade with me because I was wearing my new straw helmet with my frock-coat. I don't know what the boy is coming to.

George (1847–1912) and Weedon (1852–1919) Grossmith,
The Diary of a Nobody, 1894

A FAMILY VAULT

One morning in the hot summer of 1921 I was walking with my
father in the park at Renishaw, where great patches of shadow lay
under the old trees and at the edges of the plantations. He was wearing a very neat, pale grey suit and a grey wide-awake hat. As we were
approaching a fence with a wooden gate, he suddenly took a little run
and vaulted lightly over it. I was astonished, for he was over sixty
years of age, complained always that the slightest exertion tired him
out, and, additional cause for wonder, I had never seen him do this
before. He must have noticed my surprise, for he said to me: 'I try to
keep up my vaulting, to amuse my friends.'

Osbert Sitwell (1892–1969), *Tales My Father Taught Me*, 1962

FARVE AND THAT POPISH NONSENSE

Farve's deepest ire, however, was reserved for a proposal to reform
the House of Lords by limiting its powers. The Lords who sponsored
this measure did so out of a fear that, unless such a course was taken,
a future Labour Government might abolish the House altogether.
Farve angrily opposed this tricky political manoeuvre. His speech was
widely quoted in the Press: 'May I remind your Lordships that denial
of the hereditary principle is a direct blow at the Crown? Such a
denial is, indeed, a blow at the very foundation of the Christian faith.'
To Farve's annoyance, even the Conservative Press poked fun at this
concept, and the Labour Press had a field day with it. 'What *did* you
mean to say?' we asked, and he patiently explained that just as Jesus
became God because He was the Son of God, so the oldest son of a
Lord should inherit his father's title and prerogatives. Nancy pretended to be surprised at this explanation: 'Oh, I thought you meant
it would be a blow at the Christian faith because the Lord's son would
lose the right to choose the clergyman.'

The right to hire and fire the clergy was one which my father would
have been loath to relinquish. He had the 'living' of Swinbrook, which
meant that if the incumbent vicar died or left the parish it became
Farve's responsibility to interview and choose among prospective
replacements. Shortly after we moved to Swinbrook such choice was

made necessary by the death of the Reverend Foster, the parish clergy-man. Debo and I managed to eavesdrop on at least one of the inter-views that followed. A pallid young man in regulation dog-collar was admitted by the parlour-maid. 'Would you come this way, sir? His Lordship's in the Closing Room,' she explained. My father's study had once been known by the more usual terms for such rooms – library, business room, smoking room – but I pointed out to Farve that since he spent virtually his entire life within its walls one day, inevitably, his old eyes would close there, never to open again. Thus it came to be called the Closing Room, even by the servants. The Closing Room was a pleasant enough place to spend time in if one was not there under duress; it was lined from floor to ceiling with thousands of books amassed by Grandfather, and there was a lot of comfortable leather-covered furniture and a huge gramophone – but the idea of being summoned for an interview with Farve filled us with vicarious terror.

'Oh, poor thing! There he goes. He's for it,' Debo whispered from our hiding-place under the stairs. We heard Farve explaining that he would personally choose the hymns to be sung at Sunday service. 'None of those damn' complicated foreign tunes. I'll give you a list of what's wanted: "Holy, Holy, Holy", "Rock of Ages", "All Things Bright and Beautiful", and the like.' He went on to say that the ser-mon must never take longer than ten minutes. There was little danger of running over time, as Farve made a practice of setting his stop-watch and signalling two minutes before the allotted time was up.

'Do you go in for smells and lace?' he suddenly roared at the aston-ished applicant. 'Er?' Questioning sounds could be heard through the walls of the Closing Room. 'Incense, choir robes and all that Popish nonsense! You know what I'm driving at!' Debo and I squirmed in sympathy.

Jessica Mitford, *Hons and Rebels*, 1960

MURDER IS DISCUSSED WITH A WIDOWER-PAPA

Sometimes, in the course of this winter, my Father and I had long cosy talks together over the fire. Our favourite subject was murders. I won-der whether little boys of eight, soon to go up-stairs alone at night, often discuss violent crime with a widower-papa? The practice, I cannot help thinking, is unusual; it was, however, consecutive with us. We tried other secular subjects, but we were sure to come round at last to 'what do you suppose they really did with the body?' I was told, a thrilled listener, the adventure of Mrs. Manning, who killed a gentleman on the stairs and buried him in quick-lime in the back-kitchen, and it was at this time that I learned the useful historical fact, which abides with me after half a century, that Mrs. Manning was hanged in black satin, which thereupon went wholly out of fashion in England. I also heard about Burke and Hare, whose story nearly froze me into stone with horror.

These were crimes which appear in the chronicles. But who will tell me what 'the Carpet-bag Mystery' was, which my Father and I discussed evening after evening? I have never come across a whisper of it since, and I suspect it of having been a hoax. As I recall the details, people in a boat, passing down the Thames, saw a carpet-bag hung high in air, on one of the projections of a pier of Waterloo Bridge. Being with difficulty dragged down – or perhaps up – this bag was found to be full of human remains, dreadful butcher's business of joints and fragments. Persons were missed, were identified, were again denied – the whole is a vapour in my memory which shifts as I try to define it. But clear enough is the picture I hold of myself, in a high chair, on the left-hand side of the sitting-room fire-place, the leaping flames reflected in the glass-case of tropical insects on the opposite wall and my Father, leaning anxiously forward, with uplifted finger, emphasising to me the pros and cons of the horrible carpet-bag evidence.

Edmund Gosse (1849–1928), *Father and Son*, 1907

STINKBOTTOM

Papa's best practical joke on his son was played in my first term at All Hallows, when I was still very nervous. He told me that he proposed to change his name to Stinkbottom. When he had done so, the headmaster would summon the school together and say: 'Boys, the person you have hitherto called Waugh will in future be called Stinkbottom.' I understood perfectly well that he was joking, but one never knew how far he would be prepared to go with his jokes. School assembly was held every morning, and every morning I felt a slight tightening of the chest as Mr Dix came forward to make his morning announcements.

Auberon Waugh, *Will This Do?*, 1991

HE IS NOT IN HIS SENSES

'My dear John, – You will be much grieved to hear that your poor mother, after sitting in the corner for nearly two years waiting for the millennium, appeared to pine away; whether from disappointment or not I do not know; but at last, in spite of all Dr Middleton could do, she departed this life; and, as the millennium would not come to her as she expected, it is to be hoped she is gone to her millennium. She was a good wife, and I always let her have her own way. Dr Middleton does not appear to be satisfied as to the cause of her death, and has wished to examine; but I said no, for I am a philosopher, and it is no use looking for causes after effects; but I have done since her death what she never would permit me to do during her life. I have had her head shaved, and examined it very carefully as a phrenologist, and most curiously has she proved the truth of the sublime science. I will give you the result. Determination, very prominent; Benevolence, small; Caution, extreme; Veneration, not very great; Philo-progeni-tiveness, strange to say, is very large, considering she has but one child; Imagination, very strong: you know, my dear boy, she was always imagining some nonsense or another. Her other organs were all moderate. Poor dear creature! she is gone, and we may well wail, for a better mother or a better wife never existed. And now, my dear boy, I must request that you call for your discharge, and come home as soon as possible. I cannot exist without you, and I require your assistance in the grand work I have in contemplation. The time is at hand, the cause of equality will soon triumph; the abject slaves now hold up their heads; I have electrified them with my speeches, but I am getting old and feeble; I require my son to leave my mantle to, as one prophet did to another, and then I will, like him, ascend in glory.

'Your affectionate Father,
'NICODEMUS EASY.'

From this it would appear, thought Jack, that my mother is dead, and that my father is mad. For some time our hero remained in a melancholy mood; he dropped many tears to the memory of his mother, whom, if he had never respected, he had much loved: and it was not till half an hour had elapsed, that he thought of opening the other letter. It was from Dr Middleton.

'My dear boy, – Although not a correspondent of yours, I take the right of having watched you through all your childhood, and from a knowledge of your disposition, to write you a few lines. That you have, by this time, discarded your father's foolish, nonsensical philosophy, I am very sure. It was I who advised your going away for that purpose, and I am sure, that, as a young man of sense, and the heir to a large property, you will before this have seen the fallacy of your father's doctrines. Your father tells me that he has requested you to come home, and allow me to add any weight I may have with you in persuading you to do the same. It is fortunate for you that the estate is entailed, or you might soon be a beggar, for there is no saying what debts he might, in his madness, be guilty of. He has already been dismissed from the magistracy by the lord-lieutenant, in consequence of his haranguing the discontented peasantry, and I may say, exciting them to acts of violence and insubordination. He has been seen dancing and hurrahing round a stack fired by an incendiary. He has turned away his keepers, and allowed all poachers to go over the manor. In short, he is not in his senses; and, although I am far from advising coercive measures, I do consider that it is absolutely necessary that you should immediately return home, and look after what will one day be your property. You have no occasion to follow the profession, with eight thousand pounds per annum. You have distinguished yourself – now make room for those who require it for their subsistence. God bless you. I shall soon hope to shake hands with you.
'Yours most truly,
'G. MIDDLETON.'

There was matter for deep reflection in these two letters, and Jack never felt before how much his father had been in the wrong.

Captain Marryat (1792–1848), *Mr Midshipman Easy*, 1836

THAT DEEP INDIAN NIGHT

My father made me a wooden castle big enough to get into, and he fixed real pistol barrels beneath its battlements to fire a salute on my birthday, but made me sit in front the first night – that deep Indian night – to receive the salute, and I, believing I was to be shot, cried.

T.H. White (1906–64), unpublished journal, quoted by Sylvia Townsend Warner,
in *T. H. White* 1967

SUGAR DADDY

I would say my father did not prepare me well for patriarchy; himself confronted, on his marriage with my mother, with a mother-in-law who was the living embodiment of peasant matriarchy, he had no choice but to capitulate, and did so. Further, I was the child of his mid-forties, when he was just the age to be knocked sideways by the arrival of a baby daughter He was putty in my hands throughout my childhood and still claims to be so, although now I am middle-aged myself while he, not though you'd notice, is somewhat older than the present century.

I was born in 1940, the week that Dunkirk fell. I think neither of my parents was immune to the symbolism of this, of bringing a little girl-child into the world at a time when the Nazi invasion of England seemed imminent, into the midst of death and approaching dark. Perhaps I seemed particularly vulnerable and precious and that helps to explain the over-protectiveness they felt about me, later on. Be that as it may, no child, however inauspicious the circumstances, could have been made more welcome. I did not get a birthday card from him a couple of years ago; when I querulously rang him up about it, he said: 'I'd never forget the day you came ashore.' (The card came in the second post.) His turn of phrase went straight to my heart, an organ which has inherited much of his Highland sentimentality.

He is a Highland man, the perhaps atypical product of an under-developed, colonialized country in the last years of Queen Victoria, of oatcakes, tatties and the Church of Scotland, of four years' active service in World War One, of the hurly-burly of Fleet Street in the twenties. His siblings, who never left the native village, were weird beyond belief. To that native village he competently removed himself ten years ago . . .

He has partitioned off a little room in the attic of his house, con-structed the walls out of cardboard boxes, and there he lies, on a camp-bed, listening to the World Service on a portable radio with his cap on. When he lived in London, he used to wear a trilby to bed but, a formal man, he exchanged it for a cap as soon as he moved. There are two perfectly good bedrooms in his house, with electric blankets and everything, as I well know, but these bedrooms always used to belong to his siblings, now deceased. He moves downstairs into one of these when the temperature in the attic drops too low for even his iron constitution, but he always shifts back up again, to his own place, when the ice melts. He has a ferocious enthusiasm for his own private space. My mother attributed this to a youth spent in the trenches, where no privacy was to be had. His war was the War to end Wars. He was too old for conscription in the one after that.

When he leaves this house for any length of time, he fixes up a whole lot of burglar traps, basins of water balanced on the tops of doors, tripwires, bags of flour suspended by strings, so that we worry in case he forgets where he's left what and ends up hoist with his own petard.

He has a special relationship with cats. He talks to them in a soft chirruping language they find irresistible. When we all lived in London and he worked on the night news desk of a press agency, he would come home on the last tube and walk, chirruping, down the street, accompanied by an ever-increasing procession of cats, to whom he would say good night at the front door. On those rare occasions, in my late teens, when I'd managed to persuade a man to walk me home, the arrival of my father and his cats always caused consternation, not least because my father was immensely tall and strong.

He is the stuff of which sitcoms are made.

His everyday discourse, which is conducted in the stately prose of a thirties *Times* leader, is enlivened with a number of stock phrases of a slightly eccentric, period quality. For example. On a wild night: 'Pity the troops on a night like this.' On a cold day:
Cold, bleak, gloomy and glum,
Cold as the hairs on a polar bear's –

The last word of the couplet is supposed to be drowned by the cries of outrage. My mother always turned up trumps on this one, interposing: 'Father!' on an ascending scale.

At random: 'Thank God for the Navy, who guard our shores.' On entering a room: 'Enter the fairy, singing and dancing.' Sometimes, in a particularly cheerful mood, he'll add to this formula: 'Enter the fairy, singing and dancing and waving her wooden leg.'

Infinitely endearing, infinitely irritating, irascible, comic, tough, sentimental, ribald old man, with his face of a borderline eagle and his bearing of a Scots guard, who, in my imagination as when I was a child, drips chocolates from his pockets as, a cat dancing in front of him, he strides down the road bowed down with gifts, crying: 'Here comes the Marquess of Carrabas!' The very words, 'my father', always make me smile.

Angela Carter, *The Granta Book of the Family*, 1995

SELF CRITICISM

'There's really nothing to restaurant criticism,' said Daddy, as I visualised the patricide scene in Pasolini's *Oedipus Rex*. 'Mind you, we used to have Raymond Postgate's *Good Food Guide* when you were a boy – terribly bourgeois, I suppose.' He paused for a moment, spoon en route. 'Of course, they say fish is good for the brain.'

'Who says fish is good for the brain?' I snapped.

'P G Wodehouse.'

We lapsed into silence. I regarded our fellow diners. They were a robust, chunky lot. At the table next to ours, seven men with moustaches were fishing 'out. Ipswich has had strong American connections since the war, and what with the décor, the waitresses dressed as waitresses and the empty quay outside, the impression of being Stateside was strong.

Daddy opted for the char-grilled marlin with garlic butter and I, propitiating our tutelary spirit, decided on the grilled whole mullet with dill and melon. We shared a side salad. The salad was a tightly furled bunch of rather hard leaves. The impression it gave was that the chef had once had an extremely unhappy affair with a cabbage and was trying to forget it. Both fish were garnished with more leaves and a clutch of those distinctly penile-looking new potatoes.

My mullet was a charming fish: delightful figure and just the right size. Like all my favourite creatures, its body fell open upon being pressed in the right places, to reveal firm flesh with a slightly woody bouquet. I was ravishing this when Daddy came up with his conversational bombshell of the evening: 'You know,' he said, eyeing me over a forkful of marlin, 'I had a peripheral part in the expansion of Ipswich.'

You can depend on Daddy to say things like this. An academic who specialises in the theory and practice of urban regional development, it's fair to say that wherever you eat in south-east England, you won't be far from a Daddy-influenced conurbation. Yes, you could tuck into roast pork in Peterborough, masticate mangetouts in Milton Keynes or nosh Neufchâtel in Northampton, safe in the knowledge that my Daddy has had – no matter how peripheral – an input into the local environment.

Daddy went on to discourse about the cusp of new town development in the late 1960s. I was disconcerted; while clumsy in almost every aspect of manual operations (his doctoral students have been known to tie his shoelaces for him), when at trough Daddy's hands almost blur with speed. I just managed to swipe the last chunk of the marlin before it was ingested. It was worth it. Marlin has dark, heavy flesh and unless it's grilled to perfection it can become either rigid or exhausted. But the chef at Mortimer's had this fish's number and it was now playing a peripheral part in Daddy's development.

Will Self, *Observer*, 15 October 1995

A VERY SMALL TAIL

It was rather awful being the youngest in my father's household, never quite sure if things were fact or fiction and always afraid to ask. When I was very young, my father told me that Hungary used to be called 'Yumyum' but that they changed it to Hungary because they thought it was more dignified. He told us both, when we slurped our soup, that King Ludwig of Bavaria used to do that and his courtiers had him locked up as insane. Was it true? There was a mad King Ludwig of Bavaria, of course, but did he bubble in his soup? Had my father made it all up or had he read it somewhere in some out-of-the-way book, of the sort he so often discovered? I never asked him, and now I shall never know.

The worst story, though, was about the Duke of Wellington's tail. My father told us one day that the Duke of Wellington had had a very small tail, which did not usually show under his coat, though he had to have a special hole made in his saddle in order to be comfortable on a horse. This sounded quite plausible to me, so I filed it away among the many facts of history I gleaned from my father's conversation. Some years later, after I had gone away to boarding school, I studied the period of the Napoleonic Wars in history. Anxious to share my special knowledge, I assured the teacher that the Iron Duke had had a tail: my father had told me so, and his grandparents had known the Duke. The teacher remained skeptical, so I applied to my father for confirmation. First he smiled, then he laughed, then he said 'Well . . .,' and I lost a beautiful illusion, along with a fragment of my faith in my father.

Katherine Tait, *My Father Bertrand Russell*, 1975

UNUSUAL POSITIONS IN BED

The next morning he departed unexpectedly for Scarborough, where a day or two later he slipped the cartilage in his knee, had it operated on, but refused to be given any kind of anesthetic ('No one ever dreamt of taking an anesthetic in the Middle Ages. It is most self-indulgent'). And on being subsequently told by the surgeon not to move, but to lie still, he treated this injunction in so conscientious a manner that as a result he developed pleurisy and was confined to his bed for three weeks.

During this period he alleged that he suffered from insomnia; which led Henry Moat to remark:

'Naturally Sir George can't sleep all night as well as all day.'

But my father had determined to make use of valuable time that would otherwise be wasted, and explained, when I came on leave, and went to visit him in a nursing home, that he had spent the previous nights in experimenting with the various unusual positions in bed that he had found to be the most conducive to sleep. Of what might prove to be this valuable addition to human knowledge he had no intention of depriving the world. He sent for me the next morning and, when he heard my footsteps, called out to me:

'Come in at once, and shut the door. I've had an idea.'

'About sleeping?' I enquired.

'Yes . . . The descriptions of my attitudes are difficult to follow in words alone, so I have decided to issue an illustrated pamphlet. I propose to call it *The Twenty-seven Postures of Sir George R. Sitwell*. Do you think that is a good title: will it sell the book, and whom shall I get to illustrate it?'

'Undoubtedly it will sell the book,' I replied, my mind first flying to the famous *Postures* of Aretino, then, more innocently, to the book of

Lady Hamilton's Attitudes, and also to the parodying volume of car-icatures which followed its publication. 'I will try to think of a suit-able artist,' I went on, 'but there's so little of that kind of work being done at present. It's a pity Aubrey Beardsley is dead. It would just have appealed to him.'

My father looked pleased.

'By the way,' I continued, 'I tried one of your positions last night. It certainly helped me to sleep.'

'Which one?' he demanded.

'The one you told me about, where you lie with your nose over the edge of the bed. It's easier to remember than most of the postures.'

'That's *not meant* to make you sleep,' he snapped angrily. 'It's just to pass the time.'

Osbert Sitwell (1892–1969), *Tales My Father Taught Me*, 1962

THE INVENTOR OF THE OUTDOOR SLEEPING BAG

Worldly rationalist though he was, or liked to think he was, my father had an eccentric side, which expressed itself every decade or so in A New Invention. He spoke often of the 'genius' of the man who invented Cat's-eyes for night driving, and he aspired to a similarly grand scientific breakthrough. His first effort, or the first he thought worth approaching the patents office about, was the electric tooth-brush anti-gunge protector. When he enthusiastically bought an elec-tric toothbrush shortly after they were introduced in Britain, his one complaint was that the water and toothpaste tended to slide down the brush into the battery-operated base and to reduce efficiency. He designed a new sort of brush with a series of spiky protrusions which would deflect the gunge away from the base, and he sent off his design to the manufacturers. Disappointingly, they seemed to have felt that as well as deflecting gunge, the spiky protrusions would also tear into, perhaps even tear apart, the mouth and gums of the user – at any rate, my father received only a polite acknowledgment of his 'interesting proposal, which we have passed on to the relevant department' . . .

. . . my father kept his next, and last, invention to himself.

Throughout my childhood he had been in the habit of sleeping out-doors whenever the weather was warm enough to permit it, and sometimes when it wasn't. He slept on the back lawn, outside the front porch, down the drive and (when I was grown up) on the roof terrace of my flat in Greenwich. But his favourite venue was the terrace of his chalet. Baden-Powellishly full of the joys of the alfresco kip – 'Marvellous. Fresh air. Nothing between you and the sky. Can't beat it' – he seemed to spend more and more of each summer away from his bed. I worried what it signified, but my mother never complained of his habit, beyond a wry comment or two when clear night skies turned to rain by morning. *His* one complaint was that his sleeping-bag, which he would sleep in fully dressed on a camp-bed, always ended up damp and clammy, whatever: 'It's either rain or condensation. No bloody way round it.'

But finally he thought of a way. Suppose he were to place the sleeping-bag inside *another* sleeping-bag, made of plastic, like an envelope slipped inside a second, tougher envelope. He got hold of a reject roll of plastic from Armorides, the local factory, and cut it into two coffin-sized strips. Then he taught himself how to operate my mother's sewing-machine, a victory of will-power over instinct, since my father had not previously mastered, or shown signs of wanting to master, any domestic task he considered 'feminine'. He had never, to my knowledge, darned a sock, sewn on a button, boiled an egg, washed or ironed a shirt, swept the floor, cleaned the cooker or vacuumed the carpet. And it was only once he'd retired that, after a fashion, he attempted the washing-up: spurning the Fairy Liquid bottle, he'd hold items of cutlery or crockery one at a time under a trickling hot tap and scrub them shiny-clean with a nail-brush. But he did always insist on dressing crabs: no one else, he thought, could be trusted to remove the dead men's fingers. And now in his fifties he taught himself to sew.

His first sleeping-bag took some time to complete. But having succeeded, he decided he might as well make three more, 'for all the family', then another two, 'for when you have friends down . . . Pity to waste the plastic.' He was so pleased by what he saw he'd have gone on to make a seventh, but he had run out of material. I have a photograph of him grinning like a crazed scientist at the wheel of the sewing machine. The first time I made use of his invention, with him eagerly monitoring my reactions from the next camp-bed, must have been around the time the photograph was taken.

'What a spectacle,' he said as we lay in our outdoor sleeping-bags looking upwards into a night slashed and grazed by shooting stars, 'doesn't it make you feel small?'

It was a Saturday night, and for once, instead of the wind clinketyclanking in the boat rigging like a Hare Krishna troupe, the air was silent, the sea calm as stone.

'Have you ever thought,' my father went on, 'that just as we are like tiny atoms in the universe, so the universe itself might be just a tiny atom in another universe? Or that each atom in your body might be a universe in a different dimension? Weird thought – sort of scares the shit out of you, space does.'

There were shrieks from the shoreline: someone larking about, a swim in the phosphorescence.

'When you look up there and think that the light from those stars set off hundreds of years ago, and then beyond them are the millions of stars you can't see except with a telescope, and they're thousands of light years away. We can't be the only intelligent life in the universe. It's a matter of making contact: if we keep sending signals from Jodrell Bank and so on, in different codes and languages, some day something will come back.'

Another shriek: salt water, a gentle swell, the surprising warmth of two bodies meeting . . .

'What do you think life can have been like at the start? You look up there and it's obvious the stars are different bits of the one thing that blew apart when time began. Imagine them rushing together again. Imagine reassembling that first planet or universe.'

'Reassembling?' I said, playing God's advocate. 'So it must have been assembled in the first place, someone invented it.'

A woman's cry, a man's guffaw.

'No, it just happened – primeval soup, a sudden spark, then, bang, time began. No one could have *made* all those stars.'

'Oh, I don't know,' I said, straining to catch the sound of someone, two people rather, in the sand below us. 'Think of all the frog-spawn that comes out of a single frog.'

'Oh, so you think someone *laid* the universe, like a bloody great bird laying an egg? And what's a shooting star supposed to be then? An egg falling out of the nest?'

We bickered on a bit about creation. Below us, the sighs and moans and sand-scuffles ebbed away, to be replaced by my father's immense snore – so immense I imagined it setting in motion a cosmic rhythm which would rock the stars backwards and forwards in unison. Across the bay, the lighthouse on St Tudwall's island flashed through the night, went out while I counted to twelve, then swung round into sight again, slicing up the darkness like a cake-knife. I shivered and wished I were man enough to be able to fall asleep, or, if not that, man enough to tell my father I'd had enough and was going in to my bed.

I woke at six, not only cold but damp. My father was awake already.

'All right, son?'

'Hum. My sleeping-bag feels wet.'

'Yes. When it's a clear night, there's condensation on the inside of the plastic as well as the outside – I suppose it's soaked through to your sleeping-bag as well.'

'So the outdoor sleeping-bag isn't working.'

'Course it is – it'd be much worse if you didn't have it. And on rainy nights you don't get condensation.'

'But on rainy nights you wouldn't want to sleep out.'

'Christ, you *have* got out of the wrong side of the bed, haven't you?'

'I'm still in it, Dad – and I'm soaked through.'

We squabbled some more. I told him I'd never use one of his sodding sleeping-bags again.

Blake Morrison, *And When Did You Last See Your Father?*, 1993

IN PURSUIT OF CHILDREN

I went into Farve's business room with Sibell one evening before dinner to say goodnight, and there was Mr. Norman sitting in an armchair, reading. He put down his book and talked to us for a few minutes. As we went up to bed I said to Sibell: 'Does your father often read?'

'Oh yes,' she replied.

'I've never heard of a *man* reading,' I said.

'Oh haven't you,' said Sibell. 'Lots of Fa's friends read.'

Until that moment I had always imagined reading was for women and children only, though I knew that men wrote. Even my grandfathers had published several books apiece, and at that very time there were vague murmurings, which reached us, among the uncles and aunts and Farve about Sir Edmund Gosse, who had written an 'insolent' (so they said) preface to Grandfather Redesdale's third volume of memoirs; Gosse was getting this book ready to be published posthumously. The insolence consisted in a hint that Grandfather found no intellectual companionship within his numerous family, which was of course perfectly true.

[226]

Muv's brother, Uncle George, pleased Farve with an epitaph sup-
posed to be suitable for this literary enemy:
Here lies Gosse,
No great loss.

Uncle George made this couplet rhyme, while Farve pronounced
loss to rhyme with horse, as we all did, which rather spoilt the joke.

Farve was now back from 'the front'; he was Assistant Provost
Marshal at Oxford, and lived in rooms at Christ Church. We used to
visit him there; he had installed a pianola; Muv laughed but we
thought it made the most heavenly sounds. Farve put some rainbow
trout in Mercury, and generally made himself at home in Tom Quad.

When he came to Batsford we played hide and seek all over the
house. All the lights were put out except in the library where Muv sat
with the youngest children. There were five staircases up and down
which we thundered, but during the silent moments I nearly died of
fright, straining my ears to hear a creaking board, somebody creeping
quite near. Then there came the sound of footsteps thumping down
the corridor, a distant scuffle and scream and Farve's triumphant roar
when he caught someone.

Diana Mosley, *A Life of Contrasts*, 1977

VAGUE LORD SALISBURY

He found it hard to recognize his fellow men, even his relations, if he
met them in unexpected circumstances. Once, standing behind the
throne at a Court ceremony, he noticed a young man smiling at him.
'Who is my young friend?' he whispered to a neighbour. 'Your eldest
son,' the neighbour replied.

David Cecil (1902–85), *The Cecils of Hatfield House*, 1973

A DOG WRITES

February 16, 1945

Dear Art,

Your father was telling me that in the letters you receive, nobody mentions my name. This is not unusual; it happens to many dogs. You know, it's a strange thing, but once you walk around on four legs instead of the orthodox two, people begin to suspect that you don't know what's going on. I don't know whether you have ever been a dog – I know you look like one – but it has certain advantages and disadvantages. As you know, your father and I both live under the same roof. He is not a bad guy, despite the fact that he kicks me occasionally, especially those days when the market goes down. When he strokes me affectionately, I know that the stocks are on the upswing. I watch your old man very closely, although I don't imagine he thinks I do, and he is quite a character. He reads the paper every morning, worries about the war, and all the other problems that the morning paper presents. Your father and I have many run-ins these days. You see, he can't get it into his thick skull that I have come of age and that sex is just as important to me as it is to him. There's a beautiful collie in the 500 block on Palm Drive who thinks I'm a pretty hot dog. I'm crazy about her, and although it isn't good for my social prestige to be seen around with a bitch from the 500 block, I try to be broad-minded about it and not too dogmatic in my views.

I've done considerable running away in recent months – sometimes for days! It isn't that I don't like your father but my freedom is terribly important and I am not going to relinquish it for that mangy pound-and-a-half of horse meat that he tosses at me each evening. I may not even go with him when he moves to Westwood. The back-yard is exceedingly small and there is a hell of a high steel picket fence surrounding it. I am convinced that if I try to scale this enclosure I will probably be disemboweled, so I may solve the whole thing by just remaining in Beverly, feeding out of garbage cans and living a dog's life with my collie.

Well, I could go on and tell you many tales of my adventures in the hills of Beverly but I don't want to bore you. The only reason I wrote you at all was because I didn't want you to think that I was an out-of-sight, out-of-mind dog. As a matter of fact, I miss you a lot and if you could send me a few bones, even those of a Jap, I certainly would appreciate it.

By the way, when you write to your father again, remember, not a word about this letter – he doesn't know I can write, in fact, he thinks I'm a complete schmuck.

Well, take care of yourself. That's the leash you can do.

Your old pal,
Duke Marx

Groucho Marx (1895–1977), <i>The Groucho Letters –
Letters to and from Groucho Marx</i>, 1967

OSWALD MOSLEY DRESSES UP

Sometimes my mother and father would come up to the night nursery to say goodnight before they went out to dinner. I have more memories of my father than my mother at these times, perhaps because he tried to be funny. Once he was going to dinner at Buckingham Palace and he was wearing full evening dress with medals: he showed us how he had pinned these medals on his behind. I remember thinking this enormously funny.

Nicholas Mosley, <i>Rules of the Game and Beyond the Pale</i>, 1994

NEW GROUND

We played Scrabble wrong for years.
We counted the Double and Triple Word Scores
as often as we liked.
We had to move aside the letters
to see what colours they were on.

My father was out of work
and we were moving again. He stared at the board,
twisting his signet ring.
He liked adding 's' to a word
and scoring more points
than the person who thought of it.

He wanted 'chinas'. He said they were ornamental

bricks from Derbyshire, hand-painted.
He cheated from principle, to open up new ground
for his family. Not 'God feeds the ravens',
but *Mundum mea patria est*. We were stuck

at the end of a lane in Sussex
for two winters. My father threw down
his high-scoring spelling mistakes and bluffs
and started counting.
He would have walked all over us
if we'd let him have the last word –

'aw' as in 'Aw, hell!', 'ex' with the 'x' falling
on the last Triple Letter Score.
We made him take everything back.
What was left in his hand counted against him.

Hugo Williams, *Writing Home*, 1985

THE GREATEST CRIME OF ALL

Renoir was opposed to all efforts to train young children. He wanted
them to make their first contacts with the world around them on their
own. If absolutely necessary, he would tolerate applying a little bitter
aloes to a baby's thumb, though he thought that might be an abuse of
authority. But then he would contradict himself by insisting on a child
having just the right kind of colours and objects in its surroundings.
His ideas on the subject were not theoretical. He would not have
approved of an 'artistic' environment. His chief desire was to bring us
up amidst good plain things, with as few as possible of them made by
machines. Nowadays, the price of such hand-made objects would be
prohibitive. He liked to think of a baby's eyes gazing at the light-
coloured bodices of women, at cheerfully painted walls, at flowers,
fruit, a mother's healthy face. He did disapprove, however, of the custom prevalent in the south of hanging bright objects on the side of a
cradle, for he thought it was apt to make a child cross-eyed. He
objected to extremes such as letting glaring artificial light shine in a
child's eyes, or leaving it completely in the dark. As children, we slept
with a night-light in the room. He was very sensitive to unusual or
loud noises, especially gunfire, asserting that it harmed the child's del-

icate sense of hearing. But in Renoir's opinion artificial feeding of infants was the greatest crime of all – 'not only because mother's milk has been invented, but because a child should bury its nose in its mother's breast, nuzzle it, and knead it with its chubby hand.' In his way of thinking, bottle-fed babies grew up into men 'lacking all the gentler feelings: anti-social beings who would take drugs to calm their nerves – or worse yet, wild animals always fearing they are going to be attacked.' He insisted that babies need animal protection and comfort from the warmth of a living body. 'By depriving them of those advantages, we are paving the way for generations of mentally deranged.'

Jean Renoir (1894–1979), Renoir, My Father, 1962

BAD LOW TOAD

GREEN BANK HOTEL,
FALMOUTH,
10th May 1907

MY DARLING MOUSE,

Have you heard about Toad? He was never taken prisoner by brigands at all. It was all a horrid low trick of his. He wrote that letter himself – the letter saying that a hundred pounds must be put in the hollow tree. And he got out of the window early one morning, & went off to a town called Buggleton, & went to the Red Lion Hotel & there he found a party that had just motored down from London, & while they were having breakfast he went into the stable-yard & found their motor-car & went off in it without even saying Poop-poop! And now he has vanished & every one is looking for him, including the police. I fear he is a bad low animal.

Goodbye, from
Your loving Daddy.

Kenneth Grahame (1859–1932), *First Whisper of* The Wind in the Willows,
1944

He was a very large man, tall and heavily built, the heaviness of his frame increasing with age. As a trooper he had been almost perfectly proportioned, I believe, according to Army standards, able to hold sixpences between his thighs, knees, calves and ankles when he stood upright with his legs close together, but the broad shoulders sagged forward more and more in late middle age until he acquired a top-heavy, unwieldy look. Upon these shoulders was set a large head, which may be called grand, with a wide, intelligent forehead, a prominent supraciliary ridge, and the strong features of an elder English statesman. My mother called him 'Punch', but that suggests an exaggeration of feature he did not possess; his nose and chin were both strong but there was nothing nut-crackery about them. His face was fleshy and venous, becoming rather jowly, his complexion ruddy. Thin on top, his greying hair was full at the sides and back; a thick moustache adorned a pleasant mouth in which, most of the time, a Jamaican cigar was tucked. I don't remember him as a smiling man, though he was a cheerful one; he would laugh and chuckle, but his mien generally was serious and attentive; the smile, if he were pleased or amused, was conveyed more by voice, manner, and small facial movements than by any display of teeth. In one of his eyes, which were wide and blue and greatly magnified by his horn-rimmed spectacles, he had a pronounced cast.

Strangely enough, considering the condition of his own, my father held decided views, often stated, of where eyes should be placed and what they ought to do. He was liable, in the early 'twenties, to come out with a number of maxims, old adages common to his generation, perfectly absurd for the most part and out of which we managed to joke him, a process to which he was easily amenable. Among them were two 'chaps' who came in for very severe strictures: there was the 'chap who doesn't look you straight in the eyes' and there was the 'chap whose eyes are too close together': neither could be trusted. These quaint fancies, which I reported among my friends, had upon us all a somewhat self-conscious effect: should we pass muster? I have said elsewhere that I did not find it altogether comfortable to look my father in the eye; this was partly due to his maxim, partly to the fact that I myself don't much like looking people straight in the eyes, and partly to his cast or squint which made it difficult, in his case, to do so. The consequent tests were sometimes unnerving. His own gaze, which perhaps he supposed straight, was ever full, thoughtful and prolonged, and it was his habit, according to the distance from him one happened to be sitting, sometimes to lower his head and regard one over the rims of his spectacles, a cross-examining look, sometimes to tilt back his head for a better focus. Thus with his magnified blue eyes swimming behind the lenses, he fixed one, yet not, as it were, quite in one's place, his cast causing the beams of his lamps to intersect too soon and pull one in, so that one sometimes felt not merely scrutinised but trapped at an uncomfortable distance, at too close quarters. My own eyes, I remember, when I was younger, often felt as though they were starting from their sockets under the strain of bravely meeting his; if my self-conscious gaze so much as wavered, I thought, the game would be up, my guilt established.

J.R. Ackerley (1896–1967), *My Father and Myself*, 1968

THE TALE OF A LEARNED PIG

My dear Thomas More,

You are not able to read writing yet – but whenever you have been quite a good boy and your kind Mamma has time – I dare say she will read you some of this letter. I wanted to write you another letter but did not know whether you had been quite a good boy minding all your Mamma said to you AT THE MOMENT – for I should not wish to write a letter to a boy who did not mind what was said to him – but a letter came yesterday from your Mamma who tells me that you mind all she says. You cannot think how glad I was to hear it. – I longed to take you up upon my knee and kiss you a great many times – and I wished that your Mamma and you and Sarah and little sister could take a walk with me upon these high hills – and see all these villages farms and woods – with oxen ploughing and farm yards full of sheep – Your Mamma will explain my words which you do not understand. St Catherine's Hill near Guildford is a pretty place with the ruins of a church upon it [*Two sketches*] Well! on the round hill where the church stands, there was a FAIR the other day – they built tents there with large poles [*Sketch*] The day before the Fair. The Dancing Bear. They built tents there with long poles which they then covered with cloth called canvas (your Mamma will show you a bit) – with canvas to keep out the winds and the rain. Then they put into these tents all the curious people and curious beasts and curious things they had to show. There were little men not so high as the table – and standing by them you would see a great giant almost as tall as the grand pianoforte in my study – and men without arms that could hold a pen between their toes and write anybody's name – and a learned pig that knew his letters – and had some laid upon the ground (like those in your box of letters) and then if you asked him which was H for Hog or P for pig or g for grunter – he would point to the right letter with his nose. And among these great tents there were numbers of smaller tents called booths filled with all manner of curious things for good boys who had learned their book well and minded what was said to them at the moment – there were playthings without number – Drums and tamborines and penny trumpets and poppet shows a half-penny each – kites to fly and boats to swim in a basin – song books and picture books and – O! the cakes! Pies made in the shape of little pigs and filled with sweetmeats – with a currant for each eye and a curly tail which bit crisp in the mouth – and ginger bread nuts and gingerbread and *gilded* gingerbread made into the shape of crows and crowing cocks and stars . . .

. . . I am delighted to hear that you have been such a good boy – and shall soon I hope – come home and give you a great many kisses – Ask your Mamma to give you a few kisses

from Your affectionate FATHER

SAMUEL PALMER

P.S. Your Mamma has seen one of the greatest fairs in the world – the carnival of Rome – perhaps she will tell you about it – they throw sugar plums at each other and go about in masks.

Samuel Palmer (1805–81), letter to Thomas More Palmer, 6 October 1844

A LOVER OF LOST CAUSES

My father used to take me through the hop-fields sitting in a little wicker basket which was strapped to the handlebars of his bicycle. One day we went to Chislehurst caves, which had been used to store ammunition during the war. I was at once frightened and embarrassed when he leaned over a well and shouted: 'Are there any Germans down there?'

One night I awoke to find my father alone in the room, opening a tin of sardines. No sign of my mother. She had gone to a hospital, he told me, to get me a little sister called Pamela. It turned out to be a little brother called Terry.

In fact my mother had hoped that I too should be a little girl called Pamela. I turned out otherwise, so she left my father to choose a name for me. Like many fathers at that time, he picked Denis for my first name. He wanted something more substantial to follow it. Winston Churchill had been his idol for many years. In 1917 Churchill was in disgrace for his part in the Dardanelles disaster. Like many Irishmen, my father was a lover of lost causes. So my middle name is Winston – a source of much ribald comment when I entered politics.

Denis Healey, *The Time of My Life*, 1989

THAT WONDERFUL PERSON OF SPARTA

There was an Old Person of Sparta,
Who had twenty-five sons and one daughter;
He fed them on snails, and weighed them in scales,
That wonderful person of Sparta.

Edward Lear (1812–88), *The Complete Nonsense*, 1947

NINE

Fatherhood – the Anguish and the Joy

The fundamental defect of fathers, in our competitive society, is that they want their children to be a credit to them.

Bertrand Russell (1872–1970), *Sceptical Essays*, 1928

PARENT TO CHILDREN

When you grow up, are no more children,
Nor am I then your parent:
The day of settlement falls.

'Parent,' mortality's reminder,
In each son's mouth or daughter's
A word of shame and rage!

I, who begot you, ask no pardon of you;
Nor may the soldier ask
Pardon of the strewn dead.

The procreative act was blind:
It was not you I sired then –
For who sires friends, as you are mine now?

In fear begotten, I begot in fear.
Would you have had me cast fear out
So that you should not be?

Robert Graves (1895–1985), *Collected Poems*, 1975

PARENTAL FEELING IS COMPLEX

Ever since the day, in the summer of 1894 when I walked with Alys
on Richmond Green after hearing the medical verdict, I had tried to
suppress my desire for children. It had, however, grown continually
stronger, until it had become almost insupportable. When my first
child was born, in November 1921, I felt an immense release of pent
up emotion, and during the next ten years my main purposes were
parental. Parental feeling, as I have experienced it, is very complex.
There is, first and foremost, sheer animal affection, and delight in
watching what is charming in the ways of the young. Next, there is
the sense of inescapable responsibility, providing a purpose for daily
activities which scepticism does not easily question. Then there is an
egoistic element, which is very dangerous: the hope that one's children
may succeed where one has failed, that they may carry on one's work
when death or senility puts an end to one's own efforts, and, in any

case, that they will supply a biological escape from death, making one's own life part of the whole stream, and not a mere stagnant puddle without any overflow into the future. All this I experienced, and for some years it filled my life with happiness and peace.

Bertrand Russell (1872–1970), *Autobiography, 1914–1924*

THE VEXING QUESTION OF PATERNITY

CAPTAIN [*getting up*]: Margret, who was the father of your child?

NURSE: Oh, I've told you time and time again: it was that scamp Johansson.

CAPTAIN: Are you sure it was he?

NURSE: You're talking like a child! Of course I'm sure, seeing he was the only one.

CAPTAIN: But was *he* sure he was the only one? No, he couldn't be, even though *you* were sure. That's the difference, you see.

NURSE: I don't see any difference.

CAPTAIN: No, you can't see it, but the difference is there all the same. [*He looks through a photograph album on the table.*] Do you think Bertha's like me?

[*He looks at a picture in the album.*]

NURSE: Why yes – you're as like as two peas.

CAPTAIN: Did Johansson admit that he was the father?

NURSE: Well, he had to!

CAPTAIN: How terrible. Here's the doctor. [*The* DOCTOR *comes in.*] Good evening doctor. How's my mother-in-law?

DOCTOR: Oh, nothing serious – only a slight sprain in the left ankle.

CAPTAIN: I thought Margret said it was a cold. There seems to be quite a difference of opinion about the case. Go to bed, Margret. [*The* NURSE *goes. Pause.*] Do sit down, doctor.

DOCTOR [*sitting*]: Thanks.

CAPTAIN: Is it true that you get striped foals if you cross a zebra with a mare?

DOCTOR [*surprised*]: Perfectly true.

CAPTAIN: Is it true that further foals may also be striped, even if the next sire is a stallion?

DOCTOR: Yes, that's true, too.

CAPTAIN: So that, under certain conditions, a stallion can sire striped foals – and vice versa?

DOCTOR: So it seems, yes.

CAPTAIN: Therefore a child's likeness to the father means nothing?

DOCTOR: Well –

CAPTAIN: That is to say, paternity cannot be proved.

DOCTOR: Hm – well

CAPTAIN: You are a widower? And you've had children?

DOCTOR: Ye-es.

CAPTAIN: Didn't being a father sometimes make you feel ridiculous? I know of nothing more absurd than seeing a father lead his child through the street, or hearing a father talk about 'my children'. He ought to say 'my wife's children'! Didn't you ever realize what a false position you were in? Weren't you ever afflicted with doubts . . . I won't say suspicions, for, as a gentleman, I assume that your wife was above suspicion.

DOCTOR: No, as a matter of fact, I never was. And anyhow, Captain, wasn't it Goethe who said 'A man must take his children on trust'? . . .

. . . since I don't believe in a life to come, my child was my after-life. She was my idea of immortality – perhaps the only one that has any foundation in reality. Take that away and you wipe me out . . .

. . . Who is the father?

LAURA: You are!

CAPTAIN: No, I am not. There's a crime lying buried here that's beginning to stink – and what a hellish crime it is! You women pity black slaves and set them free, but you keep white ones. I've worked and slaved for you and your child, your mother, and your servants. I've sacrificed my career and promotion, I've been racked and tortured, I've endured sleepless nights, worrying about your future till my hair has turned grey, and all so that you could enjoy a carefree life, and when you grew old, live it again through your child. I've borne all this without complaining because I imagined that I was the father of that child. It was the lowest kind of theft – the most brutal slavery. I've served seventeen years' hard labour though I was innocent. What can you give me in return for that?

LAURA: Now you're really mad!

CAPTAIN [sitting]: That's what you hope. I've seen how you've struggled to hide your sin. I've sympathized with you, realizing what caused your anxiety; I've often lulled your guilty conscience to rest, thinking that I was chasing away some morbid fancy. I've heard you cry out in your sleep, and I've refused to listen. Now I remember the night before last – it was Bertha's birthday. It was between two and three in the morning and I was sitting up reading. You screamed 'Keep away, keep away!' as if someone were trying to strangle you. I knocked on the wall because – because I didn't want to hear any more. I'd had my suspicions for a long time, but I dared not hear them confirmed. That's how I've suffered for your sake; what will you do for me?

LAURA: What can I do? I swear before God and all that I hold sacred that you are Bertha's father.

CAPTAIN: What use is that, when you've already said that a mother can and should commit any crime for her child's sake? I implore you, for the sake of the past – I implore you, as a wounded man begs for the death-blow – tell me everything. Don't you see that I'm as helpless as a child? Can't you hear that I'm calling to you as if you were my mother? Won't you forget that I'm a grown man – a soldier whose word of command both men and beasts obey? I am a sick man, all I ask is pity; I surrender the symbols of my power, and pray for mercy on my life.

LAURA [coming to him and laying her hand on his forehead]: What's this? A man, and crying?

CAPTAIN: Yes, I'm crying, although I'm a man. Has not a man eyes? Has not a man hands, organs, dimensions, senses, affections, passions? Fed with the same food, hurt with the same weapons, warmed and cooled by the same winter and summer as a woman. If you prick us, do we not bleed; if you tickle us, do we not laugh; if you poison us, do we not die? . . .

It's all to be found here – in every one of these books. So I wasn't mad after all. Here it is in the *Odyssey* – Book I, line 215; page 6 in the Uppsala translation. Telemachus is speaking to Athene. 'My mother indeed declares that he – meaning Oddysseus – is my father; but I myself cannot be sure; since no man ever yet knew his own begetter.' And it was Penelope, the most virtuous of women, whom Telemachus was suspecting. That's a fine thing, eh? And then we have the prophet Ezekiel: 'The fool saith: Lo, here is my father, but who can tell whose loins have engendered him?' That's clear enough, isn't it? And what have we here? Merzlyakov's *History of Russian Literature*: Alexander Pushkin, Russia's greatest poet, died in agony caused much more by the rumours going round of his wife's infidelity than by the bullet wound in his chest from a duel. On his death-bed he swore that she was innocent. Ass! Ass! How could he swear to that.

August Strindberg (1849–1912), *The Father*, translated by Peter Watts

SONS, WHAT THINGS YOU ARE

See, sons, what things you are,
How quickly nature falls into revolt
When gold becomes her object!
For this the foolish over-careful fathers
Have broke their sleep with thoughts,
Their brains with care, their bones with industry;
For this they have engrossed and pil'd up
The canker'd heaps of strange-achieved gold;
For this they have been thoughtful to invest
Their sons with arts and martial exercises;
When, like the bee, tolling from every flower
The virtuous sweets,
Our thighs pack'd with wax, our mouths with honey,
We bring it to the hive; and like the bees
Are murder'd for our pains. This bitter taste
Yields his engrossments to the ending father.

William Shakespeare (1564–1616), *Henry IV*, Part 2, Act IV, sc. V, 64–79

DEVOTION AND CARELESSNESS

The relations between fathers and children are one of the perpetual
great tragedies of life. The devotion of the old, the carelessness of the
young. The agonised way in which the former sees the only joy of his
life yearning only to leave him, without a thought or a comprehension
of how all the light of the old man's life proceeds from the young; the
selfish concentration with which the latter looks only at the world and
his future without even a word of sympathy for the old heart which
he breaks by a departure which he makes all the more bitter by the joy
with which he conscientiously strikes wound after wound into the old
soul who is too weak to allow his son to depart without a protest.

Extract from 1921 diary of Glubb Pasha (1897–1986), from Trevor Royle,
*Glubb Pasha – The Life and Times of Sir John Bagot Glubb,
Commander of the Arab Legion*, 1992

BAD HABITS

'I have a sone, and by the Trinitee,
I hadde levere than twenty pound worth lond,
Though it right now were fallen in myn hond,
He were a man of swich discrecioun
As that ye been! Fy on possessioun,
But if a man be vertuous withall
I have my sone snybbed, and yet shal,
For he to vertu listeth nat entende;
But for to pleye at dees, and to despende
And lese al that he hath, is his usage.
And he hath levere talken with a page
Than to comune with any gentil wight
Where he myghte lerne gentillesse aright.'

Geoffrey Chaucer (c.1343–1400), 'The Squire's Tale', *The Canterbury Tales*

POEM

My arms are rivers heavy with raw flood,
And their white reaches cry though flesh be dumb,
And I am ill with sudden tenderness
For him – I had not known such duress
Of thorny sweetness fell to fatherhood.
Arms can be torrents; little creature, come
And in the river-banks of my caress

Find you a coign for conies, or a nest
Under the overhanging of my head
For wildfowl, or curl here, ah close, and be
In hearing of the tides that flood in me,
And listen to the boulders in my breast,
And dare the compass of my arms, nor dread
The pools of shade they spill for you, so gently.

How vernal, how irradiant is his face
Lit up as though by stars or a quick breeze
Of lucent light that nowhere else abides,

Save in his features lambent like a bride's
And more unearthly than my crass embrace
Can share or hope for now . . . the rivers freeze
And my idiot arms fall, heavy, to my sides.
(c. 1944)

Mervyn Peake (1911–68), *Peake's Progress*, 1978

FATHERS WAIT

Every time I see my father I have new and complicated feelings about
how much of the deprivation I felt with him came willingly and how
much came against his will – how much he was aware of and unaware
of.

Jung said something disturbing about this complication. He said
that when the son is introduced primarily by the mother to feeling, he
will learn the female attitude towards masculinity and take a female
view of his own father and of his own masculinity. He will see his
father through his mother's eyes. Since the father and the mother are
in competition for the affection of the son, you're not going to get a
straight picture of your father out of your mother, nor will one get a
straight picture of the mother out of the father.

Some mothers send out messages that civilization and culture and
feeling and relationships are things which the mother and the
daughter, or the mother and the sensitive son, share in common,
whereas the father stands for and embodies what is stiff, maybe brutal, what is unfeeling, obsessed, rationalistic: money-mad, uncompas-
sionate. 'Your father can't help it.' So the son often grows up with a
wounded image of his father – not brought about necessarily by the
father's actions, or words, but based on the mother's observation of
these words or actions.

I know that in my own case I made my first connection with feeling through my mother. She provided me my first sense of discrimi-
nation of feeling. 'Are you feeling sad?' But the connection entailed
picking up a negative view of my father, who didn't talk very much
about feelings.

It takes a while for a son to overcome these early negative views of
the father. The psyche holds on tenaciously to these early perceptions.
Idealization of the mother or obsession with her, liking her or hating

her, may last until the son is thirty, or thirty-five, forty. Somewhere around forty or forty-five a movement toward the father takes place naturally – a desire to see him more clearly and to draw closer to him. This happens unexplainably, almost as if on a biological timetable.

A friend told me how that movement took place in his life. At about thirty-five, he began to wonder who his father really was. He hadn't seen his father in about ten years. He flew out to Seattle, where his father was living, knocked on the door, and when his father opened the door, said, 'I want you to understand one thing. I don't accept my mother's view of you any longer.'

'What happened?' I asked.

'My father broke into tears, and said, "Now I can die."' Fathers wait. What else can they do?

Robert Bly, *Iron John, a Book about Men*, 1990

HE INCARNATES THE WORLD OF ADVENTURE

The life of the father has a mysterious prestige: the hours he spends at home, the room where he works, the objects he has around him, his pursuits, his hobbies, have a sacred character. He supports the family, and he is the responsible head of the family. As a rule his work takes him outside, and so it is through him that the family communicates with the rest of the world: he incarnates that immense, difficult and marvellous world of adventure; he personifies transcendence, he is God.

Simone de Beauvoir, (1908–86) *The Second Sex*, 1949

NO CONSOLATION FOR NEGLECT

But business, official cares, duties, you say! Duties indeed! the last, doubtless, is that of a father! Let us not think it strange that a man whose wife disdains to nourish the fruit of their union himself disdains to undertake its education. There is no more charming picture than that of family life; but the lack of one trait disfigures all the others. If the mother has too little strength to be a nurse, the father will have too much business to be a teacher. The children sent from home and dispersed in boarding-schools, convents, and colleges, will carry otherwheres the love of home – or, rather, they will bring home the habit of being attached to nothing. Brothers and sisters will scarcely know one another. When they are all assembled in state, they can be very polite and formal, and will treat each other as strangers. The moment that intimacy between parents ceases, the moment that family intercourse no longer gives sweetness to life, it becomes at once necessary to resort to lower pleasures in order to supply what is lacking. Where is the man so stupid as not to see the logic of all this?

A father who merely feeds and clothes the children he has begotten so far fulfills but a third of his task. To the race, he owes men; to society, men of social dispositions; and to the state, citizens. Every man who can pay this triple debt and does not pay it, is guilty of a crime, and the more guilty, perhaps, when the debt is only half paid. He who can not fulfill the duties of a father has no right to become such. Neither poverty, nor business, nor fear of the world, can excuse him from the duty of supporting and educating his own children. Reader, believe me when I predict that whoever has a heart and neglects such sacred duties will long shed bitter tears over his mistake, and will never find consolation for it.

J.J. Rousseau (1712–78), *Emile*

SOME DISAPPOINTING SONS

It is not always the case that a 'wise father makes a wise son,' nor is it always the case that a son is 'a chip of the old block.' The subject is a very long one, but the following examples will readily occur to the reader: –

English History: Edward I, a noble king, was the son of Henry III, and the father of Edward II, both as unlike him as possible. Richard II, the fop, was the son of the Black Prince. Henry VI, a poor, worthless monarch, was the son of Henry V, the English Alexander. Richard Cromwell was the son of Oliver, but no more like his father than Hamlet was like Herculês. The only son of Addison was an idiot.

In France: The son of Charles V, *le Sage*, was Charles VII, the imbecile.

In Greek History: The sons of Pericles were Paralus and Xantippus, no better than Richard Cromwell. The son of Aristidés, surnamed *The Just*, was the infamous Lysimăchus. The son of the great historian Thucydĭdés were Milesias the idiot and Stephanos the stupid.

The kings of Israel and Judah give several similar examples. But it is not needful to pursue the subject further.

Rev. E. Cobham Brewer, *A Reader's Handbook*, 1880

OF PARENTS AND CHILDREN

The joys of parents are secret: and so are their griefs and fears. They cannot utter the one, nor they will not utter the other. Children sweeten labours, but they make misfortunes more bitter. They increase the cares of life, but they mitigate the remembrance of death. The perpetuity by generation is common to beasts, but memory, merit, and noble works are proper to men. And surely a man shall see the noblest works and foundations have proceeded from childless men, which have sought to express the images of their minds, where those of their bodies have failed. So the care of posterity is most in them that have no posterity. They that are the first raisers of their houses are most indulgent towards their children, beholding them as the continuance not only of their kind but of their work; and so both children and creatures.

The difference in affection of parents towards their several children is many times unequal and sometimes unworthy, especially in the mother; as Salomon saith, *A wise son rejoiceth the father, but an ungracious son shames the mother*. A man shall see, where there is a house full of children, one or two of the eldest respected, and the youngest made wantons, but in the midst some that are as it were forgotten, who many times nevertheless prove the best. The illiberality of parents in allowance towards their children is an harmful error; makes them base; acquaints them with shifts; makes them sort with mean company; and makes them surfeit more when they come to plenty. And therefore the proof is best, when men keep their authority towards their children, but not their purse. Men have a foolish manner (both parents and schoolmasters and servants) in creating and breeding an emulation between brothers during childhood, which many times sorteth to discord when they are men, and disturbeth families. The Italians make little difference between children and nephews

[248]

or near kinsfolks; but so they be of the lump, they care not though they pass not through their own body. And to say truth, in nature it is much a like matter, insomuch that we see a nephew sometimes resembleth an uncle or a kinsman more than his own parent, as the blood happens. Let parents choose betimes the vocations and courses they mean their children should take, for then they are most flexible, and let them not too much apply themselves to the disposition of their children, as thinking they will take best to that which they have most mind to. It is true that if the affection or aptness of the children be extraordinary, then it is good not to cross it; but generally the precept is good, *Optimum elige, suave et facile illud faciet consuetudo.* Younger brothers are commonly fortunate, but seldom or never where the elder are disinherited.

Francis Bacon (1561–1626), *The Essayes or Counsels*

HOW MANY DELICIOUS ACCENTS

No man can tell but he that loves his children how many delicious accents make a man's heart dance in the pretty conversation of these dear pledges: their childishness, their stammering, their little angers, their innocence, their imperfections, their necessities, are so many emanations of joy and comfort to him that delights in their persons and society; but he that loves not his wife and children feeds a lioness at home, and broods a nest of sorrows.

Jeremy Taylor (1613–67), *XXV Sermons*

TEN

Feuds, Quarrels and Reconciliations

And, ye fathers, provoke not your children to wrath: but bring them up in the nurture and admonition of the Lord.

Ephesians 6:4

And he said, A certain man had two sons:

And the younger of them said to *his* father, Father, give me the portion of goods that falleth *to me*. And he divided unto them *his* living.

And not many days after the younger son gathered all together, and took his journey into a far country, and there wasted his substance with riotous living.

And when he had spent all, there arose a mighty famine in that land; and he began to be in want.

And he went and joined himself to a citizen of that country; and he sent him into his fields to feed swine.

And he would fain have filled his belly with the husks that the swine did eat: and no man gave unto him.

And when he came to himself, he said, How many hired servants of my father's have bread enough and to spare, and I perish with hunger!

I will arise and go to my father, and will say unto him, Father, I have sinned against heaven, and before thee.

And am no more worthy to be called thy son: make me as one of thy hired servants.

And he arose, and came to his father. But when he was yet a great way off, his father saw him, and had compassion, and ran, and fell on his neck, and kissed him.

And the son said unto him, Father, I have sinned against heaven, and in thy sight, and am no more worthy to be called thy son.

But the father said to his servants, Bring forth the best robe, and put *it* on him; and put a ring on his hand, and shoes on *his* feet:

And bring hither the fatted calf, and kill *it*; and let us eat, and be merry:

For this my son was dead, and is alive again; he was lost, and is found. And they began to be merry.

Now his elder son was in the field: and as he came and drew nigh to the house, he heard musick and dancing.

And he called one of the servants, and asked what these things meant.

And he said unto him, Thy brother is come: and thy father hath killed the fatted calf, because he hath received him safe and sound.

And he was angry, and would not go in: therefore came his father out, and intreated him.

And he answering said to *his* father, Lo, these many years do I serve thee, neither transgressed I at any time thy commandment: and yet thou never gavest me a kid, that I might make merry with my friends:

But as soon as this thy son was come, which hath devoured thy living with harlots, thou hast killed for him the fatted calf.

And he said unto him, Son, thou art ever with me, and all that I have is thine.

It was meet that we should make merry, and be glad: for this thy brother was dead, and is alive again; and was lost, and is found.

Luke 16: 11–32

DADDY

You do not do, you do not do
Any more, black shoe
In which I have lived like a foot
For thirty years, poor and white,
Barely daring to breathe or Achoo.

Daddy, I have had to kill you.
You died before I had time –
Marble-heavy, a bag full of God,
Ghastly statue with one gray toe
Big as a Frisco seal

And a head in the freakish Atlantic
Where it pours bean green over blue
In the waters off beautiful Nauset.
I used to pray to recover you.
Ach, du.

In the German tongue, in the Polish town
Scraped flat by the roller
Of wars, wars, wars.
But the name of the town is common.
My Polack friend

Bit my pretty red heart in two.
I was ten when they buried you.
At twenty I tried to die

And get back, back, back to you.
I thought even the bones would do.

But they pulled me out of the sack,
And they stuck me together with glue.
And then I knew what to do.
I made a model of you,
A man in black with a Meinkampf look

And a love of the rack and the screw.
And I said I do, I do.
So daddy, I'm finally through.
The black telephone's off at the root,
The voices just can't worm through.

If I've killed one man, I've killed two –
The vampire who said he was you
And drank my blood for a year,
Seven years, if you want to know.
Daddy, you can lie back now.

There's a stake in your fat black heart
And the villagers never liked you.
They are dancing and stamping on you.
They always *knew* it was you.
Daddy, daddy, you bastard, I'm through.

Sylvia Plath (1932–63),*Collected Poems*, 1981

HIS IGNORANT BARBARIC CARCASS

Oh, this father! this kindly, anxious, uncomprehending, constipated
father! Doomed to be obstructed by this Holy Protestant Empire! The
self-confidence and the cunning, the imperiousness and the contacts,
all that enabled the blond and blue-eyed of his generation to lead, to
inspire, to command, if need be to oppress – he could not summon a
hundredth part of it. How could he oppress? – he *was* the oppressed.
How could he wield power? – he *was* the powerless. How could he
enjoy triumph, when he so despised the triumphant – and probably
the very idea. 'They worship a Jew, do you know that, Alex? Their
whole big-deal religion is based on worshipping someone who was an

established Jew at that time. Now how do you like that for stupidity? How do you like that for pulling the wool over the eyes of the public? Jesus Christ, who they go around telling everybody was God, was actually a Jew! And this fact, that absolutely kills me when I have to think about it, *nobody else pays any attention to.* That he was a Jew, like you and me, and that they took a Jew and turned him into some kind of God after he is already dead, and then – and this is what can make you absolutely crazy – then the dirty bastards turn around afterwards, and who is the first one on their list to persecute? who haven't they left their hands off to murder and to hate for two thousand years? The Jews! who gave them their beloved Jesus to begin with! I assure you, Alex, you are never going to hear such a *mishegoss* of mixed-up crap and disgusting nonsense as the Christian religion in your entire life. And that's what these big shots, so-called, believe!'

Unfortunately, on the home front contempt for the powerful enemy was not so readily available as a defensive strategy – for as time went on, the enemy was more and more *his* own beloved son. Indeed, during that extended period of rage that goes by the name of my adolescence, what terrified me most about my father was not the violence I expected him momentarily to unleash upon me, but the violence I wished every night at the dinner table to commit upon his ignorant, barbaric carcass. How I wanted to send him howling from the land of the living when he ate from the serving bowl with his own fork, or sucked the soup from his spoon instead of politely waiting for it to cool, or attempted, God forbid, to express an opinion on any subject whatsoever . . . And what was especially terrifying about the murderous wish was this: if I tried, chances were I'd succeed! *Chances were he would help me along!* I would have only to leap across the dinner dishes, my fingers aimed at his windpipe, for him instantaneously to sink down beneath the table with his tongue hanging out. Shout he could shout, squabble he could squabble, and oh *nudjh*, could he *nudjh*! But defend himself? against *me*? 'Alex, keep this back talk up,' my mother warns, as I depart from the roaring kitchen like Attila the Hun, run screaming from yet another half-eaten dinner, 'continue with this disrespect and you will give that man a heart attack!' 'Good!' I cry, slamming in her face the door to my room. 'Fine!' I scream, extracting from my closet the zylon jacket I wear only with my collar up (a style she abhors as much as the filthy garment itself). 'Wonderful!' I shout, and with streaming eyes run to the corner to vent my fury on the pinball machine.

Philip Roth, *Portnoy's Complaint*, 1969

My old friend James Harrington esq. (*Oceana*) was well acquainted with Sir Benjamin Ruddyer, who was an acquaintance of Sir Walter Ralegh's. He told Mr J.H. that Sir Walter Ralegh being invited to dinner to some great person where his son was to go with him, he sayd to his son 'Thou art expected to-day at dinner to goe along with me, but thou art such a quarrelsome, affronting . . . that I am ashamed to have such a beare in my company.' Mr. Walter humbled himself to his father, and promised he would behave himselfe mighty mannerly. So away they went (and Sir Benjamin, I think, with them). He sate next to his father and was very demure at least halfe dinner time. Then sayd he, 'I, this morning, not having the feare of God before my eies but by the instigation of the devill, went to a whore. I was very eager of her, kissed and embraced her, and went to enjoy her, but she thrust me from her, and vowed I should not, for your Father lay with me but an hour ago.' Sir Walter being strangely surprized and putt out of his countenance at so great a table, gives his son a damned blow over his face. His son, as rude as he was, would not strike his father, but strikes over the face the gentleman that sate next to him and sayd 'Box about: 'twill come to my father anon.' 'Tis now a common-used proverb.

John Aubrey (1626–97), Brief Lives

I DID CALL HER IMPUDENT BAGGAGE

Sept. 13. [1671] After night shut I went to my daughter Mohun, she and her husband being desperately out again. I cannot but blame both, but her most being my ungracious daughter and breaking all my advices and carrying herself irreligiously. Among other expressions she said she would be a common whore before she would submit to her husband's will in what I thought fit; if she had not been married I had beat her, I did call her 'impudent baggage', and said she carried herself like a whore, and left her with resolution to see her no more. This was after her husband had sworn never to strike her nor give her ill words.

Dec. 2. Spent most of the day in reconciling my daughter Mohun and her husband, and supt with them and left them in bed.

Arthur Annesley, 1st Earl of Anglesey (1614–86), Diary

A DIVIDED DUTY

Brabantio. . . . Come hither, gentle mistress:
Do you perceive in all this noble company,
Where most you owe obedience?
Desdemona. My noble father,
I do perceive here a divided duty:
To you I am bound for life and education,
My life and education both do learn me
How to respect you, you are lord of all my duty,
I am hitherto your daughter: but here's my husband:
And so much duty as my mother show'd
To you, preferring you before her father,
So much I challenge, that I may profess,
Due to the Moor my lord.
Brabantio. God bu'y, I ha' done:
Please it your grace, on to the state-affairs;
I had rather to adopt a child than get it;
Come hither, Moor:
I here do give thee that, with all my heart,
Which, but thou hast already, with all my heart
I would keep from thee. For your sake (jewel)
I am glad at soul I have no other child,
For thy escape would teach me tyranny,
To hang clogs on 'em; I have done, my lord.

William Shakespeare (1564–1616), *Othello*

THOU LOV'DST ME NOT

Prince. I never thought to hear you speak again.
King. Thy wish was father, Harry, to that thought;
I stay too long by thee, I weary thee.
Dost thou so hunger for mine empty chair
That thou wilt needs invest thee with my honours
Before thy hour be ripe? O foolish youth!
Thou seek'st the greatness that will overwhelm thee.
Stay but a little, for my cloud of dignity

Is held from falling with so weak a wind
That it will quickly drop; my day is dim.
Thou hast stol'n that which after some few hours
Were thine without offence, and at my death
Thou hast seal'd up my expectation.
Thy life did manifest thou lov'dst me not,
And thou wilt have me die assur'd of it.
Thou hid'st a thousand daggers in thy thoughts,
Which thou hast whetted on thy stony heart,
To stab at half an hour of my life.
What, canst thou not forbear me half an hour?
Then get thee gone, and dig my grave thyself,
And bid the merry bells ring to thine ear
That thou art crowned, not that I am dead.
Let all the tears that should bedew my hearse
Be drops of balm to sanctify thy head,
Only compound me with forgotten dust,
Give that which gave thee life unto the worms;
Pluck down my officers; break my decrees;
For now a time is come to mock at form -
Harry the fifth is crown'd! Up, vanity!
Down, royal state! All you sage counsellors, hence!
And to the English court assemble now
From every region, *apes* of idleness!

William Shakespeare (1564–1616), *Henry IV*, Part 2

NOTHING WILL COME OF NOTHING

Lear. . . . what can you say to draw
A third more opulent than your sisters? Speak.
Cordelia. Nothing, my lord.
Lear. Nothing?
Cordelia. Nothing.
Lear. Nothing will come of nothing: speak again.
Cordelia. Unhappy that I am, I cannot heave
My heart into my mouth: I love your Majesty
According to my bond; no more nor less.
Lear. How, how, Cordelia! Mend your speech a little,

[259]

Lest you may mar your fortunes.
Cordelia. Good my Lord,
You have begot me, bred me, lov'd me: I
Return those duties back as are right fit,
Obey you, love you, and most honour you.
Why have my sisters husbands, if they say
They love you all? Happily, when I shall wed,
That lord whose hand must take my plight shall carry
Half my love with him, half my care and duty:
Sure I shall never marry like my sisters,
To love my father all.
Lear. But goes thy heart with this?
Cordelia. Ay, my good Lord.
Lear. So young, and so untender?
Cordelia. So young, my Lord, and true.
Lear. Let it be so; thy truth then be thy dower:
For, by the sacred radiance of the sun,
The mysteries of Hecate and the night,
By all the operation of the orbs
From whom we do exist and cease to be,
Here I disclaim all my paternal care,
Propinquity and property of blood,
And as a stranger to my heart and me
Hold thee from this for ever. The barbarous Scythian,
Or he that makes his generation messes
To gorge his appetite, shall to my bosom
Be as well neighbour'd, pitied, and reliev'd,
As thou my sometime daughter.
Kent. Good my Liege, –
Lear. Peace, Kent!
Come not between the Dragon and his wrath.
I lov'd her most, and thought to set my rest
On her kind nursery. Hence, and avoid my sight!
So be my grave my peace, as here I give
Her father's heart from her!

William Shakespeare (1564–1616), *King Lear*

Lear. It may be so, my Lord.
Hear, Nature, hear! dear Goddess, hear!
Suspend thy purpose, if thou didst intend
To make this creature fruitful!
Into her womb convey sterility!
Dry up in her the organs of increase,
And from her derogate body never spring
A babe to honour her! If she must teem,
Create her child of spleen, that it may live
And be a thwart disnatur'd torment to her!
Let it stamp wrinkles in her brow of youth,
With cadent tears fret channels in her cheeks,
Turn all her mother's pains and benefits
To laughter and contempt, that she may feel
How sharper than a serpent's tooth it is
To have a thankless child! Away, away!

William Shakespeare (1564–1616), *King Lear*

THE TOYS

My little Son, who looked from thoughtful eyes,
And moved and spoke in quiet grown-up wise,
Having my law the seventh time disobeyed,
I struck him, and dismissed
With hard words and unkissed,
– His Mother, who was patient, being dead.
Then, fearing lest his grief should hinder sleep,
I visited his bed,
But found him slumbering deep,
With darkened eyelids, and their lashes yet
From his late sobbing wet.
And I, with moan,
Kissing away his tears, left others of my own;
For on a table drawn beside his head,
He had put, within his reach,
A box of counters and a red-veined stone,

A piece of glass abraded by the beach,
And six or seven shells,
A bottle with bluebells,
And two French copper coins, ranged there with careful art,
To comfort his sad heart.
So when that night I prayed
To God, I wept, and said:
Ah, when at last we lie with trancéd breath,
Not vexing Thee in death,
And Thou rememberest of what toys
We made our joys,
How weakly understood
Thy great commanded good,
Then fatherly not less
Than I whom Thou has moulded from the clay,
Thou'lt leave Thy wrath, and say,
'I will be sorry for their childishness.'

Coventry Patmore (1823–96), in *The Oxford Book of Victorian Verse*, 1922

THE MOST LOATHSOME AND DISGUSTING
RELATIONSHIP

Carter's Hotel,
Albemarle Street,
1 April 1894

Alfred,

It is extremely painful for me to have to write to you in the strain I must; but please understand that I decline to receive any answers from you in writing in return. After your recent hysterical impertinent ones I refuse to be annoyed with such, and I decline to read any more letters. If you have anything to say do come here and say it in person. Firstly, am I to understand that, having left Oxford as you did, with discredit to yourself, the reasons of which were fully explained to me by your tutor, you now intend to leaf and loll about and do nothing. All the time you were wasting at Oxford I was put off with the assurance that you were eventually to go into the Civil Service or to the Foreign Office, and then I was put off with an assurance that you were going to the Bar. It appears to me that you intend to do nothing. I utterly decline, however, to just supply you with sufficient funds to enable you to leaf about. You are preparing a wretched future for yourself, and it would be most cruel and wrong for me to encourage you in this. Secondly, I come to the more painful part of this letter – your intimacy with this man Wilde. It must either cease or I will disown you and stop all money supplies. I am not going to try and analyse this intimacy, and I make no charge; but to my mind to pose as a thing is as bad as to be it. With my own eyes I saw you both in the most loathsome and disgusting relationship as expressed by your manner and expression. Never in my experience have I ever seen such a sight as that in your horrible features. No wonder people are talking as they are. Also I now hear on good authority, but this may be false, that his wife is petitioning to divorce him for sodomy and other crimes. Is this true, or do you know of it? If I thought the actual thing was true, and it became public property, I should be quite justified in shooting him at sight. These Christian English cowards and men, as they call themselves, want waking up.

Your disgusted so-called father,

Queensberry

'What a funny little man you are! Alfred Douglas.'

Queensberry: You impertinent young jackanapes. I request that you will not send such messages to me by telegraph. If you send me any more such telegrams, or come with any impertinance, I will give you the thrashing you deserve. Your only excuse is that you must be crazy. I hear from a man at Oxford that you were thought crazy there, and that accounts for a good deal that has happened. If I catch you again with that man I will make a public scandal in a way you little dream of; it is already a suppressed one. I prefer an open one, and at any rate I shall not be blamed for allowing such a state of things to go on. Unless this acquaintance ceases I shall carry out my threat and stop all supplies, and if you are not going to make any attempt to do something I shall certainly cut you down to a mere pittance, so you know what to expect.

28 August

You miserable creature,

I received your telegram by post from Carter's and have requested them not to forward any more, but just to tear any up, as I did yours, without reading it, directly I was aware from whom it came. You must be flush of money to waste it on such rubbish. I have learned, thank goodness, to turn the keenest pangs to peacefulness. What could be keener pain than to have such a son as yourself fathered upon one? However, there is always a bright side to every cloud, and whatever is is light (sic). If you are my son, it is only confirming proof to me, if I needed any, how right I was to face every horror and misery I have done rather than run the risk of bringing more creatures into the world like yourself, and that was the entire and only reason of my breaking with your mother as a wife, so intensely was I dissatisfied with her as the mother of you children, and particularly yourself, whom, when quite a baby, I cried over you the bitterest tears a man ever shed, that I had brought such a creature into the world, and unwittingly had committed such a crime. If you are not my son, and in this Christian country with these hypocrites 'tis a wise father who knows his own child, and no wonder on the principles they intermarry on, but to be fore-warned is to be fore-armed. No wonder you have fallen prey to this horrible brute. I am only sorry for you as a human creature . . . You must be demented; there is madness on your mother's side, and indeed few families in this Christian country are without it, if you look into them. But please cease annoying me, for I will not correspond with you nor receive nor answer letters, and as for money, you sent me a lawyer's letter to say you would take none from me, but anyhow until you change your life I should refuse any. It depends on yourself whether I shall ever recognise you at all again after your behaviour. I will make allowance; I think you are demented, and I am very sorry for you.

Queensberry

Marquess of Queensberry (1844–1900), letters to Lord Alfred Douglas

A BREACH OF FILIAL PIETY

During the last visit which the Doctor made to Lichfield, the friends with whom he was staying missed him one morning at the breakfast-table. On inquiring after him of the servants, they understood he had set off from Lichfield at a very early hour, without mentioning to any of the family whither he was going. The day passed without the return of the illustrious guest, and the party began to be very uneasy on his account, when, just before the supper-hour, the door opened, and the Doctor stalked into the room. A solemn silence of a few minutes ensued, nobody daring to inquire the cause of his absence, which was at length relieved by Johnson addressing the lady of the house in the following manner: 'Madam, I beg your pardon for the abruptness of my departure from your house this morning, but I was constrained to it by my conscience. Fifty years ago, Madam, on this day, I committed a breach of filial piety, which has ever since lain heavy on my mind, and has not till this day been expiated. My father, you recollect, was a bookseller, and had long been in the habit of attending Uttoxeter market, and opening a stall for the sale of his books during that day. Confined to his bed by indisposition, he requested me, this time fifty years ago, to visit the market, and attend the stall in his place. But, Madam, my pride prevented me from doing my duty, and I gave my father a refusal. To do away the sin of this disobedience, I this day went in a postchaise to Uttoxeter, and going into the market at the time of high business, uncovered my head, and stood with it bare an hour before the stall which my father had formerly used, exposed to the sneers of the standers-by and the inclemency of the weather; a penance by which I trust I have propitiated heaven for this only instance, I believe, of contumacy toward my father.'

Rev. Richard Warner (1763–1857), *Tour through the Northern Counties*, vol. I, 1802

DO NOT LAUGH AT ME

Cordelia. O! look upon me, Sir,
And hold your hand in benediction o'er me.
No, Sir, you must not kneel.
Lear. Pray, do not mock me:
I am a very foolish fond old man,
Fourscore and upward, not an hour more or less;
And, to deal plainly,
I fear I am not in my perfect mind.
Methinks I should know you and know this man;
Yet I am doubtful: for I am mainly ignorant
What place this is, and all the skill I have
Remembers not these garments; nor I know not
Where I did lodge last night. Do not laugh at me;
For, as I am a man, I think this lady
To be my child Cordelia.
Cordelia. And so I am, I am.

Lear. Be your tears wet? Yes, faith. I pray, weep not:
If you have poison for me, I will drink it.
I know you do not love me; for your sisters
Have, as I do remember, done me wrong:
You have some cause, they have not.
Cordelia. No cause, no cause.

William Shakespeare (1564–1616), King Lear

KING LEAR'S DAUGHTER

Letter from Goneril, daughter of King Lear, to her sister Regan

I have writ my sister.
King Lear, Act I, sc. 4

THE PALACE, November

Dearest Regan,

I am sending you this letter by Oswald. We have been having the most trying time lately with Papa, and it ended to-day in one of those scenes which are so painful to people like you and me, who *hate* scenes. I am writing now to tell you all about it, so that you may be prepared. This is what has happened.

When Papa came here he brought a hundred knights with him, which is a great deal more than we could put up, and some of them had to live in the village. The first thing that happened was that they quarrelled with our people and refused to take orders from them, and whenever one told any one to do anything it was either – if it was one of Papa's men – 'not his place to do it'; or if it was one of our men, they said that Papa's people made work impossible. For instance, only the day before yesterday I found that blue vase which you brought back from Dover for me on my last birthday broken to bits. Of course I made a fuss, and Oswald declared that one of Papa's knights had knocked it over in a drunken brawl. I complained to Papa, who flew into a passion and said that his knights, and in fact all his retainers, were the most peaceful and courteous people in the world, and that it was my fault, as I was not treating him or them with the respect which they deserved. He even said that I was lacking in filial duty. I was determined to keep my temper, so I said nothing.

The day after this the chief steward and the housekeeper and both my maids came to me and said that they wished to give notice. I asked them why. They said they couldn't possibly live in a house where there were such 'goings-on.' I asked them what they meant. They refused to say, but they hinted that Papa's men were behaving not only in an insolent but in a positively outrageous manner to them. The steward said that Papa's knights were never sober, that they had entirely demoralized the household, and that life was simply not worth living in the house; it was *impossible* to get anything done, and they couldn't sleep at night for the noise.

I went to Papa and talked to him about it quite quietly, but no sooner had I mentioned the subject than he lost all self-control, and began to abuse me. I kept my temper as long as I could, but of course one is only human, and after I had borne his revilings for some time, which were monstrously unfair and untrue, I at last turned and said something about people of his age being trying. Upon which he said that I was mocking him in his old age, that I was a monster of ingratitude – and he began to cry. I cannot tell you how painful all this was to me. I did everything I could to soothe him and quiet him, but the truth is, ever since Papa has been here he has lost control of his wits. He suffers from the oddest kind of delusions. He thinks that for some reason he is being treated like a beggar; and although he has a hundred knights – a hundred, mind you! (a great deal more than we have) – in the house, who do nothing but eat and drink all day long, he says he is not being treated like a King! I do hate unfairness.

When he gave up the crown he said he was tired of affairs, and meant to have a long rest; but from the very moment that he handed over the management of affairs to us he never stopped interfering, and was cross if he was not consulted about everything, and if his advice was not taken.

And what is still worse: ever since his last illness he has lost not only his memory but his control over language, so that often when he wants to say one thing he says just the opposite, and sometimes when he wishes to say some quite simple thing he uses *bad* language quite unconsciously. Of course we are used to this, and *we* don't mind, but I must say it is very awkward when strangers are here. For instance, the other day before quite a lot of people, quite unconsciously, he called me a dreadful name. Everybody was uncomfortable and tried not to laugh, but some people could not contain themselves. This sort of thing is constantly happening. So you will understand that Papa needs perpetual looking after and management. At the same time, the moment one suggests the slightest thing to him he boils over with rage.

But perhaps the most annoying thing which happened lately, or, at least, the thing which happens to annoy me most, is Papa's Fool. You know, darling, that I have always hated that kind of humour. He comes in just as one is sitting down to dinner, and beats one on the head with a hard, empty bladder, and sings utterly idiotic songs, which make me feel inclined to cry. The other day, when we had a lot of people here, just as we were sitting down in the banqueting-hall, Papa's Fool pulled my chair from behind me so that I fell sharply down on the floor. Papa shook with laughter, and said: 'Well done, little Fool,' and all the courtiers who were there, out of pure snobbishness, of course, laughed too. I call this not only very humiliating for me, but undignified in an old man and a king; of course Albany refused to interfere. Like all men and all husbands, he is an arrant coward.

However, the crisis came yesterday. I had got a bad headache, and was lying down in my room, when Papa came in from the hunt and sent Oswald to me, saying that he wished to speak to me. I said that I wasn't well, and that I was lying down – which was perfectly true – but that I would be down to dinner. When Oswald went to give my message Papa beat him, and one of his men threw him about the room and really hurt him, so that he has now got a large bruise on his forehead and a sprained ankle.

This was the climax. All our knights came to Albany and myself, and said that they would not stay with us a moment longer unless Papa exercised some sort of control over his men. I did not know what to do, but I knew the situation would have to be cleared up sooner or later. So I went to Papa and told him frankly that the situation was intolerable; that he must send away some of his people, and choose for the remainder men fitting to his age. The words were scarcely out of my mouth than he called me the most terrible names, ordered his horses to be saddled, and said that he would shake the dust from his feet and not stay a moment longer in this house. Albany tried to calm him, and begged him to stay, but he would not listen to a word, and said he would go and live with you.

So I am sending this by Oswald, that you may get it before Papa arrives and know how the matter stands. All I did was to suggest he should send away fifty of his men. Even fifty is a great deal, and puts us to any amount of inconvenience, and is a source of waste and extravagance – two things which I cannot bear. I am perfectly certain you will not be able to put up with his hundred knights any more than I was. And I beg you, my dearest Regan, to do your best to make Papa listen to sense. No one is fonder of him than I am. I think it would have been difficult to find a more dutiful daughter than I have always been. But there is a limit to all things, and one cannot have one's whole household turned into a pandemonium, and one's whole life into a series of wrangles, complaints, and brawls, simply because Papa in his old age is losing the control of his faculties. At the same time, I own that although I kept my temper for a long time, when it finally gave way I was perhaps a little sharp. I am not a saint, nor an angel, nor a lamb, but I do hate unfairness and injustice. It makes my blood boil. But I hope that you, with your angelic nature and your tact and your gentleness, will put everything right and make poor Papa listen to reason.

Let me hear at once what happens.

Your loving
GONERIL

P.S. – Another thing Papa does which is most exasperating is to quote Cordelia to one every moment. He keeps on saying: 'If only Cordelia were here,' or 'How unlike Cordelia!' And you will remember, darling, that when Cordelia was here Papa could not endure the sight of her. Her irritating trick of mumbling and never speaking up used to get terribly on his nerves. Of course, I thought he was even rather unfair on her, trying as she is. We had a letter from the French Court yesterday, saying that she is driving the poor King of France almost mad.

P.P.S. – It is wretched weather. The poor little ponies on the heath will have to be brought in.

Maurice Baring (1874–1945), *Lost Diaries and Dead Letters*

AUDEN'S BAD ADVICE

I remember once discussing my father and my difficult relationship with him. Wystan was adamant. 'Those people just batten on one, real emotional harpies, they've got to be taught a lesson. Stand up to him, make him see you don't need him any more.' ('From the immense bat-shadows of home deliver us.') Shortly afterwards my father lunched with me in Soho, a treat he always enjoyed, and on the way back I stopped the taxi outside my door in Chelsea (he lived in South Kensington). He clearly expected to be invited in for a talk and a brandy but I bade him an abrupt farewell and gave the driver his address. Clutching his two thick cherrywood sticks with the rubber ferrules, his legs crossed, his feet in pumps, for owing to arthritis he could not stoop to do up laces, he fingered his grey moustache while a tear trickled down his cheek. I don't know which of us felt more unhappy.

Cyril Connolly (1903–74), *Some Memories of W.H. Auden: A Tribute*, 1974

YOU LOOK LIKE A MALE WHORE

My father hated me chiefly because I was revolting but also because I was expensive. Sometimes he would turn on me at the dinner table and hiss, 'Don't eat so much butter on your bread.' To such injunctions I paid even less heed than usual for our life now seemed to be luxurious. I have since decided that with the move out of London my father had abandoned common sense altogether and plunged into a financial gamble that in his own way he was shortly to win.

We occupied what I would now call a very ordinary four-bedroom house and employed a housemaid and a gardener. This last feature of opulence was due not so much to the size of the garden as to the fact that nothing would have induced me to till or even to scratch the soil. I don't hold with flowers even when they are as good as artificial ones.

We also had a car but this could hardly be looked upon as a status symbol. Every car that my father bought was broken-down. He chose them like this deliberately so that he could spend almost all the week-end in the garage repairing them. This was a way of avoiding being with his family. Man goes and buys a car and lies beneath. When he was not tinkering with it, he was making the car the subject of one of our recurring Strindberg dramas. Every Sunday afternoon he asked my mother if she would like to go for a drive. She, who had learned her lines perfectly, said that she would.

'Where would you like to go?'

My mother then ploughed her way conscientiously through the list of places that were within driving distance. She was told that they were too far away or at the top or bottom of hills that were bad for the car. Then she was allowed to say, 'Well, anywhere. I don't mind.'

'If you don't care where we go,' my father would conclude, 'we might as well stay at home.'

But we didn't and the whole afternoon was hell.

About eighteen months after we moved to High Wycombe, the dreary ritual of our lives was interrupted by my mother going away for a few days. What caused this to happen, I can't remember. Perhaps she left in self-defence. This was a very rare occurrence as neither my father nor I could boil a kettle unless conditions were favourable. This was further evidence of the rigid sexual structure of the world at this time. Men fetched coal from cellars and hammered nails; women boiled kettles. You knew where you were even though you hated it.

My father and I got on shakily but, to my amazement, not badly. We spoke to each other. He asked me what I intended to do with my life and at last I understood that the future was now. Neither of my parents ever said to me, 'You're mad but, when you go out into the world, you will doubtless meet people as mad as you and I can only hope that you get on all right with them.' Such words as these would have been a great help. Instead, my mother protected me from the world and my father threatened me with it. My feeling of inadequacy increased steadily. I remember a day when my mother and I stood beside the road at Loudwater station and waited for my father to emerge from the London train. As we stood there, a stream of men in dark suits and bowler hats went by us. I thought, 'I'll never be able to get into step with them.' I felt as I had in childhood when two other children turned a skipping-rope and urged me to run under it and start jumping. I couldn't do it.

Hateful was the dark-blue serge . . . O, why should life all labour be? Perhaps I was a born lotus-eater suffering from permanent symptoms of withdrawal.

At the end of one of the ominous but not hostile conversations with my father that took place during my mother's absence, he said, 'The trouble is you look like a male whore.'

This cheered me up a little as I had not then taken my final vows. I was in a twilit state between sin and virtue. The remark was the first acknowledgment that he had ever made of any part of my problem. In gratitude I promised that when I went up to London at Christmas, I would try not to come back.

Quentin Crisp, *The Naked Civil Servant*, 1968

A QUARREL OVER RUSKIN

I began to read Ruskin's *Unto This Last*, and this, when added to my interest in psychical research and mysticism, enraged my father, who was a disciple of John Stuart Mill's. One night a quarrel over Ruskin came to such a height that in putting me out of the room he broke the glass in a picture with the back of my head. Another night when we had been in argument over Ruskin or mysticism, I cannot now remember what theme, he followed me upstairs to the room I shared with my brother. He squared up at me, and wanted to box, and when I said I could not fight my own father replied, 'I don't see why you should not'. My brother, who had been in bed for some time, started up in a violent passion because we had awaked him. My father fled without speaking, and my brother turned to me with, 'Mind, not a word till he apologizes.' Though my father and I are very talkative, a couple of days passed before I spoke or he apologized.

W.B. Yeats (1865–1939), *Autobiography*, 1972

AN IMPERFECT CONFLAGRATION

Early one June morning in 1872 I murdered my father – an act which made a deep impression on me at the time. This was before my marriage, while I was living with my parents in Wisconsin. My father and I were in the library of our home, dividing the proceeds of a burglary which we had committed that night. These consisted of household goods mostly, and the task of equitable division was difficult. We got on very well with the napkins, towels and such things, and the silverware was parted pretty nearly equally, but you can see for yourself that when you try to divide a single music-box by two without a remainder you will have trouble. It was that music-box which brought disaster and disgrace upon our family. If we had left it my poor father might now be alive.

It was a most exquisite and beautiful piece of workmanship – inlaid with costly woods and carven very curiously. It would not only play a great variety of tunes, but would whistle like a quail, bark like a dog, crow every morning at daylight whether it was wound up or not, and break the Ten Commandments. It was this last-mentioned accomplishment that won my father's heart and caused him to commit the only dishonourable act of his life, though possibly he would have committed more if he had been spared: he tried to conceal that music-box from me, and declared upon his honour that he had not taken it, though I knew very well that, so far as he was concerned, the burglary had been undertaken chiefly for the purpose of obtaining it.

My father had the music-box hidden under his cloak; we had worn cloaks by way of disguise. He had solemnly assured me that he did not take it. I knew that he did, and knew something of which he was evidently ignorant; namely, that the box would crow at daylight and betray him if I could prolong the division of profits till that time. All occurred as I wished: as the gaslight began to pale in the library and the shape of the windows was seen dimly behind the curtains, a long cock-a-doodle-doo came from beneath the old gentleman's cloak, followed by a few bars of an aria from *Tannhäuser*, ending with a loud click. A small hand-axe, which we had used to break into the unlucky house, lay between us on the table; I picked it up. The old man seeing that further concealment was useless took the box from under his cloak and set it on the table. 'Cut it in two if you prefer that plan,' said he; 'I tried to save it from destruction.'

He was a passionate lover of music and could himself play the concertina with expression and feeling.

I said: 'I do not question the purity of your motive: it would be presumptuous in me to sit in judgment on my father. But business is business, and with this axe I am going to effect a dissolution of our partnership unless you will consent in all future burglaries to wear a bell-punch.'

'No,' he said, after some reflection, 'no, I could not do that; it would look like a confession of dishonesty. People would say that you distrusted me.'

I could not help admiring his spirit and sensitiveness; for a moment I was proud of him and disposed to overlook his fault, but a glance at the richly jewelled music-box decided me, and, as I said, I removed the old man from this vale of tears. Having done so, I was a trifle uneasy. Not only was he my father – the author of my being – but the body would be certainly discovered. It was now broad daylight and my mother was likely to enter the library at any moment. Under the circumstances, I thought it expedient to remove her also, which I did. Then I paid off all the servants and discharged them.

That afternoon I went to the chief of police, told him what I had done and asked his advice. It would be very painful to me if the facts became publicly known. My conduct would be generally condemned;

the newspapers would bring it up against me if ever I should run for office. The chief saw the force of these considerations; he was himself an assassin of wide experience. After consulting with the presiding Judge of the Court of Variable Jurisdiction he advised me to conceal the bodies in one of the bookcases, get a heavy insurance on the house and burn it down. This I proceeded to do.

In the library was a book-case which my father had recently purchased of some cranky inventor and had not filled. It was in shape and size something like the old-fashioned 'wardrobes' which one sees in bedrooms without closets, but opened all the way down, like a woman's night-dress. It had glass doors. I had recently laid out my parents and they were now rigid enough to stand erect; so I stood them in this book-case, from which I had removed the shelves. I locked them in and tacked some curtains over the glass doors. The inspector from the insurance office passed a half-dozen times before the case without suspicion.

That night, after getting my policy, I set fire to the house and started through the woods to town, two miles away, where I managed to be found about the time the excitement was at its height. With cries of apprehension for the fate of my parents, I joined the rush and arrived at the fire some two hours after I had kindled it. The whole town was there as I dashed up. The house was entirely consumed, but in one end of the level bed of glowing embers, bolt upright and uninjured, was that book case! The curtains had burned away, exposing the glass doors, through which the fierce, red light illuminated the interior. There stood my dear father 'in his habit as he lived,' and at his side the partner of his joys and sorrows. Not a hair of them was singed, their clothing was intact. On their heads and throats the injuries which in the accomplishment of my designs I had been compelled to inflict were conspicuous. As in the presence of a miracle, the people were silent; awe and terror had stilled every tongue. I was myself greatly affected.

Some three years later, when the events herein related had nearly faded from my memory, I went to New York to assist in passing some counterfeit United States bonds. Carelessly looking into a furniture store one day, I saw the exact counterpart of that book-case. 'I bought it for a trifle from a reformed inventor,' the dealer explained. 'He said it was fireproof, the pores of the wood being filled with alum under hydraulic pressure and the glass made of asbestos. I don't suppose it is really fireproof – you can have it at the price of an ordinary book-case.'

'No,' I said, 'if you cannot warrant it fireproof I won't take it' – and I bade him good morning.

I would not have had it at any price: it revived memories that were exceedingly disagreeable.

Ambrose Bierce (1842–c.1914), The Eye of the Panther, 1928

A VIOLENT BLOW

I spend a couple of hours with Mr. George Young. I took courage to relate to him an anecdote about himself. Nearly forty years ago, I happened to be in a Hackney stage-coach with Young. A stranger came in – it was opposite Lackington's. On a sudden the stranger struck Young a violent blow on the face. Young coolly put his head out of the window and told the coachman to let him out. Not a word passed between the stranger and Young. But the latter having alighted, said in a calm voice, before he shut the door, 'Ladies and gentleman, that is my father'.

Henry Crabb Robinson (1775–1867), Diary

CURSED FROM BIRTH

My father was Polybus, King of Corinth:
my mother Merope, a Dorian. As Prince,
I was highly regarded among the people.
But one day something . . . strange occurred, out of
the blue, a curious thing, which for some reason
worried me deeply. It was at a banquet.
A man who had had too much to drink called me
a bastard – said I was not my father's son!
I was so incensed I could scarcely contain myself!
Next morning I went straight to my mother and father
and told them. They were outraged at the insult.
This . . . reassured me, but the story was spreading,
and deep inside me it still rankled.
Unknown to my mother and father I went to Delphi;

and Apollo . . . instead of answering my questions,
told me of other things – showed me a future
of horror, of sorrow, of pain beyond belief!
He said I was fated to sleep with my own mother!
To have children by her, a ghastly, incestuous breed!
And to murder my father!
When I heard this – I ran!
I left Corinth for good, got right away,
trying to find some far off place where I
would never see those oracles come true!
And in my wanderings I came to the region where
you say the late king died. Listen, Jocasta,
this is the truth: as I came near the place
where three roads meet, I came face to face
with a herald, followed by a horse-drawn carriage,
and riding in it a man – all just as you have described!
And the one in front and the old man himself
tried to force me off the road, out of their way!
Well, I was angry. I hit out at the driver,
and the old man, waiting for me to pass him,
brought down his stick and caught me flush on the head!
But he paid for that. With one blow of my staff
I knocked him out of his seat and down he came,
flat on his back. I killed him – killed them all,
the lot of them! But, god! If he, this stranger,
by some crazy coincidence – was Laius,
what man on earth is more accursed than I am?
What man more hated by the gods? I am the man
no citizen or alien may shelter!
I am the one no-one may speak to! I am
the one they must all drive from their homes!
And all these curses I laid on myself!
And . . . I pollute the bed of the man I killed!
I touch his wife with the hands that shed his blood!
Oh god! I must have been cursed from my birth –
a monster, an abomination! I must
face exile, never to see my people again,
never set foot in my homeland – or I am doomed
to marry my mother and murder my father –
Polbus, who gave me life, who cared for me . . .!
But why? What can I think but that some god,

some cruel power has planned all this for me?
O no!
O never let me see the day!
Hear me, you gods on high! – O let me vanish
from the sight of men, from the face of earth before
I see the stain of such defilement on me!

Sophocles (496–406 BC), *Oedipus the King*, translated by Christopher Stace

THAT UNFEATHER'D, TWO-LEG'D THING, A SON

why should he, with Wealth and Honour blest,
Refuse his Age the needful hours of Rest?
Punish a Body which he could not please;
Bankrupt of Life, yet Prodigal of Ease?
And all to leave, what with his Toyl he won,
To that unfeather'd, two Leg'd thing, a Son:

John Dryden (1631–1700), *Absalom and Achitophel,* 165–70

HOW EASIE 'TIS FOR PARENTS TO FORGIVE

But oh that yet he woud repent and live!
How easie 'tis for Parents to forgive!
With how few Tears a Pardon might be won
From Nature, pleading for a Darling Son!
Poor pitied Youth, by my Paternal care,
Rais'd up to all the Height his Frame coud bear:
Had God ordain'd his fate for Empire born,
He woud have given his Soul another turn:

John Dryden (1631–1700), *Absalom and Achitophel,* 957–64

AN ACCURSED PLUM-PUDDING

On Christmas Day of this year 1857 our villa saw a very unusual sight. My Father had given strictest charge that no difference whatever was to be made in our meals on that day; the dinner was to be neither more copious than usual nor less so. He was obeyed, but the servants, secretly rebellious, made a small plum-pudding for themselves. (I discovered afterwards, with pain, that Miss Marks received a slice of it in her boudoir.) Early in the afternoon, the maids, – of whom we were now advanced to keeping two, – kindly remarked that 'the poor dear child ought to have a bit, anyhow,' and wheedled me into the kitchen, where I ate a slice of plum-pudding. Shortly I began to feel that pain inside which in my frail state was inevitable, and my conscience smote me violently. At length I could bear my spiritual anguish no longer, and bursting into the study I called out: 'Oh! Papa, Papa, I have eaten of flesh offered to idols!' It took some time, between my sobs, to explain what had happened. Then my Father sternly said: 'Where is the accursed thing?' I explained that as much as was left of it was still on the kitchen table. He took me by the hand, and ran with me into the midst of the startled servants, seized what remained of the pudding, and with the plate in one hand and me still tight in the other, ran till we reached the dust-heap, when he flung the idolatrous confectionery on to the middle of the ashes, and then raked it deep down into the mass. The suddenness, the violence, the velocity of this extraordinary act made an impression on my memory which nothing will ever efface.

Edmund Gosse (1849–1928), *Father and Son*, 1907

A SHARED LAVATORY CONDEMNED

At home our own obsessions had changed. My brother was now the centre of attack; my father was merely sarcastic to me, saying things like 'How is Professor Know-all?' or 'What is in the superior mind of my sentimental son?' His sarcasm was often, I think, a form of shyness . . .

Suddenly, no doubt to win my father's affection, he went after a job in Father's own trade, a silk firm. He got the job and Father was not very pleased: it looked like an outflanking movement. Within six months, the firm (which was French), sent my brother to Lyons to work in the factory and to learn the trade. Father could not believe the outrage: it was one of the best firms in the trade. To punish my brother he sent him off without money and for six months the boy half-starved on the low wage and bad food of a poor apprentice. He came back after six months, exuberantly happy, Frenchified and covered with a rash. He arrived at the front gate on a Sunday morning just after Father got back from church. Father stared at him in fury.

'Your train arrives at five'.

'I came by the earlier one'.

'You can't have done – that is for first-class passengers'.

'I came first class'.

'You travelled first class', cried Father. 'What d'you mean by that? Where did you get the money?'

'The firm paid'.

'You're not asking me to believe that one of the biggest firms in the trade allows its factory hands to travel first class?'

'The manager told me'.

'He was joking'.

'He came on the same train'.

'You didn't have the impudence to travel with the manager?' shouted Father. Now they had advanced to the lawn just inside the gate of the house. Mother was standing at the door, listening to the rumpus.

'Oh dear, what's he done?'

'Only from Calais. I met him in the lavatory on the boat. We came to London together'.

'You used the same lavatory as the manager?' screamed Father.

'Walt, what is it?' cried Mother.

'Look at his face', said Father in disgust.

'The filthy hound has been going with prostitutes', moaned Father. 'He has got a disease'.

We stood on the lawn gazing at the delinquent.

'You'd better get inside', said Father wretchedly.

The rash was the effect of bad food, but my brother had enjoyed himself. He was soon showing Father he knew more about silk than my father did and – height of social dreams – had lunched often on Sundays with the British Vice-Consul – a 'hellish' lad my brother murmured to me. Father contained his jealousy: on the Monday my brother would be sacked for his presumption.

'I cannot understand your lack of judgement', he said. 'You go to the same lavatory and then – it's past belief – you travel in the same first-class compartment to London with him.'

'He asked me to. He doesn't speak English.'

'What! You little fool, every Frenchman speaks English!'

On Monday morning my backward brother was promoted.

Father was sad. He could see what it was. His son, his own son, preferred to work for a Frenchman rather than for himself.

V.S. Pritchett, *A Cab at the Door*, 1968

LOVE IS SPURNED

Her recollections of the dear dead boy – and they were never absent – were itself; the same thing. And oh, to be shut out: to be so lost: never to have looked into her father's face or touched him, since that hour!

She could not go to bed, poor child, and never had gone yet, since then, without making her nightly pilgrimage to his door. It would have been a strange sad sight, to see her now, stealing lightly down the stairs through the thick gloom, and stopping at it with a beating heart, and blinded eyes, and hair that fell down loosely and unthought of; and touching it outside with her wet cheek. But the night covered it, and no one knew.

The moment that she touched the door on this night, Florence found that it was open. For the first time it stood open, though by but a hair's-breadth: and there was a light within. The first impulse of the timid child – and she yielded to it – was to retire swiftly. Her next, to go back, and to enter; and this second impulse held her in irresolution on the stair-case.

In its standing open, even by so much as that chink, there seemed to be hope. There was encouragement in seeing a ray of light from within, stealing through the dark stern doorway, and falling in a thread upon the marble floor. She turned back, hardly knowing what she did, but urged on by the love within her, and the trial they had undergone together, but not shared: and with her hands a little raised and trembling, glided in.

Her father sat at his old table in the middle room. He had been arranging some papers, and destroying others, and the latter lay in fragile ruins before him. The rain dripped heavily upon the glass panes in the outer room, where he had so often watched poor Paul, a baby; and the low complainings of the wind were heard without.

But not by him. He sat with his eyes fixed on the table, so immersed in thought, that a far heavier tread than the light foot of his child could make, might have failed to rouse him. His face was turned towards her. By the waning lamp, and at that haggard hour, it looked worn and dejected; and in the utter loneliness surrounding him, there was an appeal to Florence that struck home.

'Papa! Papa! speak to me, dear Papa!'

He started at her voice, and leaped up from his seat. She was close before him, with extended arms, but he fell back.

'What is the matter?' he said, sternly. 'Why do you come here? What has frightened you?'

If anything had frightened her, it was the face he turned upon her. The glowing love within the breast of his young daughter froze before it, and she stood and looked at him as if stricken into stone.

There was not one touch of tenderness or pity in it. There was not one gleam of interest, parental recognition, or relenting in it. There was a change in it, but not of that kind. The old indifference and cold constraint had given place to something: what, she never thought and did not dare to think, and yet she felt it in its force, and knew it well without a name: that as it looked upon her, seemed to cast a shadow on her head.

Did he see before him the successful rival of his son, in health and life? Did he look upon his own successful rival in that son's affection? Did a mad jealousy and withered pride, poison sweet remembrances that should have endeared and made her precious to him? Could it be possible that it was gall to him to look upon her in her beauty and her promise: thinking of his infant boy!

Florence had no such thoughts. But love is quick to know when it is spurned and hopeless: and hope died out of hers, as she stood looking in her father's face.

'I ask you, Florence, are you frightened? Is there anything the matter, that you come here?'

'I came, Papa –'

'Against my wishes. Why?'

She saw he knew why: it was written broadly on his face: and dropped her head upon her hands with one prolonged low cry.

Let him remember it in that room, years to come. It has faded from the air, before he breaks the silence. It may pass as quickly from his brain, as he believes, but it is there. Let him remember it in that room, years to come!

He took her by the arm. His hand was cold, and loose, and scarcely closed upon her.

'You are tired, I daresay,' he said, taking up the light, and leading her towards the door, 'and want rest. We all want rest. Go, Florence. You have been dreaming.'

The dream she had had, was over then, God help her! and she felt that it could never more come back.

'I will remain here to light you up the stairs. The whole house is yours above there,' said her father, slowly. 'You are its mistress now. Good-night!'

Still covering her face, she sobbed, and answered 'Good-night, dear Papa,' and silently ascended. Once she looked back as if she would have returned to him, but for fear. It was a momentary thought, too hopeless to encourage; and her father stood there with the light – hard, unresponsive, motionless – until the fluttering dress of his fair child was lost in the darkness.

Let him remember it in that room, years to come. The rain that falls upon the roof: the wind that mourns outside the door: may have fore-knowledge in their melancholy sound. Let him remember it in that room, years to come!

The last time he had watched her, from the same place, winding up those stairs, she had had her brother in her arms. It did not move his heart towards her now, it steeled it: but he went into his room, and locked his door, and sat down in his chair, and cried for his lost boy.

Charles Dickens (1812–70), *Dombey and Son*

AN ALTERED HEART

Autumn days are shining, and on the sea-beach there are often a young lady, and a white-haired gentleman. With them, or near them, are two children: boy and girl. And an old dog is generally in their company.

The white-haired gentleman walks with the little boy, talks with him, helps him in his play, attends upon him, watches him, as if he were the object of his life. If he be thoughtful, the white-haired gentleman is thoughtful too; and sometimes when the child is sitting by his side, and looks up in his face, asking him questions, he takes the tiny hand in his, and holding it, forgets to answer. Then the child says:

'What, grandpa! Am I so like my poor little Uncle again?'

'Yes, Paul. But he was weak, and you are very strong.'

'Oh yes, I am very strong.'

'And he lay on a little bed beside the sea, and you can run about.'

And so they range away again, busily, for the white-haired gentle-man likes best to see the child free and stirring; and as they go about together, the story of the bond between them goes about, and follows them.

But no one, except Florence, knows the measure of the white-haired gentleman's affection for the girl. That story never goes about. The child herself almost wonders at a certain secrecy he keeps in it. He hoards her in his heart. He cannot bear to see a cloud upon her face. He cannot bear to see her sit apart. He fancies that she feels a slight, when there is none. He steals away to look at her, in her sleep. It pleases him to have her come, and wake him in the morning. He is fondest of her and most loving to her, when there is no creature by. The child says then, sometimes:

'Dear grandpapa, why do you cry when you kiss me?'

He only answers, 'Little Florence! Little Florence!' and smooths away the curls that shade her earnest eyes.

The voices in the waves speak low to him of Florence, day and night – plainest when he, his blooming daughter, and her husband, walk beside them in the evening, or sit at an open window, listening to their roar. They speak to him of Florence and his altered heart; of Florence and their ceaseless murmuring to her of the love, eternal and illim-itable, extending still, beyond the sea, beyond the sky, to the invisible country far away.

Never from the mighty sea may voices rise too late, to come between us and the unseen region on the other shore! Better, far better, that they whispered of that region in our childish ears, and the swift river hurried us away!

Charles Dickens (1812–70), *Dombey and Son*

6th November 1661
Wt a deale of patience is requiste to beare any converse wth our little children. How peevish and foolish are they! & wt fits doth our heavenly Father beare with us in!

19th February 1662
I had an occasion yt might have sadden mee this eveninge. My son D: in his passion spoke very irreverently & sinfully to mee. I did desire to deale wth him as well as I could to make him sensible of his sin, & I prayed to God to forgive him poore childe.

Rev. Henry Newcombe (1627–95), *Diary*

A GUERILLA WARFARE

Captain Thicknesse, as soon as his son Philip had attained his seventeenth year, arranged and staged a highly satisfactory quarrel between the two brothers, and in the interests of virtue, took the younger son before magistrates to swear that his elder brother had set him upon a runaway horse with the intention of killing him and inheriting his fortune – a wicked story which had, quite undoubtedly, originated in the mind of Captain Thicknesse, and which was afterwards proved to be a lie. Then after a while, to the Captain's great discomfiture, the brothers became friends, and from that time their indignant father could think of nothing bad enough to say about either of them. He was, in addition, grieved that he could not possess himself of their fortunes. For years a guerilla warfare was carried on. Eventually, Captain Thicknesse brought off a master coup of strategy. He was, by now, living at 'The Hermitage'. His younger son, hearing that his father intended to live abroad, offered to buy the property for £100, but, being only eighteen years old, he was not, as yet, in possession of his fortune, and so gave his father an acceptance for this sum. A short while after, having obtained the money in question, he paid Captain Thicknesse the £100, but presented him with an extra £100. He must therefore have been a little surprised when, some years after, having spent large sums of money upon the house, and having offered to allow his father to rebuy the house on the repayment of the £100, that virtuous old gentleman produced the original acceptance with a flourish, and denied that he had ever been paid . . .

Meanwhile Captain Thicknesse kept up a guerilla warfare with both his sons, and announced that his brother, who was High Master of St. Paul's school and who had had these errant youths under his charge, years before, disapproved of the eldest so strongly that he had determined to change his name unless his nephew did so. This gentleman was extremely sensible and an admirable instructor of youth; for according to the Captain: 'My brother always endeavoured to check the disposition of all ingenious men who were under him, when they betrayed a tendency to poetry. I recollect I have heard him say that he declined Dr. Johnson's acquaintance, as he deemed him then only a poet.' To this strong criticism Captain Thicknesse, who was as just as he was severe, added the footnote: 'He since, however, became a great moralist.'

But Captain Thicknesse was growing older, and his sons would take little or no notice of his attempts to quarrel with them, and Mrs. Catherine Macaulay, whom he had attacked in another work, had left Bath, and a crowd had attacked the Captain's house because he had caused his man-servant to be taken by a press-gang as a punishment for seducing a maid. His creditors besieged the house, too. The Captain was growing older, and he was growing tired – even of quarrelling. The frills on his shirt-front still bristled like the fins of a fish, his wig and profile looked as martial as ever, but some joy had gone out of life. So the Captain announced that he intended to 'set out for Paris; a journey far preferable, I think, to see the wrangling there than to stay to wrangle here with an old superannuated hero and a mad Doctor'.

So, accompanied by the long-suffering Mrs. Thicknesse and by the aged Jacko, who still rode the chaise horse postillion-wise, mopping and mowing, making queer gestures of anger and defiance at the gathering dust, the Captain set out for France where he spent the remainder of his life. In 1792, just as he was about to start on a journey to Italy, this remarkable old gentleman died, leaving a will which began thus:

'I leave my right hand, to be cut off after my death, to my son Lord Audley; I desire it may be sent to him, in hopes that such a sight may remind him of his duty to God, after having so long abandoned the duty he owed to a father, who once so affectionately loved him.'

Edith Sitwell (1887–1964), *The English Eccentrics*, 1933

'I think myself happier now than the greatest monarch upon earth. He has no such fire-side, nor such pleasant faces about it. Yes, Deborah, we are now growing old; but the evening of our life is likely to be happy. We are descended from ancestors that knew no stain, and we shall leave a good and virtuous race of children behind us. While we live, they will be our support and our pleasure here; and when we die, they will transmit our honour untainted to posterity. Come, my son, we wait for a song: let us have a chorus. But where is my darling Olivia? That little cherub's voice is always sweetest in the concert.' Just as I spoke Dick came running in. 'O Papa, Papa, she is gone from us, she is gone from us forever.' – 'Gone, child!' – 'Yes, she is gone off with two gentlemen in a post-chaise, and one of them kissed her, and said he would die for her: and she cried very much, and was for coming back; but he persuaded her again, and she went into the chaise, and said, 'O what will my poor Papa do when he knows I am undone!' – 'Now then,' cried I, 'my children go and be miserable: for we shall never enjoy one hour more. And O may Heaven's everlasting fury light upon him and his! – Thus to rob me of my child! – And sure it will, for taking back my sweet innocent that I was leading up to heaven. Such sincerity as my child was possessed of! – But all our earthly happiness is now over! Go my children, go and be miserable and infamous; for my heart is broken within me!'

. . . The next morning we missed our wretched child at breakfast, where she used to give life and cheerfulness to us all. My wife . . . attempted to ease her heart by reproaches. 'Never,' cried she, 'shall that vilest stain of our family again darken these harmless doors. I will never call her daughter more. No, let the strumpet live with her vile seducer: she may bring us to shame, but she shall never more deceive us.'

'Wife,' said I, 'do not talk thus hardly: my detestation of her guilt is as great as yours; but ever shall this house and this heart be open to a poor returning repentant sinner. The sooner she returns from her transgressions, the more welcome shall she be to me. For the first time the very best may err; art may persuade, and novelty spread out its charm. The first fault is the child of simplicity, but every other the offspring of guilt. Yes, the wretched creature shall be welcome to this heart and this house, though stained with ten thousand vices. I will again hearken to the music of her voice, again will I hang fondly on her bosom, if I find but repentance there. My son, bring hither my Bible and my staff: I will pursue her, wherever she is; and though I cannot save her from shame, I may prevent the continuance of iniquity.'

Oliver Goldsmith (1730–74), The Vicar of Wakefield

BLOCK CLAIMS CHIP

Among Macmillan's many critics was his own son, Maurice, who once wrote a letter to *The Times* attacking the government in general and his father in particular. By way of reply, Macmillan announced in the House of Commons, 'The member for Halifax [Maurice Macmillan] has intelligence and independence. How he got them is not for me to say.'

L. Harris, The Fine Art of Political Wit, 1965

PAPA OUT OF HUMOUR

27TH DECEMBER, 1883
The third day of Christmas, and not a bit like Christmas; Mamma not well all the time, facial neuralgia, Papa out of humour and hostile to me, so that on every possible occasion he tries to find something nasty to say to me. The other day I was unwell, so that I could not dress even for dinner, and he kept making a mock of me and saying I was like a tipsy soldier's grass widow; I nearly howled and left the table. To-day he told me I was the worst of all his children. There was a time when such treatment would have hurt me more than it does to-day: to-day it enrages me – I do not know why. I must have changed for the worse.

Tatiana Tolstoy (1864–1950), Diary

A LUDICROUSLY GLARING UNFITNESS

. . . the Matador proposed to appoint his son Colonel of the Middlesex Milita. Since he himself had loved soldiering, he thought no doubt that this was a piece of luck for his son. His son took a different view. 'Your proposition gave me a stomach-ache all this morning,' he wrote to him. 'I do not know whether I have sufficiently recovered my equanimity to write intelligibly, but I will try. First then as to my inclinations. I detest soldiering beyond measure. As far as taste goes I would sooner be at the treadmill.' He went on to say that he would not be able to combine his duties as a soldier with those at the House of Commons as his health would not stand it, and he ended: 'I have said nothing about my unfitness for the post for that is your responsibility not mine; and it is so ludicrously glaring that you cannot have overlooked it. The only point that affects me, the exposure to extreme contempt that I must face, will be rather a benefit to me than otherwise; for spite of many strenuous efforts at self-steeling, I care much too much for other people's contempt; and therefore the more I meet with it, the better for me.'

His father accepted his refusal; but it cannot have improved relations between the two.

David Cecil (1902–85), *The Cecils of Hatfield House*, 1973

GEORGE III IS NOT AMUSED

From an early age, the Prince of Wales irritated his father, thus giving some portents of the traditionally stormy relationship between King and heir. When shut out of his father's dressing-room one day, as a boy of ten, the Prince of Wales retaliated by shouting 'Wilkes and Liberty!' through the keyhole. To His Majesty, the radical journalist John Wilkes was the devil incarnate; but whether the King was infuriated by his son's impudence, or laughed it off 'with his accustomed good-humour', depends on whose version one reads. The boy particularly resented being made to wear a baby's cambric frock with lace cuffs, long after seeing other children of his age wearing more suitable clothes. To servants, he would complain in exasperation how his father treated him, seizing his lace collar and complaining bitterly that he was to be kept looking like a baby.

This mischievous child grew up to be a mischievous adult. When he was twelve, the King complained to Holderness that the Prince did not apply himself to his work; he showed 'duplicity' and had a 'bad habit . . . of not speaking the truth.' Naturally intelligent, he was inclined to be lazy, unlike the more honest, lively and industrious Frederick, whose conduct and progress pleased his father and tutors far more.

King George loved his children when they were small, but as they grew up he became less fond of them. As a parent, he was over-protective, attempting to teach his sons the virtues of rigorous simplicity, hard work and punctuality. The boys must be beaten at the first signs of laziness, and it distressed their sisters to see their two eldest brothers being held by their tutors and thrashed with a long whip.

John Van Der Kiste, *George III's Children*, 1992

HE WOULD NOT YIELD . . .

At 50, Wimpole Street marriage was a forbidden subject. Browning, who detested underhand methods, had to be convinced that it would be worse than useless to ask for Mr. Barrett's consent. 'If a Prince of Eldorado should come,' Miss Barrett once remarked to her sister, 'with a pedigree of lineal descent from some signory in the moon in one hand, and a ticket of good behaviour from the nearest Independent Chapel in the other -' (for Mr. Barrett was a staunch Nonconformist) – 'Why, even *then*,' said Arabel, 'it would not *do*.' 'You might as well think,' Miss Barrett assured her lover, 'to sweep off a third of the stars of heaven with the motion of your eyelashes. He would rather see me dead at his feet than yield the point; he will say so and mean it, and persist in the meaning.'

W. Hall Griffin, *The Life of Robert Browning*, 1938

. . . AND HE NEVER WOULD FORGIVE

The prisoner of Chillon, we are told, 'regained his freedom with a sigh.' As much may be said, with a difference, of Mrs. Browning. Her sighs were all for her father's unrelenting temper. Neither then nor later did he forgive his daughter. She wrote repeatedly to him, but no reply was vouchsafed. Five years later, being on a visit to London with her husband and her child, she made a final and ineffectual appeal. Browning also wrote. To him a violent answer was returned, accompanied by all the letters which his wife had written, unopened and with the seals unbroken. There is no need to say more upon this painful topic. Mrs. Browning had counted the cost of her action, and was not unprepared for its results. What she gained was immeasurably greater than what she lost. 'By to-morrow at this time,' she had written to her husband, the night before they left London, 'I shall have *you* only, to love me . . . You *only!* As if one said *God only*. And we shall have *Him* beside, I pray of Him.' Her choice was triumphantly vindicated; and the letters which she wrote to her friends during the remainder of her life are the best and most illuminative comment on these impassioned and most touching words.

W. Hall Griffin, *The Life of Robert Browning*, 1938

PAPA WILL PREACH

I understand the old boy is exceedingly out of humour and I am in hourly expectation of a thunderstorm from that quarter. Fatherly admonitions at our time of life are very unpleasant and of no use; it is a pity he should expend his breath or his time in such fruitless labour. I wonder which of us two he looks upon with least eyes of affection.

Prince William (1765–1837), to the Prince of Wales, 16 February 1788

NO APPROBATION

[?*Aug. 1784*] By your letter of the 2d of last month I see by the good management of Major General de Budé he has been able to assist you in discharging some debts you have made. I cannot too strongly set before your eyes that if you permit yourself to indulge every foolish idea you must be wretched all your life, for with thirteen children I can but with the greatest care make both ends meet and am not in a situation to be paying their debts if the[y] contract any, and to anyone that has either the sentiments of common honesty or delicacy, without the nicer feelings which every gentleman ought to possess, the situation of not paying what is due is a very unpleasant sensation. In you I fear that vanity which has been too predominant in your character has occasioned this, but I hope for the future you will be wiser. I cannot conclude without saying that I wish you had profited as much by my sending you to Hanover as Frederick has the commendation of all ranks of people. His civility and propriety are remarked by all that come from thence, but I am sorry to say your manners are still compared, as I too well saw when you returned from America, to the frequenters of the forecastle, and your love of improper company, particularly of some ill behaved Englishmen that have been at Hanover. This intelligence does not come from any that attend you, and therefore I have not hinted to Budé that I know this, but you may easily believe nothing can pass at Hanover that I am not acquainted with. I mention this that you may reflect on your conduct and consider that a Prince is to be an example to others, that by the propriety of your conduct I can alone with justice to my country advance you in your profession; that the levity which was natural in a boy must ill become you now that when you return to sea you must be the Prince, the gentleman and the officer, which requires ideas I fear as yet you have not turned your mind to. I have here given you the advice of an affectionate father. It is not by promises I am to be lulled; I shall by your future conduct watch whether my advice takes any real effect and then you will ever find me [etc.]

George III (1738–1820), to Prince William

TH'UNGUIDED DAYS

King. Most subject is the fattest soil to weeds,
And he, the noble image of my youth,
Is overspread with them; therefore my grief
Stretches itself beyond the hour of death.
The blood weeps from my heart when I do shape
In forms imaginary th'unguided days
And rotten times that you shall look upon
When I am sleeping with my ancestors.
For when his headstrong riot hath no curb,
When rage and hot blood are his counsellors,
When means and lavish manners meet together,
O, with what wings shall his affections fly
Towards fronting peril and oppos'd decay!

William Shakespeare (1564–1616), *Henry IV*, Part 2

Frank Gilmore could love his sons until they defied or challenged his rule. Once that happened, he treated them as his worst enemies. It was as if my father perceived any act of defiance by his sons as a denial of their love for him, and love's denial had already cost him his heart too much in his life. As a grown and strong man, he did not have to abide such a refusal from children.

The pattern of my father's temper hadn't changed all that much from the previous years when the family was on the road – that is, any infraction or displeasing act was enough to invoke a punishment – but the methods of correction had changed considerably. Instead of spankings, my father now administered fierce beatings, by means of razor straps and belts, and sometimes with his bare, clenched fists. With each blow that was thrown, my father was issuing the command that his children love him. With each blow that landed they learned instead to hate, and to annihilate their own faith in love.

'This is something you never really saw about him,' my brother Frank told me one day. 'When Dad got angry at somebody he knew no limits. He wouldn't have cared what he did. He would come at you with his razor strap, and he'd really bring that thing down on you. He was merciless at those times. We would end up with cuts and bruises all over us, though he was careful not to leave marks on our faces, or anyplace else where other people might see them.'

Apparently the beatings were commonplace affairs – that is, if you can ever call the pounding of a child commonplace. On an at least weekly basis, my father would whip either Frank Jr. or Gary, or more likely both of them at the same time, until my mother would insist that the beating stop. Usually the punishments were the result of small matters – for example, one of the boys forgetting to mow the lawn behind the backyard tree – but just as often they seemed to occur as the result of my father's bad whims. Frank Jr. gave me an example of such an occasion. 'One time,' he said, 'when Gary and I came home from school, Dad was hiding behind the door and we didn't even know it. We got in the door, we heard the door shut, and the next thing we knew we were getting razor-strapped across the back. He really went wild that night, because we were something like five minutes late – and I'm not kidding when I say five minutes. I don't even remember *why* we were late, maybe the schoolteacher stopped us and talked, or maybe we visited with a friend. I can't remember. I just remember he was hiding behind the door with the razor strap. We didn't even get a chance to give an explanation, and we got whacked I don't know how many times.'

On another occasion, some money had been stolen off my father's desk. He gathered Frank and Gary before him and asked which of them had taken it. Frank knew Gary had stolen the money, and though he was angry at his brother for doing so, he wasn't about to tell on him. 'If that's the way you want it, then you'll both get the whipping,' my father said, with the logic of a gym teacher or army sergeant or some similar small-time despot. That night he doubled up the strap – it could do more damage that way – and flailed his sons until they bled through their jeans. With each thrash, he called them thieves. Later, Frank asked my father if he would still have whipped him if he'd said that Gary had stolen the money. 'Of course I would have whipped you,' my father said. 'Nobody likes a damn squealer.' That night Frank learned that, one way or another, he was bound to pay for his brother's crimes.

'When Dad would grab the razor strap and go haywire on us,' Frank told me, 'he wasn't talking to us about anything that we'd done wrong, nor was he telling us how we needed to improve our behavior. It was simply that we had upset him. He was angry with us and this was his way of getting revenge. He wasn't doing it to teach us anything, except possibly to fear him. That was the reason he punished us: not to make us better, but to make us sorry.'

Mikal Gilmore, *Shot in the Heart*, 1994

A NAUSEOUS BEAST

Frederick Louis had remained in the background for some years after his arrival in England from Hanover on the death of George the First. Once, however, he had learnt the English tongue, and become aware of his own importance as Prince of Wales, he entered with avidity into opposition against his parents. He was a weak character, fond of adulation, and easily led by flatterers. He had cast himself in the royal family drama, of which he was the author, as a man of intrigue; but he so overacted his part that he finally found himself expelled from his father's Court, and an enemy of the King and Queen for life.

The reason for George the Second's decision to be rid of his son is explained in the following letter that he wrote to the Prince of Wales following the latter's treatment of his wife – Augusta of Saxe-Gotha – during her pregnancy. Frederick Louis had no comprehensible explanation for his actions, and left his parents to suspect that Augusta's first-born had been brought in to the lying-in chamber in a warming-pan, as was suggested of Mary Beatrice of Modena's son. 'That nauseous beast,' exclaimed Princess Caroline, 'is capable of anything – even *that*!'

September 10, 1737

The professions you have lately made in your letters of your particular regard to me are so contradictory to all your actions that I cannot suffer myself to be imposed upon by them.

You know very well you did not give the least intimation to me, or the Queen, that the Princess was with child or breeding, until within less than a month of the birth of the young Princess. You removed the Princess [Augusta] twice in the week immediately preceding the day of delivery from the place of my residence, in expectation, as you have voluntarily declared, of her labour; and both times upon your return, you industriously concealed from the knowledge of me, and the Queen, every circumstances relating to this important affair. And you at last, without giving any notice to me, or the Queen, precipitately hurried the Princess from Hampton Court in a condition not to be named. After having thus, in execution of your own determined measures, exposed both the Princess and her child to the greatest perils, you now plead surprise and tenderness for the Princess, as the only motives that occasioned these repeated indignities offered to me and the Queen, your mother.

This extravagant and undutiful behaviour, in so essential a point as the birth of an heir to my Crown, is such an evidence of your premeditated defiance of me, and such a contempt of my authority, and of the natural right belonging to your parents as cannot be excused by the pretended innocence of your intentions, nor palliated or disguised by specious words only.

But the whole tenor of your conduct for a considerable time has been so entirely void of all real duty to me that I have long had reason to be highly offended with you.

And until you withdraw your regard and confidence from those by whose instigation and advice you are directed and encouraged in your unwarrantable behaviour to me and to the Queen, and until you return to your duty, you shall not reside in my Palace; which I will not suffer to be made the resort of them who, under the appearance of an attachment to you, foment the division which you have made in my family, and thereby weaken the common interest of the whole.

In this situation I will receive no reply; but when your actions manifest a just sense of your duty and submission, that may induce me to pardon what at present I most justly resent.

In the meantime, it is my pleasure that you leave St. James's with all your family, when it can be done without prejudice or inconvenience to the Princess. I shall for the present leave to the Princess the care of my granddaughter until a proper time calls upon me to consider of her education.

George II (1683–1760), Intimate Letters of England's Kings,
ed. M. Sanders, 1959

A NEW MANIFESTO FOR MARX

I feel myself suddenly invaded by doubt and ask myself if your heart is equal to your intelligence and spiritual qualities, if it is open to the tender feelings which here on earth are so great a source of consolation for a sensitive soul; I wonder whether the peculiar demon, to which your heart is manifestly a prey, is the Spirit of God or that of Faust. I ask myself – and this is not the least of the doubts that assail my heart – if you will ever know a simple happiness and family joys, and render happy those who surround you. . . .

Alas, your conduct has consisted merely in disorder, meandering in all the fields of knowledge, musty traditions by sombre lamplight; degeneration in a learned dressing gown with uncombed hair has replaced degeneration with a beer glass. And a shirking unsociability and a refusal of all conventions and even all respect for your father. Your intercourse with the world is limited to your sordid room, where perhaps lie abandoned in the classical disorder the love letters of a Jenny and the tear-stained counsels of your father . . . And do you think that here in this workshop of senseless and aimless learning you can ripen the fruits to bring you and your loved one happiness? . . . As though we were made of gold my gentleman-son disposes of almost 700 thalers in a single year, in contravention of every agreement and every usage, whereas the richest spend no more than 500.

Heinrich Marx (1782–1838), letter to his son Karl Marx, November 1837

It was not long after the episode of *The Picture of Dorian Gray* that I attempted to murder my father. The attempt was, unfortunately, unsuccessful.

Of all the failures in my life, and there have been many, this is the one that I regret most keenly. Had I succeeded I should have had no spark of pity or remorse; my sleep, for many years would have been easier. As Wilde said, through the lips of Lord Henry . . . 'All the great crimes of the world are committed in the brain.' (Perhaps he had forgotten that Christ on a previous occasion had expressed the same conviction.)

In my brain I murdered my father, not once, but many times.

On one of his frequent visits, the family doctor reproved my father for taking four tablets of aspirin. 'In your present condition,' he said, 'it is putting a strain on your heart.' Here, I thought, was a method in which I might well make some experiments – the classical tradition of the overdose.

Fate was kind, on that long summer holiday which marked the beginning and the climax of my efforts. My brothers were both away; our staff had been reduced, by one of the recurrent financial crises, to a single maid, of a somnolent disposition. It therefore devolved upon me to take up the tray containing my father's evening meal, which was usually some form of soup or broth, as he could not eat anything solid.

Here, then, was a chance. I bicycled over to the neighbouring town of Newton Abbot, and purchased a bottle of aspirin from an obscure chemist. I chose a market day, for safety's sake, and as I entered the shop I held a handkerchief over my face as though my nose were bleeding, and turned away my head as I handed the money across the counter.

From this bottle, which I hid in an old pair of shoes, I extracted sixteen tablets of five grains each, making a total dose of eighty grains. This was four times the amount against which the doctor had warned him.

Just before the bell rang for dinner, at seven-thirty, I took a toothglass, crushed the tablets to a powder, and poured water on them. Then I ran downstairs and concealed the glass behind a bowl of flowers. It would be an easy matter to take it up with the tray, to pause outside the door and to mix the aspirin with the broth.

Everything seemed to be working perfectly; I felt calm, almost disinterested, and certainly in no way guilty. Does any man feel guilty when he strikes at the fangs of a snake, particularly when the snake is creeping towards one he loves? As I took the tray from my mother I smiled. 'You are very cheerful this evening,' she said. I nodded and went out whistling. I remember that I whistled the first few bars of an intermezzo by Brahms; I also remember that the glass containing the aspirin had been hidden behind a silver bowl filled with fuschias, and that a single scarlet petal had fallen into it. It was the work of a moment to mix the drug. A few seconds later I had opened the door and was standing by his bed.

Good. He was sitting up, which meant that his great body would not have to be heaved into position. He looked even more repulsive than usual, for he was feeling sentimental. At any moment he might break into the familiar, maudlin theme of 'I'm no good to anybody . . . I'm a bad father . . . you'd be better off without me . . .' – a theme which always reduced my mother to tears. Studying his face, which I hoped would soon be twitching in its last convulsions, I thought of the picture of Dorian Gray, and the subtle line of hypocrisy which had been the first sign of corruption to fall across the canvas.

'You're too good to me,' he moaned, holding out his hands.

Better than you guess, I thought.

Usually, when he absorbed his soup, I turned away, even at the risk of spilling it. I have always been physically fastidious; too easily nauseated by the leprous side of Nature's face; at the sick-bed and in hospitals I am a coward. But on this occasion I watched every detail with pleasurable attention – the red, loose lips closing over the edge of the bowl like some questing slug, the gulp, gulp of the thick neck – even the drops of fluid that congregated on the fringe of his moustache.

He lay back, licking his lips, sucking in the last drops.

'Too good to me,' he murmured.

Should I stay and watch? No. There might be unpleasant manifestations. I carried the bowl to the wash-stand, swilled it with water, and tiptoed out of the room.

'He drank it all,' I said to my mother, when I returned to the dining-room.

'Let's hope so.'

'Shall we have some music? Would it disturb him?'

'Not if you play softly.'

I played the first movement of Beethoven's Moonlight Sonata, for this is a piece which any intelligent child can play with his eyes shut, and my fingers had begun to tremble. After that I played some of the transcriptions of César Franck's organ chorales; they had a piercing purity; they built ladders of song to the throne of God. One had the right to such music, at such a time.

Then the dream was broken; there was a cry in the distance.

My mother started to her feet.

I stopped playing. 'What is it?'

'I thought I heard something.' She was looking up towards the ceiling.

'It was nothing.'

'Yes . . . there it is again. I must go to him.'

I put my hand on her arm: I was playing for time; every second counted now; the longer he was left alone the greater chance that he would die.

'You'll only distress yourself,' I said.

'I can't help that.'

'Let *me* go, for once.'

'You . . . you really want to?'

'I'll see to everything.'

I sped up the long dark staircase; panic was close on my heels, but even so, there was hope as well. 'Oh, God, please let him die!' I whispered. 'Please let him die!'

I flung open the door.

He was sitting on a chair in the middle of the room, clad only in a shrunken vest. He was tugging on his boots.

I stood in the doorway, open-mouthed. What had happened? My eyes wandered from him to the bed, where I had expected to see his corpse.

Then I understood. The bed was not a pretty sight; he had been violently sick. Whatever had been inside him a few minutes ago was certainly there no longer.

I wanted to laugh and to cry; most of all, with that beastliness a few feet away, I wanted to be sick myself.

'Clear up that bloody mess.'

I gulped. 'Yes, father.'

He looked up with a start; I had been standing in a dim light and his back had been half turned to me; he had been under the impression that he was addressing my mother.

'Oh, it's you, my dear?' he whined, with a quick change of tone, for he was cadging for favour. 'I'm afraid I've been rather ill.'

'So I see.'

'Can't think what it was. Perhaps it was the soup.'

'D'you feel better now?'

'Quite all right . . . quite all right. Thought I'd come downstairs for a bit.'

I went to clear up the mess.

On the following day my father was in very good spirits. He walked for two miles in the early morning, devoured an enormous breakfast, and in the afternoon he rolled the lawn.

So ended my first attempt at murder. There were to be others, but never again would I try my luck with any sort of poison. It was like trying to poison an ox. This man's stomach – apart from being stronger than steel, must obviously have a special technique of its own, merely through his extraordinary capacity for vomiting. He had trained himself to be sick as easily and as casually as the average man would comb his hair . . .

The occasion of the third attempt to murder my father can be precisely dated. It was shortly before eleven o'clock on the night of Saturday, March 31st, 1929. This is not a date that I am likely to forget.

He was at the end of Stage Four – the delirium stage – on Monday, March 26th. This, as I observed to my mother, hanging up my coat in the hall of the Haunted House at the end of a long day's rehearsal, was most propitious. Yes, she agreed – and it is a sign of our lunatic existence that she said it with no irony – nothing could have been more fortunate. She counted on her fingers. Yes. It meant that on Wednesday, March 28th, he would be up and about again. And that on the following Monday, April 2nd, the day of the first night, he would be right in the middle of his 'good' period.

Then she said this fatal thing. 'Do you think he might go up to the cottage for a few days? To . . . to recuperate?'

'By himself?'

'It might be better if he went alone, just for once. Besides, he'll have the Watsons to look after him.'

The Watsons were a couple whom I had engaged a few weeks before. They had settled down very well. Mrs Watson was an adequate cook and her husband was a competent rough gardener. More important, as far as the present circumstances were concerned, he was a tough ex-Guardsman, who would be able to deal with any emergency requiring physical force.

Although the conception was revolutionary, I accepted it. On the morning of Wednesday, March 28th, my father, with a great deal of trembling and fussing and polishing of his eyeglass, was lumbered into a hired motor-car, and set off for the rural delights of Huntingdonshire.

Had he only known it, he was driving very near to his death.

. . . I headed for the Great North Road. If I drove fast I should be in time to 'make the tour' – to walk down the paths, bending low over every bed, alert for the signs and tokens of spring. Of all the pleasures that life has offered, this has been the keenest – returning to a garden that one loves, finding out what has happened while one has been away – how many buds have broken, how many green spears have thrust through the expectant earth. Even in the depths of winter I have gone out in the small hours of the morning with a lighted torch, to scrape away the snow from some distant corner, in the hope of finding a glint of early gold.

Dusk was falling when I turned into the lane leading to the cottage and, as always, there was a sense of leaving the cares of life behind, of stepping into a secret world – a world where a hush lay over the meadows, like the mists that drifted from the wide meandering streams, where the ancient willows spoke in whispers. Now came the familiar bend in the road, the glimpse of a thatched roof, the sudden view of white walls sturdily timbered. If I had to choose the happiest moment in my life I should take this moment. Half past five, or thereabouts, on the evening of March 31st, 1929. Behind me the sweet smell of success, all around me, peace, ahead of me the chance of a miracle – the chance that I might meet the man who was my father, actually *meet* him as a father. What would he be like? If it came to that, what would it be like to have a father at all?

The answer was not long in coming.

Something was wrong. The cottage was not welcoming me. There were no lights in the windows; the door was not opened by a beaming housekeeper. The cottage was hostile, possessed by an evil spirit. This was no matter of imagination; it was the communication of a psychic fact. I knew.

I leant back in the car, noting with the acumen of a trained reporter the familiar spasms and contractions in my stomach. So we were home again – home, sweet home. Home to the refuge that I had built so painfully, and tried to make so beautiful.

I drove the car into the wooden garage. Yes, there was something very wrong. A pile of peat lay in a corner, carelessly spilt over an oily floor. Stacked against the wall was a bundle of shrubs, their roots exposed and dry. Watson would never have let this happen. As I closed the doors and walked round to the front entrance I noticed that no smoke was coming from the chimneys.

I opened the door. The cottage was silent, with the curious acid silence that lingers in the wake of a violent quarrel. No lamps were lit, but there was enough light to see a sheet of paper glimmering on the old oak table in the hall. I took it up and read it by the light of a torch – the same torch that had been designed for a happier purpose. It was a letter from the Watsons, informing me that my father's behaviour had been so monstrous that they could no longer stay in the house, that they had been obliged to give immediate notice, that they had left their keys at the village post office, and that though they regretted being forced to take such a drastic step, they were sure that I would 'understand'.

Of course I 'understood'. They had been forced to endure for three days the society of a man whom I had suffered for thirty years. It was more than 'understandable' that he had been too much for them. Meanwhile, I stood there alone with something waiting in the next room. Well . . . one had been through it all before. I kept the torch alight, and walked in.

He was lying in a heap by the empty grate. His fly-buttons were undone; he had been sick on his waistcoat, and the room was filled with a most unpleasant odour. I was so accustomed to this sort of situation that these details hardly seemed important; it would be merely a question of routine – doing-up the fly-buttons, wiping-up the vomit, rinsing-out of the clothes under the tap. And all the rest of it.

But what suddenly gave a touch of drama to these familiar chores was the sight of a shattered ornament lying in his hand. This was the small china figure on which I had set particular store – the figure of a shepherdess with rosy cheeks, whom I had discovered walled up in a secret cabinet some months before. She was a person of great sweetness and distinction, and I had planned to write a story about her. Now she lay shattered, with his hairy fingers round her neck. It was a small consolation that in falling, a fragment of china had cut into his wrist, so that his dark blood oozed on to the coconut matting.

Home sweet home. I walked over to the window and looked out. There would still be time to 'make the tour'.

Included in my abundant literary output over the years are a number of detective novels, and I sometimes wonder whether they may have gained authenticity from the fact that they were composed by a man who has actually planned a murder in cold blood.

My first thought was that I might leave him there to die. The fire was out; for several hours he would be unable to hoist himself off the coconut matting; and in the meantime the windows could be opened to let in the cold. (It was growing colder every minute. There was snow in the air.) I could wrench off his jacket and tug off his shoes and force another glass of whisky down his throat, so that he would stay there long enough to freeze to death.

But would it be cold enough? And *would* he die? Might it not be necessary to call in a doctor? Might he not recover, and the whole hideous cycle begin again? Might I not be faced with some difficult problems about why I had delayed seeking medical assistance?

All these questions I pondered while standing over him, shivering, hungry, and very much alone (still remembering my ludicrous ideal of 'meeting my father', an hour ago).

No, I decided, it would not be cold enough. I must get him outside, and keep him there. This meant giving him a double dose of the sleeping pills which my mother had packed for him. They had been prescribed by the latest in the endless succession of his doctors, and he had been warned that in no circumstances must he combine them with alcohol. So much the better. Nobody could prove that he had not taken them himself. I went upstairs, and found them in his sponge-bag, which he had not troubled to open since his arrival. Then I came down and thrust them into his mouth, under the damp black moustache.

As I started to tug him across the floor, one of his eyes opened, and blinked. It reminded me of the eye of an octopus. (Many years later, in a book written, ironically enough, for children, I was to use the eye of an octopus as an instrument of terror.) But the going was hard; it was like dragging a ton of bricks. He weighed seventeen stone and was proud of it. He gloated in his stomach and puffed out his belly on social occasions; obesity, to him, was synonymous with bonhomie.

I dragged this seventeen stone of flesh through the french windows, into the night. His close-cropped head bumped on the kerb of the porch, and as it did so, the octopus eye opened again for a moment. There was life in the old boy yet. Where to deposit him? Not too far. There would be footprints to explain. And many accusing pointers, written in mud and slush, for now it had begun to snow in earnest. The best place would be just outside the window, among the tangled branches of an old rose-bush. They would lacerate his face, and if there were any odd blood-stains to be accounted for, they would confuse the issue.

A few last heaves and tugs and seventeen stone of paternity was deposited in a prickly shrub, with the snow coming down. No octopus eye, this time. Not a sound. Not a movement.

Then I went into my study, lit the fire, sat down at the piano, and set it all to music. It came out as a sort of furious and disjointed étude, and because I had been denied the opportunity to learn the elementary grammar of composition, it was a thing of shreds and tatters, with sharps where there should have been flats, with rests in the wrong places, and quavers where there should have been semi-quavers. I had an aching desire for musical relief . . . it was all there, in my mind, in my heart, in my soul. But He had tied my fingers and broken, or almost broken, my spirit. But not quite. The hours went by and at last the first draft of the piece was finished. It was rough and amateurish but some of the pain and the passion came through. Which is why I shall publish it at the end of this book; some pianist with the necessary technique may care to study it, if only as a musical curiosity.

By now it was past midnight. The fire had died in the grate, and in my heart. But I had said my say, through the only medium in which I was qualified to say it, and I was no longer cold. I closed the piano, and prepared to go outside.

And then – there was a crash and a splintering of wood, and he fell into the room, covered with snow, with blood streaming down his face.

Beverley Nichols (1901–83), *Father Figure*, 1972

ELEVEN

In Memoriam

After my father died I had slept for two days without interruption. I wrote, at the end of a play: 'I'd been told of all the things you're meant to feel. Sudden freedom, growing up, the end of dependence, the step into the sunlight when no one is taller than you and you're in no one's shadow. I know what I felt. Lonely.'

John Mortimer, *Clinging to the Wreckage*, 1972

WHEN DID YOU LAST SEE YOUR FATHER?

When did you last see your father? Was it when they burnt the coffin? Put the lid on it? When he exhaled his last breath? When he last sat up and said something? When he last recognized me? When he last smiled? When he last did something for himself unaided? When he last felt healthy? When he last thought he might be healthy, before they brought the news? The weeks before he left us, or life left him, were a series of depletions; each day we thought 'he can't get less like himself than this,' and each day he did. I keep trying to find the last moment when he was still unmistakably there, in the fullness of his being, *him.*

When did you last see your father? I sit at my desk in the mortuary-cold basement of the new house, the one he helped me buy, his pace-maker in an alcove above my word processor, and the shelves of books have no more meaning than to remind me: these are the first shelves I ever put up without him. I try to write, but there is only one subject, him. I watch the news: Yugoslavia, the General Election, the royal separations – the news he didn't live to see. I've lost sight not only of his life, what it meant and added up to, but of mine. When my three children come back from school, their cries echo emptily round the house and I feel I'm giving no more than a stranger could give them – drinks, attention, bedtime stories. Never to have loved seems best: love means two people getting too close; it means people wanting to be with each other all the time, and then one of them dying and leaving the other bereft. A fox comes trotting up the lawn towards my window, printing itself in the dew, as though it owned the place. I feel as if an iron plate had come down through the middle of me, as if I were locked inside the blackness of myself. I thought that to see my father dying might remove my fear of death, and so it did. I hadn't reckoned on its making death seem preferable to life.

Blake Morrison, *And When Did You Last See Your Father?*, 1993

WOUNDS

Here are two pictures from my father's head –
I have kept them like secrets until now:
First, the Ulster Division at the Somme
Going over the top with 'Fuck the Pope!'
'No Surrender!': a boy about to die,
Screaming 'Give 'em one for the Shankill!'
'Wilder than Gurkhas' were my father's words
Of admiration and bewilderment.
Next comes the London/Scottish padre
Resettling kilts with his swagger-stick,
With a stylish backhand and a prayer.
Over a landscape of dead buttocks
My father followed him for fifty years.
At last, a belated casualty,
He said – lead traces flaring till they hurt –
'I am dying for King and Country, slowly.'
I touched his hand, his thin head I touched.

Now, with military honours of a kind,
With his badges, his medals like rainbows,
His spinning compass, I bury beside him
Three teenage soldiers, bellies full of
Bullets and Irish beer, their flies undone.
A packet of Woodbines I throw in,
A lucifer, the Sacred Heart of Jesus
Paralysed as heavy guns put out
The night-light in a nursery for ever;
Also a bus-conductor's uniform –
He collapsed beside his carpet-slippers
Without a murmur, shot through the head
By a shivering boy who wandered in
Before they could turn the television down
Or tidy away the supper dishes.
To the children, to a bewildered wife,
I think 'Sorry Missus' was what he said.

Michael Longley, *Poems, 1963–1983,* 1986

HE PLAYED AT BEING A FATHER

He never gave his whole heart to anyone, though he tried. 'My most profound feelings have remained always solitary and have found in human things no companionship,' he wrote. 'The sea, the stars, the night wind in waste places, mean more to me than even the human beings I love best, and I am conscious that human affection is to me at bottom an attempt to escape from the vain search for God.'

We who loved him were secondary to the sea and stars and the absent God; we were not loved for ourselves, but as bridges out of loneliness. We were part of a charade of togetherness acted by a fundamentally solitary person. He played at being a father in the same way, and he acted the part to perfection, but his heart was elsewhere and his combination of inner detachment and outer affection caused me much muddled suffering.

Katherine Tait, *My Father Bertrand Russell*, 1975

THE LESSON

'Your father's gone,' my bald headmaster said.
His shiny dome and brown tobacco jar
Splintered at once in tears. It wasn't grief.
I cried for knowledge which was bitterer
Than any grief. For there and then I knew
That grief has uses – that a father dead
Could bind the bully's fist a week or two;
And then I cried for shame, then for relief.

I was a month past ten when I learnt this:
I still remember how the noise was stilled
In school-assembly when my grief came in.
Some goldfish in a bowl quietly sculled
Around their shining prison on its shelf.
They were indifferent. All the other eyes
Were turned towards me. Somewhere in myself
Pride like a goldfish flashed a sudden fin.

Edward Lucie-Smith, *A Tropical Childhood and Other Poems*, 1961

A GREAT BROODING PRESENCE

One detected his presence as soon as one walked into the pretty hall, with its white and black stone floor, its glass chandelier in the well of the staircase. His presence sometimes exuded from the library on the left in a sort of miasma compounded of Havana cigar smoke and gin, or it might come bursting out of the drawing-room on the right, in a great shout of laughter accompanied by the smell of lavender; he always put Yardley's Lavender Hair Tonic on his head when he changed for dinner – a line long since discontinued, I believe. One might have thought he would have preferred some expensive preparation from Trumper's of Curzon Street, where he went to have his hair cut. It was a gentle agreeable smell which I always associated with the more festive aspects of home life.

In the pink bathroom, to which I was taken within minutes of my first arrival in this strange house, there was a printed postcard stuck above the cistern: *From Mr Evelyn Waugh, Piers Court, Stinchcombe, Nr Dursley, Gloucestershire. Dursley 2150.* Underneath it, in his own handwriting, was written: 'Should the handle fail to return to the horizontal when the flow of water ceases, please agitate it slightly until it succeeds.'

I read that message every time I urinated at home for the next eleven years, and never ceased to resent it. The downstairs lavatory in the front of the house, decorated with Abyssinian paintings, with an armchair seat upholstered in leopard skin, was out of bounds to children. So was the butler's lavatory immediately behind the business room on the other side of the baize door. Every servant had his lavatory, according to degree, down to some outside earth closets for the gardeners. Quite possibly they all had notices in my father's handwriting, with instructions about what to do at every stage of the process.

The presence, as I say, was overwhelming. He was a small man – scarcely five foot six in his socks – and only a writer, after all, but I have seen generals and chancellors of the exchequer, six foot six and exuding self-importance from every pore, quail in front of him. When he laughed, everyone laughed, when he was downcast, everyone tiptoed around trying to make as little noise as possible. It was not wealth or power which created this effect, merely the force of his personality. I do not see how he could have been pleased by the effect he produced on other people. In fact he spent his life seeking out men and women who were not frightened of him. Even then, he usually ended up getting drunk with them, as a way out of the abominable problem of human relations.

Which is a little sad when one reflects that all he really wanted to do in company was to make jokes, to turn the world upside down and laugh at it, to enrich and enliven this vale of tears with a little fantasy. The important questions of man's relationship to God and man's responsibility for material or spiritual welfare of his fellow men could be left to private contemplation. The main purpose of human association was to share enjoyment of the world's absurdity.

One can easily forget the times when he was happy and witty and gay. He was a master of farcical invention: anything pompous or false would be turned on its head, magnified a thousand times and reduced to absurdity, usually by a process of exaggerated agreement. He would invent elaborate fantasies about the neighbours – how the local dentist, called McMeekin, had a face like a ham, and shook hands so violently that he invariably crushed the fingers of his patients. He would train us to make 'poop, poop' noises every time we passed the house of a neighbour called Lady Tubbs. But it is impossible to do justice to this fugitive art by quotation, as Boswell proves time and again, and I certainly will not try. Timing and immediacy are essential to it, but so is atmosphere. Unlike Sydney Smith, Evelyn Waugh left a corpus of beautifully polished writing as a permanent memorial to his genius, and that must suffice. But he needed an audience which could respond intelligently; whenever he met incomprehension he was liable to be reduced to the most appalling gloom. It was this, more than anything else, which he dreaded, and which made him shun strangers with a rudeness which never failed to make people gasp. 'Why do you expect me to talk to this boring pig?' he would suddenly shout at his hostess about some fellow guest. 'He is common, he is ignorant and he is stupid, and he thinks Picasso is an important artist.'

It was this fear which accounted for the coldness and exasperation towards his children when they were young, although at least one of them gave him further reason to be exasperated. There could be no mistaking the relief of his children when he was absent, the great brooding presence was removed. Children could charge through the house, making as much noise as they liked. Outrageous breakages could be perpetrated, and the chances were that my mother would try to cover them up and conceal them before the monster's return.

The most terrifying aspect of Evelyn Waugh as a parent was that he reserved the right not just to deny affection to his children but to advertise an acute and unqualified dislike of them. This was always conditional on their own behaviour up to a point, and seldom entirely unjustified, but it was disconcerting, nevertheless, to be met by cool statements of total repudiation.

As the number of children increased – by 1950 there were six of us – he spent longer periods away from home, much to the relief of us all. As I have said, even at the time, I half-suspected that he was aware of the relief we felt when he was away, that his great act of disliking his children and shunning their company was at any rate in part an acknowledgement of his tragic inability to relax with them.

In fact the most welcome aspect of him, as a parent, was his lack of interest in his children, at any rate until they were much older and became fit subjects for gossip. I have described how no noise could be made in the front of the house, but that was as far as the reign of terror extended. So long as we were out of sight and sound, we could do whatever we wanted. In that sense, he was a permissive, even indulgent parent. At the age of ten or eleven I announced that I was interested in chemistry – I never studied it at school, but neither of my parents would have known that – and wished to make some chemical experiments for Christmas. Papa thought this a capital idea, and asked for a list.

In addition to the usual glass tubing and spirit lamps, I wanted a Wolff jar for distilling alcohol, large quantities of sulphur, saltpetre and charcoal, for making gunpowder some concentrated sulphuric and hydrochloric acids for various unspecified experiments I had in mind, and large quantities of nitric acid and glycerine as I was interested in the idea of going into the commercial production of nitroglycerine as an explosive. All these things were acquired for me from a chemical supplier in London at extraordinarily low cost, and the Court Room at the back of the house was set aside for my experiments. The only substance on which he failed me was prussic (or hydro-cyanic) acid which the supplier refused to produce. Papa said I was not to worry, he was sure he could get some through the porter at White's, but none ever materialized.

Not many parents, I believe, would be prepared to give their sons of nine or ten bottles of concentrated sulphuric, hydrochloric and nitric acid to play with unsupervised. Some will decide that this was a deliberate, Charles Addams-like plot to get rid of me, but my parents were similarly unconcerned about firearms, which presented a greater threat to everyone else. From my earliest years I stalked our forty acres alone looking for small animals, or blasted away at targets around the house. Similarly, they were unconcerned about school rules and school reports, holding all authority in derision until the threat of expulsion brought with it the danger that children might be returned home.

Auberon Waugh, *Will This Do?*, 1991

LOVED, REVERED AND HONOURED

Later, in the evening of this day, at ten minutes past six, we saw a shudder pass over our dear father, he heaved a deep sigh, a large tear rolled down his face and at that instant his spirit left us. As we saw the dark shadow pass from his face, leaving it so calm and beautiful in the peace and majesty of death, I think there was not one of us who would have wished, could we have had the power, to recall his spirit to earth.

I made it my duty to guard the beloved body as long as it was left to us. The room in which my dear father reposed for the last time was bright with the beautiful fresh flowers which were so abundant at this time of year, and which our good neighbours sent to us so frequently. The birds were singing all about and the summer sun shone brilliantly . . .

At midday on the fourteenth of June a few friends and ourselves saw our dear one laid to rest in the grand old cathedral. Our small group in that vast edifice seemed to make the beautiful words of our beautiful burial service even more than usually solemn and touching. Later in the day, and for many following days, hundreds of mourners flocked to the open grave, and filled the deep vault with flowers. And even after it was closed Dean Stanley wrote: 'There was a constant pressure to the spot and many flowers were strewn upon it by unknown hands, many tears shed from unknown eyes.'

And every year on the ninth of June and on Christmas day we find other flowers strewn by other unknown hands on that spot so sacred to us, as to all who knew and loved him. And every year beautiful bright-coloured leaves are sent to us from across the Atlantic, to be placed with our own flowers on that dear grave; and it is twenty-six years now since my father died!

And for his epitaph what better than my father's own words:
'Of the loved, revered and honoured head, thou canst not turn one

hair to thy dread purposes, nor make one feature odious. It is not that the hand is heavy and will fall down when released; it is not that the heart and pulse are still; but that the hand was open, generous and true, the heart brave, warm and tender, and the pulse a man's. Strike! shadow, strike! and see his good deeds springing from the wound, to sow the world with life immortal.'

Mamie Dickens (1838–96), *My Father as I Recall Him*

SQUARING UP

When I was thirteen and crimping my first quiff
Dad bought me a pair of boxing-gloves
In the hope that I would aspire to the Noble Art.

But I knew my limitations from the start:
Myopia, cowardice and the will to come second.
But I feigned enthusiasm for his sake.

Straight after tea, every night for a week
We would go a few rounds in the yard.
Sleeves rolled-up, collarless and gloveless

He would bob and weave and leave me helpless.
Uppercuts would tap me on the chin
Left hooks muss my hair, haymakers tickle my ear.

Without gloves, only one thing was clear:
The fact that I was hopeless. He had a son
Who couldn't square up. So we came to blows.

Losing patience, he caught me on the nose.
I bled obligingly. A sop. A sacrifice.
Mum threw in the towel and I quit the ring.

But when the bell goes each birthday I still feel the sting
Not of pain, but of regret. You said sorry
And you were. I didn't. And I wasn't.

Roger McGough, *Defying Gravity*, 1992

Gary's final comment about his father said much regarding the cost he had paid for being Frank Gilmore's son. 'My father was the first person I ever wanted to murder,' Gary told our Uncle Vern in his last few hours. 'If I could have killed him and got away with it, I would have.' . . .

Years later, I would learn what my brother's last words were. They stunned me when I heard them, they haunt me still. Gary Gilmore's final words, before the life was shot out of him, were these: 'There will always be a father.' . . .

It is funny. For years I think I was as close to my father as anybody has ever been – as my mother said, I was the only one in the family who still loved him at his death. Though I would spend my adolescent years living with my mother, it was my father – more than anybody else – who raised me, and it was my father I felt safe with. But now when I look at this picture of his face, I think of the things he did to my mother and brothers during this time and the time to come. I try to reconcile my sense of him, and the sanctuary I felt in his presence, with his brutality and his abandonments of his other children. I cannot understand how a man who could be so loving could also leave a baby of his on a park bench while he went off to try and pass a bad check – because that is what truly happened on that day in Atlantic, Iowa, when he lost custody of Gary to a state orphanage. I cannot believe that man was my father, that I once loved him more than anybody else in my world. That I still love him, because I don't know how not to.

My father feels so close, and yet so far. He's the biggest enigma in this history, and I'm worried that if I can't solve him – if I can't uncover his secrets and explain his fears – I have no right telling this story. Maybe to know my father, I'm going to have to examine my own heart and face up to the part of him that dwells there. At the same time, *my* greatest fear is that I am too much like the man, that I already own his sins.

Mikal Gilmore, Shot in the Heart, 1994

MY DEAR DEAF FATHER

My dear deaf father, how I loved him then
Before the years of our estrangement came!
The long calm walks on twilit evenings
Through Highgate New Town to the cinema:
The expeditions by North London trains
To dim forgotten stations, wooden shacks
On oil-lit flimsy platforms among fields
As yet unbuilt-on, deep in Middlesex . . .
We'd stand in dark antique shops while he talked,
Holding his deaf-appliance to his ear,
Lifting the ugly mouthpiece with a smile
Towards the flattered shopman. Most of all
I think my father loved me when we went
In early-morning pipe-smoke on the tram
Down to the Angel, visiting the Works.
'Fourth generation – yes, this is the boy.'
The smell of sawdust still brings back to me
The rambling workshops high on Pentonville,
Built over gardens to White Lion Street,
Clicking with patents of the family firm
Founded in 1820 . . .
When lunch-time brought me hopes of ginger-beer
I'd meet my father's smile as there he stood
Among his clerks, with pens behind their ears,
In the stern silence of the counting-house;
And he, perhaps not ready to go out,
Would leave me to explore some upper rooms –
One full of ticking clocks, one full of books;
And once I found a dusty drawing-room,
Completely furnished, where long years ago
My great-grandfather lived above his work
Before he moved to sylvan Highbury.
But in the downstair showrooms I could find
No link between the finished articles
And all the clatter of the factory.
The Works in Birmingham, I knew, made glass;
The stoneworks in Torquay made other things . . .
But what did *we* do? This I did not know,

[316]

Nor ever wished to – to my father's grief.
O Mappin, Webb, Asprey and Finnigan!
You polished persons on the retail side –
Old Mag Tags, Paulines and Old Westminsters –
Why did I never take to you? Why now
When, staying in a quiet country house,
I see an onyx ashtray of the firm,
Or in my bedroom, find the figured wood
Of my smooth-sliding dressing-table drawers
Has got a look about it of the Works,
Does my mind flinch so?
Partly it is guilt:
'Following in Father's footsteps' was the theme
Of all my early childhood! With what pride
He introduced me to old gentlemen,
Pin-striped commercial travellers of the firm
And tall proprietors of Bond Street shops.
With joy he showed me old George Betjeman's book.
(He was a one-'n' man before the craze
For all things German tacked another 'n'):
'December eighteen seven. Twelve and six –
For helping brother William with his desk.'
Uninteresting then it seemed to me,
Uninteresting still. Slow walks we took
On sunny afternoons to great-great-aunts
In tall Italianate houses: Aberdeen Park,
Hillmarton Road and upper Pooter-land,
Short gravel drives to steepish flights of steps
And stained-glass windows in a purple hall,
A drawing-room with stands of potted plants,
Lace curtains screening other plants beyond.
'Fourth generation – yes, this is the boy' . . .
Atlantic rollers bursting in my ears,
And pealing church-bells and the puff of trains,
The sight of sailing clouds, the smell of grass –
Were always calling out to me for words.
I caught at them and missed and missed again.
'Catch hold,' my father said, 'catch hold like this!',
Trying to teach me how to carpenter,
'Not *that* way, boy! When will you ever learn?' –
I dug the chisel deep into my hand.

'Shoot!' said my father, helping with my gun
And aiming at the rabbit – 'Quick, boy, fire!'
But I had not released the safety-catch.
I was a poet. That was why I failed.
My faith in this chimera brought an end
To all my father's hopes. In later years,
Now old and ill, he asked me once again
To carry on the firm, I still refused.
And now when I behold, fresh-published, new,
A further volume of my verse, I see
His kind grey eyes look woundedly at mine,
I see his workmen seeking other jobs,
And that red granite obelisk that marks
The family grave in Highgate Cemetery
Points an accusing finger to the sky.

John Betjeman (1906–84), *Summoned by Bells*, 1960

SILENCE

My father used to say,
'Superior people never make long visits,
have to be shown Longfellow's grave
or the glass flowers at Harvard.
Self-reliant like the cat –
that takes its prey to privacy,
the mouse's limp tail hanging like a shoelace from its mouth –
they sometimes enjoy solitude,
and can be robbed of speech
by speech which has delighted them.
The deepest feeling always shows itself in silence;
not in silence, but restraint.'
Nor was he insincere in saying, 'Make my house your inn.'
Inns are not residences.

Marianne Moore (1887–1972), *Collected Poems*, 1963

THE SIGN OF THE CROSS

Ivor had evolved a radical system for dealing with trauma and blocked experience and had been treating Lyn. She had discovered in one of the sessions that she was raped as a child, a totally blocked experience, something she had never remembered before. This was all new to me; I did not know that such things were possible. A few times we talked about it late into the night, Ivor explaining how patients experienced their birth as though for the first time, or grief, or a trauma from childhood. And over these weeks the idea came up that I should do a few sessions with Ivor. I'm sure I laughed and tried to change the subject. I might have said that I was afraid.

In the years that followed I often had dinner in the house that Ivor and June bought in Ranelagh, near the centre of Dublin. I don't know what year it was, but it was towards the end of the 1980s, and there was a crowded table and a lot of talking, when Ivor, who has no small talk, was sitting beside me and asked me if my parents were still alive. I was surprised at the question: I thought he knew that my father was dead. I told him that my father had died when I was twelve.

I can see him watching me, holding my gaze, as he asked if this had affected me very deeply. I must have shrugged as I tried to explain that my father was a secondary teacher, and he died just before I was due to go to his secondary school, and I dreaded him teaching me, so in a way, when he died I was relieved. Did you know him well? Ivor asked me. No, I said, no, there were four other children, three older than me, and he was very sick for the last four years of his life. But did you ever have a relationship with him? Ivor continued. Oh yes, I said, when I was younger before he became sick, I used to go down to the museum he had founded in the town every day with him after school, and when I was even younger I used to go and sit at the back of his class, or write on the blackboard. Suddenly, as I spoke, as Ivor still watched me – his look was always even and open – my eyes filled up with tears. Do you realise, he asked me, that you have blocked the experience of his death, all your grief, and you're going to have to do something about it?

In May 1992 June telephoned me. She herself wanted to do one of the sessions and she needed someone to come with her, as you had to work in pairs. She needed someone that she could trust, she said. I knew that she had had her own troubles, and she probably needed to do the session. I said I would do it. I made it clear that I was terrified. So was she, she said.

It would take from Friday morning to Sunday afternoon and there was accommodation in the hospital for those attending. Some of them were Ivor's patients, people who had been disabled by traumas which they had not fully experienced; others were merely people interested in the workshop, or whose reasons for being there were not entirely obvious. I put myself in the last category as I drove into the hospital early on that Friday . . . I'm not sure at what moment it happened but I had suddenly moved into a different state of consciousness. I don't know if some of the crying and moaning sounds came from the *pa* system or from the people around me, but I think from both.

I was in terrible distress. I knew that June was there beside me. I could ask her for Kleenex if I needed it, or to hold my hand, or to stay close. I knew that I could stand up and go out to the toilet if I needed to. But I had entered another world which was more urgent and real than the one I had left. I had to breathe hard, breathe like hell, to stay there. It was all dark in the church, but sometimes lights came on; there were always heavy drum sounds and wild music and cries, babies crying, someone moaning in pain.

And I was moaning too and screaming. I was in my parents' bedroom on the morning that my father died. My mother was downstairs. It is difficult to know how time passed, or how long things went on for. I know that I screamed 'I cannot deal with this' over and over. I know that I screamed at the top of my voice. I know that June grew worried about me and Ivor came over to look at me. I know that I would ask for Kleenex and blow my nose and then start screaming and thrashing around on the mattress. I was not afraid. June's being close was important, but she was outside of what was happening to me. What was happening was real, and the distress was absolute. I started to shout, 'Will you put your arms around me?' I had to gesture to June that I did not mean her, that I was all right. I was a twelve-year-old boy in the front upstairs bedroom of a small house, with neighbours and friends visiting downstairs, expressing their condolences in quiet voices, with my aunt having told me that my father had died during the night in a hospital not far from the town. I was crying all of the time now and shouting out to my father and my mother 'Will you put your arms around me?' 'Will you please?' 'Please?' June and I had agreed to give each other space and never to interfere and touch only when invited. Sometimes, the crying sounded terrible, like howling, but I couldn't stop, or at least I did not know whether I could or not because I did not try: I seemed to want this to happen.

It was a summer's morning in 1967. I was in one bed and my older brother in another bed across the room. I pretended to be asleep when my aunt came into the room and whispered something to him. He said nothing, but quietly got up and put on his clothes and left the room. My father was in hospital, and we knew that he was bad. He had had a stroke, and maybe a heart attack, I'm not sure. But I did not know that he was going to die. I lay in bed listening for some sign. Eventually, I got out of bed and went into my parents' bedroom. My mother had been in the hospital all night; my aunt had stayed to mind myself and my two sisters and two brothers. I watched from the window as one neighbour crossed the street to talk to another. They looked up at our house; and I knew by the way they were talking that one was telling the other that my father was dead. I knew that my mother was downstairs, and I dreaded the idea that she would have to tell me the news. I wanted to hide. I remember that I was turning to go back to my bedroom when my aunt appeared and she told me that my father had died in the hospital during the night, her voice catching and breaking as she explained that if my father had lived he would have been incapacitated, and he would not have wanted that. He had gone to heaven, she said, and my mother, who had shared her life with him, was going to need us all now. I turned away from her crying, but she told me I wasn't to cry. I went into my room and got dressed.

I was back there now in that bedroom, on that summer morning. An hour, two hours must have gone by. I kept blowing my nose and calming down and then starting off again. I felt the shock and the powerlessness and the grief; fierce, absolute things; the realisation that he was dead would cause me to seize up on the mattress and start to scream and cry out. Ivor came over at one stage and I thought he was going to take me out of this ordeal – sometimes I wanted desperately to stop – but he made me turn on all fours and he held my stomach. 'Get it all up now,' he said as he pushed in my stomach muscles. He had brought a metal bowl with him and I screamed so hard I started to vomit mucus into the bowl, and when I lay down he told me to breathe heavily again. The whole terrible pain came back; like before, I began to sob and then cry and then call out and then scream, but it was worse now, this sense of pure loss, of being abandoned, of someone being torn away forever, of being utterly forlorn, but more than anything of not being able to deal with it.

It was almost time for the next session. I still expected this to be about something else. I thought that I could not delve any further into the experience of my father's death. I thought that something new would arise, as we fetched the mattresses and rolled them out. I lay down just as I had done the previous evening. And it began again.

I would blow my nose and start to breathe heavily and then the crying would begin and become uncontrollable and I couldn't stop myself shouting and screaming. The music was always there, constantly changing, throwing out violent and disturbing sounds against snatches of opera and classical music, but I was only barely aware of it. I held June's hand, and shouted out 'Will you let me go?' and started to cry as though no answer was coming or would ever come, as though I would be held all of my life by something which had happened all that time ago.

It began to change. The change was gradual and soft. But I started shouting, 'I will let you go.' I lay on my back and made gestures as though releasing air from my mouth, and then whispering 'I will let you go' and repeating it again and again in whispers. I don't know whether I did let him go or not, but I felt happy as I lay there, saying something that I had never dared to think.

Once more, it is hard to judge how much time passed, but the change from shouting out 'Will you let me go?' to 'I will let you go' seemed to happen fast, in maybe twenty minutes or half an hour. I still lay there making gestures with my hands as though releasing something from my mouth.

I thought that I had come to the end, I could see no other way in which this could develop. I signalled to June that I'd had enough and she got Ivor. I was content, thinking that I had gone through enough. But Ivor said I should go on, I should start the fast breathing again. There was more, he said.

So I lay on the mattress and took deep breaths and began to listen to the sounds all around me. I went straight back into my private, hidden world. Now I felt warmly towards my father rather than frightened by his death. I became overwhelmed by a compulsion to thank my father for life, but I was embarrassed by it. It sounded like the sort of thing you hear at a bad funeral service. But I needed to do it. I lay there feeling it, trying to let myself do it, say the words, thank my father for life. I held back: I had to let myself use language that I would not normally use. I had to say: 'Thank you for giving me life' and I had to say it over and over until I was sure that I meant it and was no longer embarrassed by it.

In the end I wanted to bless him. It was the first time in my life I had ever thought of anything like this. I wanted to make the sign of the cross over him. It was not just an idea that came into my head for a moment. It was a compelling need, something I had to do. But I did not want to be seen doing it; I did not want to see myself doing it. I was shamed by this need to bless my dead father, to make the sign of the cross over him. I tried to hold back. I couldn't do this. I was, for the first time, embarrassed that June was beside me. I would find this hard to explain.

And then I did it. I made the sign of the cross in the air, over and over. I had no choice. I knew afterwards that I could go no further. Ivor told me to rest.

Before it all ended we sat around in a ring as we had at the beginning and talked. We were warned not to go to pubs or mix with large groups of strangers over the next few days. We were all too open, too raw. We talked about the symbols we had conjured up the first day. Mine was a cross. I saw it now as the cross which the altar boy had carried in front of my father's coffin as it was wheeled down the centre aisle of Enniscorthy Cathedral, but I was not sure.

Colm Tóibín, *The Sign of the Cross*, 1994

THOSE WINTER SUNDAYS

Sundays too my father got up early
and put his clothes on in the blueblack cold,
then with cracked hands that ached
from labor in the weekday weather made
banked fires blaze. No one ever thanked him.

I'd wake and hear the cold splintering, breaking.
When the rooms were warm, he'd call,
and slowly I would rise and dress,
fearing the chronic angers of that house,

Speaking indifferently to him,
who had driven out the cold
and polished my good shoes as well.
What did I know, what did I know
of love's austere and lonely offices?

Robert Hayden (1913–80), *Collected Poems*, 1985

ALL MY PRETTY ONES

All my pretty ones?
Did you say all? O hell-kite! All?
What! all my pretty chickens and their dam
At one fell swoop? . . .
I cannot but remember such things were,
That were most precious to me.
                                    Macbeth

Father, this year's jinx rides us apart
where you followed our mother to her cold slumber,
a second shock boiling its stone to your heart,
leaving me here to shuffle and disencumber
you from the residence you could not afford:
a gold key, your half of a woollen mill,
twenty suits from Dunne's, an English Ford,
the love and legal verbiage of another will,
boxes of pictures of people I do not know.
I touch their cardboard faces. They must go.

But the eyes, as thick as wood in this album,
hold me. I stop here, where a small boy
waits in a ruffled dress for someone to come . . .
for this soldier who holds his bugle like a toy
or for this velvet lady who cannot smile.
Is this your father's father, this commodore
in a mailman suit? My father, time meanwhile
has made it unimportant who you are looking for.
I'll never know what these faces are all about.
I lock them into their book and throw them out.

This is the yellow scrapbook that you began
the year I was born; as crackling now and wrinkly
as tobacco leaves: clippings where Hoover outran
the Democrats, wiggling his dry finger at me
and Prohibition; news where the *Hindenburg* went
down and recent years when you went flush
on war. This year, solvent but sick, you meant
to marry that pretty widow in a one-month rush.
But before you had that second chance, I cried
on your fat shoulder. Three days later you died.

These are the snapshots of marriage, stopped in places.
Side by side at the rail toward Nassau now;
here, with the winner's cup at the speedboat races,
here, in tails at the Cotillion, you take a bow,
here, by our kennel of dogs with their pink eyes,
running like show-bred pigs in their chain-link pen;
here, at the horseshow where my sister wins a prize;
and here, standing like a duke among groups of men.
Now I fold you down, my drunkard, my navigator,
my first lost keeper, to love or look at later.

I hold a five-year diary that my mother kept
for three years, telling all she does not say
of your alcoholic tendency. You overslept,
she writes. My God, father, each Christmas Day
with your blood, will I drink down your glass
of wine? The diary of your hurly-burly years
goes to my shelf to wait for my age to pass.
Only in this hoarded span will love persevere.
Whether you are pretty or not, I outlive you,
bend down my strange face to yours and forgive you.

Anne Sexton (1928–74), Collected Poems, 1962

WRITE SO I MAY COME TO YOUR ARMS

Vienna
4 April 1787

This very moment I have received a piece of news which greatly distresses me, the more so as I gathered from your last letter that, thank
God, you were very well indeed. But now I hear that you are really ill.
I need hardly tell you how greatly I am longing to receive some reassuring news from yourself. And I still expect it; although I have now
made a habit of being prepared in all affairs of life for the worst. As
death, when we come to consider it closely, is the true goal of our existence, I have formed during the last few years such close relations with
this best truest friend of mankind, that his image is not only no longer
terrifying to me, but is indeed very soothing and consoling! . . . I hope
and trust that while I am writing this, you are feeling better. But if,
contrary to all expectation, you are not recovering, I implore you . . .

not to hide it from me, but to tell me the whole truth or get someone
to write it to me, so that as quickly as is humanly possible I may come
to your arms. I entreat you by all that is sacred – to both of us.
Nevertheless I trust that I shall soon have a reassuring letter from you;
and cherishing this pleasant hope, I and my wife and our little Karl
kiss your hands a thousand times and I am ever your most obedient
son

W.A. Mozart

Wolfgang Amadeus Mozart (1756–91), letter to his father

29 May 1787

... I inform you that on returning home to-day I received the sad news
of my most beloved father's death. You can imagine the state I am in.

Wolfgang Amadeus Mozart, letter to Baron Gottfried von Jasquin

WOODS

My father who found the English landscape tame
Had hardly in his life walked in a wood,
Too old when first he met one; Malory's knights,
Keats's nymphs or the Midsummer Night's Dream
Could never arras the room, where he spelled out True and Good
With their interleaving of half-truths and not-quites.

While for me from the age of ten the socketed wooden gate
Into a Dorset planting, into a dark
But gentle ambush, was an alluring eye;
Within was a kingdom free from time and sky,
Caterpillar webs on the forehead, danger under the feet,
And the mind adrift in a floating and rustling ark

Packed with birds and ghosts, two of every race,
Trills of love from the picture-book – Oh might I never land
But here, grown six foot tall, find me also a love
Also out of the picture-book; whose hand
Would be soft as the webs of the wood and on her face
The wood-pigeon's voice would shaft a chrism from above.

So in a grassy ride a rain-filled hoof-mark coined
By a finger of sun from the mint of Long Ago
Was the last of Lancelot's glitter. Make-believe dies hard;
That the rider passed here lately and is a man we know
Is still untrue, the gate to Legend remains unbarred,
The grown-up hates to divorce what the child joined.

Thus from a city when my father would frame
Escape, he thought, as I do, of bog or rock
But I have also this other, this English, choice
Into what yet is foreign; whatever its name
Each wood is the mystery and the recurring shock
Of its dark coolness is a foreign voice.

Yet in using the word tame my father was maybe right,
These woods are not the Forest; each is moored
To a village somewhere near. If not of to-day
They are not like the wilds of Mayo, they are assured
Of their place by men; reprieved from the neolithic night
By gamekeepers or by Herrick's girls at play.

And always we walk out again. The patch
Of sky at the end of the path grows and discloses
An ordered open air long ruled by dyke and fence,
With geese whose form and gait proclaim their consequence,
Pargetted outposts, windows browed with thatch,
And cow pats – and inconsequent wild roses

Louis MacNeice (1907–63), Collected Poems, 1966

MY PAPA'S WALTZ

The whiskey on your breath
Could make a small boy dizzy;
But I hung on like death:
Such waltzing was not easy.

We romped until the pans
Slid from the kitchen shelf;
My mother's countenance
Could not unfrown itself.

The hand that held my wrist
Was battered on one knuckle;
At every step you missed
My right ear scraped a buckle.

You beat time on my head
With a palm caked hard by dirt,
Then waltzed me off to bed
Still clinging to your shirt.

Theodore Roethke (1908–63), *Collected Poems*, 1968

POOR DEAR MAN

. . . all my childish affection and love was given to my father. I worshipped him. He was always a friend. If ever there was a saint on this
earth, it was my father. He got bullied a good deal by my mother and
she could always make him do what she wanted. She ran all the family
finances and gave my father ten shillings a week; this sum had to
include his daily lunch at the Athenaeum, and he was severely cross-
examined if he meekly asked for another shilling or two before the end
of the week. Poor dear man, I never thought his last few years were
very happy; he was never allowed to do as he liked and he was not
given the care and nursing which might have prolonged his life. My
mother nursed him herself when he could not move, but she was not a
good nurse. He died in 1932 when I was commanding the 1st Battalion
The Royal Warwickshire Regiment in Egypt. It was a tremendous loss
for me. The three outstanding human beings in my life have been my
father, my wife, and my son. When my father died in 1932, I little
thought that five years later I would be left alone with my son.

Field-Marshal Montgomery (1887–1976), *Memoirs*, 1958

OTHER MEMORIES

Father, I've been unjust to you.
Less than fair. Large with my own self.
Janus, the two-faced god, is always true;

There were other times. We had other selves.
Now I remember how in slippers you padded
To our room, to turn out the gas light.
The small gashed globe went ember-red
And briefly smouldered on into the night.
As the purring faded our room regained
Its attic silence. And then you quietly came
To both our sides. You made the sign of Christ
Upon our sleepy heads. And said 'God bless'.
Now in the greater darkness, the small light out,
Your clumsy silent hands seem, almost, eloquent.

Peter Abbs, *Icons of Time*, 1991

THE LARGEST MAN I EVER SAW

'I may here add a few pages about my father, who was in many ways a remarkable man.

'He was about 6 feet 2 inches in height, with broad shoulders, and very corpulent, so that he was the largest man whom I ever saw. When he last weighed himself, he was 24 stone, but afterwards increased much in weight. His chief mental characteristics were his powers of observation and his sympathy, neither of which I have ever seen exceeded or even equalled. His sympathy was not only with the distresses of others, but in a greater degree with the pleasures of all around him. This led him to be always scheming to give pleasure to others, and, though hating extravagance, to perform many generous actions . . .

'My father used to tell me many little things which he had found useful in his medical practice. Thus ladies often cried much while telling him their troubles, and thus caused much loss of his precious time. He soon found that begging them to command and restrain themselves, always made them weep the more, so that afterwards he always encouraged them to go on crying, saying that this would relieve them more than anything else, and with the invariable result that they soon ceased to cry, and he could hear what they had to say and give his advice . . .

'My father possessed an extraordinary memory, especially for dates, so that he knew, when he was very old, the day of the birth, marriage, and death of a multitude of persons in Shropshire; and he once told me that this power annoyed him; for if he once heard a date, he could not forget it; and thus the deaths of many friends were often recalled to his mind. Owing to his strong memory he knew an extraordinary number of curious stories, which he liked to tell, as he was a great talker . . .

'My father was very sensitive, so that many small events annoyed him or pained him much. I once asked him, when he was old and could not walk, why he did not drive out for exercise; and he answered, "Every road out of Shrewsbury is associated in my mind with some painful event." Yet he was generally in high spirits. He was easily made very angry, but his kindness was unbounded. He was widely and deeply loved . . .

'My father's mind was not scientific, and he did not try to generalise his knowledge under general laws; yet he formed a theory for almost everything which occurred. I do not think I gained much from him intellectually; but his example ought to have been of much moral service to all his children. One of his golden rules (a hard one to follow) was, "Never become the friend of any one whom you cannot respect."'

Charles Darwin (1809–82), autobiographical 'Recollections', c.1877 or 1878 in *The Life and Letters of Charles Darwin*, ed. Francis Darwin, 1887

EFFORTS AT TRUTH

The last time I saw my father was in November 1980, ten days before he died. I had gone over with my second wife to spend a weekend with him and Diana; now more than ever he seemed anxious to talk. He would be up in the mornings long before his usual time, and when I appeared in the drawing room he would say – Have some pink champagne! I would say – Now Dad? and then – Yes! It was quite like, after all, the times I had visited him in Holloway. Then we would talk for most of the day – of the past, of life before the war, of my mother, of her sisters. He wanted, I think, to make something clear about the past: he told me – as he had used to tell me so many years ago – how good his first marriage had been; how now of course his second marriage was very good, but what he wanted now, with and for everyone, was reconciliation. He said – Throughout the thirties, you know, it was as if I had two wives: do you think that was immoral? I said – Ah,

Dad, immoral! He was this very old man who had Parkinson's disease; he took pills to make himself stop shaking. Sometimes when standing he would lose his balance and topple over like an enormous tree; from the floor he would explain, laughingly – 'It's these pills, you know; it's a wonder what can be done by modern science!' I told him that I wanted to write something about his life; that I wanted to try to write the truth; that no one of course ever quite caught the truth, but if one made efforts then these could stand for it. I said that I thought however peculiar his life had been – or just because of this – the story of it would be best served by truth; there had had to be prevarications in the past perhaps, but his life had been passionate enough and a struggle enough and concerned with real things enough for it to be proper that there should now be efforts at truth.

Nicholas Mosley, *Rules of the Game and Beyond the Pale*, 1994

FATHER AND SON

Only last week, walking the hushed fields
Of our most lovely Meath, now thinned by November,
I came to where the road from Laracor leads
To the Boyne river – that seemed more lake than river,
Stretched in uneasy light and stript of reeds.

And walking longside an old weir
Of my people's, where nothing stirs – only the shadowed
Leaden flight of a heron up the lean air –
I went unmanly with grief, knowing how my father,
Happy though captive in years, walked last with me there.

Yes, happy in Meath with me for a day
He walked, taking stock of herds hid in their own breathing;
And naming colts, gusty as wind, once steered by his hand,
Lightnings winked in the eyes that were half shy in greeting
Old friends – the wild blades, when he gallivanted the land.

For that proud, wayward man now my heart breaks –
Breaks for that man whose mind was a secret eyrie,
Whose kind hand was sole signet of his race,
Who curbed me, scorned my green ways, yet increasingly loved me
Till Death drew its grey blind down his face.

And yet I am pleased that even my reckless ways
Are living shades of his rich calms and passions –
Witnesses for him and for those faint namesakes
With whom now he is one, under yew branches,
Yes, one in a graven silence no bird breaks.

F. R. Higgins (1896–1941), *The Oxford Book of Irish Verse*, 1958

AN AGED NURSLING

Miss Weston,
Lichfield, March 20, 1787.
Respondent to your kind inquiries, I have the pleasure to tell you, that
my dearest father, though weaker than ever in his limbs, and amidst
the fastfading powers of memory, has had no relapse since his dreadful epileptic seizures in December; while his affection for me seems to
increase as the other energies of his mind subside. When I administer
his food, his wine, and even his medicines, which indeed are few, cordial and palatable, he looks at me with ineffable tenderness; and with
an emphatic, though weak voice, 'thank you, my dear child, my darling, my blessing;' and not seldom he calls me 'the light of his eyes'.
The sensations of melting fondness which such expressions awaken in
my bosom, are of unutterable pleasure. But, alas! soon or late, we
generally pay an high price for whatever has been cordial to our
spirits, and sweet to our hearts. This augmented tenderness, from a
parent always affectionate, – O! how will it embitter the parting hour,
which I must consider as perpetually impending!

You are aware by how slight a thread the life of my aged nursling has
been long suspended. His drop into the grave is an event which, I fear,
will baffle my resolution to sustain with the cheerful resignation
which reason and religion dictate. That entire dependence upon my
care and attention, resulting from the decay of his corporeal and intellectual faculties, has doubled our bond of union, and engrafted the
maternal upon filial tenderness. He seems at once my parent and my
child; nor shall I suffer less, perhaps even more, from the loss of him,
than if he had died while power, and authority, and exertion were in
his hands.

Anna Seward (1747–1809), *The Letters of Anna Seward, Swan of Lichfield*, 1936

DAD

Your old hat hurts me, and those black
fat raisins you liked to press into
my palm from your soft heavy hand:
I see you staggering back up the path
with sacks of potatoes from some local farm,
fresh eggs, flowers. Every day I grieve

for your great heart broken and you gone.
You loved to watch the trees. This year
you did not see their Spring.
The sky was freezing over the fen
as on that somewhere secretly appointed day
you beached: cold, white-faced, shivering.

What happened, old bull, my loyal
hoarse-voiced warrior? The hammer
blow that stopped you in your track
and brought you to a hospital monitor
could not destroy your courage,
to the end you were
uncowed and unconcerned with pleasing anyone.

I think of you now as once again safely
at my mother's side, the earth as
chosen as a bed, and feel most sorrow for
all that was gentle in
my childhood buried there
already forfeit, now for ever lost.

Elaine Feinstein, *Ain't I a Woman*, 1987

MY FATHER MOVED THROUGH DOOMS OF LOVE

my father moved through dooms of love
through sames of am through haves of give,
singing each morning out of each night
my father moved through depths of height

this motionless forgetful where
turned at his glance to shining here;
that if(so timid air is firm)
under his eyes would stir and squirm

newly as from unburied which
floats the first who,his april touch
drove sleeping selves to swarm their fates
woke dreamers to their ghostly roots

and should some why completely weep
my father's fingers brought her sleep:
vainly no smallest voice might cry
for he could feel the mountains grow.

Lifting the valleys of the sea
my father moved through griefs of joy;
praising a forehead called the moon
singing desire into begin

joy was his song and joy so pure
a heart of star by him could steer
and pure so now and now so yes
the wrists of twilight would rejoice

keen as midsummer's keen beyond
conceiving mind of sun will stand,
so strictly(over utmost him
so hugely)stood my father's dream

his flesh was flesh his blood was blood:
no hungry man but wished him food;
no cripple wouldn't creep one mile
uphill to only see him smile.

Scorning the pomp of must and shall
my father moved through dooms of feel;
his anger was as right as rain
his pity was as green as grain

septembering arms of year extend
less humbly wealth to foe and friend
that he to foolish and to wise
offered immeasurable is

proudly and(by octobering flame
beckoned)as earth will downward climb,
so naked for immortal work
his shoulders marched against the dark

his sorrow was as true as bread:
no liar looked him in the head;
if every friend became his foe
he'd laugh and build a world with snow.

My father moved through theys of we,
singing each new leaf out of each tree
(and every child was sure that spring
danced when she heard my father sing)

then let men kill which cannot share,
let blood and flesh be mud and mire,
scheming imagine, passion willed,
freedom a drug that's bought and sold

giving to steal and cruel kind,
a heart to fear, to doubt a mind,
to differ a disease of same,
conform the pinnacle of am

though dull were all we taste as bright,
bitter all utterly things sweet,
maggoty minus and dumb death
all we inherit,all bequeath

and nothing quite so least as truth
– say though hate were why men breathe –
because my father lived his soul
love is the whole and more than all

E. E. Cummings (1894–1962), *Complete Poems 1913–1962*, 1962

'DADDY'

He was still with me when I awoke from a dream of him. He was
standing at the foot of the bed, smiling down on the son he had not
seen for nearly thirty years.

'Daddy,' I said.

I did not dare to believe that he would answer me. I waited, but no words came. He acknowledged that he was my father, my long-dead father, with a nod.

'Daddy,' I said again, relishing the word I had had no cause to relish for most of my life. 'Daddy, what are you doing here?'

(I assumed, madly, that he knew where I was: in the guest bedroom at 1541, 7th Street South, in Fargo, North Dakota. The house belonged to my new-found friends Hal and Alice – they called themselves, collectively, 'Halice' – who were spending the summer in Britain. Some days, I had only their ancient cat, Flipsy, for company. My principal household task was to put down bowls of beer for the slugs in the garden. It was Alice's conviction that the creatures died in an alcoholic ecstasy: 'Much kinder than crushing them underfoot.' Each morning, I had to dispose of scores of Budweisered corpses.)

I sat up in bed, to be closer to him. When I offered him my hands, he vanished.

'Daddy, please come back to me.'

That was twelve years ago, and I have not seen him since. There is now no reason for us to meet. On a hot night in July, in a country he never visited, he gave me his parting gift, the gift I had been denied one far-off November.

It was as if America had been eradicated, wiped out: in that large bed, capable of bearing two ample guests, I was in the London of my childhood, calling out for the father who had gone from me. I was a boy, once more, pleading in a boy's voice. I spoke no other word but 'Daddy', for no other word seemed necessary. I wanted nothing else but his return, and the certain comfort it would bring.

I sobbed until my boy's body ached, until the source of all my tears was dry.

The next morning, I was restored to America and manhood. I felt serene. I had accepted the gift of grief, and my acceptance, my complete acceptance, of it had released something in me of which I had been completely unaware – and might have stayed so always. If I had laughed him out of my presence as a mere illusion, if I had turned from him and gone back to sleep, then that mysterious something – a nurtured coldness; an icicle of long formation – would be mine today. I welcomed him, though, in the precious minutes he was with me, and ensured myself a night of pain. My first thought was that his vanishing meant rejection, but, as the night progressed, I came to understand its true significance. He was dying a second time – just for me, to my lasting benefit.

Paul Bailey, *An Immaculate Mistake*, 1990

My father played the melodeon
Outside at our gate;
There were stars in the morning east
And they danced to his music.

Across the wild bogs his melodeon called
To Lennons and Callans.
As I pulled on my trousers in a hurry
I knew some strange thing had happened.

Outside in the cow-house my mother
Made the music of milking;
The light of her stable-lamp was a star
And the frost of Bethlehem made it twinkle.

A water-hen screeched in the bog,
Mass-going feet
Crunched the wafer-ice on the pot-holes,
Somebody wistfully twisted the bellows wheel.

My child poet picked out the letters
On the grey stone,
In silver the wonder of a Christmas townland,
The winking glitter of a frosty dawn.

Cassiopeia was over
Cassidy's hanging hill,
I looked and three whin bushes rode across
The horizon – the Three Wise Kings.

An old man passing said:
'Can't he make it talk' –
The melodeon. I hid in the doorway
And tightened the belt of my box-pleated coat.

I nicked six nicks on the door-post
With my penknife's big blade –
There was a little one for cutting tobacco.
And I was six Christmases of age.

My father played the melodeon,
My mother milked the cows,

And I had a prayer like a white rose pinned
On the Virgin Mary's blouse.

Patrick Kavanagh (1905–67), 'A Christmas Childhood',
The Collected Poems, 1972

A KINDLY SWEET DISPOSITION

To pursue the thread of our story, my father's regiment was the year after ordered to Londonderry, where another sister was brought forth, Catherine, still living, but most unhappily estranged from me by my uncle's wickedness, and her own folly – from this station the regiment was sent to defend Gibraltar, at the siege, where my father was run through the body by Captain Phillips, in a duel, (the quarrel began about a goose) with much difficulty he survived – though with an impaired constitution, which was not able to withstand the hardships it was put to – for he was sent to Jamaica, where he soon fell by the country fever, which took away his senses first, and made a child of him, and then, in a month or two, walking about continually without complaining, till the moment he sat down in an arm-chair, and breathed his last – which was at Port Antonio, on the north of the island. – My father was a little smart man – active to the last degree, in all exercises – most patient of fatigue and disappointments, of which it pleased God to give him full measure – he was in his temper somewhat rapid and hasty – but of a kindly, sweet disposition, void of all design; and so innocent in his own intentions, that he suspected no one; so that you might have cheated him ten times in a day, if nine had not been sufficient for your purpose – my poor father died in March, 1731 –

Laurence Sterne (1713–68), *Memoirs*

. . . my dad was a . . . he was such a gentle man, my father – he died in 1975. I still have a very good . . . I have a better relationship with him than I could manage, as it were, at the time of the later stages of my so-called journey from grammar school to Oxford and all that that meant, which sort of slightly intimidated him.

MB: *What do you mean by a better relationship?*

DP: A better relationship in the sense that I see more and I feel that I understand more of his gentleness and of his desire to reach me, and I feel that I am being reached . . . I can't put it in any other way. For example, the things he used to . . . he used to be almost scared of me, when I didn't want him to be, and I used to feel irritation about that, which I didn't want to feel. You know, those sort of things. And I'd be writing in this little downstairs room, 'cos I've always, I've always had this passion for it. I have this antique – and I'm not ashamed now of being able to say, it is an antique word, and it's one that's easily scoffed at – but I do have a sense of vocation, and I have it to the, I will have it to the last ounce of my life, the last second. I had the sense, and I'm proud that I've got it, and I'm no longer ashamed of saying yes, I have had, have had a sense of vocation, and it was writing. And he would sort of hover on, in the doorway, or lean against the door jamb and, 'So . . . so, all right, our Den?' I'm writing, so I'd be irritated because, I mean, I'd go in and talk to him, I was finishing something, or I was doing, or I was engaged in something. 'Yes, Dad, sure' – you know all that, so 'Sure it's all right – mind?' That anxiety to communicate but doing it wrongly. Now of course I'd say, 'Come on in, Dad, for Christ's sake sit down and let . . .' it doesn't matter about that now, that minute, but of course I cut my cards, and yet there's a sense in which by even saying it you see I've done it, I've said it – 'Come on in, Dad' – and he, he and I, I can feel him genetically in me, and I see the waste of so much of his life because of the system that he lived through. He was shy, he was gentle, he was a bit feckless in many ways. If he had a . . . he'd always say, the pound in your pocket is your best friend, but of course as soon as he had one, it'd be drinks all round in the pub, much to my mother's dismay, but he was that kind of, you know, 'Come on, us gotta have one', that kind of man. And I . . . I plug into that now more, more easily, that's all I can say.

Dennis Potter (1935–95), interview with Melvyn Bragg,
Seeing the Blossom, 1994

PHOTOGRAPH OF MY FATHER IN HIS TWENTY-SECOND YEAR

October. Here in this dank, unfamiliar kitchen
I study my father's embarrassed young man's face.
Sheepish grin, he holds in one hand a string
Of spiny yellow perch, in the other
A bottle of Carlsbad beer.

In jeans and denim shirt, he leans
Against the front fender of a Ford *circa* 1934.
He would like to pose bluff and hearty for his posterity.
Wear his old hat cocked over his ear, stick out his tongue . . .
All his life my father wanted to be bold.

But the eyes give him away, and the hands
That limply offer the string of dead perch
And the bottle of beer. Father, I loved you,
Yet how can I say thank you, I who cannot hold my liquor either
And do not even know the places to fish?

Raymond Carver, *Winter Insomnia* 1970

IN FINDING HIM I LOST HIM

I am at home now. The jade feathers are appearing on the acacia. The
peonies are busting open in the warm border. My parrot has decided
that he trusts me, and even lets me stroke his head and throat when I
have Christopher the red cat purring loudly on my shoulder and drib-
bling down my back. There have been storms of apple blossom, and
fritillaries along the drive. There is a fog of lilac along the roadside
fence and frogs are dwelling in the pool in my wood which this year
will cast shade for the first time. I am unmoved. For this, for every
thing, I am out of tune.

There is a change – and I am poor. I cannot speak to Daddy any
more because I know he lied to me. It was not the war that destroyed
his love for me, but his charade and my censorious, scrutinising
nature. He is no longer beside me with his face turned away, but lying
in my desk drawer in tatters, a heap of cheap props. I think I know

that the people who genuinely loved him were aware that his gentle-manly carry-on was an act and loved him for the way he did it, but I, like the RAF officers he met 'overseas', am not beguiled. 'He was a character,' his old friends say when they tell stories of the amazing effrontery that reduced policemen and publicans to apologetic wrecks. He was good company, but not for me. I was never his boon companion, but a full-on pain in his neck.

In finding him I lost him. Sleepless nights are long.

Germaine Greer, *Daddy We Hardly Knew You*, 1989

EYES

My father's eyes looked into yours with love.
Time passed, he's dead, but isn't really dead.
His eyes still operate inside my head.
This is called the continuity of being alive.

The gentleness of my father is to me
Reflected in your eyes, which are beautiful
Or your lips to which he listened, or quietly
When your body lies beside me, breasts taut and full.

And the promise in that body of a child
He will never know, but who'll be someone else,
Someone who moves in a world completely wild,
But who carries blood brought from a long way off.
My father's eyes look into yours with love.

Dom Moraes, *Collected Poems*, 1957

THE ONLY MAN I EVER LOVED

Profoundly isolated in my misery, I longed for human sympathy. Slowly it dawned on me that I had created my own solitude, building with my own hands the prison walls that now surrounded me. I thought of my father, of all he had done for me, of the many times I had fended off his affection or accepted his gifts without acknowledging the love that prompted them. 'He is more than ninety years old,' I said to myself. 'Probably I shall never see him again. I must write while there is still time and tell him how much I love him, more than anyone else in the world. I must thank him for all he has done and all he has been in my life.'

So I did. I wrote, with all the 'yes, buts . . .' standing round my desk and all the old complaints crowding my pen, but I fought them off. 'Not this time,' I told them. 'You have had your day. Let me for once tell the good side, which is just as true as the bad, though you don't like to admit it. Go away. I am going to write a love letter for once in my life.' It was good that I did, for indeed there was not much time left.

One morning at breakfast the phone rang. It was a friend from Wellesley. 'If I can do anything, Kate, let me know.'

'Do anything about what?'

'You don't know? Your father died yesterday. We heard it on the news.'

'Oh . . . thank you . . . No, I didn't know . . . Yes, if there is anything you can do, I'll call . . . I don't know yet what I will do. I don't see how I can go over there, and what would be the good anyway, now he's gone?'

I hung up the phone, told the family, finished up the morning chores and went out to drive to the high school where I taught, twenty-five miles from home. It was raining. White mists hid everything but the wet road ahead of me. The heavens are weeping for him, I thought, and the truth is shrouded in mist. 'Sentimental idiot,' I told myself, but the heavens and I went on weeping. Is he really and finally dead? Is that the end of him? Was he right, after all? God, he can't be finished, can he? A man like that doesn't just stop – you will want to see him and talk things over with him – I will want to see him again, without the hindrances that have kept us apart. Bleak rain, bleak mist, grey road, leading from unhappy home to abominable school – and now he is gone. I wept as I drove, feeling utterly abandoned. Then the stubborn optimism of my parents joined with the ragged remnants of my faith: no, this is not the end; he has arrived with God and is getting all his questions answered at last, and someday I shall be there too, with both of them.

I drove on to school and went on with life in a world without my father. I had told myself often: he is so old, so deaf, so cut off from me, it's as though he were dead already; it won't be too bad when it happens. But it was too bad, and it left me with a numb ache for a long time: now I can never tell him this, never ask him that, never straighten out old confusions – never until I am dead too, and who knows how long that will be?

It was a long time before I thought of writing about him. I will tell the world what a great father he was, I said to myself, how wise and witty and kind, how much fun we always had. They mustn't think he was always a cold and rational philosopher. So I thought, and so I began to write, but it has not come out that way. The 'but's' and complaints seized my pen and forced it to record them. 'He loved truth, you know,' they urged. 'You cannot honor him with a lying memoir. You must set down all that was wrong, all that was difficult and disappointing, and then you can say: "He was the most fascinating man I have ever known, the only man I ever loved, the greatest man I shall ever meet, the wittiest, the gayest, the most charming. It was a privilege to know him, and I thank God he was my father."'

Katherine Tait, *My Father Bertrand Russell*, 1975

Envoi

DO NOT GO GENTLE INTO THAT GOOD NIGHT

Do not go gentle into that good night,
Old age should burn and rave at close of day;
Rage, rage against the dying of the light.

Though wise men at their end know dark is right,
Because their words had forked no lightning they
Do not go gentle into that good night.

Good men, the last wave by, crying how bright
Their frail deeds might have danced in a green bay,
Rage, rage against the dying of the light.

Wild men who caught and sang the sun in flight,
And learn, too late, they grieved it on its way,
Do not go gentle into that good night.

Grave men, near death, who see with blinding sight
Blind eyes could blaze like meteors and be gay,
Rage, rage against the dying of the light.

And you, my father, there on the sad height,
Curse, bless, me now with your fierce tears, I pray.
Do not go gentle into that good night.
Rage, rage against the dying of the light.

Dylan Thomas (1914–53), Poems, 1971

ACKNOWLEDGMENTS

The first person I want to thank is my dear friend Cressida Connolly who dreamt up the whole idea of an anthology of fathers. It was her encouragement which prompted me to set the project in motion in the first place and her enthusiasm and suggestions have kept me going. My sister-in-law, Rosaleen Mulji, has helped me enormously – this book is stuffed with her ideas, all of which were funny and original. Two other friends have also been especially helpful: Sophia Morrison and Matthew Connolly, who gave up their time to help both practically with scissors and paste and intellectually with advice and support. Among the many friends to whom I am grateful for suggestions are: Anthony and Laura Blond, Jessamy Calkin, Maura Dillon-Malone, Michael Gearin-Kington, John Gross, Selina Hastings, Martin Hobhouse, Sara Holloway, Barry Humphries, Helen Kime, Miles Kington, Celia Lyttleton, Jonathan Moyne, Paul Raben, Jeremy Sandford, William Sieghart and Andrew and Ruth Wilson. I would also like to thank all the saints who work at The London Library (On one occasion they even looked after my baby while I dashed up to the third floor to grab some books), John Wyse Jackson, better known as Sean, at John Sandoe's Bookshop, Jonathan Burnham at Chatto for having the courage to give me the go-ahead and my editor Jenny Uglow for her kind and efficient advice. Lastly, I want to mention my darling children Molly, Hector, Arthur, Matthew and Samuel for being so good and helpful (the eldest two) and for being so bad and distracting (the youngest three) and my husband Erskine who is the most exemplary father I know.

The editor and publishers gratefully acknowledge permission to reprint copyright material as follows:
Peter Abbs for 'Other Memories' from *Icons of Time* (1991); Desmond Banks & Co for an extract from *Scandal* by Christine Keeler, 1989; Blackstaff Press for 'Study of a Figure in a Landscape' by Paul Durcan from *Daddy, Daddy* (1990); Bloomsbury for an excerpt from Paul Bailey, *An Immaculate Mistake* (1990); Carcanet Press for 'Parent to Children' by Robert Graves from *Collected Poems* (1975); Curtis Brown Ltd, London on behalf of the Hon. Edward Plunket for an excerpt from *The Curse of the Wise Woman* © Lord Dunsany 1933, and on behalf of the Estates of Sir Winston S. Churchill and Lord Randolph Churchill for excerpts from *Winston S. Churchill* (1966) © Peregrine Churchill; Andre Deutsch Ltd for

'Song to be Sung by the Father of Infant Female Children' by Ogden Nash from *Candy is Dandy* (1983); Element Books Ltd for an excerpt from *Iron John* by Roger Bly (1991); Everyman's Library Ltd for an excerpt from *Fathers and Children* by Ivan Turgenev, translated by Avril Pyman (1962); Faber and Faber Ltd for 'Follower' by Seamus Heaney from *Selected Poems* (1980), 'Lament 5' and 'Lament 13' by Jan Kochanowski, translated by Stanislaw Baranczak and Seamus Heaney, 'Silence' by Mariane Moore from *Collected Poems* (1968). 'For a Fatherless Son' and 'Daddy' by Sylvia Plath from *Collected Poems* (1985), 'My Papa's Waltz' by Theodore Roethke from *Collected Poems* (1968), 'Missing my Daughter' by Stephen Spender from *Collected Poems* (1985) and excerpts from *The Dublin Diary of Stanislaus Joyce* (1952) by Stanislaus Joyce, *Amongst Women* (1990) by John McGahern and *Seeing the Blossom* (1994) by Dennis Potter; John Fuller for 'Fathers' by Roy Fuller from *Collected Poems* (1962); David R. Godine Inc for 'The Temple of Longing' in *New American Poets of the '90s'* ed J. Myers and R. Weingarton (1991); Victor Gollancz Ltd for an excerpt from *Hons and Rebels* (1960) by Jessica Mitford; Harcourt Brace Jovanovich for 'Advice to a son' by Ernest Hemingway, © 1979 by the Ernest Hemingway Foundation and Nicholas Gerogiannis; HarperCollins Publishers for excerpts from *Letters of Anne Fleming*, (1985) edited by Mark Amory, *The Naked Civil Servant* (1968) by Quentin Crisp, *The Poor Mouth* (1973 edn.) by Flann O'Brien, *Surprised by Joy* (1955) by C. S. Lewis, *Son of Oscar Wilde* (1954) by Vyvyan Holland and 'Remembering Golden Bells' by Chu-i Po from *Translations from the Chinese* by Arthur Waley; Wolf Rudiger Hess for an excerpt from *My Father Rudolf Hess* (W. H. Allen, 1986); Henry Holt and Company, Inc. for an excerpt from *Voices Offstage: A Book of Memoirs* by Marcus Connelly, © Marcus Conelly 1968; David Higham Associates for 'The Truisms' and 'Woods' from *Collected Poems* (1966) by Louis MacNeice, 'Do Not Go Gentle into that Good Night', from *Poems of Dylan Thomas* (1971), 'Poem' by Mervyn Peake from *Peake's Progress* (1978), 'Early Morning Feed' by Peter Redgrove from *Poems 1954-87* (1987) and excerpts from *The Prince of Wales* (1994) by Jonathan Dimbleby, *The Cecils of Hatfield House* (1973) by David Cecil, *The English Eccentrics* (1933) by Edith Sitwell, *Tales My Father Taught Me* by Osbert Sitwell and from the Journals of T. H. White; The Kavanagh Hand Press, N.Y., for 'A Christmas Childhood' from *The Collected Poems of Patrick Kavanagh* edited and with commentary by Peter Kavanagh © 1972, 1976 Peter Kavanagh; Kayak Books, Inc for 'Photograph of My Father in his Twenty-Second Year' by Raymond Carver, from *Winter Insomnia* (1970); Little Brown and Company for excerpts from *Glubb Pasha – The Life and Times of Sir John Bagot Glubb* (1962) by Trevor Royle and *My Father's*

House by Sylvia Fraser (Virago Press, 1987); Liveright Publishing Corporation for 'Those Winter Sundays', © 1966 by Robert Hayden, from *Angle of Ascent: New and Selected Poems* (1966); Macmillan Inc for excerpts from *The Fine Art of Political Wit* by L. Harris (1965); Macmillan Publishers Ltd for excerpts from *Cyril Connolly: A Nostalgic Life* (1995) by Clive Fisher and *The Prince Consort* (1949) by Rogert Fulford, and Macmillan Press for two excerpts from *Karl Marx: His Life and Thought* (1973) by David McLellan; John Murray (Publishers) Ltd for 'My Dear Deaf Father' by John Betjeman from *Summoned by Bells* (1960); W. W. Norton & Company for 'my father moved through dooms of love' from *Complete Poems 1904-1962* by E. E. Cummings, edited by George J. Firmage, © 1940, 1968, 1991 by the Trustees for the E. E. Cummings Trust; Oberon Books for an extract from *Oedipus the King*, translated by Christopher Stace (1987); *The Observer* for an excerpt from 'Self Criticism' by Will Self, 15 October, 1995; Orion Publishing Group Ltd (Weidenfeld) for excerpts from Cyril Connolly 'Some Memories' in *W. H. Auden: A Tribute* ed. Stephen Spender (1974), *The Diaries of Evelyn Waugh* ed. Michael Davie (1976) and *The Letters of Evelyn Waugh*, ed. Mark Amory (1980) and *Speak, Memory: An Autobiography Revisited* (1987) by Vladimir Nabokov; Oxford University Press for 'New Ground' from *Writing Home* (1985) by Hugo Williams; Pemberton for 'To my Children Unknown' by James Kirkup from *Facing the World – An Anthology for Humanists* (1989); Penguin Books India for 'Son' and 'I Cross the Room to Kiss My Son' from *Collected Poems 1957-1987* (1988) by Dom Moraes, and an excerpt from *My Son's Father* (1990) by Dom Moraes; Penguin Books Ltd for extracts from *Old Goriot* by Honore de Balzac translated by Marion Ayton Crawford (1951), Dennis Healey *The Time of My Life* (1990), 'The Firstborn' in *I Can't Stay Long* (1975) by Laurie Lee; *Gargantua and Pantagruel* by Rabelais translated by J. M. Cohen, *War and Peace* by Leo Tolstoy translated by Rosemary Edmonds (1957), *The Father* by August Strindberg translated by Peter Watts (1958); Penguin Books (Granta) for excerpts from Blake Morrison *When Did You last See Your Father?* (1933); Penguin Books (Hamish Hamilton) for excerpts from Germaine Greer, *Daddy We Hardly Knew You* (1989), Jean-Paul Sartre *Words* translated by Irene Clephane (1964), Paul Theroux, *The Mosquito Coast* (1981); Penguin Books (Michael Joseph) Groucho Marx, *The Groucho Letters* (1967); Penguin Books (Viking) for excerpts from *Shot in the Heart* (1994) by Mikal Gilmore; Peters, Fraser & Dunlop for 'Lord Hippo' from *Cautionary Verses* by Hilaire Belloc (1940), 'Squaring Up' from *Defying Gravity* by Rogert McGough (1992), 'Wounds' from *Poems 1963-83* by Michael Longley (1986) and excerpts from *Two Flamboyant Fathers* (1966) by Nicolette Devas, *Rules of the Game and Beyond the Pale* (1994) by Nicholas Mosely, *Renoir My Father* by Jean Renoir (1962) and *Will This Do* (1991) by Auberon Waugh; Random House UK Ltd (The Bodley Head) for an excerpt from J. R. Ackerley, *My Father and Myself* (1968); Random House (Jonathan Cape) for excerpts from Bruce Chatwin, *What Am I Doing Here?* (1989), Simone de Beauvoir, *The Second Sex* (1995) Philip Roth, *Portnoy's Complaint* (1969) and Colm Toibin *The Sign of the Cross* (1994); Random House (Chatto) for a section from 'Stargazing' from *Stones & Fires* (1996) by John Fuller, 'The Almond Tree' from *A Familiar Tree* (1969) by Jon Stallworthy and extracts from Aldous Huxley, *Brave New World* (1932), Laurie Lee, *Cider With Rosie* (Hogarth Press 1959), Stella Tillyard, *Aristocrats* (1994) and V. S. Pritchett *A Cab at the Door* (1968); Reed Consumer Books (Heinemann) for excerpts from Beverley Nichols *Father Figure* (1972); Reed (Methuen) for excerpts from *John Betjeman Letters*, Vol. I, edited by Candida Lycett Green and *The Life of Robert Browning* (1838) by Griffin W. Hall; Rogers, Coleridge & White for 'Dad' by Elaine Feinstein from *Some Unease and Angels; Selected Poems* (1977) and 'A Lesson' from *A Tropical Childhood and Other Poems* (1961) by Edward Lucie Smith; Routledge for excerpts from Bertrand Russell, *Sceptical Essays* (1928) and *The Autobiography of Bertrand Russell* (1924); George Sassoon for 'To My Son' by Siegfried Sassoon from *Collected Poems* (1947); Sterling Lord Literistic for 'All my Pretty Ones' by Anne Sexton from *All My Pretty Ones* (1962); Katharine Tait for excerpts from *My Father Bertrand Russell* (Victor Gollancz, 1975, new edn. 199, Thoemmes Press, Bristol) © Katharine Russell Tait, 1975; A. P. Watt Ltd on behalf of The Trustees of the Maurice Baring Will Trust for an excerpt from *Lost Diaries and Dead Letters* by Maurice Baring (1925), and on behalf of the Estate of Viscount Montgomery of Alamein CBE for an extract from *Memoirs* (1958) by Viscount Montgomery; Hugo Williams for an excerpt from 'What shall we do now that we have done everything?' in *Fatherhood* ed. Sean French (Virago, 1993).

INDEX